LA HABANA
CUBA
TRINIDAD
SANTIAGO
HISPANIOLA

VILLA RICA
DE LA VERA CRUZ
JALAPA
CEMPOALA
CHACHALACAS RIVER
PASS OF
NOMBRE
DE DIOS

MAP BY DAVID CAIN

NIGHT *of* SORROWS

Also by Frances Sherwood

The Book of Splendor
Green
Vindication
Everything You've Heard Is True

W. W. NORTON & COMPANY

New York London

FRANCES
SHERWOOD

NIGHT *of* SORROWS

a novel

Night of Sorrows is a work of fiction. Several
characters are real figures in history, and many events
took place as described. They were the inspiration
thanks to which an imaginative world
of its own came into being.

Copyright © 2006 by Francis Sherwood

FIRST EDITION

For information about permission to reproduce selections from this
book, write to Permissions, W. W. Norton & Company, Inc.,
500 Fifth Avenue, New York, NY 10110

Manufacturing by The Haddon Craftsmen, Inc.
Book design by Barbara M. Bachman
Production manager: Anna Oler

LIBRARY OF CONGRESS CATALOGING-IN-PUBLICATION DATA

Sherwood, Frances, 1940–
Night of sorrows / Frances Sherwood.— 1st ed.
p. cm.
ISBN-13: 978-0-393-05825-3 (hardcover)
ISBN-10: 0-393-05825-5 (hardcover)
1. Aztecs—Fiction. 2. Princesses—Fiction. 3. Conquerors—Fiction.
4. Cortés, Hernán, 1485–1547—Fiction. 5. Mexico—
History—Conquest, 1519–1540—Fiction. I. Title.
PS3569.H454N54 2006
813'.54—dc22

2006000420

W. W. Norton & Company, Inc.
500 Fifth Avenue, New York, N.Y. 10110
www.wwnorton.com

W. W. Norton & Company Ltd.
Castle House, 75/76 Wells Street, London W1T 3QT

1 2 3 4 5 6 7 8 9 0

To my son LARK WILLIAM MADOO

One by one I bring together
your songs.
I am linking the jades,
with them I make a bracelet
of everlasting gold.

Bedeck yourself with them:
they are your wealth
in the region of flowers,
they are your wealth
on earth.

—one of the ancient poets,
from FIFTEEN POETS OF THE AZTEC WORLD
by Miguel León-Portilla

PART 1

There had been signs.

The first sign was a long finger of lightning. As intent as a snake aiming for its catch, it ignited a fire in the tallest temple in the capital. On the same night prisoners mysteriously escaped their cages. A few days later a bird was found with a mirror in its wings. The lake foamed up like a cornered animal and overlapped its banks. A falling star shot out sparks like a skunk kicking out her scent from under her black-and-white skirts. A woman was seen walking the streets weeping inconsolably.

The professionals of the court told the emperor there was no better way to avert catastrophe than to have a Flowery War. Before war could be prepared, floating white temples were sighted in the Eastern Sea. From deep within their subterranean holds two-headed creatures emerged with legs as long as young trees and feet hard enough to trample a man like maize on a grinding stone. Most terrifying, however, was that humanlike creatures grew out of the backs of these monsters, their faces half hidden by thick hair. They were crowned with hard headpieces in the shape of two plates clamped together. Their upper parts were encased in carapaces. They held in their top appendages—arms, if you will—sticks that could make fire. Not only did these creatures control their own lightning, but from their floating temples they rolled out tubes that belched stone balls as loud as thunder.

Then messengers brought back reports from the eastern coast that the "things" were not whole creatures after all, but rather two separate beings, one part like large deer, and astride these gigantic animals were foreign men in outrageous costumes. Priests conjectured it was the second coming of the banished god, for it was One Reed, the year predicted for Quetzalcoatl's return.

Born in Mali, the month of grass, in the Christian year of 1500, Malintzin was a strong, healthy baby. Her delivery went according to tradition, and her birth was accompanied by the traditional words, "You will be the heart of the house, you will go nowhere." Her umbilical cord and placenta were buried in the floor near the ashes of the family dead and beside the metlatl, the grinding stone, and the comalli, the griddle, the hearth and cooking pots, the straw mats for seats and boxes for storage.

Because her father was a high official in an Aztec-held town between Nahua Mexico and Maya Yucatán in the Tabasco region, her calli was more than a windowless four-sided hut with a smoke hole in the center of the thatched roof. Her family had many rooms, the outside walls made of stone with sweet-smelling cedar beams holding up the roof and doorways opening onto a large courtyard planted with flowering bushes and medicinal herbs. Their compound included a maize granary, a sweat house, and a small shrine for worship. Her name Malin had the additional suffix *-tzin* because she was a noble's child, a princess. Her mother, lower-born than her father, kept an obsidian knife at the bottom of a bowl covered by water to protect the house from sorcerers.

Her father's only child, Malintzin proved to be talkative, which even in a noble family was not proper for a girl. Grown men had to be circumspect of speech, for only the emperor himself, who was called tlatoani, he who speaks, had that privilege, and was by tradition the spokesman for the people. Her father, however, said that because she was such an intelligent daughter, when she was of age she would be sent to the calmecac to study with a priestess with other wellborn girls before their marriages. Prancing about the courtyard, Malintzin would name each thing anew, and in their secret language things talked back to her. Sometimes she could not quiet the voices, for at night the gods of the underworld whispered to her, "Malintzin, come out and play with us." They beckoned to her with fingers of bone, clicking their teeth in their bare skulls and dancing disjointedly, their skeletons creating an eerie, knocking music. Her father was the one who would find her far from her sleeping mat and bring her back inside.

"Malintzin, my child, at night the demons, the Tzitzimitl, come out and eat little children."

The worst ones were the ghosts of women who had died in childbirth and were buried at the crossroads. Malintzin also had to be wary of the jaguar and puma, mountain lions and coyotes. Her father, after rescuing her from this treacherous night world, would rub her feet and gently command the bad spirits to stay still and not tempt his daughter out on dangerous nocturnal adventures. And he would sprinkle water on the threshold of the door and ask the sky to grant her sleep without memory so she would wake up with no knowledge of evil. Her mother thought her father indulged her and that she should be kept inside night *and* day.

Indeed her father let her neglect the loom and the grinding stone, the broom and spindle, the common activities of a woman. He let her sit beside him when he negotiated with the tax collectors from the capital every eighty days for one-third of the town's goods—cotton, seashells, pearls, salt, maize, and green quetzal feathers. Her mother said no good would come of that, that she would learn to ignore a woman's destiny. As a high official, her father was the one who saw that the maize fields were tended correctly and all was in order. He, with the priests, determined propitious dates for marriages and attended celebrations of births. And he made certain that all festivals were carried out according to custom.

When Malintzin was seven years old, it was the end of the fifty-second-year cycle and the world was again at peril from the death of the sun. She was permitted to accompany her father to Uixachtecatl to celebrate the festival of the first light. When the Pleiades reached the center of the sky, marking the time for a new fire ceremony, the sacrificial victim was first choked by garroting with a cord, then his heart was extracted with a flint knife. At that point the priest seized a wooden fire stick and small board, inserting it into the breast of the victim and twisting it until it heated, kindling new fire. Only then would the stars give the sign that the world would continue. Thereupon the priest gave thanks to the fire god, and runners, fanning out all over the empire from the capital, Tenochtitlán, and all the great cities, would light hearths in homes using sparks from the original lights. People gave thanks for the renewal of the year by piercing and bleeding their ears, tongues, and penises with cactus thorns. New sleeping mats would be brought out, floors swept, walls whitewashed.

It was on that occasion Malintzin realized for the first time that her father was a participant in the sacrificial rites, and that the scars all over his body testified to his self-inflicted piety. After that, Malintzin became aware that captives of the Flowery Wars were marched up the one hundred and fourteen steps of the tallest pyramid in Tenochtitlán, the capital of the Mexica, and had their hearts cut out without a whimper. They went to the sky immediately, she was told, to stay with the sun god, Huitzilopochtli, who was also the god of war and the patron god of the Mexica. Other dead people had years of wandering and many ordeals to go through before they joined the sun god, and it was best that they died with a piece of jade in their hair to pay the yellow dog to get them across the dark river.

Captives, like warriors, were considered heroes, and some were considered the persons of gods during the year before their sacrifice, feted and fed, brought lovely virgins, and decorated with flowers and fine clothes before they died to be reborn. These men were highly honored, Malintzin's mother told her, and were glad to be sacrificed, for they died according to the law and their duty. But in her town during the festival of the flayed ones in the early spring, Malintzin observed that the line of captives seemed sick with dread. Some had to be dragged screaming, and others, as they slowly ascended the holy steps, defecated in fear, leaving a trail of feces and urine behind them as testament to absolute terror.

And then there was the slave in her father's household, the woman who helped care for Malintzin, whose own baby was chosen by emissaries from the capital to be sacrificed for the rain god Tlaloc's festival. It was the tears of many babies as they were thrown into wells that made Tlaloc happy enough to send heavy clouds and break them open like eggshells. The rain nourished the crops and saved the people. But the slave woman did not care that it was a great privilege to have her son sacrificed for the well-being of the land. She was neither grateful nor flattered. She loved her baby above all else. Malintzin's mother pointed out that the woman was not a good citizen of the empire and should be punished without the privilege of sacrifice for her insolent ways. Telling only Malintzin, the slave mother plotted to keep her newborn hidden from the officials—a crime punishable by worse than death.

Initially the distraught mother planned to put her baby in a basket and sequester him in a clump of flowers, leaving a space for his little nose and mouth to breathe, telling the officials he had died, but surely, Malintzin reasoned, his cries would give him away. The poor woman thought of suspending her baby in the branches of a tree, keeping him in a lidded urn, or giving him to a relative to keep in another village. But they would find him in those places too, and her relatives would be killed in retaliation. So she ran away into the forest with her child. Her husband was killed, of course, but they did not find her or the baby. Malintzin's mother said that Tlaloc himself would punish the slave woman and child for disobedience. What was one baby that the crops of the empire should be jeopardized?

A year later Malintzin heard of a woman and child who lived with the monkeys in the deep jungle. They ate monkey food, it was said, never starting a fire, and did monkey things like groom each other and comb for bugs to pinch and eat on each other's bodies, and at night when the monkeys gathered together in the low branches of the trees to sleep, the mother and son slept with them. The woman's hair grew over her forehead and chin, people said, and the boy did not learn human language but spoke in howls and shrieks and walked with a low, slanted stoop, his hands dragging along the ground. All of this was not impossible, Malintzin conjectured, for dream-readers said that in sleep each person can turn into the special animal of his naming, and there were priests who could turn themselves into what they wanted by eating peyotl, the buds of northern cactus, or teonanacatl, a sacred fungus.

Then it was whispered that the boy child was killed by other monkeys when they wanted to mate with his mother. And the next year they found a set of human bones picked clean on the other side of the sweat house. Jaguars, it was rumored. The little family had not gotten far, and it was believed that the woman, fearing that a scream would give away her hiding place, had remained silent.

To Malintzin, these events served as a premonition, an ominous warning against disobeying the gods. Yet, she wondered, why did the gods live only through death, why must the earth be saturated with blood for crops to grow, why did their town, and other towns, pay such high tribute to the capital, and why did her father, who had survived many Flowery Wars and had his hair cut appropriately as one who had captured many men, sicken? Because that is what happened. He was made to eat peppers for a laxative, jimsonweed and poppy for his cough, toronjil for his upset stomach, anise leaves and tea of lemongrass to soothe his spirit. People who were knowledgeable about herbs and bad spirits were sent for, and soothsayers from the next town came to cast maize kernels and bones to read the future. His sickness made him rave with fever; his flesh wasted away. He could not rise from his mat or even hold his head up without help. Finally he could not move his mouth to eat, and he closed his eyes, only opening them to gaze fondly at his beautiful young daughter.

Nine years old, Malintzin held his hand as he died. Despite her great fear, she wished she could travel with him to the underworld. When his ashes were buried in the ground under the hearth next to Malintzin's umbilical cord and placenta, she refused to go to her own place of sleep, but must put her sleeping mat over him, and willed dreams of him standing up, his cloak billowing out behind him and the necklace of turquoise stroked by the rays of the sun as he walked through the town greeting people. The little dogs buried

with him jumped for joy at being alive. He sang poetry, xochi-
cuicatl, flower songs.

Malintzin, little flower of my heart,
Sing of me when I am gone.
Master of my song,
My tongue of feathers.

After the proper days of mourning, her mother married a man
who did not rub Malintzin's feet or take her about or let her sit by him
when he spoke to others. As soon as he moved into their house, he
threw out all of her father's weapons, his bow and arrows, his club, his
knives. Although he too was a city official, he was not wellborn with
a knowledge of writing and reading, and did not know the songs and
history of the ancestors. He was of Malintzin's mother's people, a
farmer's son who had distinguished himself by capturing many men in
the Flowery Wars. He was stern, a hard man with lips thin as a blade
of obsidian and the manners of one unaccustomed to fine food and the
froth of the cocoa bean. He regarded Malintzin's delicate fingers and
nimble step as mockery, an affront. He could not endure being presented daily with evidence that his wife had been with another man.
He did not let Malintzin escape his scrutiny, go outside, walk about.
Did she think she was as free as a bird or an animal of the forest or a
man who could speak out, learn dances and poems. Dare she rise and
stand up tall, leaving the dust of the hearth for the early morning air
or the breeze of an evening?

Her mother said:

"All your refinements have brought disharmony into our house."

Her real father had given her comfort for bad dreams, but her
mother's husband appeared in her bad dreams. Half awake, she would
be aware that he lifted her cueitl and huipilli and took her sleep-limp
hand to tighten it around his hard member, the tepolli. He was like
one of the demons she had feared, for he lurked and hovered, covering the nighttime doorway with his black shadow. Afterward she
would hear him rousing her mother, then she heard their rhythmic

sounds break the night into little pieces. During the day her mother's husband behaved as if nothing had happened, and he dutifully beat Malintzin with the bundle of sticks he kept hanging by the door. He blighted her days, haunted her sleep. Sometimes in angry words with her mother he said somebody, not him, would have to leave the house. Malintzin's mother assured him that soon her daughter would bud breasts, marry, and move into the house of a husband. Her husband fumed: Two women in the house? Two women and one man? If he had two wives it would be different.

Malintzin grew silent, dug up the stones from the floor, made holes in the earth, and ate the earth from under her fingernails. At night she shut her eyes tightly and curled up in a tight light ball so her bad night dreams would not get her—his sour breath steaming on her back, his big hands crawling around her body like heavy-shelled turtles. Do not tell your mother, it would kill her, do not tell anybody, I will kill you. Of course she would never tell. Her mother knew nothing. She slept like one who had dropped down a water hole, never to emerge. Then, when she was nearly ten years old, her mother said she was going to have the baby she and her husband had wanted for so long. It was a boy, given on his birth a little shield and bows and arrows.

One day on the day of the sign of the sun, a day everybody was expected to draw blood from ears and tongues with knotted rope and the spines of fish and cactus, and her stepfather was going house to house to check on the piety and fidelity of all the householders, Malintzin sneaked out just to run in the maize field between the tall rows of green, slippery leaves, the plants fat to bursting with the ripening maize. She rolled around like a dog scratching its back. She did somersaults as she had seen acrobats once do in a festival, and she jumped and skipped, kicking her legs straight out like the hind legs of a rabbit. Then she heard a strange sound. She held very still as a rabbit would, silently twitching its ears. The leaves rustled in one section of the field, but not in tight little snaps as in a fast wind or like the languorous sigh of a low stirring before rain or the weary, haphazard flap here and there of a farmer at work on the squash plants that grew in low vines between the maize. The sound was angry, disrespectful;

plants were being pushed aside unkindly, *whip-whap, whip-whap*, and accompanying the sound, like heavy drumbeats, was the dull thud of men tramping in heavy sandals. Then she saw the colorfulness of their cloaks, the bright feathers like the shiny black of the toucan and red parrot spray. Commoners were not allowed color and feathers.

Malintzin had seen Maya traders before, and knew that they were from the south and traded with the capital of the Mexica empire. They carried gold and silver and emeralds to be made into lip plugs and nose rings, ornamental plates, and baskets from the coast, and the black and red pottery of Oaxaca. She knew they were not supposed to be there in her mother's husband's field amid the stalks of corn.

She began to run, first slowly, for her feet would not obey her mind, then faster, and with all her might she lunged through the outside doorway of the house, ran into the patio quick, quick to find her mother, did not see her, and hurried to the cooking circle.

"Mother, Mother, help me," Malintzin cried piteously. Her brother was wrapped on her mother's back as she was tending the hearth.

"Do not let them take me." She scrambled into her mother's arms. And her mother, for the first time in a long time, held her fast to her chest, patted her back, and smoothed down her hair. But when the men entered she pushed her daughter away.

"Take her."

Malintzin kicked and screamed. Two of them grabbed her arms and another her legs.

"I am of noble blood. My father—"

Malintzin's cries and pleas fell on hatred and scorn. In exchange, the traders gave her mother a small sack of cocoa beans, a cake of honeycomb, and a bit of jade. Her mother turned her face away, did not look at her daughter, and spit into the fire.

"I will tell the neighbors my daughter walked into the forest in her sleep and was taken by the monkeys to live with them in the trees. She has been stung by scorpions, bitten by snakes, swallowed by a river lizard, disappeared. Coyotes have come down the mountain to eat her. Take her far away from me."

Did her father's ashes come to life to save Malintzin from the slavers' evil clutches?

No.

Did her umbilical cord cry out from its hole near the hearth? Did her placenta weep the tears of the womb?

No.

Did the grinding stone overturn itself in protest?

Did the spindle spin a thread of denial, and the loom weave a sorry story?

The implements of war and farm, did they come to her assistance? And the gods in the heavens in their heavy and elaborate headdresses, did they come down to do battle with the slavers? The broom, sacred symbol of order, stood in its place and did nothing. Gentle Quetzal-coatl did nothing. Malintzin's mother quickly killed a slave child nobody would miss and buried her in Malintzin's place. It was so sad, she told her neighbors, her daughter died. Fortunately Malintzin's mother had a young son to console her for her loss, a son who would inherit the land, the house, and the holdings of her two husbands.

Chapter 2

The Mayan slave traders attached Malintzin to the other slaves by a collar around her neck connected to a wooden plank which ran between the two lines of them. Only a child, very small in stature, she had to tread quickly on her tiptoes or would be dragged along, the rough wood cutting into her tender shoulders. These particular traders carried cocoa and vanilla beans, pelts of jaguar and ocelot, green quetzal feathers, shards of turquoise, bits and pieces of gold, pulque distilled from the sap of the maguey, and fiber made from the leaves of the maguey. Malintzin was sold in Baak in the shadows of the old Maya ruins where spider monkeys lived in the toppled shrines, jungle vines overtaking the steeped stairs; little lizards and the palanca viper and coral snakes banded in black and red slithered between the cracks of stone.

To get to Baak had taken many days of walking, and without cactli of either fiber or deerskin, Malintzin's feet were blistered and bloodied by the time she was sold next to cages of rabbits and small parrots, piles of red beans and shriveled chilies. She was bought by a rich Maya man with a big belly and an amber lip plug.

In her father's house Malintzin had eaten dog, fish, waterfowl, weasel, and, on feast days, turkey. Now she ate slave food: bees, scum from the lake nearby, insects, grasshoppers, worms, and whatever else she could snatch, as much cornmeal as she could spoon into her mouth when nobody was looking, scrapings from the rinds of squash, pepper stems, stolen fruit, and leftover cornmeal cake before the dogs could get at it. Her once-lustrous thick hair became lank and thin, and the warmth of her skin cooled, leaving her pale as maize tassels. She dropped things, became sleepy at her tasks, and could not be roused from her mat in the morning.

In her dreams she was still the little child in her father's house in the town of her childhood in the square facing east, west, north, and south, hearing the music of flutes and trumpets made of turtle shells. Were the gods punishing her now? Had the gods conspired to punish her for betraying her mother by having her mother betray her? Had her mother found out, after all, and sold her in revenge? Had her husband, once he had his baby son, said, Get rid of her. Malintzin tried to puzzle it out in the Nahautl language and in Maya too, for she had, despite her resistance, learned their language. She had learned their festivals and all their ways, but what words, what celebration poem, what secret sounds, what meanings in any language could make a mother who did not need food for sons sell her daughter? Perhaps the seeds of her mother's hate had been sown when she, Malintzin, was an infant toddling into her father's outstretched arms, and as a girl when she left the spindle and loom to follow her father on his official rounds. Had it been because she, the daughter, blossomed like the flower of a yucca while her mother, long picked from her plant, withered. Had she, Malintzin, perhaps talked too much, laughed too loudly, showing her teeth and the red whorls of her throat? When she learned the pictured names of things kept in the folding books, had it offended her mother, who could not decipher one glyph. Dutiful daughter that she was, her father's princess, Malintzin had been proud to learn the poems of Quetzalcoatl, understand how Smoking Mirror lured the Plumed Serpent god to look at his reflection and, recognizing his own ugliness, put on a mask.

Her mother had her own knowledge, Malintzin finally realized, for the woman knew that as the worm bides its time, lying in wait in the soil to penetrate the heel, enwrap the heart, so do all little girls pay the price of youth and absorb the lessons of age. Malintzin could only take comfort in the idea that since the worst had happened to her, she had nothing left to fear. Nothing else could hurt her.

Yet that offered poor consolation, and moreover proved untrue, for rather than becoming the sort of person who is toughened to mistreatment and ill fortune, Malintzin became prone to hurt, and each slip and slight added to her original pain. She was one who tripped over her feet, cut her hand, got lost coming home from the river, fell into the river on the way, could not be trusted to carry plates, vomited without reason, dozed standing up, had to release her bowels all through the day, had pains in her stomach as soon as she lay on her mat, and wept uncontrollably.

Thus, in the course of several years, despite harsh training, she proved herself too fragile to do her duties, not good for much, and she was once again taken to the slave block. It was the law that the third time she was offered for sale, she could be bought for sacrifice by the traders' guilds or a group of workers who did not have captives to offer for the favor of the gods. This time as she stood on the block in her pathetic state, she was hardly glanced at. But the man who bought her, another rich, haughty Maya lord with curved, cruel lips, was not concerned with her thinness. He looked at her teeth and the shape of her nose and eyes. He passed his hands along her childish hips.

"They say she is from noble blood," her seller said.

"You can tell," the Maya said. "The arch of her feet, the way she holds her neck."

"She is wellborn, well spoken, knows the Nahuatl language of the court and Chontol Maya, Yucatec. Soon she will come into her womanhood and know how to please a man."

For the first few days this new master let her sleep late into the morning, and at night another slave, a Maya girl named Cuy, brought strongly seasoned stews and meat finely chopped and enfolded with tomatoes in maize cakes, and porridge mixed with water and flavored with vanilla bean and honey. This slave, Cuy, a Maya, unlike Malintzin, had never known her parents. She told Malintzin she knew she was from a noble family, that her dear mother had died and her rich father expired soon afterward in grief. Cuy said she knew this in her bones and teeth, in her nails and the roots of her hair. She was not born to be a slave, but the wife of a wise and wealthy man, the mother of warriors and sages. But I really am a princess, Malintzin wanted to say but did not, for in her other home they all laughed at her.

Cuy had already come into her flower, and was grown enough to take the master's sons to the mat from time to time for extra food. This she did at night after she was done in the kitchen, and it was supposed to be a secret, but Malintzin, in the next hut, could hear and she knew those sounds and what they meant. There were some women who did not marry—the ones who served the young men who lived in the barracks, at the calmecac, learning to be warriors. Malintzin had also heard of women in the capital who were not affiliated with the schools or the captive prisoners; rather they wandered the streets after sundown, some floating in canoes along the channels, stopping when they saw a man, asking him if he wanted an auianime for the night. These women painted their faces and stained their teeth yellow, and were not modest but joined in the men's festival dances. Cuy was not bold at all. Small as a twig, she never looked up, holding her head at a slant, hunched her shoulders, and kept her hands in front of her chest as if shielding herself from any oncoming blows.

At first in this new household, Malintzin feared she was being fattened for sacrifice, and thus like Cuy she should stay thin and ugly, but she could not help herself. She ate and grew strong, and by the time the rains came and she had her first flower, she was a comely young woman with strong hips and full breasts. Her hair grew back thick and lustrous. Cuy brushed it for her each night so it flamed out like something alive. Her mouth was as lush and purple as a forest orchid, and her skin had the color of a fawn's coat. Her eyes, while not slanting like a Maya's, were well shaped and large, black coals smoldering in the bed of a fire.

During her first flower, Cuy warned her, "Maax Cal, Prattling Monkey, tell nobody you are a woman. I will show you how to tie yourself up and wash yourself well so they do not smell it."

But word got out. Everybody in that house was a spy. Maax suspected that Cuy had told her friend from youth, Jaguar Claw, the butcher, who told the cook, who told the first wife, who told the master. The house was full of gossip, the four sons were back from school, and all the slaves and servants could speak of was that the young men would soon go into battle.

The night her flowery flow was over, Malintzin was taken out of her own hut, dressed in a new cueitl and beautiful clean huipilli with embroidered patterns around the neck. She was allowed to wear a necklace made of white shells which against her brown skin glowed like moonflowers, and her thick hair was combed with a cactus-spine comb so that it rose from her face like the fan of a lizard that could puff up its neck. Then she was escorted to the room of the lord's first son and made to lie with him. Although he knew what to do, he cried in fear and embarrassment and huddled in a corner of the room with his hands over his face. She cried too, fearful that she would be sold again. However, the next night the next oldest brother lay on top of her and poked successfully. It did not hurt, but while he was at it she turned her face away, could hear the crickets in the tall grass and the wind singing in the trees, and wondered what good thing she would be given to eat the following morning. And so it went, as when her mother's husband touched her and made her touch him, a time she could pretend sleep and remember stories her father had told her.

Malintzin bathed every day now and dressed nicely every night. Sometimes it was one of the brothers who came or even the master himself, visiting lords, passing Aztec merchants and officials, men of her father's position. She learned many dialects of Maya, and her knowledge of court Nahuatl became useful in impressing those noble guests from Mexica. She never yellowed her face or teeth with pollen or painted her body. Her ears were pierced, but she did not have to shred them during festivals or cut lines to bleed her legs in homage to the gods. Her flesh was kept smooth, rubbed with duck fat and aloe grease. She was asked to play the whistles made of deer bone, sing, chant poems, and sometimes dance the snake dance. And Cuy showed her a secret trick necessary to her survival.

"Each time, right before, you place a small piece of rubber sap from the trees along the northern coast in the region of the Olmec rolled in a tiny ball and patted flat at the entrance to your baby cave, for while a man does not place a baby in a woman's belly—only the gods can do that—his juice is necessary to make it grow. For somebody like us, a child is worse than death. Banishment, no roof to shelter you, death alone in the jungle."

Maax grew taller than Cuy and taller also than Jaguar Claw, the butcher, Cuy's friend. As a baby, Jaguar Claw had been born so crooked he killed his mother coming out, and when his father saw him, his ill-shaped limbs, his lip split up to his nose, he sold him and left for the capital. That is what was said. Jaguar Claw's face was as round as the sun and each of his hands was as big as his face, and he said he could throttle a jaguar with just one of them if he had to. Cuy's nose was narrow as a parrot's beak with a little bump at its top, and her face was quizzical, inquiring, sharp with intelligence. And although nobody knew anything about her parents, apparently somebody had cared enough to put two boards on her head to flatten and elongate her forehead, and her eyes had been crossed in the traditional Maya way by having a small object dangled in front of her when she was a baby.

When Malintzin had been in flower for more than five years reckoned by the ceremonial count of twenty days in a month, eighteen months in a year, and five days left for the time of darkness, or in Christian fathoming nineteen years old, her master, her master's sons, and all the men of the town went to war again. There had been several wars in the last years, squabbles with neighboring towns, Flowery Wars to get captives to sacrifice to the gods. This war, however, seemed different. There was no ceremonial presentation of weapons from the enemy, no official announcement or days and nights of ritual preparation. The bows and arrows stocked in the middle of the town in the arsenal were snatched and quickly distributed. Headdresses, war paint, poems, and dances were dispensed with. In the faint light of early morning, the men marched off. A day went by, two. The women stayed in their oval thatched-roofed houses praying that their men would fight bravely and, if caught, die bravely. On the third night the cacique returned in defeat, his headdress askew, his shins scratched and bloodied, and his face smeared with sweat and dirt. Behind him trudged what remained of his bedraggled troops—the wounded, the lame, the maimed.

It seemed that twenty young women were needed as a peace offering along with a hoard of maize from the storehouse, as many turkeys as could be spared, strings of smoked fish, and golden ornaments. Every household had to comply. Cuy and Malinche were selected as two of the expendable young women; both of them were bathed and rubbed with aloe salve lightly salted so that their breasts and buttocks glistened, and their lips were darkened a deep hue with blackberry stain and their eyes rimmed with a charred stick. They were dressed in cueitls of the red cochineal dye, and their huipilli, despite the law against cotton for commoners, were white cotton.

Maax was terribly worried. Third time sold could mean sacrifice. Cuy clung to her mat, for she did not want to leave behind all she had known—the kitchen where she scrambled for scraps, the marketplace where she sold her handiwork for her master's gain, the duck pond she had to stand in until her toes became pleated as mushrooms, the temple in the middle of the square where prisoners were sacrificed, the mistress who beat her regularly.

Jaguar Claw, commanded to accompany the women as escort, was excited, nay, ecstatic. He had heard that the enemy troops were preparing to go to the Mexica capital, the imperial headquarters, the most beautiful city on earth, Tenochtitlán. His whole life he longed to see the island city of the pyramided temple in honor of Huitzilopochtli, Emperor Moctezuma's palace, the palace of Moctezuma's father, the many canals and flower gardens, the famous zoo, and the training ground and garrisons of the jaguar and eagle warriors.

Cuy pleaded with her mistress, whom she called mother, for she knew no other.

"Cuy, I will take care of you," Malintzin had offered, at that moment hating Cuy for her weakness and lack of pride.

"How can you take care of me? You are a slave too."

If Malintzin had any hope, it was to be with Nahuatl-speaking people once again before she died. "I will be your new little mother, Cuy. Do not be afraid."

"And I will be your father," Jaguar Claw added, his voice elevated to the false shrill of a woman.

Maax did not want to hear that from him even in mockery, for although she had tried to be cordial for Cuy's sake, she suspected that Jaguar Claw was not truly Cuy's fast friend and protector; Jaguar Claw betrayed her to the mistress whenever it was advantageous.

"Our new master must be a man of consequence, a mighty warrior to merit such a generous gift—twenty women, food, and glitter," Jaguar Claw said as they walked down the beach. The cacique and his entourage led the procession. Drummers kept rhythm, low and deep, a heavy boom matching the humiliation of defeat. The baskets of maize cobs were carried by bearers who wore simple loincloths, maxt-latl, the fish in strings between them, and the live turkeys hung upside down by their feet, their hapless wings flapping frantically and then, slowly, their gobbles swallowed up by the night. Behind them in two straight files were the twenty women, some sobbing, others more brave looking straight ahead at the bonfires lit on the beach. Great temples, their giant white wings illuminated by the moon, listed on the black water. Malintzin's throat constricted. These were the foreign gods sighted along the coast. The signs in the capital had foretold their arrival. It was all true. Quetzalcoatl was prophesied to return from the Eastern Sea to claim the land. Now he was here, and she would see for herself. Malintzin, first sold by her mother at ten years of age, had been a slave nine years. It was the year One Reed, spring 1519.

Chapter 3

After a terrifying few days and nights traveling up the coast in a small chamber of a winged temple, Malintzin realized that the boats were not temples and the aliens were not gods. When smaller canoes were lowered from the sides of the big boats and they paddled to shore, the strangers disembarked like outsized locusts awakened from years of cocooned sleep. In a rapacious manner, they swarmed up the beach and into the edges of the jungles as if to mow down every leaf in sight. The hard silvery shells they wore around their big bellies and up their backs to their necks made them look like stubby bean beetles, and their arms and legs covered in swaths of tight fabric reminded her, in their thinness, of green grasshoppers. Some showed skin on their legs, and that was truly disgusting, for they had as much hair as the legs of the tarantula. The strangers' heads were curiously encased in the same protective material of their chests and back. No antennae apparently, but a sprout of feathers, not a proper headdress at all, shot out of the back of their headpieces as if, despite all their ugliness, they wanted to attract the female of their kind.

"Outlandish, exotic beyond belief, but certainly not gods. If they are people, they are barbarians," Malintzin whispered to Cuy in Chontol Maya. She was afraid of them, but worse were their huge monsters that shivered and shook with the menace of underworld forces. The creatures' high braying was akin to women crying out in pain. Their gigantic caged dogs, large as men, strained and snarled and foamed at the mouth. Dogs were to be eaten by people, not the other way around.

Yet a few days before, when the cacique and his escorts disappeared down the beach, their cloaks billowing out behind them like the broad spread of eagles in flight, the torchlights fading away like

the past, Malintzin recognized that her life was to change from that
time forward. On the floor of the floating temple she had been too
frightened and tired to pay too much attention. Truthfully she had also
been so sickened by the rocking motion that she could only try to quell
the unease in her stomach. Now she could see that the savages were
massed together in a great and strange army. Would she have to lie
down for each and every one of them? She shuddered to think of their
lack of amenities. If she were not sacrificed to her own gods, was she
to die a more terrible death?

The twenty women slaves and Jaguar Claw huddled under a giant
ahuehueti tree, barely suppressing their terror. Then one of the barbarians, the head barbarian, it seemed from his commanding presence,
stepped forward, actually touched the arms of the women, and separated each from the other with his furred paws. The smell of him. And
the hairy heathen, stinking brute, could not keep his eyes still and
focused like a warrior or properly downcast like a respectful commoner. He let his eyes roll around in their sockets, they were black, the
color of bats, and he appraised the slave women like a curious monkey; then they landed on her chest like twin crows.

Not me, Malintzin begged silently, please not me.

She, of course, had kept her own eyes down, as was proper, but
long ago she had mastered the art of seeing when not looking. It was
as if she could see straight through her lids, for she observed the eyes
wander up to her hair like flies savoring seaweed rotting on the beach.
Then they came to rest on her mouth. She wanted to swallow them
whole in one gulp. Or swat them away. Let them fall at her feet where
she could stamp them down into the dust. They went up again, waist,
chest, forehead, her hair. She hated her hair. Unlike other women's,
Malintzin's hair could not be tamed with a cactus-spine brush or
pressed into neat buns over her ears or knotted in tight braids at the
sides of her head, but it must spring out free and loose, be its own tan-
gled mess.

She bent her neck and looked at Cuy's feet in her cactli. Her
friend's toenails were rough and ragged, for she chewed on them at
night, holding her limber legs in her hands and spitting the nail bits

out of the side of her mouth. Cuy teasingly called her toenails her sacrifice, for neither woman was required to bleed her ears and legs in
homage to the gods. Malintzin's feet were large and her legs slightly
bowed, for like all Indian children, she had been carried on her
mother's back until she could walk a good distance on her own. These
legs were now trembling. The master barbarian was still looking out at
her from all the fur on his face; his lips were practically hidden, but in
their thicket were disturbingly pink, like the moist inside of a woman.
How repulsive he was. And the noise he made—she supposed it was
human language—rolled from his mouth like smooth rubber balls
interspersed with the soft lulling coo of pigeons bathing themselves in
the afternoon dust. She could not hold on to any one distinct sound.

Now the head barbarian made a gesture and the women and
Jaguar Claw were herded forward into the cooking circle of the camp,
and all the savages who had been standing at attention in a formation
of sorts began to scuttle about like dazed ants released from their
grainy hill.

"How tasty big ants are when first soaked in lime and then chili
pepper sauce," Malintzin remarked to Cuy, trying to climb out of
dread by way of words. They were, all the slave women, herded into
the cooking circle. Malintzin was set to chopping, Malintzin to stirring. "But I prefer grasshopper; I like them best fried in red chili peppers and sprinkled with salt from the salt flats."

Cuy replied that she liked little ants which could be eaten raw and
alive, but they had to be eaten fast before they crawled out of your
mouth.

Malintzin's favorites were dog stew with squash and pumpkin so
rich it growled from the pot and roast ducks tender and succulent on
the inside and skin so crisp on the outside that it quacked in your
mouth. She was accomplished in making these dishes. Cuy readily
acknowledged Malintzin's many talents. She could play ceremonial
tunes on the five-toned flute well enough for the festival of green
corn; she was well versed in prayers to Chicomecoatl, the goddess of
maize; she was so gifted in sounds and talk that she could tell you the
names of everything in Nahautl and Maya, court and low. Malintzin

knew ten words in each language for the color green, going from moss to the color of the sea when the bottom is sand and the sun hits at midday, to the hard skin of limes, and the jungle tree leaves turning dark in the twilight.

"And Cuy," Malintzin reminded her, "I am gifted in being your little mother. That means what I say goes."

"You are not my mother."

"One day out of the womb and she disobeys?"

Jaguar Claw gave them a disapproving look. His job was to skin about a hundred rabbits in one morning, and it was not funny. But he knew the more indispensable he made himself, the longer he would live.

The barbarian camp, Malintzin noted, was clumsily arranged. True enough, it was on a river, yet they had pitched their cloth houses in a straggling line without regard for shade. Malintzin observed them slashing bushes and saplings, venting their rage on harmless vegetation which might, in the heat of the day and cool of the night, shelter them. Moreover, because they did not know better, their nasty morning habits brought on evening mosquitoes so thick and vicious that Malintzin, even though she rubbed bitter lime juice on her body and slippery soft aloe behind her elbows and knees, wanted to bury herself in a hole or cover all but her nose in water; nonetheless, there she was, aboveground that night, the twilight bleeding magenta and orange, a suffusion of blues blending to gray so beautifully she could not bear to speak of it. She could hear a hundred flowers she could not name sing out their scent as if it were their last night on earth. Looking out from between the flaps, she and Cuy, playing spy, saw the black seep out from the edges of the jungle and spread like ink from the octopus along the surface of the ground and to all the reaches of the sky. The loud hoots and hollers of the bigger monkeys and the chattering laughter of smaller monkeys followed. Then the calls and warbling, twittering and honks of birds took over.

"Have you seen them, the strange men who live in cloth houses and coat themselves in hard silver, are they not silly and insignificant?" cawed the scarlet macaw.

"We, here in the trees, in our jungle bowers, let us barrage them with our derision," beeped and cried the chachalacas, the jacamars, the lovely cotingas, the sleek black toucans.

"I told you so, I told you so," granddaddy parrot pointed out.

And then a hundred green parakeets that walked about in the day like little feathered fat men on an important empire errand cackled derision down on the heads of the restless conquistadors.

"God damn it to hell, damn bugs are biting me to death," Alvarado muttered in his small pup tent. "I cannot get to sleep."

"Be quiet or the devil take you." Cortés could sleep on a rock in the middle of a storm if he had to, or under the vengeful sun at midday if he was truly tired.

Meanwhile, underneath the cries of birds and the cackle of monkeys, the big cats lumbered forth silently. Lean with hunger and keen on the hunt, the pumas, the ocelots, and the jaguars were about to snatch Malintzin from her cloth house and in one pull drag her into the mouth of the underworld.

"Oh no!" Malintzin screamed in her sleep.

"Quiet, quiet, it is only a dream, Maax."

"I saw—"

"Shh, little mother, tell me a story." Cuy knew well that for Malintzin, talking calmed her fears and set her mind on a daylight path. "Tell me Quetzalcoatl."

"Quetzalcoatl," Maax began, picking each word like a stepping-stone, "this is for you, not for me, Cuy. I do not need stories."

"Yes, I know."

"Are you listening, Cuy?"

"Yes."

"Our god Quetzalcoatl was a real man for a time. He was a priest and king, a poet and feather worker, a man dedicated to piety and purity, and he spent much of his days in Tula fasting and praying in obedience to the gods. Then something happened which made it necessary for him to go out into the world and greet his fate. We can do no less, Cuy, my daughter."

"I hope to be in accord, little mother Maax, monkeygirl. You sleep. Sleep. Your eyes are getting sleepy. Sleepy. Slee . . ."

Chapter 4

In the morning Malintzin and Cuy and the other eighteen women had to assemble under the palm fronds that had been laid across tall sticks to make the cooking shelter. The corn kernels which had been soaking overnight in squeezed lime juice had to be ground, then mixed with water, balled and flattened, kneaded, patted, and roasted flat on the stone griddle. The beans, once cleaned, were put to boil early so they could soften slowly, and yesterday's beans and squash stew were warmed anew. Fresh tomatoes had to be sliced and peppers chopped. The turkeys, once killed, hung in mournful tandem, twisting right and left in each fresh breeze, and needed to be plucked, cleaned, and roasted. Caged live Gila monsters lay ready to be strangled, depoisoned, and made into tasty tidbits to be placed on the thin cornmeal cakes.

The cooking circle was in front of the lines of cloth houses. Behind the camp, in the bay, floated the galleons. No longer considered temples, they seemed more birdlike than ever to Malintzin. She could imagine them rising up, the eleven of them in a flock, and taking flight. In the meadow near the shore the huge animals the barbarians rode ate, of all things, grass. Not men, not turkeys—grass.

On the third morning, after the meal, their chief summoned all his men, the women slaves, and several Indian servants he had brought from the islands of Hispaniola and Cuba, including the darkest man Malintzin had ever seen with tiny curls nested on his head like shiny black beetles. Banners were unfurled. Several of the foreigners hit drums hanging from their necks on long cords with long pointed sticks. Others put trumpets, not of whorled conch shells, but what seemed like gold, to their mouths. A volley of sound pealed forth, notes much higher and more distinct and various than the tones any instrument Malintzin had ever heard. That music made her feel as if something wonderful was going to happen, and she pictured a woman rising from the sea on the back of a seal, or a flock of birds appearing in the sky, from far away white dots, but as they grew closer large and dropping flower petals from their beaks on them all in congratulations. She could even imagine the gods sitting on the top rim of the sun, their legs overhanging, enjoying the entertainment. And maybe this was in preparation for still one more marvel kept hidden deep in the bottom of the aliens' floating houses. Already they had revealed tricks unknown to the people of the sun. They had big tubes that belched balls so heavy they were like mountain boulders. Malintzin had seen the grass-eaters prance and dance with bells strung around their necks. One of the fire sticks had been used to kill a hapless slow-moving armadillo that did not know enough to run away.

When the trilling stopped, their chief, atop a grass-eater, galloped up and down the beach sprinkling sand in the four directions of the east, west, south, and north, and then with his long bright knife he slashed the bulbous trunks of several ceiba trees. With an exaggerated flourish, he planted a banner of blue and white, with a red mark in the middle, on the shore. Another cloth on a stick was set by its side. This one had a picture of a woman in a long blue cloak and golden head-dress. A famous goddess of theirs, no doubt. Then, on signal, the whole group of them, over several hundred, her friend Cuy estimated, the whole lot of them took off their metal hats and knelt down in the sand on one knee. A line of seagulls that had been scavenging in the seaweed for dead crabs stopped and looked up. The cormorants that had been circling about screeching their heads off went quiet.

"Now what are they going to do?" Malintzin asked Cuy.

"It is one of their rites, Maax," she whispered back.

Jaguar Claw said, "They are going to eat sand. It is their sign of politeness."

"Hush," Cuy said.

The head barbarian, their cacique, the one Jaguar Claw called "the

Cockroach," gesticulated with his sword, swooped it in a circle above him in the sky, and emitted a long string of babble.

"Let me correct myself," Jaguar Claw amended. "They are not going to eat the beach. The Cockroach is laying claim to the land like the greedy coyote who must pee on each stump and bush to make his territory known."

Then the two men who did not wear shirts of the silvery scales of the fish, one of whom went barefoot and whose robe, the color of an old tree trunk, was frayed and with an uneven hem, fell prostrate to the earth. These two strangers had their heads shaved in a circular pattern and wore an ornament of a tortured man on a string around their necks. In point of fact, the armored ones carried carvings of the same naked man spread-eagle on long staffs. These they now planted on the shore next to their banners. It was a frightening sight to Malintzin, this line of sticks bearing the resemblance of a tortured dead man affixed to them. It was as if a sacrifice had taken place on the spot and evidence must remain to scare away all newcomers, or the figures of the dead man were like clothed sticks stuck in maize fields to scare away hungry birds. The macabre staffs were like skull racks after a sacrifice.

After that the white men busied themselves with cutting down trees with an implement of jagged teeth like that of a big dangerous fish, and from those long trunks they hewed rough boards which they hammered together with nails made of a dull silver into walls. It was apparent that they were building their own city on the coast. But had they permission? Did not Moctezuma see through his many spies and runners what they were doing? Longhouses to sleep the men? A corral to keep the grass-eaters together? A building by the stream where animals could be killed and cut up? There was another square building with their torture emblem tied on the thatched roof. On the branch of a massive ceiba tree curtained with ragged moss they hung a rope made of fiber. Malintzin, who was throwing away dirty water from the morning meal in the bushes, stared at it. It dangled like a newborn snake, not knowing if it should fly or crawl.

"It is for execution," one of them said in Chontol Maya.

He was a tall, lean man almost as brown as she was, with long dangling arms like a monkey he could not keep still, and she knew he was the only one of them who could speak the Mayan tongue.

"I was on a canoe," he continued, "a big one." He pointed to the floating houses anchored in the bay. "It was dashed against the rocks." He held up one hand flat and hit it with his fist. "Crash, boom." He flailed around, then huddled his shoulders tightly together. "I was taken prisoner by the Mayans." He walked a few steps hunched over like one attached to a collar. But although he was talking in Maya, her second language after the Aztec tongue, and demonstrated all he said, she found him difficult to understand.

"I lived among the Mayans as a slave. El Capitán rescued me." He pointed to the house they had made for the Cockroach. It had the two banners planted in front of it. "Canoe. Crash. Slave. Rescue." He lifted his eyebrows up and down and danced forward and back. "Canoe. Crash. Slave. Rescue." He thrust out his arms free as a bird.

But Malintzin wanted to know where the whole army came from, what lay beyond the waters, why they were in the empire of the sun. She pretended not to be too interested, too eager, too intelligent, for that was something that would never do for a slave or a woman, and to be both meant exercising double caution. She leaned to the side as if listening for a hint of breeze or the call of a bird. She held her features without expression and was patient, for she knew that this white tribe spoke to fill the silence. They were worse than birds.

"We come to bring you the Word," the white man finally said.

Malintzin tried to think. What word? Why so many men for one word? It must be a heavy word, hard to lift and difficult to say. Many men, one word. It had to be a god. Then she pointed to the tree branch with the looped rope.

"It is *the gallows*," he said, and indicated its use with a quick jerk of his head, sticking out his long tongue to one side.

"The gal-lows."

Later Malintzin learned the gallows was used to choke you if you ran away, either a slave or one of the white men, for there were some among the group who wanted to go back to their home across the

Eastern Sea, and if you said something like that to the Cockroach, you went to the gallows. The gallows was also used if you offended their gods. In fact, there were many misdeeds requiring the gallows, particularly if you were a slave and did not know their ways. Not only could you be hanged by the neck at the gallows, but if you were not careful, you could be tied up and *burned at the stake*. At that moment she understood finally that the barbarians were not mere stumbling buffoons with confused intentions, and her dream which had been set aside returned and was born anew, born bigger. The fear crowded out everything else and she felt she had not a word left to guide her.

Chapter 5

Cortés was not afraid of dying or anything else, although truth be told, he was not overfond of public speaking. As a child, he had been sickly, the priest sent to administer last rites twice in a row. And when he was nineteen, crossing the Atlantic from Spain to Hispaniola in the West Indies, the ship lost course, and it was only when the captain spotted and followed a dove that they found shore and safe harbor. Cortés had been with Velázquez when he conquered Cuba in 1511 from the Arawak Indians. He had been in the thick of it. So while he knew the Grim Reaper, black-cloaked skull and bones, long sickle in hand, would come to mow him down in time, until then he did not fear the consequences of battle.

Composure, dignity, Hernán, remember to look them straight in the eye. Do not ramble. Do not prevaricate. Appear certain of yourself. Be charming, very charming, yet manly. Manly, genial, confident. Deliver your speech!

Cortés's usually clear mind was muddled because for the first time in his whole life he had not been able to sleep well the night before. Somewhere deep in the surrounding jungle some monkeys found something ridiculously silly enough to screech their heads off about all night, joined by annoying birds who must sing their tiny hearts out for the mere bothersomeness of it, and he would be damned if he did not notice an inordinate amount of rustling in the bushes. Lizards, snakes, rats, be gone! Who knew what it was? Cursing in the strongest terms—"On my conscience, evil betide you!"—had not put an end to the incessant racket. The only quiet time had been a few moments before sunrise. A pause, an intake of breath, the curtain of dense black lifted. Then it all started again. Jesus Christ and Mary.

Now the captains were assembling the troops. They had been instructed to gather at the shoreline by the line of crosses and banners for the occasion. Cortés planned to address them from a promontory above. He practiced a few words of his speech, examined his hands, put them behind his back, paced, wrinkled his brow. "God, king, mission." Or, "Mission, king, God"?

Precedent and disputation, discourse and argument should have been his forte. He had been trained in just that sort of thing at law school. Now he could not remember the curriculum not only because it had been some sixteen years ago, but because his halfhearted student days, supposedly studying at the University of Salamanca, had been spent in a drunken stupor. Moreover, since then he had not had occasion to address an audience, to proclaim, to remonstrate, to convince. Dissemble, yes, but speechify? No.

This occasion, which would mark a decisive turn away from the ignominy and anonymity in his heretofore wasted life, required all his faculties in fine tune. His main chance, this new world, new time, his world, his time. Cortés peeked through his narrowed eyes and saw the lot of them: his captains in half armor as he required, for it is a bad sheep that will not carry his own wool; and behind them the army three hundred strong—musketeers, pikemen, archers, poleaxers, cannon firers, those armed with mace and hammer, sailors, carpenters, drummers, trumpeters, a priest, a brother, one soothsayer-barber surgeon, a black slave, and sundry others with no talents to speak of. And the Indian slave women.

Native women, how that term summoned pleasures. It suggested submission, domination, a playful back-and-forth of, I am your master, you are my slave. Cortés, he admonished himself, keep your mind on your speech. The words he used today would be tantamount to conquest tomorrow. Indeed his position could not be stronger. He was not only a prince, so to speak, among his peers, a man among men, a commander of legions, but also the soon-to-be overseer of a multitude of brown underlings on a continent blessed with buried treasure. In a word? Gold.

Most men, he now understood, were born to their fate, having it handed to them on a silver platter or meted out to them blow by blow. Others must find their way on the path of experiencia. He was such a one. For years his parents, proud but poor, or was it poor but proud, hidalgos, had believed the worst of him. For example, his father found fault in whatever he did or did not do. And she, martyred saint of a mother, suffered for her wayward son unceasingly, her eyes filling with tears of infinite patience, regretful little sniffs matching every painful smile. Her wretched demeanor was more infuriating than his father's imprecations. Admit it, Señor Hernán Cortés, he admonished himself now, you *were* a troublesome boy, yes, and a failure at the law, disdaining the droning murmur of twice-learned lessons chanted to the slow rhythm of dragging afternoons. He returned to Medellín to take up the post of town ne'er-do-well. Medellín in the province of Extremadura in the heart of Spain, a parched and dusty harrow in the road, overlooked by a derelict nobleman's castle—a place barren of color, hot, sleepy; a blinded ox would die of boredom there. Did he mention trees? A treeless, unforgiving landscape.

Cortés had been bred of soldiers, his father distinguishing himself against the Moors. But the Moors had been defeated finally and forever in 1492 at Granada, and the country united under Queen Isabella and King Ferdinand, so who was he supposed to fight? As second best, he was toying with the idea of enrolling as a condottiere for a city-state in Italy. He was not of the sort to join the Church. What other employment was there for a young man of his time? Then the possibility of sailing to the Indies presented itself. Indeed, at age nineteen, he decided that the New World with its rumors of gold and unlimited land for the take was better than war. Yet even with a household, servants, land, and slaves, and as a notary of sorts, he had not become notable. His stay on the island of Hispaniola and then Cuba had made him rich, but not fabulously rich. It was a dull endeavor, farming, and he had not traveled all the way from Spain to dirty his own hands.

Yet in justice to his procrastination and slow blooming, that is, when one thinks on it, how many men are redeemed in one step, one move, one decision? Man has his frailty, otherwise he would be God.

His own weaknesses concerned women, but what man was not weak when it came to women. And the thing about native women, he had found out through many assignations and a few unwanted pregnancies, was this: They submitted silently. They were not like the Spanish daughters of lesser fortunes and paltry dowries sent to the islands to find their living in a population of uncouth and unmarried men. These señoritas played the game of virginity long in the teeth, desperate of eye, appearing at each and every colonial social function, such as they were: the shipment of satin or a piano from Spain, a rare wedding, a dinner party featuring wild boar or green sea turtle, and, dare he say it, dance? They went to dances strutting about like the prize imported horses, turning a well-shod foot, showing a bit of ankle, doodling, dawdling, dangling their wares, swishing hips under layers of taffeta in hopes of getting noticed. Men, in hopes of legitimate Christian progeny if nothing else, *took* notice.

Native women, on the other hand, were neither dainty nor had they airs or affectation, indeed required no courting and did not have the interfering protection of an ambitious mother. And truth be told, Indio women were wise with a knowing that caused a deep undertow, like the moon to the sea, in the loins of a man, a fully mature thirty-three-year-old man.

Speech, speech! Hernán Cortés walked back and forth thoughtfully, his eyes on the ground in front of his boots. Back, forth, back, forth. But truly, the seduction of a woman and persuasion of a man were not that different. Flattery, close attention, an appearance of resolve and competence—those were the customs of courtship. He smiled. He did like the hairstyles of the native women, their straight, shiny black hair in thick braids wrapped around their perfectly shaped heads or wound into two little topknots in the front like little horns, oh, the devil take them! However, the woman who truly attracted him wore her hair fanned out from her face in black wings, prostitute style. Hawk of the night. Mistress of evil. Eighteen, nineteen, she was a fully grown woman with the splayed feet of a sailor, lips of a plum stain, animal eyes, onyx—wary, unmoving—an aristocratic nose. Slave girls, twenty of them, and one ill-tempered butcher with a harelip.

"Gentlemen . . . ," he began, the moment having finally arrived, the peal of the trumpets subsiding.

Dramatically clearing his throat and staring out at his minions, he placed the cone-shaped, taut, tight skin to his lips to project his voice far down the beach. Careful to speak slowly, he stopped at the end of every sentence so that his words could be repeated up through the ranks by a soldier assigned to every forty men. The echoing effect was exhilarating, the power of his speech brought fresh blood to all his parts.

"My loyal followers . . . citizens of the Villa Rica de la Vera Cruz, the rich town of Vera Cruz." Thus far they had a fine stockade, a prison, of course, a gallows, a small chapel, and a slaughterhouse, although he had yet to spot a pig, cow, or sheep in this godforsaken land. "Destiny awaits us." Sweat was running in rivulets down his back, and some mosquitoes seemed to have crept into his codpiece.

"Destiny, destiny," ran through the ranks.

"Mis compañeros, never forget God, and know that only with him is Fortuna to be found." Cortés's picture of Fortuna was a waterwheel, its buckets so full they brimmed over as they ascended. His fortunes clearly were on the way up, and if ever those buckets began a descent, emptying as they went down, he intended to put a nail in the apparatus and stop it in its tracks. He changed his position, put one foot up on a rock, posed his profile to dignified advantage, and kept his sword ready at a rakish angle on his left side, his dagger tucked into his right side, and deep in his boots a sheath knife in the event that he was disarmed. On his back he had his crossbow and bag of arrows, and beside him the harquebusiers had set up their guns on tripods in the event that somebody did not like what he said.

Meanwhile busy bee Bernal Díaz, record keeper excelente, sat on an adjacent rock, his ink mixed in a jar beside him and his supply of seagull quills tucked in a row at his belt.

CINCO DE MAYO, AÑOS DE NUESTRO SEÑOR 1519

That went in the upper right-hand corner of the first page. He wondered if he should start with "His Majesty" or "My name is Bernal Díaz del Castillo."

Someday the whole world would read his account:

The Conquest
by BERNAL DÍAZ DEL CASTILLO

When future generations would ask "Who was Cortés?" Bernal Díaz would tell them. "Our commander in chief was a man who was at the forefront of every battle, did not hang back or seek cowardly refuge in a commander's tent. Noble in demeanor and actions, a man who feared God wisely and carried his Word to the heathen, a man . . ." Perhaps his opening should be: "I am the esteemed Bernal Díaz del Castillo, official scribe, loyal recorder, the one and only writer of the adventures of the one and only Hernán Cortés, a hidalgo from Spain, resident of Hispaniola and Cuba, sent by the governor of Cuba, one Velázquez, to explore, to trade . . ." Or: "We, valiant men, in our eleven ships left Cuba bound for the mainland on March 4, 1519 . . . After many threats from the tumultuous sea, we saw land, first of all the island Cozumel, and then in the area of Tabasco, where we fought hand to hand some vicious, bloodthirsty savages, we won the day, were rightfully awarded some female slaves, came up the coast, and established the town of Vera Cruz, the True Cross . . ."

Bernal Díaz thought it crucial to catalogue all fourteen horses brought on the expedition, their names and colors. Each horse was more expensive than the lone black African slave, Adu.

"Gentlemen . . . ," Cortés began again.

"He calls us gentlemen," Don Quintaval murmured to Adu, "as if we were princes of the realm." Besides being a fencing master, Quintaval was the owner of a very fine horse, which made him a prized candidate for the trip, and he owned a magnificent sword of tempered

Toledo steel, boots made of Córdoba leather, the Negro slave, and two Indian servants from Hispaniola, Manuel and Juan. Slight of frame, fastidious in dress, with a carefully trimmed beard, Don Quintaval had all the accouterments of a Spanish grandee. Adu, some sixteen years old, was dressed in a suit of clothes matching his master's, as if he too hailed from Europe. His half armor was fashioned in France by a German smith, his green velvet tunic was made in Italy, a brocade doublet with a ruffed neck came from the Low Countries, and the wool stripped stocking was originally sheared from the back of a British sheep. The only discordant note in his attire was that he wore no shoes.

"Men, I intend to make you princes of the realm, for we are on the most honorable mission." Cortés paused, licked his lips, swallowed, and made ready to announce in public what he had already decided privately when still negotiating with that fool the Cuban governor, his so-called patron, Velázquez: "We are here not merely to trade, investigate, pick up a new supply of slaves, and rescue shipwrecked sailors. No, we have come here for the highest cause of all—king, country, and God."

Bernal Díaz worded that "God, king, and country," or should it be "country, God, king, and empire," for not only was Spain united and freed from the Moors in 1492 during the reign of Queen Isabella and King Ferdinand and had expelled the Jews, but King Charles V, Queen Isabella's grandson, was rumored to be bribing his way to the crown of Holy Roman Emperor, which would make him the richest landowner in all of Europe.

"We are on a crusade of conquest!" Cortés exclaimed, doubling his fists and raising them heavenward as if daring the heavens. The pilot, mapmaker, carpenter, and keeper of the one and only clock, Raphael Núñez, did not like the word "crusade." The Crusaders had killed everything in sight, the Jews in Europe and the Muslims in Jerusalem, leaving a river of blood in their wake. Regarded as a converso by Cortés and the others, Núñez glanced warily at the newly set-up gallows, took out his handkerchief, a nicety foreign to the others, took off his spectacles, and wiped his lenses, which were steaming up in the heat.

"My brave soldiers."

"Brave soldiers." Quintaval smirked. "I tell you."

Adu nodded in agreement, hoping his master would stop drawing attention to himself.

"Gentlemen?" Quintaval muttered on regardless. "Failed farmers from the colonies whose supply of slaves has been exhausted to death, a few unemployed craftsmen, a soothsayer who calls himself an apothecary, a Dominican and a Franciscan—those are the gentlemen he addresses. The whole of us, four hundred weak, do not even contain the hardy qualities of buccaneer, swashbuckler, pirate, or bandit."

Adu put his finger to his lips and lifted his eyebrows in warning.

"They make the announcement, then they kill you," Jaguar Claw, the Mayan butcher, whispered to Maax.

"Have you been killed yet?" Malintzin asked, for she knew that in the Maya household the three of them came from, their mistress beat Jaguar on a daily basis. The woman started on Cuy in the morning and finished with Jaguar Claw at night. She, Malintzin, was spared because her body had to be kept unmarked for her nocturnal duties.

"Have you ever gutted a fish, Maax?" Jaguar Claw replied sweetly. "Men are easier."

Malintzin doubted that Jaguar Claw had ever killed anything more dangerous than chortling turkeys, docile dogs, and lazy lizards. With his lips split and twisted to his nose, his speech garbled and nasal, he missed his calling as a clown in the emperor's private entertainment, she thought.

"There have been two previous expeditions to this continent. They were the shortest of visits, unsuccessful, and they scuttled back to Cuba, their tails between their legs, but each of these trial trips returned to Cuba with rumor, nay, reliable word, of gold, definite information that there is a splendid city to the west of this shore, its streets paved in gold. I am so certain of this that I make this promise: I shall make you in a very short time the richest of all men who have crossed the seas." Cortés flung his left arm out to indicate all that lay before them. Glory, gold, a continent ripe for the picking. The Italian, Christopher Columbus the Unlucky, had touched down on various western coasts and established island colonies still dreaming of Asia and failing to open his eyes. Cortés was a mature man. He did not delude himself that he was standing on the legendary Atlantis, or the domain of the Great Khan, the island kingdom of Cipango, or that he had "discovered" the sea route to Marco Polo's eastern potentates. On the contrary, this was a New World to become New Spain.

He looked over at Captain Alvarado, his second-in-command, and found affirmation in his face. Captain Alvarado, called "the Beautiful" for his golden red hair and boyish features, returned Cortés's glance with a smile he hoped conveyed fortitude and courage. He lifted his chin and prayed that this "New World" was not filled with snakes. Their seamless motion, dry scales, and most of all their yellow eyes, not counting of course their long forked tongue, inspired horror in his heart, and the way they could curl their bodies before the strike, may God save him from the sight. And who knew what else lay behind a tree, beneath the foot, dangling in the air? Standing there, one of the four hundred-some strong, the sun making his armor into a roasting pan, Alvarado twiddled his fingers and tapped his foot nervously, for he was of such a humor and blood that if he was not moving in some small way, his mind would fritter to pieces. At night he could not get to sleep unless he drank two full wineskins, and without fail he woke in dread and darkness.

He thought he concealed his apprehensions well and had tight control over his little tics. Alvarado remembered well jumping from a table into what he thought was his father's open arms and falling on his face. The world was a hard and bitter place, his father informed him, let him never forget it. So how did he get here, how could he have been so stupid? One day when he was sitting on the veranda thinking about what to eat next, Cortés's men, their steeds kicking up clouds of dust, approached his encomienda, his rancho, his Cuban horse farm, and asked him if he wanted to join up. Yucatán was unex-

plored, they said, wild, and free for the taking. The next day Alvarado
left his horses in charge of an assistant who had no feeling for animals
at all, like a simpleton closed the door, and rode to Santiago. Impul-
siveness was another of his faults. Now, standing in the unmerciful
sun, he would give the whole of the New World for his horses. He had
brought the mares and one stallion to the islands from Extremadura,
Spain, some five years before—a terrible crossing, with half their cargo
having to be thrown overboard like slaves. Pure Arabians. Poor
Arabians.

"We have come far and not fallen off the edge of the earth." And
with a sweeping gesture of his right hand Cortés indicated Europe,
Africa, and Asia.

Father Olmedo, the priest assigned to the expedition, disapproved
of the words "We have come far" because their trip from Cuba to the
coast of New Spain had not taken long at all, and was only one hundred and twenty miles away. Furthermore, everybody nowadays knew
the earth was not flat with a terra incognita marking the edge and the
Oceanus Occidentalis and Mare Tenebrosum below swallowing up
men and land alike. The astrolabe, magnetic compass, sextant, quad-
rant, lead line, the most up-to-date instruments, and the graphs and
maps of astronomers ensured that a good pilot could find his way on
open sea.

"We have withstood sea monsters."

"What utter bosh," Don Quintaval whispered. "We have withstood minnows. I have heard that a certain Magellan is bargaining
with the Spanish for an expedition which will circumnavigate the
whole globe."

Nonetheless, some of the men *had* feared Neptune's wrath even in
the small crossing from Cuba to the coast of Yucatán. Botello, the
soothsayer, had to cast his dice, study tea dregs, and soothe their fears
with gypsy incantations. And Captain Alvarado the Beautiful *had* seen
mermaidlike creatures, not maids truly, more mermatrons, with tough
leathery skin, wrinkled brows, fat necks, and whiskers. Harmless
really, yet not what you want to meet while taking a leisurely swim. In

deeper waters a squid the size of a ship had been sighted. All it would take for a squid to destroy a ship was a simple wrap around and down, down, down.

Brother Francisco, the monk assigned to assist Father Olmedo in winning new souls in the new land, his bare pate burning under the relentless sun, wondered if he could love the monsters of the deep as he tried to love every animal just like St. Francis, save that very bad pig St. Francis encountered who bit a lamb and later died belly up, bloated and moldering in a puddle. Brother Francisco had to struggle with the idea of loving a squid, particularly the huge one sighted by Puertocarrero off the bow.

"Squid ahoy!" Puertocarrero had warned from atop the crow's nest.

Brother Francisco had wondered if he should understand that squid as a message from God, that is, like the story of Jonah and the whale. Pride and disobedience put one in the belly of a beast. Did St. Francis love the beast too?

Señor Isla, standing by Brother Francisco, at the mention of sea monsters leaned over and could not resist telling the gentle brother that boa constrictors in Yucatán could eat a man whole, two men if it was really hungry, and that the deadliest thing alive, scorpions, got in your boots, and "in the case of you, Brother Francisco, with no shoes, between your toes." Captain Isla took pleasure in teasing the innocent Francisco, gullible gull that he was.

"We have fought many battles," Cortés went on.

As far as Quintaval knew, Cortés had never fought in any battle, save the little skirmish on the beach. In the band that conquered Cuba, Cortés bragged of derring-do, but in truth the Arawak Indians in Cuba had fled from attack. Quintaval relayed these interesting facts to Adu, sotto voce, who nodded, he hoped not in a conspiratorial manner. Don Quintaval added that he, Don Quintaval, who practiced his fencing daily, could distinguish himself in any contest. Adu, his sparring partner, was all too familiar with Quintaval's feints, faux thrusts, and unexpected parries. Cortés was nothing but a lowly notary in Hispaniola, Quintaval continued, a plantation master in Cuba whose slaves had all perished from exhaustion, a man who had left law school in Salamanca before he qualified, a dissolute wastrel in Spain. It was even said that when Cortés first came to Hispaniola, he had worked as a scrivener, the kind who walked around the square helping the illiterate write letters for a maravedí or two, and indeed had to share a cloak with two others. Moreover, Quintaval knew for a fact that Velázquez, the governor of Cuba, sorely regretted his choice of Cortés as captain, and had tried to withdraw favor and funds for the expedition at the last minute. As Cortés was scuttling out of the port, barreling on toward the coast of Yucatán in his nao, the *Santa María de la Concepción*, his personal banner inscribed in Latin, "Brothers, let us follow the Cross, and by our faith shall we conquer," the governor Velázquez had sent messengers to the shore waving hastily drawn-up papers like pathetic flags of surrender, calling out, "Come back, come back."

Adu appeared to listen to his master with one ear and Cortés with another, keeping his own mouth closed. What he was thinking about was lying down on the warm sand and going to sleep. Each morning of his captivity, not including his middle passage in the hold of a boat when he wanted to die, he concentrated his mind on, How will I escape today? Once the day started, he dreamed of sleep. In sleep he was free, although Don Quintaval, who had him sleep in his bed with him, kept him long awake with renditions of his childhood in Spain and all the people in Santiago, Cuba, who were his enemies and why he hated them. If Adu dozed off, Don Quintaval would elbow him in the ribs. "Wake up, Adu, I have not finished." When he was finished, Adu was required to kneel beside his master while prayers were said for numerous Quintavals who had perished in one way or another. Adu, who did not believe in Quintaval's god, nonetheless silently said a prayer for his family in Africa, for he thought of his family as "my family," as if he owned himself.

Cortés reached in his belt and drew out a long scroll. It was the Requerimiento, a rather elaborate and lengthy missive from the pope dated May 4, 1493, including the information that all the land discovered three hundred miles west of the Azores was granted to the Spanish monarchs, and noting also that all populations would be informed that all mankind came from Adam and Eve and was one family under the authority of the pope, who was "lord, king, and superior of the universe," and that all the conquered people were under the sovereignty of the pope and Spain, some under Portugal, as it was, and not mentioned. Most importantly, should any wicked and rebellious vassals of the king of Spain rebel, they would be punished as enemies of the faith and truth and in the service of the devil.

"What is that?" Cuy asked Jaguar Claw.

"That is their book," Jaguar Claw surmised. The Mayan and Aztec books were written on bark paper and folded out like fans.

"Had I been a man, I would wish to be a scribe," Malintzin said.

"Had you been a man, you would be a warrior or captive, and probably dead," Cuy answered pleasantly.

"Our mission, stout and willing men, is to spread the Word of the Lord or die trying."

Malintzin sometimes understood the aliens' words that were repeated over and over again, such as people's names or well-used objects: sword, horse, bow, arrows, Cortés. She knew that soon more words would gather to her, and that what she heard would make more sense until meaning would sweep over her in a wave of understanding.

"Our mission is to reach the heart of the country."

Everybody dropped to their knees, crossed themselves, Father, Son, Holy Ghost, Amen, and rose up.

"Our mission is to meet their Grand Emperor, Moctezuma, face-to-face and to convert them all to Christianity." Cortés paused and took a deep breath. "And let this not go unsaid: Men, we have come to find gold . . ." Cortés lifted his head to the sun and stared fearlessly right into its eye. "Gold, mis amigos, oro."

"Finally," Señor Isla said to Brother Francisco. "Finally Cortés is saying what needs be said."

"Gold, gold, gold for the bold," echoed up and down the ranks.

Brother Francisco did not say anything, but he silently asked God to help him love Isla, for he was a man, a fellow creature, and thus worthy of being loved. Francisco could not help, however, disliking him.

Isla, fourth in command after General Cortés, Captain Alvarado the Beautiful, and Señor Quintaval the Fencer, was aware that two earlier trips to Yucatán by the Spanish revealed the presence of gold. Why else would *he* have come? Isla could taste it on the tip of his tongue. In Spain he had the chance to relieve the overrich and tottering old of their burdensome coin, sell property that had no water or existed in the mind alone, trade horses that limped, offer pigs filled with worms, old men's teeth, and women's wigs cut from the desperately sick. Isla had encouraged speculation on Portuguese slave boats filled with dead or dying slaves, cinnamon that was merely flavored oak, and bread that was pasted chaff. He meant no harm. It was simply business. But when his enemies colluded, he had to leave Spain posthaste and depart for the islands pronto. It did not take him that long in Cuba to acquire a fine suit of clothes, a sword, a horse. Maybe it had all worked out for the best.

"Gold for the bold."

"Cities of gold!" one of the men shouted, for there were rumors of such cities.

Cities of God, is what Brother Francisco thought. Although a Franciscan, he admired St. Augustine's *Cities of God,* a book about attaining a higher state.

To Father Olmedo, cities of gold meant countless new souls for the Church, particularly important these days since every weaver, upstart printer, and lowly miller in northern and eastern Europe declared he personally knew the Word and intention of God without the intercession of his priest. Father Olmedo did not want to foul his mouth, let alone clutter his mind with the likes of John Hus, the rightly burned, John Wycliffe, who dared to translate the Bible into the savage Saxon language, and now that rapscallion Luther, who argued that every man was his own priest.

"Cities of gold!" The cry, four hundred strong, picked up.

"Rivers of gold!" It was passed down among the troops until in unison they were chanting the mottoes.

"Fountains of youth."

"Beds of gems."

"Mountains of silver."

"The Indians think I am a god," Cortés shouted out, for he was stirred by the support of his troops. Was not anything possible with the support of one's men? "The indios believe I am their god Quetzalcoatl," he said. "Well, maybe I am a god."

"Cortés is a god," went the word through the ranks. "God, god, god."

Then the shouting abruptly halted. The massed men looked to their right, their left, behind their backs. God? A god? Who could presume such a thing? And a vast silence filled the air, as if the birds and animals too were aghast.

"No, I do not mean that." The insufferable heat was making Cortés giddy. Why had he brought up the Quetzalcoatl myth that the defrocked priest, Aguilar, had mentioned. "Some Indians think you are a returned god." Aguilar had related this to Cortés in the privacy of the flagship's cabin. He explained the prophecies regarding Quetzalcoatl's fair skin, beard, the year One Reed.

"Did he say Quetzalcoatl?" Jaguar Claw asked Cuy. In Maya, the name of the god was Kukulcán. The beginning of the world was noted down in the Popo Vu. "Is that who he thinks he is? If he is Quetzalcoatl, I am Huitzilopochtli."

"If you are Huitzilopochtli, then I am Coyolxauhqui," Malintzin said.

"You do not want to be Coyolxauhqui. She was dismembered," Cuy reminded her.

"Hush," Jaguar Claw said, looking over her shoulders. "Both of you are dishonoring the gods. Do you want the world to stop because of your irreverence?"

"Will it stop?" Malintzin asked.

"I am nobody," Cortés amended, taking back his vainglorious words. "I am nobody and nothing. Dust."

"We are but dust," Father Olmedo affirmed.

"Dust," the troops echoed.

"What are they going to do now?" Cuy asked.

"They are going to eat up the beach," Jaguar Claw answered. "The beach, the mountains, the jungle, the desert."

Chapter 6

J aguar Claw skinned the armadillo which with its large gunshot wound would not yield much meat. But the foreigners wanted to feast on it, mighty hunters that they were. A bunch of iguanas had been caught and, with cords attached to their scrolled necks, patiently watched.

"You for later," Jaguar Claw told them.

The beasts blinked, enjoying the morning sun.

"They are going to divide us up, each one for a different man," Cuy said to Malintzin while she slivered some frog and chewed on some cilantro leaf to be spit into the food for flavoring. She only had two hands to chop with, so she put her teeth to work too. "See the thick fur on the foreigners' faces? Are they not disgusting, Maax? Like anteaters."

Malintzin knew the Maya were an especially clean people, bathing several times a day. But the strangers *were* dirty. They had not learned to make rooms of tall reeds for defecation where one could retreat, the matter taken out at night to be dispersed in the fields for the growth of the crops. Instead, they performed without regard for modesty, squatting like dogs on the beach, in the meadow, on the embankment, loosening their strange bottom garment and dropping it around their knees. They spat gobs of mucus. Flies attended their every move. And the way they ate? Like greedy children, letting food and drink dribble down their chins and spill down their fronts. Furthermore, they talked constantly and loudly from the moment they rose from their mats in the morning. At night they sang raucously. They even talked to their big beasts, making clucking sounds into their ears, the creatures rolling their huge eyes and answering back in wild sounds. Before they knew differently, some of the women thought the great beasts could talk in the language of the men.

Their dogs, smaller than the grass-eaters, were of a kind never seen before. As puppies, Aztec and Mayan dogs slept with the children to keep them warm. When the hairless dogs were grown and fat, they were slaughtered to make stew. The foreigners' dogs were not eaten. Instead, these huge, ferocious creatures with mouths frothing could eat a man at a command, and were used, she had been warned by Cuy, Jaguar Claw, and others, to chase down runaways.

That morning a group of the foreign caterpillar-men practiced shooting arrows from bows small but very strong. The arrows, cocked on a spring and then drawn, reached great lengths. Other men were running with spears in their hands, stabbing trees. Still others had axes with long handles which they twirled above their heads before slashing bushes. Some men marched to the beach and back to the beat of a drum, chanting in unison: Izquierda, derecha, izquierda, derecha. The grass-eaters, all sixteen of them, were being washed and brushed under the direction of the beautiful one, Alvarado.

To Malintzin, the Cockroach resembled her father in stance. She would never tell Cuy or Jaguar Claw that. Nonetheless, the white man held himself as proudly as her father, and had short legs and a large upper body. He was the one man, other than her father, who looked her straight in the eye. Not that in any other way was he similar to her father. Cuy called the lot of them caterpillars for the stripped, fuzzy leggings which wrapped their legs, and when they were in their white, unsheathed nakedness, she called them grubs. Later, when Malintzin mastered their terms, she knew cockroach was la cucaracha. El mono was monkey and la oruga caterpillar and el gusano worm. Aguilar, who had pointed out the gallows of Vera Cruz, taught her a new word each day. As a foreigner and former Maya slave, he knew both their tongues, Maya and Spanish. Moreover, Aguilar's skin was brown, not pale yellow or pink or the translucent, tender white, and he ate crouching low to the ground and looked uncomfortable in the foreigners' clothes. He was almost one of them, a person of the sun, although Jaguar Claw said not to trust him any more than any of the others.

If her people could be called the people of the sun, Malintzin thought the pale barbarians could be called the people of the moon, luna, the moon wooed by the sea and the white men born of that cold union. Some of them had eyes the color of the sea, and some had hair like a thatch of dried seaweed, not neatly trimmed and cut like a warrior's. The chief's lips were like a small fish's, not a man's mouth at all, and like the others', his carapace was silvery overlapping scales.

"I wonder which one I will be given to, Maax," Cuy persisted. The women were still crowded together in one tent. "Jaguar Claw says they have habits among themselves. He has seen strange customs which are punishable by our laws."

"Jaguar Claw is very observant, Cuy."

Indeed Jaguar Claw had the furtive eyes of a rodent. A skilled butcher, he could skin rabbits and dogs the way other men peeled fruit. He believed that if he had been higher-born and not so strange-looking, he would have been a priest, one of the highly honored ones to cut the hearts out of captives, flay skin in the skin-flaying ceremony, wear newly flayed skin as a robe, be able to wear his hair long and matted with blood. At the very least he would be a warrior, a real jaguar or eagle.

"I do not care which man I am given to," Malintzin said. It surprised her that Cuy was so concerned, for did she not hate them all as did Jaguar Claw? Yet Malintzin knew that Cuy was a person who from moment to moment flopped, like a fish stranded on the shore, from happy to sad, hopeful to downcast. Sometimes Malintzin tired of the effort of knowing her, but Cuy was her only friend. The other women in the group did not care to talk during their tasks of cooking, serving, cleaning up, and cooking again. As soon as they put their heads down, they fell asleep, dropping down into dark forgetfulness, not fluttering an eyelid until they were pulled from their mats.

Malintzin and Cuy, although tired after their work, liked to watch the Spanish through the open flap of their tent. These strange men emerged like white worms, fragile pupae out of their heavy silver shells and caterpillar clothes. Lying by a huge bonfire, feet facing the flames, leaning on the back of their arms, drying their stinking toes, they laughed and spoke all at once with the abandon of old people who had drunk too much pulque at a wedding. Two of them played instruments, one a gourd with a long neck, strings tied to it, the other a flute to his lips. The one with the stringed gourd, Botello was his name, had a mop of curling black hair, making him look like he was topped by a nest of black vipers. He wore one gold earring and had a lame foot which he thrust in front of him, giving him a hopping gait. And the other musician, the beautiful Alvarado, played his flute merrily and with great flourish, his skin radiating the passion of the young, his eyes slivers of turquoise and his hair the red-yellow of the midday sun. He was a captain, one of the inner circle. At the heart was Cortés, and the others moved about him in concentric rings.

Alvarado, lovely
Quintaval, angrily
Isla, wickedly
Aguilar, nervously
Núñez, timidly
Botello, mysteriously
Puertocarrero, sloppily
Brother Francisco, goodly
Father Olmedo, holy
Adu, youthfully

The two women friends discussed their new life every night while Malintzin gently, with the care of a real mother, took down Cuy's coiled hair, ran a cactus-spine brush through it, then rubbed a smear of duck fat scented with sweet bark stick into her scalp, section by section. In the flickering light of the fire, with her slanted eyes and narrow face, Cuy looked like a princess or a witch. But Malintzin was the princess, she reminded herself, so did that make Cuy a witch? The word "cuy" in the Maya language meant small black bird, but sometimes Malintzin thought of Cuy as more crow than bunting with her small, unblinking eyes.

"The brown-gowns do not get women," Cuy mused. "I like the fat

brown-gown best. He always nods and smiles and greets us in his language. Of the others, I would like the one who is scorched as if he fell
in a fire or got too close to the sun. His hair crinkles up like little
lightning bolts trying to find their way back to the sky." Except for
his master, Quintaval, the Spanish called the black man black bitch,
perra negra.

"He is a foreigner to the foreigners, a slave like we are, Cuy. Anyway, he is just a boy. He will not get a woman."

"There is one who looks like a Maya."

Light of foot, Núñez had, like a Maya, a narrow face. He wore a
strange apparatus in front of his eyes, two round clear panes, and he
did not wear the short puffed skirts of the others, but wore breeches
to his knees of soft leather, and instead of the silver carapace across his
chest and back, he wore a sleeveless tunic with a row of bright silver
buttons over his white blouse of full sleeves. Not wearing a sword, he
carried a bag with mallets and small axes and rolls of their paper with
him on two spindles. In another bag over his shoulder he carried a
large silver object. At intervals he would take it out as requested and
check it.

"Do you want their soothsayer with an earring and black worm
hair, Maax?"

"I do not think he will get a woman either."

"The one with the golden hair, a mouth the color of a cherry stain?"

Later, when his horse was killed from under him, peppered
through with arrows like a giant porcupine, crumpling beneath him,
Alvarado took the animal's great head in his lap and slashed its throat,
crying out: "Probrecito, probrecito."

"Such beauty is dangerous, Cuy."

The one Malintzin did not want to get for certain was the wicked
one, a man who had one fingernail as long as an Aztec priest's, signifying, she thought, he did not have to use his hands or that he was a
witch in the employ of the underworld. His face was like a jade-stone
mask, fixed, without movement, holes for eyes, a sneering lift of the lip
for a smile. Isla was his name. Malintzin thought she knew a lot about
men because she was an auianime in her second Maya house, the one

that Cuy and Jaguar Claw came from too. Although she was not an auianime of the kind revered as courtesans, or the ones who accompanied young warriors in their calmecac or attended prized captives in their final year before the steps, Malintzin was nonetheless an auianime.

Jaguar Claw predicted that the chief of the captains, the one he called the Cockroach, would choose Maax for his own. He had observed the man resting his eyes on Maax, but he warned her that she should be wary of him above all. Malintzin knew Jaguar was right, for although Cortés gazed at her with longing, then moved his eyes away, and the man's face was inharmonious, his mouth deceitful in its smallness, his chin beneath all his hair with a cruel jut to it, yet his power made him attractive. His woman would be like a first wife. Malintzin could not even dream she could become a first wife, or a second. Before she was gifted to the foreigners, she would never have been fortunate enough to serve only one man. Thus she was hopeful that there would be one, only one, and although she found him frightening, to be the Cockroach's woman would be best. But instead of taking her for his own, Cortés appointed her instead to a meek man who sucked on the hair over his lip and fondled the hair on his chin and even when his helmet was off made little curls with his fingers of the hair on his head. He was Puertocarrero.

Then, before any of the twenty women were taken to their man's mat, they had to go before the carved staves of the tortured one planted in a row along the beach and were made to kneel in homage on pain of death or loss of their legs. One of the brown-clads sprinkled drops of water on them and said many words in still another language. Later Malintzin understood that the grubs could not take women with them on the pallet unless the women were declared obedient to their tortured god. Later Aguilar explained to her that the one who was tortured had a father who was a sky god who lived on a cloud, and the woman in the blue robe was the mother of the one who was tortured. She was an earth goddess but did not wear a skirt of snakes like Coatlicue or a collar of hands and hearts. Strangely, and not the other way around, the blood of their sacrificed man-god was drunk and pieces of his body eaten.

Cuy was given to the man who carried his tools on his back, Núñez.

"It looks as if he has mutilated himself with cactus spine or fish quill and done much sacrificial bloodletting with his penis," she reported the first morning. "The skin is pulled back. He put a white cloth over me with a hole in the middle. What did yours do?"

"What they do." Malintzin's had sucked her nipples, then his thumb afterward. He was a man who clearly had not been with his mother long enough.

"Mine knows how to guide their winged houses and makes marks on their paper," Cuy bragged.

"Is he also their scribe?"

"No." Cuy pointed out Bernal Díaz, who always stood near the general and followed him around like a little dog. To Malintzin, Bernal Díaz was one who had not been with his father long enough. When he was not writing, he carried his writing quill self-importantly over his ear and had others at the ready in his belt and dry ink powder in a small pouch. Whenever the general said something, he nodded in agreement and wrote it down, as if one lost word would be an unaccountable loss. Of the brown-clads Malintzin liked Brother Francisco. He had a round moon face; his body was soft and fluffy and spilled out on the sides like cotton from its stalk. He kissed flowers, bowed before trees, and smelled of roses. The Aztec holy men wore their hair long and matted with the blood of those sacrificed. They were not permitted to bathe; their cloaks were often made of the skins of the flayed ones. They smelled of carnage.

"Did you find out why they are here?" Jaguar Claw asked the two women, as if the act on the mat were sufficiently revealing to learn someone's intentions and secret thoughts.

"I think they have come to meet the great Mexica emperor, Moctezuma, in Tenochtitlán," Malintzin said. She had been able to pick out that word from time to time. And clearly the barbarians were on the march.

"*Meet* Moctezuma?" Jaguar Claw exclaimed. "With tunnels that belch balls, thunder sticks, and long knives harder than any obsidian?

With arrows and spears, and riding on top of animals that with one kick can kill a man, followed by man-eating dogs?"

Malintzin liked the grass-eaters. When she walked out to them in the meadow, they came forward to greet her, put their big mouths in her hand to touch, and nuzzled like babies in search of a breast.

"How do you know all that, Maax, about Moctezuma and gold?" Cuy asked.

"I listen, I watch, and Aguilar teaches me their words," she admitted. Aguilar, who had been the slave of the cacique in the Tabasco region, called her Malinche, not Malintzin. Her mother and father had called her Malinali for the month she was born. Cuy called her Maax, Maya for Prattling Monkey. In her heart, she did not know who she was—grass, monkey, princess, or slave.

"Have you seen them eat the gold?" Cuy asked her.

Eating gold brought to mind soft squash blossoms melting in the mouth.

"They do not eat it, Cuy. It is too hard, and when they melt it, it is too hot."

"What do they do with it then?"

"I think they keep it next to their hearts. They have heartsickness, and only gold cures it. That is why we are going to the capital to meet Moctezuma."

"They do have heartsickness, which only extraction can cure," Jaguar Claw said. But in *his* heart, Jaguar Claw had always wanted to travel to the capital, see the great city—Tenochtitlán, the tallest pyramids, the grandest nobles, and wide streets and many canals.

Near Jaguar's butcher table, on tree boughs, dead deer, strung up by their hind legs, a line of twenty of them, swayed in the morning breeze. Malintzin could smell the rainy season coming, see it in the way the light changed and how night-blooming flowers that opened for the light of the moon remained tightly closed, guarding their frail petals against the coming assault.

"Are we going to die in the capital?" Cuy asked.

"Oh, Cuy." Malintzin looked at her. Cuy, older than Maax, seemed so much the little girl sometimes. "You are not going to die soon, not until you are old."

"Do you promise, Maax?"

"I promise." Malintzin knew she could not promise anything, but what was the harm in saying it? It was possible that they would be caught by Aztecs and used for sacrifice. It was possible that the foreigners would hang them on the gallows. It was possible that one of the great volcanoes could erupt, or the earth heave open. Any number of events come to pass, wielding the sword of death.

"Their gods are very weak," Jaguar Claw added. Malintzin was confused about that too, for why would one of their gods choose to be bled and tortured? People sacrificed *themselves* to gods. The Aztec and Maya gods drank human blood, not the other way around. The taste of the white men's man-god's blood, for they all had to drink it, was like berries picked too early, tart with only the promise of sweetness.

"Of our gods, only Quetzalcoatl was not strong," Cuy said. "He was defeated, suffered in exile during the time he was a man, and does not require sacrifice except for quails and snakes."

"He was strong. He was betrayed. But he is to come again," Malintzin added.

"The foreigners' thunder sticks," Jaguar Claw continued, "they do not have many, and they can lose them easily. Water silences them."

"The thunder sticks are guarded by their huge dogs," Malintzin pointed out.

"Have you ever seen a dog die of frog?" Jaguar Claw knew poisons.

Malintzin knew that the slimy backs of certain frogs were smeared on tips of arrows and blow darts but were rarely used by hunters or warriors. The poison tainted the meat.

"We are slaves," Cuy said, "only to be exchanged. Do masters matter?"

"You were the one concerned about who was to be your master, Cuy," Malintzin reminded her.

"Masters *do* matter," Jaguar Claw put in. "They should not be foreign."

"Núñez is a good master," Cuy announced.

"And your Maya master you had in Tabasco?" Malintzin asked Jaguar Claw.

"A monster. I was once a slave of an Aztec too," Jaguar Claw said.

"And he was good to you, fed you well?"

"A demon, cruel as a viper. I admired him greatly. And a caution to you, Maax and Cuy, where your words go, your feet follow."

Chapter 7

Aguilar was not with Cortés's group when they left Cuba. He was found shipwrecked on the coast of Yucatán. It was a lovely morning, eight o'clock by Núñez's clock. The air was not yet hot and heavy, and the flowers of the scarlet bush, long red tubes, seemed to be stretching, almost luxuriating, in the light air. The twenty slave women gifted to the conquistadors the night before were bunched together near a tall chicozapote tree, whose sap was called chicle and could be chewed. Their distribution among the men was yet to take place. Meanwhile they held themselves stiffly and stayed silent. The deformed butcher was eviscerating deer, Father Olmedo had just finished saying mass, and Bernal Díaz was correcting some notes in his notebook. Botello was mashing leaves he had collected in his quest for plants that induced aphrodisiac effects. Adu and Quintaval were practicing a few moves with Quintaval's rapiers.

"En guardia," Quintaval commanded his partner. "Parry in quarte. Parry in tierce. Semicircular parry. En merchant and advance. Withdraw. Break off."

"Wild man, ahoy," Puertocarrero called out.

"Wild man," came the echo from the troops.

"Wild man here?" Quintaval asked Adu, as if he would know European modes.

"An indio?" Adu replied. "Is he armed?"

"Is he armed?" Quintaval shouted to Puertocarrero. "An indio?"

"Armed Indian," went out the cry.

"Not armed, but running fast," Puertocarrero replied.

"Not armed."

"Oh, for Christ's sake, Puertocarrero," Cortés said. "Everybody does not have to know everything. Keep something to yourself."

"Maybe one of the natives is hungry for the Word of God," Father Olmedo suggested.

"Most likely," Quintaval whispered to Adu, "hungry for a piece of bread."

"Maybe it is a trap, Señor," Isla cautioned Cortés. "And fifty others of his kind lie in wait."

"Crossbows at the ready," Cortés commanded.

"Crossbows at the ready."

"Crossbows at the ready."

The crossbowmen pulled back their arrows, prepared to pepper the lone figure.

"Draw swords."

"Draw swords," Puertocarrero relayed.

The solitary man, despite the great show of weapons, kept running toward them. Naked save for a knotted loincloth and a sack tied to his back, he did not look Indian, for he was tall, not compactly built, mere skin and bones, and his fair hair hung in matted strings down his back.

Brother Francisco thought, Here comes Adam in his original state.

"Halt!" Puertocarrero screamed out to the man. "In the name of King Carlos. En el nombre del Rey Carlos."

Amazingly the man stopped in his tracks.

"Proceed."

"Yo soy español," the man beseeched.

"A Spaniard."

"A Spaniard."

He dared to draw nearer. His head bobbed as if he were a puppet loosely attached to his neck. His bright blue eyes gleamed with tears.

"Loco, Señor," Isla said to Cortés.

Puertocarrero, overhearing, reported.

"Madman," everybody echoed.

"Yo soy cristiano. Gracias, Santa María." The man fell at Cortés's feet.

"Raise yourself up, hombre, you are a Spaniard and a Christian."
Cortés hated groveling. He grabbed the man's arms, pulled him up,
and held him firm. "I am Captain Hernán Cortés, the leader of our
expedition." Although instructed to search for shipwrecked sailors,
Cortés had no expectation of finding any Europeans on these forlorn
shores.

"Gerónimo de Aguilar at your service," the poor creature mumbled.
Bernal Díaz immediately inscribed in his notebook:

26 DE ABRIL DEL 1519

We encountered a bereft and devote Spanish grandee . . .

Shaking badly, the refugee had to be lifted into the rowboat, and
Cortés wondered how such a weakling could be of service to him.
Obviously unfit for rugged work, the man would have to be fed,
dressed, and accommodated. The other rowboats were filled with the
water kegs, fruits, dressed deer, newly caught fish, the turkeys they had
been given by the defeated cacique, and the slave women, whom
Cortés decided would be kept on ship decks under stretched canvases.
He needed his captain's quarters for strategy sessions.

"To the ships." Cortés raised his sword dramatically.

"To the ships."

"To the ships."

The horses that had been grazing and used to great effect in the
battle with the Tabascan town were swum out to the flagship. Aguilar,
peering over, seeing their great legs churn in the clear turquoise water,
thought they resembled Pegasus galloping through the air. Alvarado,
naked and muscular, swimming in front of them, seemed only tem-
porarily detached, so that Aguilar could understand how the Indians
thought of horsemen and horse, centaurlike, as one. Lifted by crane-
like contraptions with a pulley onto the deck of the *Santa María* and
led to their spot on deck, the horses were settled in. The slave women
were taken to the other ships in the flotilla and sheltered on decks

much like the horses in the flagship. Aguilar was given clothes and a piece of cassava bread. He sat down cross-legged, holding his bread to his mouth with both hands. The captains, curious to hear his story, encircled him.

"Many años ago," he began, his voice weak and tentative, "I was on board the *Santo del Niño* on the way from Jamaica to Hispaniola."

Alvarado the Beautiful had heard of shipwrecked men living on clams and crabs for years, building fires on the beaches as signals and rustic shelters out of palm branches. They quietly went mad from solitude and frustration unless some tribesman mercifully slaughtered them.

"Everybody perished, save four of us."

As Aguilar described his ordeal to the captains, the anchors were hoisted and the common soldiers and seamen assumed their particular stations adroitly, for the deck was so crowded there was hardly room to walk two steps either way. Thick hemp ropes, bolts of canvas, casks of dried pork, wine, and pickling brine, tripods used to hold the large harquebuses in place for firing, the large bronze cannons fitted on wheels and built to fire a ball of thirty pounds, a group of falconets, the smaller cannons, tightly lidded jars of gunpowder, and boxes of cheap green-glass beads from Venice took up much of the space. Yet the *Santa María* was a nao, a large galleon, square-rigged with three masts. The animal manger was right next to the captain's cabin and set near a tiny galley. The fetid hold below deck was divided into two sections—sleeping quarters for the captains and the common soldiers. The members of the expedition, however, considered themselves fortunate, for when Christopher Columbus made his journey from Spain to the Indies, his sailors had no hold to go to, but slept on deck, and there was no galley; rather the food that had to be cooked was prepared over little fires set up for the moment.

"What was your cargo?" Cortés asked Aguilar, for he could not think of anything worth shipping from Jamaica. It was a hilly and wooded island, he had heard, with no gold.

"Indian slaves on the way to Cuba. All died chained together. Four of us, white men, were captured by the Mayans. I have been a slave to the cacique for these two years, but look, look what I have"—and he extracted from his worn cotton bag a faded, leather-bound, gold-embossed *Book of Hours*. "My salvation."

"And the other three Spaniards?"

"One has become a Mayan general. He has pierced and tattooed himself, wears rings in his lips and nose, and has taken a Mayan wife and has Mayan children."

"Beyond belief," Puertocarrero declared. "How could a white man forgo civilization?"

"And the other two?" Cortés asked.

"Sacrificed."

"Well, that is highly unfortunate," Cortés said quickly. He did not want his captains and, least of all, his soldiers preoccupied with sacrifice. "You need to eat some proper food. Una comida, a good mass. Fortunately we have a padre with us, Father Olmedo, who will take confessions, and a Franciscan, Brother Francisco."

"Ah, bueno, and as soon as we get back to Spain, I must make a pilgrimage in homage to Santiago de Compostela, Santiago, who led the attack against the Moors of Granada, the decisive battle." Aguilar crossed himself, but while he was faithful to the prayers of the hours, he had no intention of making a pilgrimage. What Aguilar really wanted to do, now that he was saved, was sleep in a proper bed, sleep and sleep.

"We are not on our way back to Cuba or to Spain." Cortés turned to him and looked into those watery blue eyes. "We are here in this heathen land, mi amigo, on a very important mission. Tell me, Señor Aguilar, do you speak the language of the indios?"

Aguilar looked about apprehensively. Mission? "I speak Chontal Maya, which is the language of most of the tribes in the south, but do not speak Nahuatl, the language of the empire."

"Empire?"

"Do you know, Don Hernán Cortés, that my *Book of Hours* is not a newfangled printed copy, but hand copied and illuminated. I need to know the hour of my delivery so I can make the proper prayer. Have you an hourglass handy?"

"Núñez, what time is it?"

Núñez took the small table clock out of his knapsack. "It is ten o'clock, sir."

"Dear God, what is that?" Aguilar was aghast. "It looks like the work of the devil."

"Be comforted, Aguilar. It is neither devil-made nor miracle. It is a clock made by man, a table clock, a miniature clock powered by a key and spring, a small copy of what most cities in Europe have in the middle of the town, a tower, and in the tower a clock. Núñez with his clock is our town crier, so to speak. I have heard it said that they can make some to hang like a pendant, to sit on your wrist like a bracelet. It is a new age, a time of wonders, but more to the point, Aguilar, what do you know about gold here?"

"Clocks so small?"

"Gold, Señor Aguilar, do the Indians have gold? Rivers of gold, mountains of silver, fountains of youth? Do you have a map to the gold?"

"Ah, tristemente, no. Nor have I heard of a fountain of youth as Juan Ponce de León sought in Florida. The gold is kept farther north and controlled by the Mexica emperor, Moctezuma."

"An emperor? They have an emperor?"

"The world is a strange place," Bernal Díaz commented. "Heathens with an emperor?"

"Beyond belief," Puertocarrero added.

"You are beyond belief," Alvarado said. "And stop eating your beard."

"You are young, Bernal Díaz, and will see many more amazing things," Father Olmedo said.

Botello wondered what Father Olmedo had in mind, for all the padre had ever seen in the line of duty were the lines of his litany, the mouths of parishioners, open like birds at breakfast, and a steady parade of gowned men chanting dismal prayers. He, Botello, had been to Paris, to Madrid, to Prague, to Venice, and would, with a little gold, get to return to Europe in a fine suit of clothes and have his own horse. He would hire somebody to read to him. He would learn the secrets of the Greeks, the Romans, the Arabs of Byzantine, the Jews of northern Africa, and the Babylonian codes.

"What strikes me," Cortés said, "is how one can come across oceans to an unknown land and find a Spanish man. Does that not strike you as wonderful?"

"Although," Quintaval said, "according to the governor of Cuba, Velázquez, part of our mission was to find shipwrecked sailors."

Cortés gave Quintaval a steely stare, but reflected that to their great surprise, the troops discovered a dog, a mastiff bitch left behind on the expedition to Yucatán the year before. This animal, which had greeted them on the beach, had lived like a wild animal, hunting for itself, yet it had not forgotten white men nor had it lost a loyal pet's sweet ways. To Cortés this indicated that the larger world, the one that blasphemous astronomers said was not the hub of God's universe, *was* the hub of the universe, a familiar and not indifferent place. He took heart from such signs, and did not need his soothsayer and fortune-teller Botello to tell what they meant. In comparison, clocks were toys. This was a miracle. God was with the conquest.

And so, in honor of the first victory over the Indians, the acquisition of twenty women, and the rescue of Aguilar, their new dog, and the mild April weather, they held a raucous celebration on board the *Santa María* that night. Botello played his guitar, really an instrument brought into Spain by the Moors, and Alvarado his flute, and the men danced to the tune of "Señorita Bonita," and "Someday I Will Marry You—Algún día yo me casaré contigo," and "Kiss Me Again, You Ugly Whore—Bésame otra vez, tú puta horrible." Moreover, Aguilar was invited to Cortés's cabin as a special guest.

Entering this sanctum sanctorum, the grateful refugee tried to execute a graceful bow in the chivalric tradition, kneeling on one knee and sweeping his hat to the floor. All elbows and knees, Cortés observed, whittled lean as a whistle, the man was ungainly and clumsy, bad soldier material.

"So, my friend, sit down. Let us get to know one another."

Aguilar sat on a high stool, the one Botello used for haircuts, and Cortés sat opposite in a Dante chair of folding legs and arms made of dark mahogany from Africa, its seat and back of a choice oxblood leather. Aguilar, pitiful in his Spanish doublet, cape, ill-fitting stockings, baggy breeches, and large velvet beret with a drooping feather, did not look Cortés straight in the face, but let his eyes wander off to the side. Could Aguilar possibly be a spy in the Indios' pay? Cortés wondered.

"I lived with the Maya, not the Aztec, Comandante. Mayas occupy Yucatán and some of the south. Aztecs control the central plains and mountains, north and south."

"Call me Cortés, Don Aguilar, as all my men do. I am one of you."

"I see you are a humble man, Comandante, I mean, Cortés."

"God's servant." Cortés noticed that this Aguilar spoke in the manner of one long separated from the Spanish language. His sentences were stilted, awkward.

Aguilar noted that Cortés was not a large man, but that his presence dominated whatever space he was in. Broad of shoulders, overhanging forehead, furrowed brow, dark eyes set close to a long straight nose that dipped to the mouth, straight dark hair cut like a pageboy's, a chin hidden by a trimmed beard, he carried himself with deliberation. But his most commanding attribute was his voice, which issued from small, almost feminine, moist red lips. Incongruously, the tone was full and resonant, emotion infusing every word and wrapping you in its sonorous spell. This man, Aguilar could see, would be capable of convincing anybody of anything—that the pope had wives, that the king was mad, that paradise itself was full of knaves. Moreover, Cortés fixed you with his eyes until you had to turn away. As a slave, you were best invisible, and so long used to that condition, Aguilar was both discomfited and flattered by the commander's rapt attention.

"Chontal Mayan, not Nahuatl, that is what I speak."

"Brandy, Señor Aguilar, aqua vitae?"

"No thank you. I must get my sea legs back." Now I have offended my savior, Aguilar feared. I have forgotten proper Spanish conduct.

Cortés put his hands on his knees and leaned forward, trying to assess how well Aguilar could handle a sword, ride a horse. He wanted to query him. Was he too long with the Indians or did this bag of bones remember ballads, rhymes, the adventures of El Cid, the great Spanish hero.

"Just tell me what you know, my friend. Start with the emperor."

"Moctezuma, emperor of the Mexica people, from the priestly class, a learned man, but a warrior, ruthless ruler, humors in flux, temperament unfathomable. Poet, musician, a man who flinches at nothing, has sacrificed thousands, war strategist—"

"You sound like you know him well and admire him immensely, Aguilar."

Aguilar blinked. "I admire God, Señor Capitán General."

"Rightly." Cortés drew himself up. "Is this emperor loved by his people?"

"He is the absolute ruler, but Mexica has waged war on many other cities and other peoples, collects tax and tribute, so Moctezuma is well hated by those he has conquered. The Mayas also hate him, for the Aztec empire now eclipses theirs. Even the peoples of the empire, all brown Indians to be sure, do not consider themselves one people. There are different tribes, the Tlaxcalas of Tlaxcala, a two-day distance from the capital, who despise Moctezuma, for he has allowed them no cotton, no salt, no gems—"

"The capital? Continue."

"Moctezuma's capital, Tenochtitlán, is the most beautiful city in the world. It sits in a high mountain valley on an island in the middle of a lake, well fortified."

"Drawbridges?"

"Yes, three causeways, heavily guarded, lead into the city."

This lake, freshwater?"

"Brackish, mostly salt. Aqueduct water comes from a spring outside a city on a hill, from Chapultepec, Hill of Grasshoppers."

The captain's chamber was in close proximity to the manger for the horses, the pigpen, and the chickens. The smell was awful, but Cortés seemed oblivious. Aguilar, however, noted that the Spanish themselves were rank, and he could well believe the long-lost dog picked up on the beach was guided to Spanish rescue by smell alone.

"Tenochtitlán, the Mexica-Aztec capital, is like ancient Sparta, Comandante."

Cortés smiled. "You have been there, to Tenochtitlán?"

"Only heard of it, but the fame and envy are whispered far and wide. The Mexica are builders, artisans, traders, but most of all warriors. War is their religion, their main god, their sun god, Huitzilopochtli, is the god of war."

"So they worship the devil then?"

"Well, they have no knowledge of the Christian God."

"You mean God. God is God."

"I mean God." Of course he knew God was God.

"Can I trust you, Señor Aguilar?" Cortés moved even closer, and Aguilar got a whiff of his sour breath, could see the brown teeth in uneven rows—and his tongue. Coated a sickly white.

"Of course you can trust me, Comandante, I mean, Cortés. You saved my life."

"What position did you hold in society before your capture by the Mayans, Aguilar?"

"Priest, Comandante Cortés."

"You do not look like a priest and you do not sound like one."

Aguilar shrugged.

"Once a priest, always a priest. It is like being a Jew, Aguilar."

"Is it? I no longer consider myself worthy."

"Really. What did you do?"

"I lay with a woman, Comandante Cortés."

"And who does not?"

"She was not baptized."

"Ah, I see. Why did you not baptize her first? You have the power invested by—"

"I was in a hurry."

"And for that?"

"Yes, but they did spare my life. I was made a slave of the cacique.

If you do not mind, I would prefer that you and all your men regard me simply as a man. I am less than a man. I am your humble servant."

"All servants are men, and my men serve me well, but I take your meaning, Aguilar. Well, may I tell you something then?"

Aguilar did not know if he was to receive this information as confession, and he wanted to caution Cortés that he no longer felt qualified, no longer wanted to hear troubles and travails, and could absolve nobody, least of all himself.

"We were sent by the governor of Cuba, Governor Velázquez, on an exploratory mission, an investigation, if you will, a little trading, a little gold, nothing too ambitious."

"You have eleven ships."

"Yes, I financed some on my own."

"You have a good many weapons."

"You have eyes in your head, Señor. What I intend—and my soldiers must learn to live with, those who do not already—is that we are going to build a settlement, found a city in the name of the emperor Charles V, and then, on the emperor's behalf, lay claim to and conquer this country."

Aguilar was taken aback. "You *are* ambitious, sir."

"It is the only way, for all Indians will soon be declared official vassals of King Charles, and rebellion among subjects is punishable by death. It is God's will, the pope's desire."

"And the governor of Cuba, who sent you, is he in accord?"

"A stupid, shortsighted, fat, measly malefactor, not fit to govern his own loins, this Governor Velázquez; he knows nothing of destiny. He will be jealous of our glory, greedy for our spoils of war. He deserves nothing except disobedience."

"I see."

"Do you? Velázquez's own petty dissatisfaction may mean that he will send his own ships to stop us, bring us back in chains. Despite such obstacles, our allegiance is to Charles, the pope, and God. Are you ready for that?"

All Aguilar was ready for was a bed, and then to dine at a table, read a book by candlelight, and live out his days as a parish schoolmaster in some remote, sleepy town. He had not anticipated being involved in plotting, plunder, execution, and transcontinental betrayal when he had run away from his slave master.

"I admire you, Comandante, but am not worthy. You see, I am without talent. You, honorable sir, and your fine captains are more suited to this holy task."

"Correcto. We are the people to do this. Experiencia es todo. God, glory, and gold, there is nothing else unless you wish to dirty your hands as a farmer." Cortés, who had been striding around the small cabin in excitement, sat down again. "Tell me more of these warrior people."

Aguilar sighed. "Warfare is waged often, sometimes to appease the gods, ward away famine, or just for sport. Their combats are called Flowery Wars because captive blood nourishes, causing maize and other crops to grow."

"Ritual wars?" Cortés poured Aguilar a glass of wine; Aguilar did not take a sip. Poor fellow, Cortés mused, have the Mayans so corrupted him he cannot enjoy enlightened amenities?

"They try not to kill their enemies in their wars."

"War games?"

"Games, yes, but deadly. Capture in order to sacrifice is the order of the day, and they march captives up to the top of pyramids where priests cut out the beating heart and offer it to their sun god, Huitzilopochtli. Their warriors get to eat the limbs. Mayans have the same practice."

Cortés's quarters were furnished only with a bunk, Cortés's chair, the stool, the captain's table used for surgery if need be, and a few benches. The glass windows, dotted with seagull filth and salt spray, were curtained in dusty red velvet fringed with braided silk. These sumptuous fabrics Cortés now drew together in fearful haste. It would not do to have somebody eavesdropping on this conversation. As omnipresent as the weevil were the cursed breed of spies who could, if so inclined, sway the loyalty of the men, make them side with the wicked Governor Velázquez's interests, and encourage them to sail for home. Truth be told, Cortés knew he had cowards and malcontents in his midst. And the thought alone caused a sweat to sprout, and itches to crawl up his back. His beard harbored who knew what? Kingdoms of insects. His crotch was abysmally chafed. Only a fool could have invented the codpiece. He had lived in the tropics of Hispaniola, for God's sake, why did he find it so uncomfortable here?

"They have an elaborately written history, and their writing is very beautiful. The Mayans have a complex number system, and have invented something called zero. They are astronomers."

"Be wary, Aguilar, of admiring pagans. Since your captivity, there has been a blasphemous, heretical monk going about the German states, a villainous mountebank of a monk named Martin Luther, preaching insurrection and desecration, surely soon to be burned at the stake posthaste. He too thinks of himself as advanced, although he is of the devil's party."

Aguilar had not heard of Martin Luther.

"You see, Aguilar, we here in New Spain are the hope of the Church. Europe is a festering bed of protest. Souls awaiting conversion here are eager for the light."

"They already consider themselves children of the sun, Capitán."

"Well, so we are half there. You see I have faith in men's nature, Aguilar, that is, to want what is best for them. That is why my captains and troops have faith in me."

"Do you trust them, do they trust you?"

"To be certain. Where goes the ox who will not draw the plow?"

However, Cortés was not as certain as he proclaimed. Who indeed did *he* trust? There was that dandy Quintaval, who had opened the first Cuban fencing school. You could not walk about Havana without tripping over somebody with a rapier. Quintaval's black slave, whose big head and that rage of hair above his ruff made him look like St. John served on a platter, now what did he think of his foolish master? Blacks were literally opaque. Isla? Was he of the governor's party? He had the visage of a snake, was always on the ready to strike. Father Olmedo was neutral at best, useless at worst. The lone Franciscan, Francisco, a man of such ample proportions it was a wonder he could walk two steps, let alone tramp across a continent. Then Alvarado, whose feet could not keep pace with his restless mind, and whose pores reeked of fear. Bernal Díaz was a lackey, but how would he handle himself in battle? Núñez was extremely valuable as a mapmaker and carpenter, but the man was a Jew, and therefore not permitted to handle weapons in Spain, so he was without experience of the rudimentary moves of swordsmanship. Puertocarrero had a mouth as big as a brandy barrel. Botello, the soothsayer, fortune-teller, and doctor, was a faithless gypsy no doubt. But he was valuable as a man who could amputate and stitch, and his fortune-telling was indispensable. Cortés turned back to Aguilar.

"I do not brook betrayal, and I see you have much to contribute. I intend to make you one of my chief lieutenants."

"I, sir?"

"Why not? You have a keen mind, you are brave, and with training will make an excellent solider." Cortés paused and lifted his finger. "And you know the language."

"Only Chontal Mayan."

"An excellent start."

"I have no training in military arts."

"Hesitation is hardly the trait of a Spanish gentleman."

"I am not a gentleman, Capitán."

"Come, come, you learned to read and write from your parish priest, did you not, your catechism and then your Latin. Your humors are in balance despite your horrible ordeal. Tell me you are not squeamish. Life itself is war. Rank and position come with action."

"But I am ignorant of shield, spear and lance, musket, cannon, halberd, sling, catapult, and crossbow, Comandante."

"Already you know your weapons."

Aguilar sighed. Had he traded one master, whose aims were cruel but straightforward, for another, whose aims were cruel but complex?

"One more thing, Comandante," and Aguilar brought this piece of information up as an afterthought, although he knew it was key.

"Out with it, man, or evil betide you."

"The Aztec, the Mexica in Tenochtitlán, or at least the emperor, I have heard this said: strange as it may seem, they think you are Quetzalcoatl."

"Questa what?"

"Quetzalcoatl is the god of wind, peace, and creation. He was in the legendary past incarnated as a man, a priest-poet, the king of Tula, and because of the jealousy of the other gods, for he was a great benefactor of mankind, Quetzalcoatl was tricked and had to leave his city of Tula. It is also said that Tula could not withstand the siege of other Toltecs. At any rate, in great disgrace, Quetzalcoatl made a pilgrimage to the east, and on the Big Water of the Eastern Sea set himself on fire and became the star Venus. Quetzalcoatl, the Plumed Serpent—quetzal is a bird of green feathers and coatl means serpent—was pale-skinned and bearded, and was foretold to claim the throne of Mexica in the year One Reed. This year is One Reed."

"They think I am a god?"

"I have heard the emperor Moctezuma believes you are the One."

"You have done me a great service telling me this, Aguilar." The One, Cortés dared to think. I *am* the One. I have come from the dust, but I will ascend the throne, I will. Cortés began marching about the room, remembered Aguilar's presence, paused, and clasped his hands together. "So I am believed to be the One." Gone were the days of wearisome subterfuge in Cuba and Hispaniola, the bleak mornings of riding about his encomienda, the tedious nights of polite conversation with a woman called his wife. Reaching far back in his memory, Cortés could even envision himself a youth in his hometown, Medellín, Extremadura, Spain, the time abed through the long afternoons reading chivalric tales, longing to duplicate those adventures. Before that he lived within the close confines of his mother's womb, sloshing about in undefined darkness. Was there any choice? He had to embrace his destiny here on this continent. He was thirty-three years old.

"Have you read the four books of the Amadis of Gaul, Comandante?"

"To be certain, Aguilar." Cortés, a grown man, still thrived on romances, adored enchanted islands, dreamed of treasure troves and explorations of mysterious caves. When living in Cuba and Hispaniola, he had rushed to the docks every time a ship came in with the most recent books from Spain. He consumed them like food. He coveted kingdoms paved in jewels, and could think of nothing better than becoming a glorious knight and getting the princess.

"If there is anything in the world similar to those mythic accounts, Comandante, it is the golden capital city of Mexica, Tenochtitlán."

Chapter 8

When Aguilar and Cortés had been in Cortés's cabin discussing Cortés's plans, the lay of the land, who was a god and who was not, the ever-curious Puertocarrero had, as Cortés feared, positioned himself close by the windows and eavesdropped on every single word of Aguilar's account of Aztec atrocities, which he had quickly related to Bernal Díaz, who, sitting over the deck, was emptying his bowels of the clogging cassava bread.

"Ritual sacrifice and cannibalism," Bernal Díaz shortly whispered to Isla.

Isla knew that nobody in their right mind would want to taste the stringy flesh of Bernal Díaz if they could possibly help it. Bernal Díaz then asked a group of them who were playing dice on board if they would rather eat a man or a woman if they were on a lifeboat in the sea when there was nothing left to eat. One could hack off one's own limb and eat it if one had to, Isla informed them, although in all fairness, he would eat his neighbor before himself. Alvarado asked Botello if he would eat him if he had to. Of course, Botello said. Alvarado asked Quintaval if he had ever taken a bite of a woman in lust. Francisco said he would rather starve than eat a person. Everybody doubted that because Francisco was the farthest away from starving of any of them, and was known to sneak into the galley, scrounge up whatever he could, and put it in his mouth.

"Cannibalism is worse than sodomy," Bernal Díaz declared, turning to look at Adu.

Adu knew what he was thinking, but he had never eaten anybody, nor was that a custom he was familiar with. Where he came from, yams were the favorite food.

"The word 'cannibal' comes from the name of that flesh-hungry tribe, the Caribs, from the Caribbean tribe on the island of Grenada," Quintaval, who had studied habits of the indios, explained to the men. His own two Indian servants sat mutely by, Juan and Manuel, not blinking an eyelash.

"The Carib-European encounter was tragic, for they preferred suicide to capture and all jumped off a cliff," Brother Francisco said.

"I do not call that tragic," Isla said. "I call it a shortage of labor."

"One cacique caught before he jumped, given the opportunity to hang rather than be burned at the stake if he converted, chose to be burned since he would meet a lot of Christians in the Christian heaven." Adu could understand that, peace at any price, for who would like to spend eternity in the company of those who killed you, and as far as jumping off a cliff, while in Cuba he often pondered jumps, dangling ropes, upright swords. Temptation lay all about. But on this evening he assumed the stupefied expression of the two Indian servants, whom all thought ignorant of Spanish, indeed completely deaf and dumb.

Brother Francisco knew that when the goodly Father Las Casas took up the cause of the indios, suggesting that slaves be brought from Africa and documenting the event of cliff-jumping, he made mention of man-eating dogs chasing the people. Brother Francisco would have run after the Caribs, saying, Do not jump. I will not eat, burn, or hang you.

Botello did not think cannibals were *that* rare. He had heard it said that in the far reaches of Ireland, in the early spring, tribal chieftains were made to pay with their lives for spring crops, and then eaten. The king is dead, long live the king, was the refrain. And as far as sacrifice went, did not every old king send his young men into the front lines of battle while he stayed well away? And did not Christians, in their way, eat the flesh and drink the blood of Jesus, their man-god?

Cortés, now alone in his cabin, realized that God's hand had guided the reprobate priest, Aguilar, straight to him. Undoing his codpiece at last, he let his genitals spill out; loosening the buckles, he undid his breastplate, opened his armor like a book, and lay it on the floor. His tall boots he had to grab by the heel and pull. He unbuttoned his stockings from the loops hanging underneath his doublet and blouse. So they think I am a god, he mused. Straightening his back, throwing his hands over his head, and jutting out his chin proudly, he did a little dance, a gypsy dance, perhaps Moorish in origin. Twirling his fingers in elegant fan fashion and bringing them together like castanets, he stamp, stamp, stamped. His feet slapped the boards of his cabin, slap, slap, slap, cracks in the edifice of the empire, click, click, click. Perhaps there was a civil war on the way. What could be better? "I am a god," he sang, "a god, a god. God," he sang.

Then Cortés heard a crack of thunder. "Dear Jesus and Mary, the sky has been cloudless all day." Then another ominous roll. It sounded like mountain-sized rocks tumbling down from the heavens, bouncing against each other on the way. Cortés poked his head out the door. His men were running about, making certain the sails were rolled up and securely tied. The horses began to neigh and the pigs honked piteously. Stray chickens skittered under the canvas. The women on board the other ship, would the women be safe? Particularly the woman who looked like a prostitute with her black wings of hair and smoldering eyes. Why had he not kept her with him? There was another rumble, and then from the black cave of sky a long snake of lightning, diamond-backed, forked-tongued, lashed out at the ship. Cortés slammed his door shut and retreated to the back of his cabin. The ship listed, Cortés's codpiece of horn slid to the floor, traveled to the other side of the room, and slid back. His chair toppled over and inched along the floor sideways. His armor, like discarded husks, slid back and forth as the boat rocked first one way, then the other. We are anchored, Cortés reminded himself. One way, then the other. Back and forth. Vindictive needles of rain pierced the deck. Calme, Capitán, calme. A little squall is all. His cabin door swung open on its own, banged, banged shut, opened again. Only in his blouse, wind slashing against his face, rain pummeling his back, Cortés ventured out. He held on to the deck railing for dear life, and hand by hand approached the wheel at the stem of the vessel.

"Hold fast, hold fast!" he shouted into the deluge. "Below deck, below deck! Where is Francisco? Francisco! Francisco!" It would not hurt to have a saint next to him. Dear God, help me. He could hardly open his mouth without it filling with water, but he managed to mutter: "Hail Mary, full of grace, the Lord is with thee, blessed art thou among women, blessed is the fruit of thy womb, Jesus. Holy Mary, Mother of God, pray for us sinners now and at the hour of our death. Amen." He sloshed his way forward. Everybody but the pilot, Núñez, was below deck already.

"Núñez."

"It is bad, Capitán. Muy malo. Go back, go back inside. You will be washed over."

"Sí."

Turning to battle his way back to his cabin, Cortés saw the horses, the horses were still there, chained, upright, the chickens gathered companionably underneath the canvas with them, the pigs, all of them huddled like the passengers on Noah's ark, the corner of their protective canvas flapping at the edges. And then he saw it: Alvarado standing next to his horse, Alonzo, holding the great head, soothing the animal's fright away in the midst of the storm with soft strokes and whispered endearments. Alvarado's hair plastered flat was black in the rain. Yet to Cortés, who remembered the true color, Alvarado's head seemed wreathed in gold, was haloed with a holy fire.

"Whimsical weather. It will blow over," Alvarado said, cupping his hands to be heard.

"Bad night," Cortés shouted back, thinking perhaps Alvarado was an angel, a guardian angel, not the flighty, fidgety Alvarado.

Catch hold of yourself, Cortés, Capitán, Comandante, General, Conquistador, Cortés chided himself, and slowly, pushing against the wind, he made his way back to his cabin, and with all his force, his feet pushing, his shoulders hunched, arms locked, he closed his door. He slipped down, grabbed the leg of the table fixed to the floor, and prayed not to be taken down to the belly of the beast, as Jonah had been for his disobedience, his cocksure manner. Stop soon, dear God, make it stop. He had tried to be a good man, a just man, and do God's bidding on earth. You are my heart, my true love, my sweet, suffering Jesus. I am not Quetzalcoatl. I am nobody. I do not believe in pagan gods. Please, God, forgive me. He squeezed his eyes shut and prayed with all his might. Then suddenly he noticed a slight abatement in the wind. He held still and listened carefully. Was the fierce gale dying down, the powers of heaven placated with his prayer? Was that what he was hearing? It was stopping, it was stopping already, he could tell. Cortés started to pray again. Remember me, Hernán, who has done your will all his life. Was it blowing over? Remember, God, I came from nothing. The storm *was* passing. I am nothing, your humble slave. And indeed the boat righted, shuddered, heaved, then shook like a great animal drying its hide, settled, and stilled.

PART II

s indicated by Núñez's clock and noted by Bernal
Díaz in his book *The Conquest,* the conquistadors left their settlement
in New Spain, Villa Rica de la Vera Cruz, the Rich Village of the True
Cross, on 19 de agosto de 1519 at eight o'clock in the morning. In
three months Vera Cruz had become a garrison with a barracks,
prison, an abattoir, gallows, chapel, and the mayor's (Cortés was
elected unanimously) dwelling. Cempoala was only a day's journey by
ship from Vera Cruz, and only another day of walking from the mouth
of the river, named Chachalacas by the Spanish. This town was not
only on the route to Tenochtitlán but also, according to Aguilar,
notable for its hostility to Moctezuma.

The conquistadors entered the city in strict military formation,
Cortés with his principals, Alvarado, Isla, Puertocarrero, Quintaval,
Aguilar, Bernal Díaz, and Núñez; then came the caballeros, and these
men were followed by those with the heavy harquebuses; horses pulled
the cannons. Next came the men with lances and axed pikes. A division marched with swords aloft so Toledo steel glinted in the sun like
a forest of silver quills. The crossbowmen flanked Father Olmedo.
And the women, like camp followers, brought up the rear. The very
last person, however, was Brother Francisco, who because of his great
weight was a slow, inept walker.

"Izquierda, derecha, izquierda, derecha," the troops chanted in
unison, a legion strong. "Left, right, left, right, and a right, left. "Hurry
up, Francisco," they relayed down the line. "Hurry up, Francisco."

Although it was the rainy season, it was a gentle day. Neatly maintained maize fields radiated out from the heart of the city. The soil
being dry in that region and the weather often cold, the Cempoalans

had to cultivate their holdings with great skill and care. Yet trees and tall bushes formed variegated bowers of leaves and blooms. Nearest the town square, the zócalo, the air was scented with the many flowers which grew in studied profusion. Brother Francisco nearly swooned. Sent to Cuba from a Spanish monastery situated on an arid plain, the monastery floor dull tile and the walls shades of beige and sand, even Christ's pallor in the chapel a waxy ivory and the drops from his wounds and gashes the brown of old blood, Francisco was not accustomed to such a profligacy of green, reds so deep as to be mysterious, brilliant purple that spoke in tongues, blue so pale it wept. The flowers formed trumpets and hanging bells, and some had petals which were not modestly folded over, but wide open like outstretched little arms, and some had fuzzy yellow middles, others arcs of gently dripping sprays, clusters, and clumps; and in the shady and dappled areas pink cosmos and blue lupines waved like playful children, scarlet salvias and zinnias shot up as if popping out of the skin of the earth to greet the sun.

How had he, Francisco, a lowly monk, been so blessed as to give witness to a world such as this? One saw God's hand, felt his holy touch and his sweet breath all about. Such beauty pained him, and he realized he had been shielding himself from all that was unfamiliar on this expedition, hardening himself against the possibility of the new, and now, with a most gracious surrender, he acknowledged the whole world as home, nothing foreign to be feared.

But he should have realized that perfection belonged to God alone, for as they entered the town Francisco saw that in the middle of the zócalo the Cempoalans had built a pyramided temple. At its base was a rack of human heads in various states of decomposition. Crestfallen, the humble monk was reminded of the ill-fated Tower of Babel, the pyramid tombs of the Egyptian pharaohs, the walls of Jericho, even, dare he say it, cathedrals of soaring buttresses, gargoyles, cornices, naves, and towers—all a presumptuous groping toward and imitation of God's power.

"Francisco," Father Olmedo warned, "do not lag behind."

"Dreamer," Botello quipped.

Sometimes Francisco called the soothsayer "Señor Diablo," but he knew that the two of them, Christian and heathen, were kindred spirits. Francisco kept a little book of drawings of the new plants and animals and tried to query the slave women for the names of things in their world and language. When Botello picked a leaf, he would taste it with a slight flick of his long tongue and then scrunch it between the fingers of his fist, bringing its scent right up to his nose. His quest was for the hallucinatory, the aphrodisiac, the vision-engendering, the orgasmic. He sought buttons of joy, seeds of bliss, mushrooms of ecstasy, or, as the Aztecs called them, flesh of the gods, teonanacatl. Francisco, also an unabashed admirer of the natural world, settled for more mundane pleasures, such as classification, comparison and contrast, simple explication. He deemed himself, sometimes, a second Adam, naming the plants and beasts of the New Eden, bringing the message of God's grace to men.

"Francisco, my brother," Botello said softly, putting his arm around Francisco's heavy shoulders, "you must keep pace. Cortés will not wait for you. He is governed by the clock, the speedy passage of each day. He is intent on making his mark in the book of history."

"Did you see those heads, Botello, on the rack?"

"Yes, I did, mi amigo. Keep your wits about you, act as if nothing is strange."

Not only did the vine-entwisted flowers and tall zapote trees seem to greet them as they entered the town, but small, hairless, barkless dogs wagged their tails and jumped for joy in twists and turns, and the women and children flowed toward them in wave after wave of warm welcome, the voices in the soft Nahuatl language falling about them in soft shushing sounds, *x*'s becoming *sch*, *o*'s lulling mid-word, and *i*'s scissoring their way through still water. More awed than frightened by the horses, the people were captivated by the tinkling bells around the horses' necks and awed by the glittering Spanish splendor.

"Núñez, what time is it?"

"Evening, Señor Cortés." Even Núñez found precision too harsh for the tenderness of the people and place.

"Halt," Cortés called.

"Halt," went through the ranks.

The Spanish waited in the town zócalo for the cacique and the dignitaries of Cempoala to make their grand entrance, and shortly a group of nobles, with much introductory trilling on whistles made of bone and wood, ambled out. Francisco thought they looked like Roman philosophers with their white cotton robes knotted at their shoulders, their loincloths like short togas, and sandals. Isla noted the plugs near their chins which pulled their lower lips below the teeth. He thought they looked like jackals. Alvarado wondered why they all had their hair cut as if upside-down bowls painted with black lacquer had been placed on their heads. They could be courtiers of King Arthur, Quintaval said to Adu, who thought their hair looked like snapping turtles sitting on top of their heads or the cylindrical houses of the Hausa, who lived on the Niger River. Cortés was interested in their golden earrings, for they were so heavy they stretched the lobes to the shoulders. One of the nobles said something and some servants came out with jars of incense hung on cords which they swung back and forth in front of the Spanish as in a midnight mass on Christmas. Then four bearers appeared. Between them they carried a contraption of woven fiber with a man in it. This cacique was so large he could not walk. Indeed, Francisco noted, the man was even bigger than he, and in order to stand upright the chief had to be hoisted from his hammock by several strong men. Aguilar, linguist pro tem, took off his flat velvet beret with a plume in it, dragged it on the ground before him with much flourish, pointed his foot prettily, and bowed deeply.

"Aguilar is certainly no longer the forlorn refugee found half naked on the beach," Quintaval whispered to Adu. "He looks like a damn fool, a ridiculous fop. I liked him naked better."

Adu did too. He did not understand why the Spanish dressed as they did in a hot climate. The worst indignity for him when he had to be in full armor was the cup of wood he was required to wear around his genitals, thrusting them into prominence and exaggerating their size. A simple loincloth would be far more modest, although less protective in battle.

Francisco agreed with Quintaval, also, that Aguilar made a better presentation naked. Indeed had not St. Francis often taken off his clothes to give to the poor, and left his father's house without a stitch on his back?

When the cacique of Cempoala began talking, Aguilar leaned forward, tried to catch a familiar word in the Mayan language, strained to perceive what the man was saying, but had to shake his head. He did not understand a word.

"This town was your idea, Aguilar," Cortés said petulantly. "I thought you could understand them."

"Not Nahuatl. I speak Mayan."

"For Christ's sake, Aguilar, why do they not speak the same tongue? They are Indians. Indians are Indians."

"Do you not remember that they do *not* consider themselves one people, Comandante? The French are white, but do not speak Spanish."

"They should."

The fat cacique spoke again.

Aguilar looked helpless.

"The chief asks where you come from." The voice came from the Spanish ranks. "The cacique of Cempoala says, Are you or are you not Quetzalcoatl?"

"Who are *you*?" Cortés said. "Step forth, let your face be seen."

There was no reply.

"Aguilar, say in Mayan: 'Who are you? Step forth.'"

"Who are you?" Aguilar said in Mayan. "Step forth and be rewarded."

Nobody stepped forth, but the troops became restless and started talking among themselves.

"Cállese, shut up," Cortés commanded. "Say, Aguilar, 'Step forth or be punished.'"

The ranks parted and the speaker came forward to the inner circle of captains and the cacique and his court. It was one of the slave women from Tabasco.

"You know Nahuatl?" Cortés turned and looked at Aguilar. "She knows Nahuatl? Talk to her, she is a Mayan slave."

"I talk to her in Mayan already," Aguilar said. "I did not know she knew Nahuatl, the language of the Mexica, too."

"What is she called?"

"Malintzin."

Cortés recognized her as the one he liked, the one with the flaring hair and the eyes like midnight. He had not taken her for himself, but had given her to Puertocarrero simply to keep her away, out of sight, saved, as it were, for another day when he had more time.

"Have her tell the fat cacique, the lazy lump of lard with disgusting markings on his face, that we, Quetzalcoatl, honor and revere him," Cortés said to Aguilar in Spanish, "and we want to stay here a few days. We are all very hungry and could eat a bear."

"Our commander who is Quetzalcoatl says to the renowned and venerable cacique of Cempoala, he says that we are happy to be in Cempoala and are grateful for his hospitality."

Malintzin told the cacique in Nahuatl that the visitors came from far away, that they had heard of the wise and just, the pious and the prudent, the astute and clever High Highness, the cacique of Cempoala, and that he has honored them by receiving them in his beautiful city.

The cacique nodded and three of his men fell in front of Cortés and began to eat the ground.

"Tell them to get up, for God's sake," Cortés said. "I hate that."

"It is a sign of respect," Malintzin said.

"What did she say, Aguilar?"

"She says, Capitán," Aguilar said, "that eating earth is a sign of respect and easier than eating a bear—I mean boar."

"She did not say bear or bore, Aguilar."

"No, she did not."

Malintzin's knees were trembling. Her mouth from so much talking was parched. Her ears rang. She did not know where her voice had come from—from her chest, her mouth, through her teeth? She had never been so bold in her life, and she glanced quickly up at the sky, for perhaps she had become for one moment a god, and the god was speaking through her. Priests went into trances in order to hear the gods and then to speak for them. Special captives such as the women chosen for the festival of green corn were for a time the persons of the gods.

"Maax." Malintzin felt Cuy behind her, tugging at her skirt. "What are you doing?"

"I do not know, Cuy. Truly I do not."

"Who is that with her? What did she say?"

"She does not know, Comandante, why she is so bold."

"Jesus and all the saints, this is no time for modesty. What time is it anyway? Núñez?"

"It is eleven o'clock in the morning, Cortés."

"Hm, I have not had a good meal all day."

Francisco felt faint too. The Indians made a soft thin bread out of their cornmeal which was wonderful. They called it tlaxcalli, and the Spanish called it tortilla. And tomatoes, such a sweet fruit that was, and he had never seen a red so bright as its smooth, waxy skin, and they had an orange melon with bunches of slippery black seeds, like fish eggs, in the middle. The flavor of stews with chili peppers? Piquant.

The fat cacique, impatient with this incomprehensible jabber, began to talk loudly.

"What is he gibbering?" Cortés looked at Malintzin. She looked at Aguilar. Aguilar looked at the cacique. Cortés wondered if her nipples were the dark color of her lips. And her tongue, in contrast, was pink, her throat a whorl of pink, and he thought of a journey in such a tunnel, a sense of rawness initially surprising, then enfolding in the most delicious comfort.

"What time is it, Núñez?"

"Eleven and thirteen minutes, Don Cortés."

Jaguar Claw, who was never far from Cuy's side, mumbled, "What are they saying?"

"The cacique said something about Moctezuma," Cuy said without the least idea.

"They hate Moctezuma in Cempoala," Jaguar Claw said.

"What is she saying?" Cortés asked. "Are those slaves whispering about me?"

"The commander does not like people whispering about him," Aguilar told Malintzin.

Jaguar Claw, understanding Aguilar's use of Maya, his native tongue, said, "The general thinks it is a plot."

Then the cacique said something to Malintzin.

"The cacique would appreciate it if the Spanish did not stand so close to them. They have to burn the copal incense and wave it in front of them because of the rank barbarian smell emanating from their flesh. The cacique asks if the strangers ever bathe."

Alvarado said to Núñez, "I like it here."

Núñez said, "I too."

"What? Speak up!" Cortés was in a fluster. "I will personally cut off the head of anybody who speaks out of turn."

"Quédese callado," somebody shouted. "Be quiet."

"Silencio," rippled the command down to the last man in line.

"The cacique asks Malintzin if the Spanish are friends of the great Moctezuma." Malintzin asked Aguilar, who translated for Cortés.

"Tell the cacique of this fine city," Cortés said slowly to Aguilar, looking pointedly at Malintzin, "have her tell him that we do not know Moctezuma, and so we cannot say if we are friend or foe. We are friends to friends, foes to foes."

Quintaval smiled. Don M., Señor Machiavelli, would be proud of this master dissembler, Hernán Cortés.

Malintzin translated the Nahuatl. Aguilar translated the Mayan into Spanish.

"The cacique says that he hates Moctezuma."

"Well, tell him," Cortés replied with a big smile, "we hate who he hates, su enemigo es nuestro enemigo, su casa es nuestra casa."

After Malintzin translated this to the Cempoalans, everybody looked very pleased with themselves, and Cortés and his principals were immediately taken for baths in the steam house, which had a fire built inside to heat water and provided rushes for beating the dirt away.

Chapter 10

Why did you speak for the Cockroach, Maax?"
Cuy asked. "How could you do such a thing?" The women slaves were getting clean, too, but not in the town steam-bath house, the temazculli, rather in the tributary of the river, as cold as it was. Cuy and Malintzin squeezed limes on their skin and patted avocado paste on their hair. Their soap was made of aloe ooze.

"Do you not understand that those white men are our enemies, Maax?"

Malintzin was remembering herself in the square, the zócalo. At that moment she stood tall and spoke with confidence. Yet now, thinking about it, she realized how unaccustomed she was to being the center of attention. It frightened her. She was out of order, her order—slavery—when she was translating, but then she knew the words and could not help it. Inside, at heart, she was a princess, not a slave.

"You speak for them, you speak for war, Maax," Cuy continued.

"There is always war. The rulers say the gods have to be fed human blood, hence war."

"This will be different, Maax."

"How do you know?"

"Jaguar Claw told me. They will kill all of us unless we kill all of them."

"You want Núñez to die, the one whose mat you share, the one you like?"

Cuy hesitated. "If it must be."

"And what about the one called Francisco? He walks with us, and is like our brother."

"He is . . . like a kinkajou with sad eyes and paws padded in pink flesh."

"And Aguilar? Do you want him to die too, Cuy?"

Aguilar was teaching them Spanish. Malintzin listened, Cuy tried to appear not to be listening, and Jaguar Claw, who could not bear to hear a word of the foreign language, stalked away. While Father Olmedo showed them pictures of a man with a beard and long hair, Aguilar said they would live forever if they believed in him.

"And their soothsayer?" Botello was nice to them too. "And the black one, Cuy?" Adu ate with the slaves when he did not have to tend his master. "And the beautiful one with hair like the sun, the one we call Tonatiuh? I would like to be with him just to feel warm. Do you think his beauty could rub off? That is, if you lie by him, under him, on him, would you get beautiful?"

"You are without shame, Maax, and yes, all of them must be killed." Washing Malintzin's back, Cuy placed her hands on her friend's shoulders and turned her so that she could look straight into her eyes. "Remember who you are, Maax, remember your people. Jaguar Claw remembers. I remember."

"I remember." Malintzin looked straight back at her friend, her eyes steady. "I remember I was sold into slavery by my Aztec mother. Mayas made me wear a choking collar and walk many leagues without shoes. They took off my cueitl and huipilli so men could look at me. My first Maya master nearly starved me to death. My second Maya master made me into an auianime, so I could never live the honorable life of a wife. *My* people, Cuy? Yes, I remember them." She ducked her head under the water and stayed down as long as she could.

"That was your fate declared by the gods," Cuy said when Malintzin popped up for air.

"And what do the gods say now?" Malintzin slicked back her rinsed hair with her hands.

"You are a slave, Maax, but without our gods, our people, our ways, you would be less than nothing, Maax. You would blow away, become dust."

"The barbarians feed me well. The one man I have treats me kindly."

"The gods will punish you."

"Cuy, the gods have been punishing me all my life."

"You think you have suffered enough, that there is no more to be suffered? You may have ears, Maax, and a tongue, but eyes?"

"You wish yourself back with your mistress, your Maya 'mother,' Cuy? Is that it? You regret not getting your lashing for the day? Are you hungry for flies, Cuy, a piece of duck meat full of worms and smelling of dung? Would you rather service twenty men during the night, not just the one? You did not complain in those days, Cuy, because you were too weak."

"Jaguar Claw says—"

"Jaguar Claw is a butcher, not a prophet."

The two women came out of the water, and on the bank of the stream dried their skin with a cloth. Not saying a word, they combed each other's hair with the cactus-spine comb and rubbed the rare cream made with cocoa bean on the heels of their feet and between their toes, over their breasts and stomachs. After the meal, they would have to separate and go to their masters' mats for their nightly duty. The cacique appointed spacious rooms in the palace for the captains; the troops were put up in canvas tents in the meadow near where the horses were kept.

"I do not mean to be so harsh, Maax," Cuy finally said in the shadow of the temple after their meal when the women were cleaning and the captains were returning to their quarters. "Is it true that Moctezuma thinks the Big Cockroach is Quetzalcoatl?"

"I do not know, Cuy, what Moctezuma thinks."

"If we could all be as valiant as Quetzalcoatl, and as wise," Cuy said, meaning the dead god, not Cortés.

"We are slaves, Cuy, we have no decisions to make and nothing to think about. We do as we are told."

"We may do what people say to do, but I know you think differently. Tell me something, Maax. Let us sit for a moment." Cuy took

Malintzin's hand and drew her to the ground. "Tell it to me so I can be as strong as you."

"I am not strong."

"You are stronger than I am. Give me some words."

"The gods gathered," Malintzin began, adopting the voice of an elder, the night closing around them, "and they asked each other, 'Who shall live on earth?' Quetzalcoatl, before he was the god of wind and maize, poetry and remembering, said, 'I know.' He decided to go to the land of the dead, and to announce to Mictlantecuhtli, the god of the underworld, that he had come to fetch the old bones of dead gods to make people. But Mictlantecuhtli told him, 'You may take the bones if you blow my trumpet and circle around four times.' But the trumpet was not hollow, it had no holes and was impossible to blow. It was a trick, Cuy, a cruel joke. However, Quetzalcoatl was not without resources, and he called upon the worms to make holes and bees to fly through, making the shell sing. Mictlantecuhtli became very angry when Quetzalcoatl was successful, and he had his demons prepare a big hole in the ground for Quetzalcoatl to fall into. Quetzalcoatl did fall but was able to climb out, and he fled with the bones, ground them up, and put them in a jade-stone bowl. Then he bled his tepolli, his penis, into the bowl. It was thus that male children were made, then female children. People were born, Cuy, and the world was started. And here we are. People."

hen Malintzin returned to the mat she was to share with Puertocarrero in the Cempoala cacique's palace, her appointed man was asleep. She lay down on his mat beside him, keeping her body apart from his so it did not touch. Looking up at the strong beams that held up the ceiling and seeing only dark outlines, she tried to tell herself she had done nothing wrong by speaking out. The words she spoke were not even her words, so perhaps they did not count. She only said what Aguilar said, who said what the Cockroach said. Three sayings, two down to her, and they were not her words.

The Cockroach was Jaguar Claw's name for the man called Cortés, Señor, El Capitán, El General, El Comandante; he, like Malintzin, had many names. Most of his men called him Cortés, and she knew they liked him, for when he spoke he directed his gaze straight to your face. That startled her, for she had never been bold enough, privileged enough, to look straight at a man, except Jaguar Claw. Had she a husband, she would look straight at him. In the half-light through the doorway from the torch kept lit in the guarded hallway of the patio, Puertocarrero, her man, looked old and rumpled. She almost felt sorry for him.

But she could not get to sleep. Bad thoughts came into her head like mooyoomeh, mosquitoes, hungry for blood. Cuy may have been right. The gods might punish her for betrayal. Yet she could answer them with these questions: When my father, my only protector in the world, lay wasting away on his mat, saying incomprehensible things, his mind unclear, was that not punishment? And when I was taken away by the slavers, had the gods saved me? When people sang and danced and sacrificed to the gods for rain and crops, did she receive any bounty or favor from the gods? Moreover, while Quetzalcoatl, the hero-god, was the one who stole bones from the gods to make people, it was the people who had to pay for the original theft with their lives.

As she was thinking this, the descent of the sun to the underworld was complete. Rainy-season clouds moved across the moon's luminous face. In the hills a coyote howled out its loneliness. Then Malintzin heard steps and somebody stood in the doorway. It was Aguilar. He put his finger to his lips. No habla, do not speak. He gestured that she follow him. Stealthily, the two made their way across the main courtyard to Cortés's room. The captain general was sitting on his chair. Tubes of wax were lit so that the room was filled with a soft, gentle glow. The man had taken off his heavy silver shell and his shirt was loose over his stomach, and instead of his puffy short skirt, he wore breeches. Bare of boots, his feet looked like slabs of white turkey meat. His long, unkempt hair was lifted from his neck and tied back from his face. In the glowing light she could see his eyes shining brightly like tiny chips of flint left in the rain. Cuy's man, Núñez, was in the room too.

"What time is it, Núñez?"

"It is ten o'clock at night, Señor Cortés." Núñez wanted to say, It is time to go to sleep or it is time that all this was over. Would that he had gone to Prague to be with his Ashkenazi relatives when he had to leave Spain, and not come here, was not here in Cempoala at ten o'clock in August of 1519.

"How is it that she knows that Aztec language?" Cortés turned to Aguilar.

Aguilar asked Malintzin in Mayan. Núñez looked at her curiously. She was Cuy's friend, and for that he liked her.

"I repeat: How does she know the Aztec language?"

"Cortés says," Aguilar said, "how do you know Nahuatl?"

She answered as succinctly as she could.

"In essence, Comandante, she says she is from a Nahuatl town, that she is Aztec, and that she is of noble blood."

"In essence? I want fact, man, always fact."

"She is something like a princess."

"A princess or not? ¿Princesa o no?"

"Noble blood."

"Illegitimate?"

Aguilar conveyed that information to her.

"She says she is her father's first and only child born to his only and official wife."

"And a slave?"

Malintzin related that part of her background to Aguilar, who in turn related it to Cortés.

"Like the Hebrew Joseph sold into bondage," Núñez said. The minute the words escaped his lips, he wished them back inside his mouth.

"The -tzin suffix of her name means noble blood," Aguilar explained. "In their society, she is a princess. Her real name is Malinali."

"What do we call her?"

"Some of us know her as Malinche."

"Malinche? Was she not baptized before I gave her to Puertocarrero? What is her Christian name?"

"Marina."

"Well, she is to be Doña Marina. Tell her, Aguilar, that if she acts as our translator and interpreter in Nahuatl and Mayan, we will bestow our favor on her."

Malintzin bowed her head and looked at the large stones of the floor.

"Extra favor might mean . . ." Aguilar cleared his throat. "She is a woman, sir."

Núñez took off his spectacles, cleaned them with his unsoiled handkerchief, and put them back on. Cuy, whom he regarded as his wife, was officially his slave, as the patriarchs had their concubines, numerous wives, and, yes, slaves.

"No, no, not that, I do not mean that. What I mean is . . . Tell her that she will gain more than her liberty."

Aguilar said something to her in Mayan.

"She asks, sir, what *that* means."

"Explain to her, estúpido, that if she serves me, one day when we are through with her, she will be free. We will give her a house, land, and gold, gold too."

"They do not value gold as we do, sir."

"Well, we will think of something she values, now, will we not, Aguilar? And in the meantime, give her a room of her own."

"She is Puertocarrero's."

"Puertocarrero, that sot of a sot, is not worthy of a woman of wits, let him be without, we cannot have our princess-translator pregnant on our trip, can we?"

Malintzin strained to understand and picked up a few words, sí, sí, ¿qué? mujer, casa, oro, libertad.

"You can go now," Cortés said to Aguilar. "You too, Núñez."

The men left the room. Cortés sat in his chair looking at her. A moment before, she had felt invisible, now she was all too visible. The man moved toward her, his shadow lurching behind him. The man put one hand on her shoulders, two hands, two great hairy paws. Against the wall of the room the man's shadow was fuzzy, like the furred animals of the north.

"¿Sí?" he asked, moving his hands to her chin. He lifted her face.

"Sí," she answered, for she knew what that word meant.

He lifted her huipilli over her head and stepped back.

"¿Sí?"

"Sí."

He took her two breasts in his hands. They were a full woman's breasts nippled purple as plums as he had anticipated. She parted her lips. Her teeth were large, white, good. Bad teeth in a woman were off-putting to him.

She did not know why she was trembling. Her body was just her body. Many men had touched it.

He loosened the tie of her cueitl and let it fall. She had not worn her sandals to come to his stone-floored room. The floor suddenly felt cold. She shivered a little.

"¿Sí?" he asked.

"Sí."

He noticed that her proportions were not like a Spanish woman's. Her waist was thick, her hips narrow, and her legs strong as a man's.

"You are cold, come." He led her to his mat and draped his long cloak over her.

Moments before, she had felt she was wading in a swift stream, now her skin was on fire. When he took off his shirt and breeches, she saw that he was like all men, not a locust, an insect, a caterpillar, an anteater, a tapir, or a god. His tepolli and all his parts and pieces were a man's. He moved his feet up and down her legs, stroking her with his toes. Nobody in all her experience had done something like that to her. Did gods do this? Nobody had shown any care or affection for her. And was it his power as a god which made her surrender herself, just give herself up to him, her mind not dividing from her body, not hovering above or going into the next day. With him, her mind sank down, joined her body.

"¿Sí?" he asked.

"Sí," she answered.

Using his long eyelashes, he tickled her throat. With his strong hands, he rubbed her feet and the saddle of her back, then put his head on her chest, as if listening to her heart. Then he began to speak to her in his language, softly humming it, and when he stroked her a certain way, he would ask, ¿Sí? Sí.

She had a memory, or was it a wish, of cradling in her mother's arms, a time of tenderness thick as honey, yet distinct as the sharp fin of a fish. But he did not spill his seed in her; at the last moment he slipped out like an eel, letting the man pulque surge out on the mat. They rested together awhile on the sweet stickiness.

"No niños," he said. "¿Entiende?"

She did not understand.

He held his hand a little way from the floor. "No niños."

"Ah, sí." She nodded. From inside the folds of her skirt, lying on the floor beside them, she brought out a small, soft black object, squeezed it, and put it in his hand. Cuy had given it to her after her first flowering.

"Ulli," she said in Nahuatl.

"¿Chicle?" It looked like the sticky sap from the zapote tree.

"Ulli."

"¿Hule?"

What Malintzin meant was the sap of a tree found in the land of the Olmecs. It was the material used for balls for the ballgame, the protective covering that went around the ballplayer's body. "Ulli," she said again, and, lifting her skirt, showed him how she could put it inside her. "Ulli. No niños," she said.

Chapter 12

It was shortly after the evening meal two weeks later that Cortés and his fine captains and the cacique of Cempoala and his special entourage were settled back around the outdoor campfire the Spanish liked so much for some of those wonderful leaves. It was an important ritual. Chopped leaves were distributed along a flat larger leaf, which was then rolled tightly together. One end of this leaf combination was lit from a stick poked in the fire. The imbiber at that moment sucked in, puffed out, sucked in, puffed out. Sometimes the chopped leaves were put into small clay pipes in the shape of small elbows. Sometimes the leaves were chewed into a thick gum with honey and lime. This divine delight was good for long trips. It kept you awake and lively. Similarly this ambrosia was perfect after a large meal; it calmed you. Botello loved tobacco. So did all the captains. Cortés liked to walk around with a long thick brown roll of it in his mouth, so he looked like a walking chimney or a baby at a teat. When he took it out of his mouth, he held it between his fingers, waving it around like a scepter. Smoking was like conquering fire.

That night, unseasonably balmy with the moon full and ripe, the captains and their ladies were reclining in a garden connected to the cacique's palace, a serene spot with a pond, a small waterfall, coral trees, bougainvillea, and allamanda vines. A paradise, Francisco reflected, noting, with a twinge of fear, that he might never again be so happy. The rank and file were either at their own campfires on the outskirts of the town or in their tents with one of the young women the cacique so obligingly provided. Most of the Cempoalans were asleep because their work started at dawn each day. Cortés sat in his special Dante chair which followed him everywhere in the arms of one of Quintaval's silent servants. Malintzin and Aguilar, the translators, sat on the ground on either side of him. The fat cacique was in his portable hammock, and he was telling them through Aguilar and Malintzin about the time he ate a whole deer by himself.

"I ate, Quetzalcoatl," he said to Cortés, "the eyes, the ears . . ." With weapons which could kill at a great distance, their strange clothes, and animals never before seen in the world, the cacique of Cempoala knew the strangers had to be gods.

"The fur," one of his Aztec nobles asked, "you ate the fur too?"

This was translated for the Spanish.

"Yes, the fur. Tell the fair god, the fur." The cacique nodded. "Fur with peppers." He was very proud of his achievement.

"He ate the fur," Malintzin said in Maya and Aguilar in Spanish.

"And the hooves?" Cortés asked.

Malintzin had been given her own room and her own mat, although she usually slept with Cortés, and several Cempoala women had been engaged to attend her. She was invited to eat with the captains, and was sometimes brought special foods, for instance, frothed cocoa with vanilla bean and whipped honey. Jaguar Claw eyed these developments with strong suspicion, and Cempoalan slaves and servants, the people who washed the conquistadors' clothes, made their food, and would eventually carry their supplies on their backs to Tenochtitlán, regarded her with hate and envy, calling her Malin*tzin*, exaggerating the last syllable of her name in mockery. That she was from Aztec royalty and sold into abject slavery by her mother did nothing to endear her to them. Once a princess, always a princess, Jaguar Claw pointed out, meaning not that he was disrespectful of hierarchy, but that by accepting the favor of the Spanish, Malintzin was the Queen of Betrayal.

"Hooves are good boiled," Alvarado admitted, "made into a jelly."

Botello was telling fortunes by the lines in the hand. So far everybody was going to get rich, live long, and have many loves.

"Have you ever had goat kidney?" Quintaval asked. "Wrapped in intestines, stuffed with olives and bread crumbs, and soaked in blood first?"

This was forwarded to the cacique as best Malintzin could, for she had never seen a goat and did not know what olives were, although the bread crumbs she knew from the hard cassava bread the Spanish ate— and blood? Blood was no problem.

Francisco was almost asleep right where he sat. He and Botello, Aguilar, and Malintzin spent the afternoons, when everybody was at siesta, tramping around. Botello was particularly interested in poppies, they must have poppies in the fields, and blue morning glories, he was certain, would grow in the tropical lowlands near the coast. Yet all he took away from his wide sampling was stomachaches.

Adu, too, sometimes went on these rambling afternoon adventures with Francisco and Botello. He liked to plot the perimeters of the fields, estimate the proximity of deep jungle, and trace getaway paths. If he ran away, how far would he get? How would he live? Would the Indians watching from the bushes take him in? Would he be subject to sacrifice? Cempoala was near the coast, and while the terrain and climate there were comfortable, Adu could not predict if farther into the interior there would be mangroves, jungle, savannas, plains, deserts, or mountains, and if the animals would be dangerous.

"Adu," Quintaval said, "stop fidgeting. Otherwise you will have to go to the other campfire and stay with the troops, not the captains."

Alvarado's favorite dish, he remarked as they were going around relating culinary treats, was bull's testicles. When he said this everybody looked at Father Olmedo, whose considerable endowments had been revealed in the bathhouse. Malintzin had never seen a bull. But the cacique and all his men laughed when she tried to translate.

"Bolas," the Spanish said.

Those who were not lounging in armor grabbed themselves and made a show of it. The Cempoalans did the same through their maxt-latls. Children, Malintzin thought, niños.

"Pig's brains," Isla, in a rare show of emotion, admitted.

Adu, always alert to sounds, heard feet tramping on soft earth. It was not the omnipresent group of Mexica spies who had been trailing them from the time of their landing in Yucatán, who were like mon-keys hanging from trees, hovering behind bushes, and were now staring down on the garden from various perches. Malintzin heard the thumping too. Maybe four men? Their gait was more of a shuffling than a straight placement of the feet. Smooth-soled sandals of deer hide, she thought.

Father Olmedo wondered if there was anybody around the fire who, when a lamb's head was boiled, went for the eyes. They could be sucked out in one inhalation.

"Delicious," several in the group declared.

"Oxtail soup," proposed Botello, getting up to demonstrate by running around the fire with his fingers to his head, charging here and there.

"I hear something," Alvarado said, looking around nervously.

The Spanish dogs began to bark from their cages. The horses, in the meadow, began to neigh.

"Who goes there?" called one of the Spanish guards in Spanish, as if expecting to be answered. All the men were glad for once that Cortés had insisted they at least wear their armored breastplates, and they tumbled up awkwardly like turtles trying to right themselves, seizing the swords at their sides. Then they heard it too, the ominous sound of a low drumbeat. And as the group approached, Malintzin could see from the insignias woven into the cloth of their tunics—the eagle on the prickly pear—that they represented the empire. They were not warriors, for their hair was worn longish and loose, not tied in the proud topknot of a man who caught captives. And they did not wear the long cloak of the pipiltin, the nobility. They did not wear the lip plugs or nose plugs only permitted the nobility. They were not merchants for they carried no goods. The fat cacique tried to extricate himself from his hammock, requiring help.

"Who are they?" Cortés asked.

"Empire," Aguilar said.

"Empire," went the cry through the dark night, and the troops who had been sleeping in their tents or lolling with ladies, quickly congregated and marched to the main part of town, their hands on the hilts of their swords.

The group of outsiders advanced.

The soldiers were only a few footsteps behind them.

Two of the strangers held nosegays up to their noses.

The cacique's guards closed in formation around the cacique.

One of the intruders stepped forth. There were only four of them and they carried no shields. Their only weapons were the obsidian knives at their waists.

"Tax collectors from the capital," Malintzin whispered to Aguilar.

"Tax collectors," went the ripple of whispers in Spanish and Mayan. "They want tribute."

The leader of the four banged the ground with his wooden staff, which was elaborately carved with a scrolled pattern in the shape of a jaguar fighting a snake.

"What form is the tribute here?" Cortés wanted to know. He already had troops scouring the area for gold mines. Indeed scores of his men were assigned to gold-searching duty and had to spend their days sifting sand in the stream, and when the citizens of the town were out in the fields, they were sent in furtive search through storehouses, huts, and more elaborate houses. The palace was always guarded, unfortunately, but before they set out for Tenochtitlán, Cortés would find a way to explore the possibilities of Cempoala thoroughly, he promised his men that.

"The tax collectors want maize, salt from the salt flats, beans, chilies, squash, animal pelts, cotton—" Malintzin began to tell Aguilar when they were interrupted by a pitiful wail.

"What? What is that?" Cortés looked at Malintzin.

The cacique, his hands over his face, blubbered out a series of words filled with all the woe in the world.

"And Moctezuma wants ten maiden women," Malintzin said to Aguilar.

"For slaves? Concubines?"

"Sacrifice."

The cacique heaved himself back down on his hammock, put his feathered fan over his face, and would not look at anybody.

"It is Uey tecuilhuitl. Pure women from all over the empire are brought to the capital for the festival of the green corn. They dance in front of the Huitzilopochtli and Tlaloc pyramid. On the last night of the dance, sword men creep up behind them and cut off their heads."

The garden arrayed with flowers, which had been festive, now seemed funereal.

"What does this mean—for us I mean?" Cortés asked Aguilar.

"They are not asking *us* to sacrifice ourselves, Comandante."

"I mean strategically. Our task here in Mexico."

"Let us fete the honorable tax collectors," the cacique mumbled through his fan. "Take them to the bathhouse."

"What are they doing?" Cortés asked Aguilar.

"It is a sign of respect to be gracious to guests," Malintzin answered.

"Why not drown the tax collectors in their own bathwater, Cortés?" Isla always made certain to be at his commander's right hand, and always knew the lay of the land, so to speak, the way the wind was blowing, who was doing what, why, and where. "Or slowly boil them to death like crabs?"

Cortés rolled his eyes. "How can they? It would mean war with the capital."

Soon servants were running about fetching clean maxtlatls and preparing food and drink. The Spanish, preempted as guests of the cacique, grumpily went back to their rooms and tents, the fiesta over. And Alvarado, Núñez, Isla, Puertocarrero, Bernal Díaz, Botello, Aguilar, and Quintaval were invited for a late-night sip of brandy in Cortés's room. Puertocarrero excused himself, he was too tired, for he preferred to drink by himself without the interruption of polite conversation. Adu, however, had to stay because Quintaval needed him. Francisco, awakened by the commotion, came along because Botello liked to have somebody to talk matters over with after important meetings. Father Olmedo joined the group, for somebody might need immediate religious consolation. Malintzin came because Cortés could not bear to have her out of his sight.

"So, Aguilar . . ." Cortés asked. The men sat along the wall, for it was only Cortés who had a chair, his Dante chair imported from Spain to Hispaniola and hauled aboard the flagship *Santa María* to the new land. The Indians did not clutter their homes with furniture, and in the morning rolled up their sleeping mats and put them in a corner.

"The Cempoalans were defeated in battle by the forces of Moctezuma's triple alliance of Tacuba and Texcoco some four years before," Aguilar told them. "They pay one-third of their resources every eighty days to the capital. This visit from the tax collectors is not at the appointed time. Our presence may have something to do with it, and the cacique of Cempoala has several young virgin daughters."

"Is that so?" Cortés was under the impression that every unmarried female had already been gifted to them.

IN HIS OWN QUARTERS, the fat cacique was talking to his own courtiers. "Mexica is starving us," he moaned and groaned. As a rule, pulque was an indulgence used very sparingly, but tonight was a night it had to be brought out. The jar was passed around and taken in duty. "When we are dead, what good will that do Moctezuma? Will the new Quetzalcoatl the Fair save us?"

"THIS MIGHT BE an opportunity," Cortés said slowly to Aguilar, "to get a message to Moctezuma, to make an impression."

"What time is it, Núñez?"

"It is nine o'clock in the evening, Señor Cortés."

THE CACIQUE WAS in an absolute dither in his hammock, working his arms and legs like a baby on his back. "How can we put a stop to this? We will have nobody left to sacrifice at our own temples." He ordered three of his courtiers to bleed their ears, cut their shins, and ask the gods to forgive him for not observing their rites with the piety they required.

———

"MOCTEZUMA KNOWS WE are here." Adu mentioned softly.

"What is the black dog doing here?" Cortés asked Quintaval. "He is not a captain."

"I need a second mind," Quintaval said.

"A mind? The slave has a mind of his own?" Cortés shook his head sadly, as if to rue this day. "Where have you left your own mind, Quintaval? You bring this perro el pedazo de negro, this cur, to a captain's meeting? No sabe nada. How do you know Moctezuma knows we are here, slave?"

"His spies," Adu answered, "are all about. They are between the corn plants, at the stream, among the flowers, behind rocks. They have been following us since the coast, since the first day, el primer día."

Cortés looked at Aguilar and Isla. Should he believe a slave? ¿Es verdad?

"That must mean that Moctezuma is planning to kill us all"—Quintaval looked about in panic—"so I think the time is best for leaving, and going back to Cuba."

"Leaving, Quintaval? Unthinkable. What kind of soldier are you?"

"We are only three hundred strong. Moctezuma has thousands. It would not be battle. It would be slaughter."

THE CACIQUE RUMINATED out loud, "We may have to sacrifice some of our own men to appease our gods. Clearly our troubles with the capital stem from our neglect of the gods. That is the way it has always been. Some must die for others to live."

"AND WHY DID you come to this heathen land," Cortés asked Quintaval, "if not to fight?"

"Because Governor Velázquez of Cuba, who has sponsored our trip, is my kinsman." Quintaval seemed at a loss. "I did not come to march to the capital, seize the country for Spain and the pope, and send the gold to Spain. I know nothing of that country anymore nor do I feel allegiance for the young King Charles V, who, if I may remind you, was raised in the Netherlands and had to learn Spanish as a foreign language. His mother is Juana la Loca, who carried the corpse of her husband around with her. Why should I die for them?"

Adu held his breath, and tried to convey his concern by lifting his eyebrows. Quintaval talked altogether too much, and would get them both into trouble.

"Our weapons, why did we bring them, Quintaval?" Cortés had gotten up from his chair and walked around, pulled the seated man up, and spoke straight to his face.

"Defense, small battles, Cortés."

Cortés laughed, turned, and pointed at Alvarado.

"Alvarado, why did you come?"

"I, sir?"

"Yes, you."

"To serve my capitán."

"I came for gold," Isla said.

"Gold," the cry went up in the room, rippling out into the night, so that the men who had gone back to their tents took up the call as if being led in communal prayer. "Santiago, Santiago, St. James, the patron saint of Spain. Gold, gold, God, God, St. James. Oro, Dios, Santiago."

"There it is," Cortés said. "It is settled. We are in absolute agreement. It has to be a full invasion, no less. We will attack Tenochtitlán and root out the barbaric practice of sacrifice at its center. If you did not notice, we are cultivating the friendship of the Cempoalan cacique so that he will give us men for our worthy cause. Do you think I like lying in a hammock all day?"

"I thought we were just taking a rest before our journey to the heart, I mean center, of the country," Bernal Díaz, who had looked up from his book, said.

"There are many things you do not know, Bernal Díaz, and then some." Cortés looked around the room. "And some of you have very little faith."

"In God?" Father Olmedo asked. He looked around the room suspiciously.

"In me, your commander, captain general, and mayor of Vera Cruz, if I may remind you, the first Spanish city on this continent." Cortés's voice rose and fell as he paced back and forth. The group drew close together. Malintzin, who was only understanding every other word, felt she was part of something very important too. The cut-glass decanter of brandy was passed around not only in good fellowship but as a seal to promise, man to man. "I have a plan," Cortés said, pointing his finger heavenward, "involving the tax collectors."

"And incur the wrath of Moctezuma?" Quintaval cut in. "What about all the spies Adu told us about, Cortés?"

"Certainly you are not afraid of some peekaboo in the bushes, Quintaval?"

"I am indeed afraid, Cortés. My life is worth more than gold."

"You are a scurrilous coward, Quintaval, not a man, not one of us."

Francisco began to choke, covered his mouth, and pretended to be coughing.

"Do you think I do not know what I am doing, men?" Cortés stood still and tall, for an upright man always knew what he was doing. "We have enemies. Do you not see?"

So far the greatest danger to their group, Núñez believed, was the mosquito, and of course the hot sun. Botello had conquered those enemies to some extent by making a smelly salve from some herbs and lard brought aboard. Botello had also recommended that the men put mud on their exposed skin so that the sun's rays did not reach it. Moreover, he, Núñez, had been able to observe the Sabbath for the most part because the troops stayed up late most nights to carouse and drink and as a consequence were late in rising each morning. He left Spain for the Indies because the Jews were expelled by the new regents, Isabella and Ferdinand. He left Hispaniola because the cruelty and swagger of the island made it hardly more habitable than Spain. The atmosphere here too was now proving inhospitable. He was forty-five years, an old man.

"This is the Rubicon," Aguilar said softly.

"Speak up, Aguilar."

"This is the Rubicon," Aguilar repeated.

"It may be." If the reference was about Julius Caesar, Cortés was flattered. "Where there is gold, there is empire. The more Moors, the more spoils. Aguilar, tell the fat cacique you and I will visit him."

When everybody else retired to their mats and the sentries were posted, Malintzin and Aguilar and Cortés went to the cacique's private quarters. The cacique was swaying quietly in his hammock, a wet rag across his forehead; his feet were being massaged by a comely young woman, and his best warriors stood around him fanning him with feathers. He had a terrible headache.

"The end of our days is near, Quetzalcoatl," he said to Cortés through the two translators. "We were once a great people."

"Do not say that, dear cacique," Malintzin translated for Cortés. "You still are, and will be."

"Clearly the gods are angry with us. Quetzalcoatl, are you, too, angry with us?"

"No, revered cacique. But you must take down your idols, cease your sacrifice, and cleanse your temples of blood. You need the protection of our God. Our biggest god. He is powerful." Malintzin was reluctant to say these words, and said them very softly.

"But your young god was tortured," the cacique replied. "How can your gods protect us? And you, Quetzalcoatl, what about you?"

"No, no." Cortés looked around for help. "Tell him, Aguilar, tell Malintzin."

"Our young god after his death rose to the sky," Aguilar said. "He joined his father, who is the strongest god of all. There is nothing our father god cannot do."

Malintzin translated this with great trepidation, almost expecting the earth to quake.

"But he let his son die."

Malintzin translated that.

"Because he loved us so much." Malintzin tried to deliver words in a monotone, as if a mere conduit, for she hardly understood what Cortés was talking about.

"What?" The fat cacique looked confused.

"Quetzalcoatl," Malintzin said, hoping not to double-talk, "the old

Quetzalcoatl, I mean, he was punished by the gods, cacique, for making man and bringing the arts and crops to him."

"Gods," the cacique sighed. "What do they want, is what I want
to know."

Aguilar told Cortés the subject of discussion should be changed.
Cortés nodded.

"We do not have enough to give the tax collectors," the cacique continued. "And I am not just talking about young women for sacrifice."

"The cacique is running out of food," Aguilar told Cortés.

"We are grateful for your hospitality; you are our brothers. Her-
manos." Cortés would have given the cacique a big, reassuring abrazo
if he thought it would console him. "Tell him to take hope," Cortés
continued. "Tell him he must put the tax collectors in prison and show
Moctezuma the resistance of brave men," Cortés said.

"And have thousands of Mexica surround our town and kill us all,
Quetzalcoatl?"

"We will protect you with our powerful father god. And that is
how I, Quetzalcoatl"—here Cortés stumbled over his words—"how
you can be helped. With my plan, with our men."

"But you are so few."

"More of us are coming."

"From the clouds?"

"Most importantly, we have our thunder sticks, our belching balls,
our great horses, swords sharper than any of your knives, our man-
eating dogs."

"Yes," the cacique acknowledged.

Aguilar looked at Cortés and asked if it was true that more Spanish were coming.

"They might. Only God knows." Cortés then pulled Aguilar
aside. "She understands quite a bit of Spanish, Aguilar, have you not
noticed? We must watch our words."

"Surely you trust her, Comandante?" Aguilar was heartened by
this conversation. If another ship was arriving, he could get a ride back
to Spain. Quizás, perhaps.

"We will always be on your side, mighty cacique." Cortés gave

Malintzin a sidelong look which, like the pulque she had once sneaked at a funeral, warmed her. Such a look from Cortés convinced her that he was thinking of her as his wife. She preened a little.

"You have our word, cacique." Cortés pressed his heart, for a minute forgetting the local customs regarding that organ of the body. He looked over at Doña Marina, thinking, She is smitten, my slave in and out of bed. "Doña Marina, do you know what I am saying in Spanish?" he asked, desire making his tongue swell in his mouth.

"Sometimes," she said. "Quizás."

"¿Puedes leer mi mente? Can you read my mind?"

"No solo puedo leer su mente, también el corazón. Not only can I read your mind, also your heart." As she spoke she felt a great sense of power. To use words to express herself out loud was to remake the world to her liking and to be less at its mercy. To say, I am frightened, to be able to get her words around that feeling, was to be less frightened. To be able to name fear in three languages was almost to conquer that fear. Fear in Spanish, miedo. Not to have courage in Nahuatl was mahui. Fear in Maya was saahkil. Her slave silence, far from being a means of survival, seemed to her at that moment to be a form of complicit cooperation in her own subjugation. Speak out, be heard, Malintzin.

"We will help you put an end to the evil Moctezuma's reign of terror, cacique," Cortés said through Aguilar, through Malintzin.

"We can have a big sacrifice tomorrow with lots of blood and food," the cacique suggested.

"They are having una fiesta grande mañana," Malintzin related to Cortés.

"That is not what I meant. Tell the cacique that Quetzalcoatl does not like sacrifice. Cacique, listen to me. Arrest the tax collectors, show Moctezuma that you are not intimidated by him. How could the venerable cacique of Cempoala be frightened of anything? Moctezuma is only a man."

"They think he is a god, in a manner of speaking," Aguilar pointed out.

"Aguilar, tell him I am a more powerful god."

Malintzin said to the cacique, "Quetzalcoatl-Cortés, he is braver than Moctezuma, braver than any man. He is strong. He is mighty." Her voice grew loud as she spoke.

"That is correct," the cacique replied. "I am brave, strong, and mighty." The cacique turned to his guards. "Arrest the tax collectors. Put them in cages, let us fatten them up."

"Arrest, yes," Cortés said, stepping forth, his finger raised. "Arrest is a good idea, and the cages too, another good idea. But let us not rush to sacrifice."

THE TAX COLLECTORS, refreshed by their bath and full from a meal of roast pumpkin soup with cornmeal dumplings, delectable larval salamander—aaxoolootl—and a cool drink made of hibiscus flower and honey, had just nestled down for the night in the palace on clean mats with some comfort women when they were rudely snatched, gagged so as not to wake anybody up with their wailing, and hustled to the zócalo, where they were put in cages.

"We represent the empire," they kept saying the next day when they were on display for all to see. Little children poked at them with sticks. Dogs lifted their right hind legs and peed on the bars of their cage. Women made jokes about their genitals. Meanwhile a huge celebration was planned, for while the town was low on resources, now that they would not be paying their taxes, they could afford to splurge a little. The women were sent to their tasks of grinding and chopping and boiling, and the Cempoalan men went fishing and hunting. Jaguar Claw was kept busy wringing necks, chopping heads off, skinning, and disemboweling. Only the top warriors would get to partake of the human flesh, which was to be made into a succotash—tlacatlaolli. Quetzalcoatl, so kind as to visit, would also get to partake if he so desired.

Chapter 13

I do not like this," Jaguar Claw complained to Malintzin over a bunch of flayed rabbits, finally condescending to talk to her. "Dishonoring the tax collectors of the empire is an offense against us all. Nobody has ever not paid taxes. Unheard of. Never."

Malintzin could say "never" in Spanish. "Never, never, nunca, nunca."

Cuy said Malintzin was not in her right mind these days, that the Maax she knew had disappeared, and she pretended to look for her behind the trees and under the bushes. "Maax Cal, Maax Cal." Then she called for Princess Malintzin, looking in her room, under her sleeping mat. "Malinali, Malinali. Malinche, Malinche," she shouted into the cooking pot. Finally giving up her search, she said, "Ah, there you are, Doña Marina, I did not recognize you."

That afternoon the servants and slaves were given a short rest and the Spanish men, with the noonday sun high in the sky, having recently adopted the idea of hammocks, were being swung gently back and forth by children enlisted especially for this task. It was hot, sticky, the air thick and still with the heat. There was a hint of coming rain. The horses themselves stopped munching their grass, and for a while, except for the low moan of one cowardly captive confined to his cage, it was quiet. Even the Aztec spies in the underbrush had curled up in their places and shut their eyes for a few moments. But Cortés, Aguilar, and Malintzin, all barefoot, stealthily crept out of their rooms to the caged prisoners in the zócalo. Cuy and Jaguar, well hidden behind bushes, followed. And behind Cuy and Jaguar was the quartet of Quintaval and Adu and the two mute servants. The leader of the tax collectors was in one cage, his second-in-command locked in with him; the other two, in the other cage, were sleeping under all the garbage that had been thrown at them.

"I am going to release you," Cortés told the first two captives through Malintzin. Quietly the conquistador opened the cage secured by knotted maguey fiber. "You two whom I release now, I want you to go back to the capital and tell your emperor that I have done this for you, and that I am a friend to the empire. Tell him that I have come far to meet the great Moctezuma, whom I love and revere. I release you in his name. You must make no noise when you sneak away."

Quintaval gave Adu a meaningful look. Adu could have predicted Cortés's behavior, for he had determined some time ago that Cortés was a wily, double-dealing son of a witch.

"Moctezuma will be confused by this," Jaguar Claw whispered in Cuy's ear.

"With all his advisers and priests, do you think he will be fooled, Jaguar Claw?" Cuy whispered back. "No, he will know it is a trick."

"What I hear is that Moctezuma is not himself these days," Jaguar Claw whispered. "The omens and the appearance of the barbarians have weakened his wits and courage. Somebody should run to the capital to tell him all that has transpired, then he will know the truth. You, Cuy, you should go."

"How can I tell him?" she hissed. "I do not speak Nahuatl. As soon as I arrived I would be shackled and used for sacrifice, and if the Spanish capture me, I will be hanged as a runaway slave."

"There are Mexica spies all around us, Cuy, who will help you."

"Then Maax can tell them in Nahuatl. I only know Maya."

The two tax collectors did not understand at first that they were to be freed. They crowded to the far side of their cage and would not come out. They had to be reassured, and finally were dragged out and promised that it was not a ploy to execute them and no dishonor was intended. They were told that their national duty was to serve as messengers from Captain Quetzalcoatl-Cortés to Emperor Moctezuma.

Then, without a sound, the two tax collectors ran into the heavy underbrush and disappeared into the jungle, where, much to their surprise, many of their countrymen lay asleep in little balls under a large ceiba tree. The freed tax collectors had to kick them awake.

Cortés and Aguilar and Malintzin tiptoed back to their rooms and pretended to be napping, Cuy and Jaguar returned to the servant area, grabbed cooking pots, and pretended to be busy, and Quintaval and Adu made their way to their quarters to commence an engrossing game of chess. The two servants slept outside under a table in the cooking area. At four-thirty, according to Núñez's clock, the towns-people, the troops in the tents, and the cacique's court woke up to the hue and cry of palace guards.

"What has happened, why is it so noisy?" Cortés asked, jumping up from his mat.

"Two of the tax collectors have escaped," Aguilar announced.

"The dirty scoundrels," Cortés declared. "We must see the cacique immediately." And off they marched to confront the indignant cacique.

"Treacherous," the cacique remarked to Malintzin, who relayed it to Aguilar.

"Dog of dogs. Perro de perros," Cortés agreed, and then suggested that the two other captives who had not managed to escape be kept on board one of the Spanish boats anchored off the coast near the mouth of the river. "There may be"—and Cortés was reluctant to even men-tion it—"betrayal from within. Indeed"—he could hardly get the words out—"betrayal among the Cempoalans themselves."

"Betrayal? Never," the cacique responded.

"Nunca," Malintzin repeated.

"Maybe not." Cortés could not vouch for anybody but himself and his men. But in his life, he confided to the cacique, he had been amazed by the duplicity of supposedly loyal men. "If the two remain-ing malefactors are kept in the boat," Cortés pointed out, "they could stay caged forever."

The cacique said the people were counting on the sacrifice, and that, as cacique, he must uphold his honor. Cortés smiled, nodding as if he understood the burdens of ruling. "Honorable sacrifice would be welcomed by the wretched tax collectors, but far better for them to be humiliated." Then, as if suddenly inspired, he said, "I know what. Those mangy tax collectors could suffer the worst indignity known to man. They could be starved to death."

"Starved to death?" This had not occurred to the cacique. It was an unusual punishment.

"But their imprisonment and subsequent demise must be arranged quietly, revered cacique, that is, no one should be allowed to see them. It would be as if they disappeared from the face of the earth." Cortés, warming to his subject, paced thoughtfully. "In my own great, glorious country, recently liberated from the control of the foreign Moorish invaders and returned to the true owners of the land, Isabella and Ferdinand, there were prisons like that, on ships which never came to port." Cortés then, realizing this would confuse the cacique, said, "Precious and delightful cacique, you do not have to honor these scum by having them sacrificed. They would beg to be sacrificed rather than starved. Oh, the shame of it."

The cacique listened carefully to the best Aguilar and Malintzin could make of this rhetoric and agreed that it was a novel idea. In his culture, starving your enemy to death had never been done, and such a disruption of custom was tantamount to, well, he could not think of what. There was a possibility that the bloodthirsty gods, offered no nourishment, might be angry. The cacique had always done as his father had done, and *his* father had done, and all was prophesied, was it not, by the ancestors who had listened to the gods. It was his fate, the fate of all, to follow the rules. To do as it always had been done was the only way to do things. There was no other way.

Aguilar told Cortés that the cacique was wary of deviating from tradition.

"Yes, yes, I know all that. Remind him of who I am. Tell him I understand. I love my father, too." At best Cortés tolerated his father when he had to, although there were many times when he wanted the scruffy cur to see him here, in the New World, a commander of men. He was an only child, and after he failed to become a lawyer or magistrate and did not secure employment in Spain, his father, at his wit's end, shedding no tears, saw Hernán depart for Hispaniola with great relief. Writing to him from Hispaniola and Cuba, Cortés was always at pains to prove that he was a respected citizen, a man who had curried favor with the governor and was destined for glory. In a position of power, surely he could make his father pr   1.

"Cacique, we can fight together against   tyrant Moctezuma," Cortés added, standing up straight and narrowing his eyes, for he was trying to convince himself as well. "Against Moctezuma, with our ranks swelled by loyal, brave Cempoalans and fortified by other discontented tribute-paying city-states, there would be no defeat for us. Moctezuma would be taught a thing or two about who is mighty and who is meek," he continued, "and Cempoala, as a   .dependent nation, would prosper, and the cacique would down in the annals of history as the best leader of his city. The scribes will laud you." Cortés had seen their books. Of maguey fiber beaten into flat pages, they opened up like fans. Their writing was composed of small pictures.

The cacique began to talk rapidly to his nobles and signaled Malintzin to come over.

"The answer is yes," Aguilar said. "Yes to starving the two remaining tax collectors on board one of the boats."

"Well then," Cortés said, "tell him it will be accomplished tonight."

The remaining two tax collectors, already resigned to having their hearts cut out, were perplexed when they were made to go downstream, and after a day of walking, they reached the beach. There they found themselves being rowed out to the winged temple. Cortés put them in his very own cabin. Cuy and Jaguar Claw, Quintaval and Adu, and all the Aztec spies watched from their secret hiding places, and the representatives of the Cempoalan cacique who had accompanied the arresting parties stood on the beach, satisfied that justice was being done.

"When the Cempoalans fall asleep," Cortés said to the tax collectors through Aguilar and Malintzin, "my men will release you. You must return to your emperor and inform him that Quetzalcoatl has released you. Tell him I am his friend and wish no harm to his people or his land. Tell him I am coming in peace. I am freeing you from the nasty and irreverent Cempoalans in his name. I revere and protect the empire's tax collectors. The cacique wrongly arrested them for doing their duty. Quetzalcoatl-Cortés has put things to rights."

Malintzin told Cortés that the tax collectors were dismayed, for they felt it was their duty to get their hearts cut out at the top of the steps.

"Tell them," Cortés said, "that if they feel that way, we will kill them on the spot."

"It has to be the steps, the obsidian knife, the right ceremony."

"Tell them, Aguilar," Cortés said, "freedom or a quick, dishonorable stab in the back."

Malintzin explained, waited for their reply, and then told Aguilar, "They have decided that they want to be hero messengers, they want to tell Moctezuma of your valor and kindness."

Late the next night, back in the comfort of the Cempoalan palace, resting on his mat, Cortés asked Aguilar to have Malintzin enlighten him about his namesake, Quetzalcoatl.

"Malinche says she does not know much. She is not a priest or a scribe or even a man. The little she knows comes from her dearly departed father. It is unseemly for a woman to talk of holy things, and—"

"Aguilar, tell her we, among friends, do not have to worry about what is proper and what is not. I will not tell anybody."

"Quetzalcoatl is the god of wind and change, the Mayas called him Gucumatz, the god of corn," Malintzin began. "Divinely conceived, he is the Plumed Serpent—quetzal, from the green bird of the south, and coatl, from the serpent of the earth, the primeval snake—of both the earth and the sky, born to the virgin Chimalman. Some say he had a coatl, a twin, Tezcatlipoca, the night sky, who was jealous of him and wished him ill."

Cortés liked the divinely conceived part. *That* would show his father who was who.

"And Quetzalcoatl was also the king of the Tula, the leader of the Toltec people, whose ways the people of Aztlán, the Aztec, if you will, or Mexica, adopted. In Tula, Quetzalcoatl constructed four temples and also the house of nobles, the house of common man, and the house of serpent. He was very pious, a priest, a poet who did not believe in human sacrifice because he loved mankind so much. He only sacrificed snakes and birds and butterflies. When he disappeared in the Eastern Sea in his burning boat of snake, he ascended to the sky and became the morning star. The people said he would return to earth in the year One Reed because he left the earth in One Reed."

"Ah, very nice. A saint, a savior, second coming and all."

Malintzin began talking again.

"Malinche says," Aguilar said, "remember, however, my master, that when Quetzalcoatl was a man, he was tempted."

Cortés did not like the sound of that.

"He was exiled and set to wandering not only because of the military defeat of Tula by other tribes. He sinned grievously. You see, the envious gods were always looking for a way to punish Quetzalcoatl for stealing the bones to make people. Thus, one day the trickster god, Tezcatlipoca, came to him and offered him pulque. Sadly, Quetzalcoatl got so drunk that in his delirium he lay with his pious sister."

"Oh dear," Cortés said, "you say his sister? ¿Hermana? Fortunately, I have no sister."

Chapter 14

Núñez was a fastidious man, he not only carried a piece of cloth for wiping his brow, called a handkerchief, but wore spectacles on the tip of his nose, and, of course, he was put in charge of the clock. He did not own the clock, and how the clock was acquired was not something people talked about. Nobody really knew. The main thing was that it was on board the boat and light enough to carry on the trek inland, and, if wound every night, in perfectly calibrated working order. Very few people, even among the rich, owned their own portable house clock. As it had been for a hundred years, time in Europe was kept by large clocks on the top of municipal buildings, which provided the signals for the town criers at bridges and other central points. Churches had tower clocks to indicate the hours for prayers, services, and the ringing of bells. Sundials were still used in gardens, hourglasses on desks, and courses at sea were plotted by observing the stars with astrolabes and sextants and many hourglasses.

Núñez's clock, made in Nuremberg, could be held in the human hand and was fastened with hinges. A thin ribbon of steel was the spring, which was wound with a key worn around Núñez's neck. The hours were appointed by Roman numerals, the hands like heraldic spears, the minutes by little gold strokes, and the brass body was etched in a pattern of skeletons, Death in hooded robe, memento mori engraved beneath. Boxed in oxblood leather, it was carried by Núñez on his back in a canvas sack.

"What time is it, Núñez?"

"It is eight o'clock, Don Cortés, in the morning."

"What time is it now?"

"It is two minutes after eight."

Botello, of course, only had to stare upward for a fairly accurate gauge, but Francisco and Father Olmedo, who felt bound to say prayers on the hour, were delighted that their religious observances would be exact, and knew without fail when to open their breviaries and recite the correct prayers, psalms, lessons, and hymns necessary for office. And Aguilar, despite his disaffection and retirement from the cloth, kept up with his *Book of Hours*, and must kneel down at Matins, the last night prayer, Lauds, the coming of light, Prime, the beginning of day, Terce, marking the Annunciation to the shepherds, Sext, marking the Adoration of the three magi, None, marking the Presentation in the Temple, Vespers, marking the flight into Egypt, and Compline, marking the coronation of the Virgin. The event of each hour was illustrated in his book by small, perfect images enclosed in frames of twisted vines and tiny gold flakes—the Madonna Enthroned, the Virgin Weaving, the Virgin of Mercy, and scenes from the Old Testament, such as David and Goliath.

That very morning, at eleven o'clock sharp, after the Spanish had lingered over their breakfast—cornmeal mush, trout roasted on the open fire, flavored with desert sage, lime, and salt from the southern salt flats, and a compote of cherries and melon—smoked a little, and held mass, the cacique made ready to present Cortés with a very precious gift. He wished to express his gratitude. The tax collectors were languishing on the boat in the bay; it was a new day in Cempoala, and must be noted.

"Get Doña Marina," Cortés said when he saw the cacique and his entourage approach.

Flustered, her hair flying behind her, she arrived drying her hands on her skirt, wet from washing the bowls and plates, for her position as someone pampered and privileged, exempt from women's work, was not acceptable to the other slaves, and to appease them, and also because she was a person who had to keep busy, she had returned to her responsibilities of cooking, cleaning, and sweeping. Usually adept at interpreting, this time she heard the cacique's words and hesitated. Indeed for a moment she lost her voice. They were very hard words for her to say.

"Malinche?"

"I am speechless, Aguilar."

"Just one sentence," Aguilar begged.

"Must I be the mouthpiece of my own destruction?"

"What is going on?" Cortés hated not to understand.

"He says he wants Quetzalcoatl-Cortés to take his beautiful niece as wife," Malintzin choked out, her body cold as the stream in the black of night. "He would be most happy to have Quetzalcoatl-Cortés as part of his family." The niece, Bernal Díaz, the chronicler, noted in his book, resembled the uncle in the feminine form. She too could barely walk and had to be held on both sides by her handmaidens. Her many chins reached her chest and her breasts fell to her waist and her belly to her knees. Underneath her voluminous skirt two dainty little feet stuck out. The lobes of her ears were stretched out of proportion by the weight of her earrings. Her hair was matted flat to her head with clay and covered with feathers. Her eyes were lost in the folds in her face. Truthfully, Bernal Díaz could find no redeeming feature to write about.

"She is ugly, no?" Aguilar said to Cortés. "Fea. Like her uncle."

"¿Fea?" Cortés observed her perfect little teeth—two rows of pearls—and her nose was delicate, pinched, like a little fruit bat's. On all of her plump little sausage fingers she wore rings. He could imagine the pleasure of her voluminous body, what it would be like to fondle and sink into it, each pucker an utter delight, the rippling rolls a joy, flesh to spare, flesh to revel in. Women with irregular noses, wide girths, long legs and arms, flat bottoms, twisted toes, and many faults, save bad teeth, fascinated him. Such women were mysterious, as if marked by God to go through life with difficulty, daring you to look at them with, if not admiration, consideration. They knew something the beautiful ones did not. Some were no less haughty than the beautiful ones, and some were so modest it was as if they felt responsible and guilty for their own appearance. This one was imperious like her uncle, with a wicked look in her tiny enfolded eyes. Oh, the devil take her, she was darling.

"You have never met a woman you do not like," Alvarado commented.

"True, true."

"You have a wife in Cuba, Cortés," Quintaval said.

"As you say, in Cuba. Tell Doña Marina to tell the cacique I am well pleased, Aguilar. Tell him never in all my travels have I ever, ever seen such a woman."

"Malinche does not like to talk about it."

"Nonsense, this translating is her official duty." Cortés tried to catch Malintzin's eye, then shrugged, as if to say, I am a man, what can I do about it? He wanted to justify himself by asking, What would Quetzalcoatl do? Insult the cacique? Quetzalcoatl, the man-god, she had told him, was not an ordinary man. For God's sake, the god-king-poet-priest had slept with his own damn sister. Malin, Malinche, Malintzin, Maax, my own Doña Marina, he felt like muttering, do you want me to imperil our alliance with the cacique over something of such small import? If he did not know better, Cortés would say his little fox was jealous, but how could that be? In her culture men had many wives, concubines if they could afford it. Moreover, these primitive women did not have sentiments regarding men. Romantic love was a European notion, the lines of lyrics and romances, stories of tragedy such as Celestina, Heloise and Abelard, and Paolo and Francesca in Dante's *Inferno*. He was familiar with that tradition from his voluminous reading. If she were jealous, she would be just like a Spanish woman. Moreover, she was an expatriate slave, belonged nowhere, and did not own a thing. How could she complain?

Malintzin's throat felt pinched and parched for want of water. Her tongue felt as if it had been stung by a scorpion and swollen to the size of a pumpkin. She felt as if her stomach had been scooped out with a sharp shell. She wanted to disappear forever for shame.

"You see, you see," Jaguar said, gloating, nudging Cuy as they watched the cacique's niece being presented. "Look at your little Maax. She is like the dog fed from his master's hand, then kicked out of the way."

Cuy was bothered too. As Maax's throat clenched, Cuy felt she had not eaten all that day. As Maax looked like somebody had put a lizard in her mouth, Cuy felt somebody had put a rock on her chest. "Be quiet," she said to Jaguar Claw.

"Tell the mighty cacique I thank him for his niece," Cortés said.

Aguilar said, "Thank you."

Malintzin said, "Thank you."

The niece simpered and smirked. Her uncle passed wind.

"Cortés says he is highly flattered by so generous an offer and will cherish the cacique's niece as his dear wife," Aguilar said to Malintzin.

"He is"—Malintzin felt she was breaking in two—"marrying her?"

Isla whispered to Francisco, "Cortés is married already."

"He cannot marry her," Father Olmedo whispered in Francisco's other ear, making certain Malintzin did not hear.

"It would not count if it is not a Christian marriage." Francisco was surprised that he had to make such a fine point to a priest, he a mere monk.

"But he cannot . . ." Here Father Olmedo sought a word, then decided not to say it. "Yes, I know what you mean. He will baptize her first."

Francisco wondered at Cortés's readiness in these situations. He supposed such inclinations were blunted in him by the brutality of his young life. To Francisco, marriage, and liaisons of that nature, were a license to kill, thus he had never experienced the quickening in his loins that other men did, even monks and fathers, who were often fathers themselves. His love of God and all his creatures, including men and women, hardly necessitated the conjoining of bodies. Contrary to what one might think, he found that his neutrality, if you will, inspired distrust in men. But women trusted him. He looked at women's *faces*. And, in truth, his special fondness for women was inspired by the need among the downtrodden, those who were beaten and neglected, for recognition and sympathy.

"So since she must be baptized a Christian before he . . . Cortés . . ."

"In war," Isla mentioned, "civilized manners are dispensed with."

"Some people walk away from war," Francisco said.

"Well, little brother, you are walking right into one," Isla countered. "Fine feelings aside."

Francisco had been sitting in his monastery in Spain, then packed off to convert the heathen in Cuba, and then, well, here he was in the New World. Sometimes, to take holy orders meant you gave your life to Caesar, that is, cardinals, bishops, priests, kings, governors.

Quintaval, who knew of Cortés's wife in Hispaniola, had to muffle his laughter at these goings-on. Doña Cortés, he knew, was a dour and spoiled young lady. Without a dowry, with no chance of marriage in Spain, she was one of the women whose mothers brought them and their sisters to a place where there was a shortage of young Spanish ladies in hopes that their daughters would be admired and courted, marry, be legally bedded, and procreate. She was a relative of Velázquez, who had forced the marriage when she had lost her virginity to Cortés.

Alvarado, on his part, was surprised at the generosity of the Indians. Excellent hosts, they provided for your every need. Each captain had a woman given to him, indeed several, not that the captains were constant, that is, all the women, save Malintzin and Cuy, were passed around, sampled, as it were. His original woman was now with Isla, but were they not all brothers in arms, although he could not think of one man in the bunch he liked. In Spain and the islands, you had to ask the father for the woman's hand. One woman, one hand, well, really two hands, and then you had to get them servants so that their hands were never dirtied. A man's hands were tied. He had believed that in war—for this is what it was, was it not, although a unique one at that—women were "taken." That was part of conquering, was it not—rape, pillage, a right to all, a rite of conquest.

After her baptism, which Aguilar told the cacique was the Spanish form of marriage, the sprinkling of water, a few words, the new bride was led to Cortés's quarters.

Not even waiting until siesta time, Cortés was eager to show "that I prize my gift. It would not do to insult our generous benefactor."

The wedding party passed by Malintzin's room. She had taken refuge on her mat and turned her face to the wall.

"Buenos días, Doña Marina," Cortés said politely.

"Buenos días." Her reply was muffled.

"Ah, señorita, you are learning more Spanish every day." He turned to Aguilar. "The young lady will put you out of a job, no?"

"It would not do to have the wench learn too much Spanish, Cortés," Isla, part of the wedding party, warned. "Women can turn on you in the blink of an eye."

Cortés had his arm around his new bride. "If there is anybody who knows the human heart, it is I, Hernán Cortés. Women must be tamed. It does not do for them to take any man for granted. Keep them unsettled. It is the only way."

The cacique's niece thought they were commenting on her beauty, and she pursed her lips petulantly. Cortés gave her a little squeeze to reassure her that she was in good hands. A lovely day lay ahead for them, a roll in the mat, the afternoon meal, the dinner meal, and a nice tobacco session. He leaned over and whispered to her in Spanish.

"I will fuck you, fuck you, and fuck you. Te lo voy a joder."

She thought he said, I admire you, you will be my number one wife, you are my favorite wife, you are precious, precious. Yo te admiro, tú serás mi esposa numero uno, tú eres mi, favorita, tú eres preciosa, preciosa.

Chapter 15

Malintzin managed to carry on during the daytime, pretending nothing was amiss, although she knew that people were laughing at her, some glad that she was no longer Cortés's woman. But when she returned to her own single room at night, the one beside Cortés's, she cried piteously, hoping that with enough tears she could drown her sorrow. She cried in embarrassment and because she had a terrible pain in her chest as if she had walked the steps to sacrifice and had her heart cut out. She thought of herself as a corn husk without the maize inside; she had lost her joy on waking up each morning within the circle of his arms. Without Cortés's attention, she did not feel alive. So when Alvarado's eyes followed her like two dogs lapping at her feet, she was grateful that somebody was affirming her life. Alvarado, watching her, he who was so watchable himself, gave her a body again and said she was alive. And she could wear Alvarado like a flower in her hair. His long body, his hair the color of sea coral, his turquoise-chip eyes were secrets, her own dark knowledge. To look upon Alvarado was to feel bestowed with his beauty. It was like the privilege of eating an avocado or hearing a flute, which he played as prettily as an emperor's attendant. To have *him* return *her* gaze was to ascend to the sky and dwell with the sun like a war hero.

The rains had come by then. It was late October by the Christian calendar and the conquistadors had been in Cempoala since September, each day more drizzly and dismal than the last, but at night the clouds would move east and the men piled up dry wood, lit bonfires, brought their mats to encircle it, and reclined. The captains had their campfire in the middle of the zócalo by the temple, their backs to the rack of skulls, and the little fires of the common soldiers ringed the outskirts of the city.

That night the moon in the misty air was full and closer and bigger in Cempoala than anywhere else in the world. It formed a halo around Malintzin's body as she stood in the doorway of Alvarado's room. Malintzin was so brown, so smooth, she looked like a seed squeezed out of a giant melon. Her hair stood up on either side of her head in kinky snakes, and her eyes flashed like embers emitting red sparks in little pops.

"I have come," she said.

He said nothing.

She dropped her clothes.

Alvarado shed his various skins without a word.

Led by his lust, he pressed on and inside her, beads of sweat ringing his waist, dripping down from his neck, forming a V from chest to navel. His breathing came hard, and her back, scratched by the ridges where the adobe bricks fitted to make the wall, broke in matched lines of bright blood. His crotch was afire. Then, suddenly, it was as if cold water had been thrown on it. Alvarado lost courage. He stepped back and stared down at his wilted tepolli.

"God forgive me, what have I done? My best friend, my fellow soldier-at-arms, my commander." He crept to a corner of the room and, naked, crouched in misery, began to cry.

If it was possible, she felt less than nothing. She scrambled to get her clothes.

"Lamb of God," Alvarado moaned, "wash away the sins of the world."

Grabbing up her clothes, she wrapped her cueitl around her, threw her huipilli over her head, and ran out. The rancid taste in her mouth made her want to purge herself up the evening meal of venison stewed with plums. Hardly knowing where she was going, she wound her way through the catacombs of rooms lining and layering the palace patios. She cursed Cortés. See what you have brought me to, she hissed, spitting into the earth as she went.

At the captains' bonfire the wineskin was being passed man to man while Botello was serenading them, composing as he went along, a song about a hidalgo who fell in love with a prostitute, and how they both came to grief. Some of the men danced with each other, linking arms. One man who had taken a cloth and made it into a woman's skirt knocked his heels together, the others whooping and hollering encouragement. Cortés, as always on his nightly rounds, checking the sentries at their posts, the horses saddled, muskets, arrows, axes, and spearing weapons at the ready, and the cannons properly cleaned, dropped in on the captains' campfire. He noticed that Alvarado was not there, nor was Quintaval there with his black slave, and where the hell was Isla? Núñez, he knew, was enraptured with his Indian slave, Cuy, and spent his evenings with her. But there was Puertocarrero the sot, Botello the soothsayer, Brother Francisco, Father Olmedo, and the rescued Aguilar already fattening up on Cempoalan tamales.

"Buenas noches." He sat down on the damp earth by Botello, rolled some of the cut tobacco leaf inside a large whole leaf, and began to smoke. Then, positioning his back on a log thrust out for his comfort, he began to regale his captains with stories of the wonderful adventures of El Cid, such as the one about the time El Cid spared the life of a Muslim sultan, the time El Cid won the liberty of a city in a joust, and the time El Cid was ignored by his lady love.

"This is the life," Puertocarrero said.

"Yes, it is," and a toast was had all around. "La vida."

"La vida, la guerra y las mujeres."

"Is it true that the French armies were led by a maid?" Puertocarrero asked Cortés, for he was unread and only knew things through the telling. To oblige him, Cortés solemnly recounted that sixty-two years before 1492, when the last stronghold of the Moorish infidels was wrested from them in the famous battle for Granada led by St. James, Santiago, and the same year when that irascible Italian, Christopher Columbus, discovered the Indies for Queen Isabella and King Ferdinand, the same year when Queen Isabella was presented with a Spanish grammar book and told that language was conquest, sixty-two years before so many things in the modern world happened, the Maid of Orléans, hearing voices in the sky, was burned at the stake.

"Joan of Orléans thought she was an Amazon. Loca." Cortés shook his skin like a horse with flies on his hind.

"Loca, like Juana la Loca, King Carlos's mother? I heard Juana carried the dead body of her husband, Philip the Fair, around with her, even though he died of too much fornication . . . with other ladies, that is, not his wife of course." Botello, also unread, was, however, privy to much that was said in whispered tones.

"Gossip," Cortés replied. "Everybody speaks of it, but it is pure gossip. Only the French do such abomination." He then lowered his voice and addressed himself exclusively to Botello. "Where is Alvarado? I saw you sitting with the men last night at the campfire. Were your ears open as I instructed?"

"I heard King Carlos V, soon to be the next Habsburg emperor if all the bribes work out, has such a big, deformed chin, he drools in five languages."

"Do not say such things, soldier." But Cortés knew Botello did not mean to mock a regent. It was the wine, the fact that it was late. It was the warmth of fellowship which eased his tongue. On such an evening, what was a little irreverence, even a little blasphemy? There was give and there was take. He could do both. Let his men feel he was one of them, and they would die for him. Anyway, Botello, as a gypsy, was never quite serious or to be taken seriously unless officially engaged in his duties as company soothsayer.

"Last night I left you alone with Quintaval. Did he express his usual discontent?" Cortés regarded Botello as an excellent soothsayer, for he had predicted Cortés's own victory in all battles and future wealth. It was as if truly he, Cortés, was born to brocade.

"Quintaval speaks on behalf of his kinsman Governor Velázquez, mi amigo, but he speaks, how should I say? Quintaval is a man of pride, that is for certain, but he is not greedy merely on his own behalf or even for his kinsman, but out of genuine concern for the capabilities of our force, that is, he does not believe us of sufficient number and strength for the task ahead."

"Fermenting rebellion, I see, the villain. May evil betide him."

"He is saying aloud what many feel. The men are fearful and restless."

"Fie on that, and may the saints weep." Cortés drew closer. "Two things, Botello. You are the one who has delayed us here when the men are eager for the march. We sit here waiting for your propitious 'signs.' Every day in Cempoala is a day lost for gold. And you know, Botello, you can be replaced." Cortés said this to instill a little fear in the gypsy, so as not to have him grow confident and cocky.

"Señor Cortés, is there another soothsayer to replace one of my keen perception?"

"Speaking of Quintaval, punishment for treason has to be judicious. We would not like to begin our expedition by making martyrs." Cortés never tarried on another's point of view.

"Treason is a word I would not use in this situation, mi amigo."

"I have been keeping my eye on him, Botello. Sometimes an example must be made."

"And there are times that small disputations blow over with the clouds in the sky."

"You are a good fellow, Botello, maybe too good for your own good." Cortés was going to say "good Christian," but Botello, the swarthy fellow, if not a heathen, was not a true believer. Cortés observed that whatever room or tent Botello inhabited, he set up shrines—little wreaths made of herbs, pieces of cloth which could be relics if he were Christian, a saint's bone, a splinter from the true cross, but Cortés doubted it, thinking such shreds might be a patch of Botello's mother's dress or something disquieting and disgusting, a witch's curse rag, for example. Once Cortés had seen Botello sleeping during the hot afternoon with many tiny green lizards sunning themselves on his face. He was smiling.

"People are bored, aburrida, and I too am sick of Cempoala. We are getting pampered." When smoking his chopped leaves wrapped within a large dried and moistened leaf, Cortés liked to take the thing out of his mouth, gaze at the smoldering end, and tap the ashes with a delicate touch of the finger. "We are all going to get as fat as the cacique. Each day we spend here we are leagues from the capital. We will rot here." Cortés had had a bad dream recently in which he was trapped by moss growing from his head to his toes.

Botello started to say something but thought better of it. Personally he was not eager to get on the warpath.

"Do not be too hasty, correcto? Is that what you think, Botello? Be merciful to Quintaval? Piadoso, Cortés? Truly, Botello, I mean no harm. It is I, Cortés, who commands you, Cortés, your friend, friend to my men." No point in scaring the poor fellow, Botello the big bear, bugbear. As a child, Cortés had seen a bear put in a ring with a bull. The bull had won.

"I mean no harm, Botello, you know that. I will see you in the morning, no?"

When Cortés approached his room after his talk with Botello, of course he had to see Bernal Díaz, who, if not in Cortés's room on his three-legged stool, was habitually seated on a stone outside Cortés's room.

"My lord, what is the matter?"

"It is nothing, Bernal Díaz, nothing. But tell me something." Cortés ushered his faithful retainer into his room, sat down in his Dante chair, and stretched out his legs.

"My lord?"

"Who are Botello's friends?"

"Francisco the monk, Adu the Negro, Malinche la Lengua."

"They call her the Tongue?"

"Well, some do, sometimes."

"And Botello? What is his greatest pleasure?"

"He likes certain herbs, certain seeds, certain molds, certain—"

Cortés waved his hand. "So, Botello, in your estimation, is he somebody to be trusted?" He fingered his codpiece. Cloth when not part of armor, it still pinched his thighs and chafed his loins.

"Botello to be trusted? As far as I know, my lord."

"Fetch Quintaval, will you?"

"Is something wrong?"

"Leave off, Díaz. Fetch Quintaval. Do so—and now." Cortés wondered why he put up with Bernal Díaz, he was so tedious. No matter. He got up and walked around his desk, merely a smoothed piece of wood on two wine casks. There were no doors, no curtains, nothing for privacy in the rooms which ringed a courtyard on the first floor of the Cempoalan cacique's palace. Doors were considered rude.

Anybody can spy on me, Cortés huffed.

"You wished to see me, Cortés?" Quintaval at his service, Quintaval the dandy.

"In Spain, Quintaval, was not your grandfather a thief, and is there not a Moor or two hanging from the family tree, and perhaps a Jew? Surely the darkness of your complexion would indicate such a possibility. A Morisco, a judío-converso?"

"I am no darker than you, my lord. My father was a grandee who fell on hard times, but honest to his dying breath. My mother was a virtuous woman, a mother."

"You know, Quintaval, you know well that I do not care who your father was, or if your mother was a whore, what they did or did not do, if they were nobles or paupers."

Quintaval narrowed his eyes. He knew Cortés cared very much about *his own* family connections and served his king as best it served him.

"I do not care if you had to carry your mother over the mountains on your back over the Pyrenees to get to Spain like Alvarado did."

"Sir?"

"What I mean is Núñez is a converso, and while I care as much as the next Castilian about the faith, I only ask absolute loyalty to me and our holy mission here in New Spain. What you do in your room, on your mat, in the cellar of your soul, and what memories you carry within the recesses of your small Quintavalian mind, or what portrait miniature you gaze upon each night, were it a faithful rendition of the devil himself, is not for me to inquire."

"You are a new man, then, a modern man?"

"You could say that. I believe in honor, of course, but the larger honor beyond individual and family."

"You believe strongly in the individual, however, the power of the man to make his own life?"

"We are not here to parse sentences, my friend. But treasonous actions, inciting mutiny, conspiring with others against me, will cost you your life. I know you are a protégé of the so-called governor Velázquez, and perhaps you came as his spy. However, I have given you ample chance to prove yourself to me. Stand warned. Do not mock me, Quintaval, do not push me, do not connive or work against me. We are on a mission for God and Crown."

"You take me amiss, Cortés. I love you well and will serve you to my death."

"You will indeed. No more needs to be said. Summon Alvarado." Cortés got up from his chair, came over, and gave Quintaval a hearty abrazo. "I am glad we understand each other."

As soon as Quintaval left, the cacique's niece appeared at his doorway, a flirtatious little smile fixed on her face.

"No, no, not tonight. Can you not see I am occupied? Jesucristo y todo los santos."

She puckered her lips, as if saying, Kiss me, my dear man, kiss me hard, and waddled on her way. Then Alvarado appeared in his doorway.

"Ah, Alvarado, I have been waiting for you. I will make this quick and blunt. Are you aware that Quintaval, bastard son of twenty generations back of mongrel dogs, is up to no good? You know it, I know it, now the whole camp knows it; maybe even the fat cacique of Cempoala knows it. We have discussed it, have we not?"

Alvarado could not remember but he nodded his head and did not look his commander in the face. "Quintaval talks too much," he said.

"Yes, and Puertocarrero drinks too much, Alvarado. But he rises in the morning, can get up on his horse and do his maneuvers." Puertocarrero did not even protest when he had taken his woman, Malinche, away from him and made her his own. As for her, he could hear her sobbing in the next room, as she did every night since he had acquired the cacique's niece. Initially Cortés had thought Doña Marina had enough tears to fill a puddle, now he wondered if her store could make a lake.

"Soon, if not already doing so, Quintaval will be recruiting other malcontents and grab-me-mores. They are like worms to rotten bread, the greedy bunch."

Alvarado stood first on one foot, then on the other, and stared at Cortés's feet. The commander had taken off his boots, and Alvarado noticed his toes were pink.

"What is it you love best, Alvarado, may I ask?"

Alvarado was going to say his horse but caught himself.

"God, sir, then king, then . . ."

"Out with it, man."

"You may think this forward, but you next; my father, a fine man, is dead."

"You do not love me first and foremost?"

"Well, I was going to say so, but I thought I should mention God, you know . . ."

"Right, right, I am playing the fool for you. Let me tell you this in the utmost confidence. Velázquez, our venerated governor, wants us to fail, but only after we have sent all the gold. Listen well, it is this: Velázquez does not understand that he does not come before God and king. Alvarado, do this for me. Follow Quintaval, keep a close eye on him, report to me daily what you hear and see . . . Let us find him out. Do I hear some shuffling? Who is that outside the door?"

"It is only I, your humble servant, Capitán General."

Isla, the quiet one. What the hell could he want? Cortés had started out the night peacefully. Now everybody and his fleas were dropping in.

"Go now, Alvarado. Remember what I said. And tell Malinche in the room next door to stop crying her heart out. She thinks she is a princess. She is just a woman. Basta. Basta."

Chapter 16

Isla had a roundabout way of speaking. He circled his point like a bee aiming to sting.

"It only rained twice today. It has been a lovely day here in Cempoala, Cortés."

"I just said the same." Cortés had ferreted out treason, he had had to extricate himself from one woman and another one was ruining his night with her childish crying, and he was stuck with his troops in a heathen enclave in the middle of nowhere. Lovely day indeed.

"And what is on your mind, Isla?" Isla played very close to the chest; a solitary one, he did not share words, did not eat like a pig or drink like a fish. He must indulge in something, Cortés reasoned. He must, the mischievous devil, have a fatal flaw he could exploit. The man was circumspect, cold, calculating. Truth be told, Cortés did not like the fellow one little bit for all his fawning.

"Do not take offense, Capitán General, if I tell you something is disturbing me, impeding my sleep, wringing out my heart with worry . . . It concerns you."

"Come now, man. I am without vanity." That Isla had a heart was interesting. Perhaps Isla was the king's spy, the emperor's man. But he was good with sword and horse. You need a cool head in battle in order to keep it on your neck.

"Your little paramour."

"Which one?"

"Malinche, Malinali, Malintzin, La Lengua, la puta."

"Ah yes, Doña Marina, a treasure. She is crying for me."

"She is cohorting with Alvarado."

"Beg pardon."

"She is doing the dirty deed with Alvarado. He puts—"

"I heard you." Cortés jumped up from his chair, went over to his sleeping mat, took out his sword, stabbed it in its stuffing again and again, then slit it up and down so the corn husks tumbled out, and then swung it against the wall, emptying all its sacking. Then he saw a parade of ants making their way across the floor, and instantly crushed them flat with his bare feet. He looked around for something else to kill. Somebody had put a vase of flowers on his desk. Who had done that? He threw it out the door, was inclined to stamp on the shards of pottery, but restrained himself. Damn Indians. Flowers everywhere. He hated flowers.

The crying next door abruptly ceased.

"It is not true," he hissed in Isla's face, keeping his voice down. "How dare you present me with such scurrilous gossip," the pernicious vulture.

"I hate to be the messenger of bad tidings."

"I am certain you do." Cortés gave Isla a steely stare. Botello had warned it was going to be a terrible day. All signs concurred, he had said, that Cortés should not get up from his sleeping mat.

"Alvarado is my most loyal man. I just saw him. Such a dastardly deed would show on his face, contort his features, dim his eyes, make him stutter. He would fall down dead. He would not betray me if Doña Marina was the last woman on earth. Doña Marina is my concubine. Such accusations come from malicious rumor, backbiting, backstabbing, jealousy, nibbling rats. This camp is a stinking stew of tattletales. People with nothing to do all day sit around spreading misleading comments about others like rotten jam on moldy bread. Is there not a commandment against false witness?" Cortés scratched himself.

"It is true. Would that it were not, Capitán General." Isla stood at attention as if he were before a military tribunal questioning his conduct.

"Why are you telling me this?" The man was malicious to the core.

"For your own good."

"Really?" Cortés did not feel good at all. His mouth tasted of cornmeal, which was coating his teeth with slime. He had not had a good slab of beef since he could remember. Why were there no cows in this country? No horses to ride? Unthinkable.

"When you are with the fat cacique's fat niece, she creeps into Alvarado's room. She is like a treacherous cat. He is like a lion."

"I ask you again. Why are you telling me this nonsense?"

"Because, Capitán General, she is your interpreter and translator. Her lack of loyalty could jeopardize our whole mission here. And Alvarado, is he not your second-in-command?"

"I promised the girl more than her freedom."

Isla was now in a relaxed stance. At ease, he stood with his feet a little apart, his hands behind his back. He was a tall man, taller than most, much taller than Cortés, and of a robust build. Yet his head, on the end of his long stalk of a neck, was curiously small. It was odd, outlandish. He had the eyes of a hawk, deep-set, but so far on the sides of his narrow face that he had to turn his head to look one way and the next, and worse, his eyes were unblinking. His mouth was long, his top lip almost invisible, his lips usually pressed together. With his hair combed back from his face and greased down flat to his skull, he looked like an eel, una ángula. And his fingers were extraordinarily white and fragile, like a woman's. The nail of the pinkie on his left hand was very long. What was that supposed to mean? Was he a witch or something? Cortés would have to ask Botello.

"What did you do before you came to Cuba, Isla?" Cortés had met him at the docks. He seemed a man of breeding. More importantly, he owned a horse.

"I was a rope maker in Seville, Spain, come to make my fortune in the Indies."

"In truth?" Cortés did not believe a word of it. Rope makers did not own horses and learn swordplay. He had come from Spain with means.

"Yes, my father had a shop."

"So you did not go to university? You are without rank or place?"

"I can read Latin. I am loyal to the emperor, Capitán General, Comandante Cortés. I am a Christian and I can handle a sword. I am not afraid."

"Would you kill a man on my command?"

"Of course."

"Not an enemy, but a man who was your compadre?"

"Do you want me to kill Alvarado and the slave girl?"

"No, no . . ." Cortés was up and pacing, his head lowered. "Not right now. I was just asking." So the man was not only a soldier but a killer. Was he perhaps a paid assassin? "For now, just follow Alvarado. Observe him closely and report to me."

There was a slight rustle.

"Jesucristo y todos los santos, y ahora qué."

"Señor?" Francisco poked his head in the door.

"Can you not see that I am talking to Isla, Francisco?"

"A delegation has arrived. They are gifts from the capital, from Moctezuma."

"More women?" Cortés rolled his eyes. "We have enough."

"They bring gold."

"Gold?"

Cortés dismissed Isla and quickly followed Francisco, urging the brother to quicken his pace. A large crowd had gathered in the zócalo. A contingent of bearers with the empire's ensign on their robes, the eagle on the cactus, carried many beautiful things in their arms which they set down before Cortés:

Two disks of gold and silver
A golden necklace with pearls and gems
Another necklace of twisted strands of gold with one hundred and two
small rubies and one hundred and seventy-two small emeralds
A helmet full of gold
A wooden helmet plated with gold
A beaver hung with twenty-five bold gold bells
A chest encircled with gold plate
A bracelet of thin gold
A wand with two gold rings at its end adorned with pearls
Hooks covered in feathers fastened with gold thread
Deerskin sandals sewn with gold thread
Leather shoes ornamented with silver, pearls, and gold

A shield with brass bells about its rim and its boss a plate of gold
Four fish of gold
Ducks cast in gold
One large mirror with gold trimmings
Fans and flyswatters of feathers and gold
Mantles with gold threads

The cacique of Cempoala, who of course had to see what the commotion was all about, immediately arrived in his hammock litter. Malintzin, who up to a moment before had been sobbing, stood at her post next to Aguilar, ready to interpret and translate. Cortés, seeing her, could barely contain himself. He wanted to leap on her, hands outstretched, and choke the life out of her right there, in front of everybody, but in light of all the golden objects set before him and needing her skills, he settled for an angry look.

"Tell him," Cortés said to Aguilar, "tell the cacique outside of the hearing of the messengers and bearers that we can see this display of wealth is only a bribe from the capital for our favor. Cortés will not be bribed. We intend to return it as soon as we can."

Aguilar related this to Malintzin, who solemnly walked over to the cacique and told him quietly in his ear what Cortés wanted him to hear. Cortés tried to detect adultery in the way she swung her hips, the way she put forth her chest, but she looked as she always did, modest, quiet on her own behalf, a willing slave, a beautiful slave. She was a woman, a smart woman no doubt, but he wanted to whip her so that the blood ran down her back and her skin hung in fringes. He wanted to strip all her skin off, quarter inch by quarter inch, so that she looked like a peeled tomato, raw and soft. He wanted to make her wince and cry for mercy. He wanted to cut her heart out even though she was heartless. And Alvarado, that was simple enough, just chop his head off. On the other hand, that would be too kind. Hanging was the most ignoble way to be executed, burning the most painful. He would decide later. The hapless fools.

"The delegation has a message for Cortés," Malintzin said.

The spokesman for the group from the empire stepped forward

and said something directly to Malintzin. She turned, said it to Aguilar, and Aguilar translated it to Cortés.

"He says, Malinche says," Aguilar said, "that Moctezuma greets the great captain Malintzin with respect."

"I am not Malintzin."

"They just say it that way. It is their way. She speaks for you and so she is you, you are she. You are her lord. Malintzin's lord. Malintzin and you speak as one."

"We speak as Cortés, not Malintzin. Are you sure her translation is faithful?"

"As far as we know. We have not been harmed yet."

"Go on, Aguilar."

Malintzin translated to Aguilar in a quiet voice so the cacique could not hear.

"Warrior to warrior," Aguilar said in Spanish, "you to Moctezuma, Moctezuma to you, he thanks you for sparing his men from the clutches of the nefarious and despised Cempoalan cacique, who is an ungrateful and perverted subject known for his preference for young boys, spider monkeys, and venomous snakes. He is dirty in all his habits, born senseless, and in every way disreputable and expendable. And with these gifts Emperor Moctezuma is courteously suggesting that Quetzalcoatl understand the empire's appreciation for his great generosity in saving his tax collectors. Take them, Moctezuma suggests, in cheerful spirit, for he wants Quetzalcoatl to be happy and prosperous, to enjoy these gifts to their full extent, and to forever remember the Mexica as a generous people, and—"

"Aguilar, get to the point."

"He says go back where you came from and leave them alone even if you are Quetzalcoatl."

"Go back where I came from? Go to that crummy island Hispaniola, where there is no gold and there are no longer any slaves? Cuba? That hellhole?"

"Maybe he means Spain, home to *your* emperor," Aguilar suggested.

"Spain? To sit in some decaying old town, hoping to get the next boat out?"

"Mi capitán," Alvarado said. "¿Está usted bien?"

The next thing Cortés was going to say was, Alvarado, you, you dog of excrement, tú, tú perro de mierda, but he contained himself, as was fitting for a gentleman, captain, general, commander, master, lord, mayor.

"I thought the Cockroach liked gold," Jaguar Claw said to Cuy.

Cuy looked at Núñez. He arched his eyebrows in question. She shrugged her shoulders. They were adopting each other's mannerisms, Francisco noted, the wandering Jew and his Mayan slave, shrugging, lifting their eyebrows, standing at a slant, respectful yet always questioning. Were those the gestures of exile? But then, Francisco reasoned, since Eden we are all exiles, all wanderers. Yet did not this town in its beauty resemble Eden, shortly to be spoiled. Like Adam and Eve, nobody can leave anything well enough alone.

"Adu," Cortés said to the black slave, "enlist the help of Juan and Manuel, Quintaval's servants, and move the kind gifts into my quarters. We will keep them there until we can return them. Tell that to the cacique, Aguilar, that we refuse the gifts and will send them all back with a very angry note. No, we will not be bribed. But until they go back, we will store them at our own expense."

Cortés turned to Bernal Díaz and said: "You estimate the total worth of this stuff in your record book, Bernal Díaz. We will count it, weigh it, melt it down, and one-fifth will go to King Carlos. Keep a few objects as curiosities to show the esteemed emperor what his vassals in far-off America are capable of sending to Spain. My share next, and when their expenses are deducted for armor and food, the rest to the men."

Then Cortés turned to Botello and said, "I do not care what the signs say on the morrow; come what may, we are preparing to leave."

Then he shouted to Puertocarrero, "And, my friends, gold for all, all for gold."

"And, my friends . . ." went through the ranks.

"To the capital," went out the cheer. "On to gold, more gold."

"Aguilar." Cortés pulled him away from the group. "Tell Malinche I wish to see her in my quarters tomorrow morning after our breakfast meal, and keep the damn niece away from me." Then he walked up to Alvarado and spit in his ear, "Touch her again, and I will kill you like a dog on the street."

"I did not want to . . . she came . . ."

"Another word and I will cut off your right hand finger by finger." What Cortés wanted to say was, How could you, my dearest Alvarado, do this to me?

Cortés gave Malintzin a look as if to say, You are a whore and a dung-smeared slattern.

She lifted her chin defiantly.

Cortés muttered, "We will see who rules this roost." He wanted to kill her slowly.

The next morning, however, he no longer wanted to kill her at all. Seeing her standing before him like a proud peacock in front of his desk, maintaining her bravado and haughtiness despite the consequences, he could not help admiring her. Here was a woman after his own heart. Whatever befell her, he realized, she was going to brave it out with style and distinction.

Inside, however, Malintzin was trembling. A hundred different tortures tumbled through her mind. But she bit her lip, held her tongue, and stared straight back into his dark eyes, which, hooded and deep-set, were often at variance with his words.

"I am going to cut out your tongue, woman. I am going to silence you once and for all. And you understand perfectly what I am saying." He got up from his chair, came over to her side of the desk, and stood very close to her. She could see his chest, which usually stuck out like a turkey's, heaving, and his breath was uneven, catching at times in what could almost be considered a sob. His eyes were crusted. His lips were dry and cracked. He was wearing his overshirt, not his boots or stockings, the silly hard shell or armor over his member. His hair was disheveled. She lifted her chin and gave him an arrogant smile.

"You are not afraid?" He stepped up to her and took out his dagger from his boot.

She lifted her chin higher. Her father was a warrior, she came from a warrior people.

"You are *not* afraid." He shook his head in sadness and admiration.

She was afraid, but would rather die than show it on her face.

"Why are you doing this to me?" he moaned. "¿Por qué me esta haciendo esto a mí?"

Limítese a respirar, just breathe, but do not speak, Malintzin said to herself. Silence was the rule and power of the slave. Muédase la lengua, bite your tongue, Cómase sus palabras, eat your words.

"You are a slave. Not everybody's slave, only mine, and if you would like to know, other people in my troops are learning Nahuatl. We can find people who know Nahuatl and Mayan on the borders of every town. I do not need you."

"They do not know as much as I do. You will not trust them."

"I do not trust you."

"You do."

"How can I trust you? You just betrayed me."

"You betrayed *me*." If she knew the power of silence, she had also come into the knowledge that words were golden. To say gold was to say everything.

"Remember, Doña Marina, I am a man. Betrayal is a man's prerogative."

"I am a woman."

"You know what I mean. Usted sabe lo que yo quiero decir." He addressed her formally.

"I know what you mean." She nodded. "Yo sé que usted quiere decir."

"Malinche." Cortés put his hand on her shoulder. "What am I going to do with you? ¿Qué hacer con usted?"

She had him, she exalted. I have him. El es mio ahora.

PART III

It was not hard to be Francisco's friend. He called her by her real name, Malintzin, he listened to her carefully, and when she had finished saying what she had to say, he would sit quietly for a few moments, press his lips together, bring his hands flat together in their gesture of prayer as if he were trying to find the right words deep inside himself, and then, with great thoughtfulness, he would reply.

"Yes, yes, I see, Malintzin."

Although their talks might begin with his god, Jesus, the young one, and Mary, his mother, they soon came to the subject of what Brother Francisco called "the earthly family."

Time and again Malintzin spoke of her own father, Maxtl, how kind he was, the many things he had taught her, and how much she still missed him.

"It seems to me, Malintzin," Brother Francisco said one day, "that you need to speak more of your mother."

"She is the one who sold me into slavery. She hated me, I hate her." Malintzin did not really want to say anything else. How could she, there was nothing more to be said. Her mother had done the unthinkable.

Francisco replied gently, "That is true, your mother did sell you. But have you ever thought there was a need for her to do so?"

"She did it because of my brother, his inheritance. Because of her new husband, how he hated me."

"Did your mother's husband only hate you?"

"He hated me more than anything."

"Because?"

"Because . . ." here Malintzin faltered. "Because."

"Because why?"

"Because he would kill me if I told, because it would kill my mother to know."

"That makes me so sad, my dear."

"It is not *that* sad," she said, bursting into tears. She did not know if she felt sad because Francisco felt sad, or if she felt sorry for herself, or if what happened was sad enough to be sad about. There were many sad things—the mother and baby who ran away to die in the jungle, the ones who get sacrificed, warriors who died in war. What had happened to her was not the worst thing that could happen to anybody. Perhaps she did not have a right to be sad at all.

"Anyway, it was a long time ago," she said in an effort to comfort Francisco.

"Our memories can be very powerful."

"Well, I am not sad now." She smiled through her tears.

"You are not sad because . . . ?"

"Because Cortés loves me."

"Oh, child." Francisco shook his head. "Cuidado. Be careful."

INSTEAD OF PROCEEDING inland from Cempoala, the expedition returned to Vera Cruz. It was late August and raining every day, but they had not returned because of the weather. Cortés said he wanted to check on the progress of the fifty men in Vera Cruz in charge of building, protecting, and maintaining the town. Vera Cruz, on the eastern coast, was a fortified foothold in New Spain, and as mayor of a settlement elected by a council, his claim in the name of Spain to the new country was firmly entrenched. In the pouring rain, Cortés had men gather and pile rocks for a wall to fortify the city. On dry days new foundations were poured. On damp days they did army maneuvers in the muck. And on rainy days Adu and Quintaval practiced fencing with their clothes drenched and their swords slick.

Food went moldy in a day, and water dripped through the thatched roofs of the buildings in an unrelenting monotony. Spirits were low. After three balmy weeks in Cempoala, they were stuck back where they started, Vera Cruz. Six months in the country, and the only gold, gifts from Moctezuma, was being saved, so said Cortés, for the Spanish monarch as proof of the expedition's necessity.

"One of the problems is that Cortés pays the king first and himself second," Quintaval said to Adu. They were practicing in the rain. "What about us? Our patrón, Governor Velázquez."

Adu knew the pronoun "us" did not refer to him. He would never be paid, whatever the circumstances.

"Move in a little closer, Adu. Cross, cross, cross." Quintaval always began their session together as if it were a first session, calling out the basic classical moves. In Spanish-style fencing, the lunge was forbidden, but Quintaval considered himself a proponent of the French tradition, an internationalist, if you will, and thus featured lunges and other cosmopolitan niceties.

"Forward, move, move."

Sometimes Botello and Francisco, on one of their botanical jaunts in the rain, traveling with small canvas canopies over their heads and looking like a caravan, would pause to watch the two swordsmen practice. And this morning the meadow outside the Vera Cruz fort was full of men going through their paces; those who were not swordsmen worked their horses, running them, having them stop quickly and pick up speed again, the wound-run maneuver. Alvarado directed.

"Elected, and I use that word with irony, my friend," Quintaval persisted. "*Elected* captain of the expedition and now mayor of Vera Cruz. Keep close, keep close, Adu, move out, in."

Adu would rather join Botello and Francisco on a flower hunt than wear out his wrists in this foolish game. With them he did not feel like a slave, protégé, father confessor, go-fetcher.

Jaguar Claw, meanwhile, was shielding himself from the rain in the doorway of the cookhouse as he stitched tanned deer hides together into a cloak for himself. For a needle he was using a maguey spine, and his thread was from the agave too. Maguey was a plant that should be worshiped, he believed. Its fibers made a coarse cloth used for cloaks and other clothes for poorer people. Pulque was made from its fermented sap and induced a happy state. How the ancestors had penetrated the mystery of its many gifts was a wonder to him. That they knew to spin the soft wool of the cotton plant into thread, grind flour from the hard kernel of a maize cob, make dyes from snails and insects, and had discovered that the hard rind of a papaya concealed a delicious soft fruit.

"I am sure other people will be with us, Adu—Rivera, Cortázar, Cabeza de Vaca, Manito, Arturo, and ourselves—and who knows how many others will join against Cortés. And all of the men mentioned have their own men to come along."

Adu tried to signal with his eyebrows and little lifts of his head that Quintaval should not be so bold or loud in his speech while playing swords in the meadow. Bernal Díaz was nosing about and had situated himself on a rock not far away, the drizzle dripping from the broad-brimmed hat which sat on his head like a flat plate. His full-blown ears, rimmed with hairs, were poised to absorb every drop of conversation.

"Adu, no, no, do not come in so close, do you want to get yourself killed? Pull back."

"Master," Adu said softly, their sword hilts touching in the criss-cross, "the record keeper is listening to you. Be wise."

Quintaval turned and saw Bernal Díaz.

"Perhaps he will be of our party."

"It is highly unlikely, Master Quintaval. Do you not note how he takes down every word as if he could save it and eat it later? He is fastened to Cortés's purse and lips and has pinned his hopes like a proud broach upon Cortés's chest. Do not cast your trust so far afield."

"Do not say 'do not' to me, Adu. Remember your place."

Ah yes, his place, the wrong place, for not only was he without power, he would be drawn into Quintaval's plot and forced to play the role and serve the punishment of conspirator by their unnatural bond. He knew also that to remain silent would be to betray both his master and his enemy, and that to speak would be to betray his master and give ammunition to his master's enemy. To be free of blame would require complete freedom. Daily he considered the odds. If he set out for a walk with Francisco and Botello and disappeared, could he get a morning's start unnoticed or would Francisco worry and alert every-body, thinking Adu had lost his way and been captured by Indians? Or if left alone in the forest, far away from the society of men, would he be eaten by animals? A high price to pay for freedom.

That night, clear and dry, they made a campfire in the middle of the cleared square, the only open, smooth area of Villa Rica de Vera Cruz. Everybody was tired and discouraged, and Quintaval, as if he felt obligated to fill the silence, drunk on pulque, let his tongue wag on. Moths were darting in and out of the firelight, some getting too close to the center, the edges of their brown wings singeing. Then they would dive to their fiery fate. At the servant's campfire, now swelled by the many bearers from Cempoala, Jaguar Claw grabbed at moths in flight, popped them into his mouth, letting them bat their soft wings against the sides of his throat, and then, opening his lips, let them go. Adu, also with the Cempoalans and slaves, outdid Jaguar Claw's example by swallowing his plucked moths whole. Then, of course, Jaguar Claw had to do the same. Everybody in the servant's circle enjoyed this entertainment, betting cocoa beans on who could put more in his mouth at once.

Alvarado, ordinarily one of the wits and troubadours of the captains' circle with his songs and flute, was silent and petulant. Cortés had barred Alvarado from speaking to him. If only he could explain to his captain that Malintzin was just a woman, hardly a point of contention among two able horsemen.

"And so, Alvarado, how goes it?" Quintaval asked.

Alvarado turned his head, spat a gob of sour mucus into the darkness, and sighed.

"The slave girl?" Quintaval asked. "An unfortunate incident."

"A slave is a slave, am I right?"

"Alvarado, you are right, a slave is a slave." Quintaval looked over at Adu, who at his campfire was jamming moths into his mouth, and mused: This was the man I taught to fence like a gentleman?

"Women are by nature slaves, deceitful. She was naked, can you blame me?"

"Indeed not. Cortés is a lunatic."

Alvarado started a bit. *Was* Cortés a lunatic? He looked up at the moon. Lunatics were supposed to be governed by her phases, and in Spain and Italy, and particularly France, there were people who turned into ferocious wolves by the light of the full moon. They would lie down on the bed as people and as the moon became brighter, hair would grow on their faces, first a patch here, a patch there, then on their whole heads and necks. Their ears would prick up and up, their nails would lengthen to claws. When they sat up in bed, they would see that they did not have the hands of a human, and on all fours they would jump out the window and run into the woods to hide and hunt, never to be men again.

"Cortés a lunatic, Quintaval? That is a rather damaging charge."

"I mean he loses his senses when a woman appears."

"Exactly." Alvarado then fell silent and looked at his feet, which had taken on the color of his boots, a reddish brown. "I wish I were back in my encomienda in Cuba with my horses. I had seven Andalusians, and I am hoping to get some Arabians. A beautiful bay, a roan stallion, a chestnut, two creams, can you imagine, a roan mare, and a dun. I am thinking of going into the horse-breeding business. Very lucrative in the Indies because of the shortage. You know there is not a homegrown horse to be found there or here as a matter of fact, so it is no wonder they do not use the wheel, no pack animals at all. Sad to say, the imported ones, well, few survive the trip across the Atlantic, so those that do should be bred. On the trip from Spain, they were like the black slaves who had to be thrown overboard when they sickened and died. A great pity."

Quintaval inched closer. "Some of us, and I say this in the most utmost confidence, feel as you do, that is, that our best interests, and our governor's best interests, are not served here on this farcical 'expedition.' The king of Spain, I hear, eager to be the emperor of the Holy Roman Empire, is hardly in Spain at all, mostly traveling with his full court. His chin is so sharp that to dare to get close puts one at risk of a stabbing. Did you know that?"

"No, I did not."

"'Tis true. He was raised in the Netherlands, a cold-blooded northerner, where they preach blasphemy against the Church, and the gold that costs us our lives allows the pretender to live in style. Some say he is as mad as his mother, Juana the Loca. Can you think of that?"

"I try not to think too much. It usually leads to melancholy."

Quintaval moved even closer to Alvarado and whispered in his ear. "What I am about to tell you, Alvarado, you must swear to keep in confidence on your mother's life."

"I do, I do." Alvarado's mother had been quite dead for many years, alas.

"Some of us want to go no farther and return to Cuba."

"Is that true?"

"It is, and by my judgment, Cortés is leading us into a pit of certain death. Have you not heard how many men Moctezuma can command? All the city-states that pay tribute, his whole empire, which is extensive by any reasoning."

"But God is not on their side, Quintaval."

"Tell me, Alvarado, whose side was God on when the Muslims captured Constantinople in 1453, Serbia in 1459, and then Albania in 1470? I am not even mentioning Spain."

"That is different."

"Is it?"

"What adventure is there in staying at home in Cuba, Quintaval?"

"That of a long life and, as you say, horses. I have a fencing school."

Alvarado looked at Quintaval sleepily. He hated complications. How inconsiderate of Quintaval to confide in him when he had his own difficulties.

"We are meeting tomorrow at nightfall behind the chapel, and then we are going to the ships. We have enough to crew one boat to Cuba, and that is all we need. The following morning, by the time they notice we are no longer in our huts and one boat is no longer anchored, we will be long gone."

"And then?"

"It is a short time to Cuba given good weather, and then, well,

Velázquez, once he knows what is happening, will want to arrest Cortés for fraud, treason, and insubordination. He will send his own forces to rightfully take over the conquest."

"You are going to take over the conquest?" Alvarado was irritated.

"I have no interest in continuing this fiasco. Let somebody else get killed."

"We have only been here a matter of five months or so." It seemed like forever to Alvarado too, but he was not going to complain about Cortés. So far his commander had spared his life.

"Six months is time enough to see that the wind blows toward the House of Habsburg."

"But once we—"

"This is no Cathay with silk, the islands of Cipongo. This is not India with spices. We are not Christopher Columbus fooling ourselves. What little gold we find will have to be dug out of the earth, and will be shipped to Europe or kept by Cortés."

"There are streams which run with gold, and other gems too, and lots and lots of fertile land, and many brown-skins for slaves. There is their delicious cocoa, sweet potatoes, maize, tomatoes. Is there any fowl more meaty than turkey? And tobacco is going to be the balm of civilization. As we are soldiers in the army, we must accept the chain of command." Alvarado recalled sharply that the penalty for treason was death.

"An army? You call us an army?" Quintaval swept his hand, indicating the men who had fallen asleep by the fire in their armor like beached sea crabs, their dirty feet bare, fleas in their beards, and who knows what in their ears and noses, and other recesses of their bodies. The Cempoalans, on the other hand, were clean-shaven, and were seated around their bonfire in neat formation, their knees to their chest, shields and spears at their sides, their quivers across their chests, and a packet of arrows on their backs.

"Do you not see? There is going to be a civil war, Alvarado, between Moctezuma's forces and the discontented cities that pay tribute. Indian against Indian. That is the only way it can be fought. We have stepped into internal turmoil. Even if the Aztec empire were crushed, our 'allies' could then turn against us, the foreigners, the white men. We are so few."

"But if we win, it is the conquest, Quintaval, winner take all. Think of all those who will be brought to God, all those souls saved for Jesus. Is that not beyond price?"

"You want to be in Bernal Díaz's little book of remembrance? Who will remember, who will care whether we prosper or die? Brought to God? We will be thrown to the devil."

Alvarado fingered his beard. "You say it well, Quintaval."

"And so you are with us. It is settled. Tonight then."

Chapter 18

The Cempoalas had called her Malintzin Tenepal, tenepal meaning one who possesses speech, and the Spanish called her La Lengua, the Tongue, but if they really wanted to know, she was more ears than tongue. Everything had a language if you listened hard enough. The food on the plate hummed and sizzled and called out temptingly, Eat me, eat me, and it would tell you how you would feel with your belly full and warm, and it would settle down at the base of your belly, murmuring happiness. Each animal had its voice, and even stones were not entirely mute, telling of their long, silent dwelling on the earth.

In Malintzin's room in the newly built sleeping quarters in Vera Cruz, she had an obsidian mirror and a small platform for her hairbrush and paints for her face. The Spanish had made chairs from barrels, tables with hewn boards, and chairs of twigs with hide stretched over them. Some of the men had fixed up little shrines in various places. Malintzin liked their gods, for they did not require bloodletting or sacrifice, but she considered belief in their power naïve, for what good could come of planting crosses and reciting strange words? Francisco said that she should consider their mother Mary her mother, and their father god her father. If she did, she would never be lonely. She feared for Francisco, for despite his strong belief in his gods, he, like all people, and perhaps more than most, was at the mercy of the men around him. Isla taunted him. Father Olmedo, who should have been his closest friend, seemed indifferent to him. Cortés himself disdained him. But when Malintzin brought this up, Francisco objected, saying that if you love, you are loved. If that were so, she had not observed it.

The word "love" in Nahuatl was tetlazohlaliztli, in Maya yaakun-
tik, and in Spanish amar. Malintzin knew that the word described a
doing, a feeling, *and* an idea. However, she did not think that the act,
the emotions, and the thought were always together at one time.
Cortés loved her, he said so, and he treated her with great gentleness.
And she loved him. That word made her feel silly, childish, on the one
hand, and on the other hand was not a sufficient description for what
she truly felt. Cortés was the first man who paid attention to her body.
Well, almost the first. Her mother's husband had looked at it and used
it for his pleasure, and those she served as auianime did look upon her
body to make certain she was a young woman. The point was that
since she was a little girl and her mother bathed and attended to her
and her father rubbed her feet at night, nobody had handled her with
care. Secretly she despised the men who used her body for their own
pleasure, going numb with distaste, although she could feign a smile,
a sigh, as well as the next woman. When the moment came, the sword
unsheathed, the tepolli in active form, she squeezed her eyes shut and
thought of other things, other events, another time and place, so that
she could suffer them gladly and not run away in disgust. She would
retreat to yesterday or the day before or the time she had a good meal
or the time she and Cuy laughed together or when she was a little girl
under the protection of her father's house. The first time she was penetrated she did pay attention, for she was curious upon realizing that
this was what her mother's husband did to her mother after he had
excited himself with her, Malintzin. He went from her mat in her
room to her mother's mat ready to make children. When her brother
was born, her mother said that she and her husband had been trying
for a long time to have a baby. When she looked at the baby, Malintzin
thought, You have me to thank.

Cortés did not let her be numb or dumb or float off to tomorrow
or up to the ceiling. He kept her right then and there, flesh on flesh.
Time, in their embrace, compressed to that moment, and the grinding
circle of inevitability, the cycle of seasons and years, were of their gen-
eration and spun to the beat of their rhythm. Disengaging, disentan-
gling, getting up from the mat and leaving the room was stepping back

into the other world, the one not of her making, and to be again at the mercy of its vagaries and indifference. Yet all it took to step into safety again was to cross the threshold of his room, and to crawl into the core of time and being again was to touch his arm, put her head on his neck, have him tickle her ears, wrap her body with his lean legs, and kiss her on the mouth. She could hide her eyes in his stomach, and she would rest in utter stillness while the world all about their mat would pick up speed, swirl around and around, and go through its paces—harvest, famine, war, peace, the death of the sun, the birth of the sun, sacrifice, resurrection, the eternal return. It was all up to them.

On this night she combed her hair smooth and shiny, and was now rubbing the petals of flowers she had picked during the day up and down her arms. Less than a week before, she had been in tears. She thought of herself, sometimes, as a rubber ball, the kind the ballplayers played with in their narrow field between two walls. Like a ball, she was also the one who wore a band of rubber to protect him against falls. His task was to get the ball through a small hoop on the side of the court without touching the ball with his feet or hands. Losing ballplayers lost their heads, and were sacrificed. She had kept her head. More than that, she believed Cortés wanted to make her his wife. There could be no other explanation for his forgiveness for her indiscretion with Alvarado, which was really born of her great love of Cortés. She had merely wanted to block Cortés out of her mind, to remind him that she was still alive despite his disregard, that she loved him so much she was going with another man to prove it. It was hard to explain, and he would not let her explain, shushing her if she wanted to apologize. Now she realized what he meant when he said he would grant her more than freedom. She knew his intentions. She would no longer be an auianime, a mere slave. He was going to marry her, and she would be an honored married woman, a wife, a mother, a matron.

As she watched herself in his polished obsidian mirror, finding herself beautiful, not ugly, as Quetzalcoatl had been tricked into thinking with the mirror Tezcatlipoca put before him, she heard the

shuffling of shoes. Spanish shoes, the leather of boots, and their sandals, which, made of rope, had thick soles, each step a plop and a suck
in the damp earth. Only a thin wall of palm and plastered mud separated the rooms; the outer walls, made in the Spanish way of mud
bricks they called adobe, were thicker. She put her ear up to the
between wall.

"Botello, roll your dice," Cortés commanded. "Tira los dados."

"I do not want to roll my dice for something so serious, Capitán."

"Cast them. I call one to hang, two to burn, three to drawing and
quartering, four to dismemberment."

"Cortés," Alvarado protested, smoothing his orange hair down,
"banishment, imprisonment, is not that sufficient?"

"Banishment only to summon forces to overtake us? Imprisonment only to waste a guard, and then on top of that feed him at our
expense? Alvarado, we are grateful for the information you brought us,
your vigilance, your loyalty, and now we do not wish to deny the
importance of your contribution to our holy undertaking."

"Quintaval will see the error of his ways," Father Olmedo argued,
"and reform accordingly."

Puertocarrero was nervously sucking on the strands of his beard.

"Once a thief, always a thief. Once a traitor, twice the influence.
Infidelity . . . need I continue with the man's sins?" Cortés was
crouched low. The men made a circle around him.

"Executed, he is a martyr," Botello pointed out.

"An example of what happens to those who defy authority. Be
strong, Botello."

"But he is a valuable soldier, an excellent swordsman," Aguilar put
in, his knobby knees sticking out awkwardly. Sometimes he regretted
being rescued on the beach.

"Of Velázquez's party, not ours. He preaches mutiny to the troops
and puts fear in their hearts, he is hardly somebody we can make
use of."

"Perhaps if you spoke to him," Núñez suggested. Núñez inched
up his spectacles with his knuckle. They often slid low on his nose. In

the jungle they steamed up. On board ship, they were speckled with spray. Still he persisted in wearing them, and could not even hear without them.

"About what? He has had fair warning. What time is it, Núñez?"

"It is ten o'clock at night, Señor Cortés." A time to put a stop to this, Núñez thought, fearful that once executions among the ranks started, it would not cease until even those who accused were put to death; and, of course, he was particularly wary of talk linking obedience to Christian duty or war-making to a holy crusade.

"You could ship Quintaval to Spain," Father Olmedo suggested.

"I would go with him as his watchman," Aguilar offered.

"Go to Spain to build a private insurrection there for us here ready to make the supreme sacrifice for God and country?" Cortés had not meant to use the word "sacrifice." But no matter, for everybody was too rattled, too anxious, to pay close attention to vocabulary.

"He is merely young, headstrong, that is his sin. Furthermore, he has a horse," Aguilar pointed out. "Let us be practical."

"You suggest we forgive heinous crimes because somebody is young? We will take his horse, Aguilar, one more horse for us. With Moctezuma to contend with, men, we can ill afford a rearguard action by Velázquez, or dissension in the ranks. We would be crushed in the middle. Do not flinch from making a hard decision, men. Think of yourselves as well as Quintaval. In war, we often have to choose the lesser of two evils, and always, always, protect yourself first and foremost, is that not one of the commandments?"

"I am not sure," Núñez ventured. "It is now ten minutes after ten. I think it is a good time for sleeping."

"Putting yourself first and foremost is not one of the commandments," Francisco said.

"It should be. Did you not see Velázquez's horsemen gallop to the edge of the docks as we left Cuba. He was going to call us back. The next thing to interfere with us will be a boat arriving from Cuba under the command of Velázquez or one of his lackeys."

"I humbly propose a trial," Núñez said, "to determine guilt or innocence. Justice and fairness hand in hand." Núñez had to be careful not to venture too far astray of current sympathies. First the accused, next the one who spoke in his defense, where would it stop?

"A trial? A public debate? Did not Judas wash his hands, Núñez? There is no question here. The penalty for treason is death."

"Treason is against God," Bernal Díaz added, giving Núñez a pointed look.

"I think I might be the judge of what is against God," Father Olmedo said. Father Olmedo made a point of keeping out of discussions, but an execution was going too far.

"Soft of heart, mush for brains," Cortés concluded.

"Well, Capitán Cortés," Father Olmedo said, "I have not heard it said that 'Soft of heart, mush for brains.' I have not heard that said in any mass, sermon, missive, hymn, epistle, gospel, or motto. And my Latin, if you will, is well in place. I may be age thirty-five, but I can still conjugate a verb or two, say my Ave Maria." Father Olmedo had escaped Spain by the skin of his teeth, for its spirit of orthodoxy since the reconquest of Granada was a menace to all those who thought for themselves. Here he was, leagues away, an ocean away, confronted with the same misuse of holy mission. A New World Inquisition.

"What say you, Isla?"

"I say you are the commander, Capitán General, and what you say is law."

"Well said."

"You will demoralize the men by the severity of it," Father Olmedo persisted, "if I may say."

"To my mind, there is nothing so rousing as a good execution."

"We should not kill one of our own." Alvarado, who had only mentioned Quintaval's confidential words as a means of regaining Cortés's good graces, was dismayed at what he had set in motion. If only he could take back his original words, swallow them whole. To gain favor, he had betrayed a man whose only real crime to date was to drink too much and be loose of tongue. For that Quintaval had to die? It seemed to Alvarado that he, no matter what he did or whatever side he took, could do no good. One mishap led to another.

"You brought this one on, Alvarado. What you begin, finish. Where are your cojones? Pressed against my concubine, Doña Marina?"

Alvarado's testicles retracted deep inside his belly. If he could keep from wetting his pants, he would serve God for the rest of his miserable life.

Malintzin, in the darkness of her room, holding herself still and tightly gripping her stomach, understood that Cortés was not as forgiving as he had appeared to her, and given that her betrayal was deeper, greater, perhaps for a woman the greatest, why had Cortés refrained from punishing her? It was because he loved her too much. That was it. Or perhaps, and this was a terrible thought, he was merely delaying the penalty for her crime, adding anxiety to her torture. He would not do that. Or perhaps by punishing Quintaval, Cortés was showing Alvarado the might of his power. Cortés would not carry out an execution. Killing in battle was dictated by duty and necessity. The thing with Quintaval? A ruse.

"I will not be a party to this," Francisco announced, leaving the room.

"You *are* a party to this and everything that goes on here whether you like it or not," Cortés shouted out after the monk. "Your presence on our march is your assent. You are one with us, do not think otherwise." Cortés went to the doorway. "Did you not come with us, Brother Francisco? Are you not Spanish, a person, dare I say it, of God."

Malintzin, glancing up from her mat, saw Francisco hurry down the hallway, his face drained with worry. She waited another moment or so, straightened herself, pressed down her hair, then stepped out of her room and went the few paces to Cortés's room. The light from the candles made the faces of the captains glow as if their necks had bloomed into grotesque roses. Aguilar's face was pinched as a dried cherry. Alvarado's cheeks were puffed as those of a beaver chomping on wood. Father Olmedo's long face had the look of a horse, a haunted, bony stallion. Núñez's face was flushed with the cast of too much pulque. Bernal Díaz looked as if his cheeks were full of rotten teeth and inflamed gums. Isla looked as if somebody had just given him a bag of gold and he was proving he could eat it. Botello's pox-marked, pitted face was stained like a strawberry.

"Doña Marina," Cortés said gently, "I will be with you shortly. Please, go back to your room. This is man's work here, my dear."

"But Hernán . . ." She said this with a coyness not at all in her usual manner of speaking, which was straightforward and without guile. And she thrust out her hip and took her tongue and licked her lips, adopting the manner of the auianime on the street.

"Un momento." Cortés came over, gave her bottom a little pat, and shooed her out. "Later, my little puma."

"You are not going to hurt anybody, are you, Hernán?"

"You know me, Doña Marina, on my conscience, I would not hurt a fly."

"I will be in my room." She gave him a hopeful smile.

"Women," he said, turning back. "Las mujeres."

"Aye," Puertocarrero agreed, then, realizing that he and Cortés had tasted of the very same one, looked down at his big feet.

"Cast," Cortés commanded Botello again.

Botello, crouched low to the floor, appearing no better than a raggedy beggar on the streets of Seville, held back his arm. He never wore armor, trusting to fate, nor did he own a fancy cloak, broach, or doublet. His was a long shirt of sacking, a rope for a belt, breeches, no hose, and a necklace made of shells. Even when he was standing upright, his back was hunched, so that bending over, he was most like a rounded possum playing dead. His gait, with his injured foot, was more of a hobble than a walk. He was not born pretty and life had treated him harshly. Yet here he was, imperfect, he realized, and the instrument of another man's fate.

"Cast."

"Haz la apuesta," Isla said. "Place your bets."

"It is late," Núñez said. "Too late."

Botello had only one die, but he shook it in his fist dramatically, frantically mouthing a prayer to whatever, whoever might help. Father Olmedo said a little prayer too: Please, God, no, do not allow this. Alvarado tried to think of pleasant things—horses galloping in the wind. Puertocarrero thought of a nice bottle of wine.

The single die landed faceup on one.

"Hanging it is," Cortés announced. "God is merciful."

Even though it was one of the less painful forms of execution if the hangman was good enough to instantly break your neck, the men left Cortés's room without looking at each other or saying a word. Indeed they could not get away fast enough. Alvarado, heading toward his room, looked to see if anybody was following him. Nobody was, so, trembling like a leaf in a high wind, he tiptoed straight to where Quintaval slept. Having been the one to inform, he understood he would be directly guilty of Quintaval's death, and thus should be the one to alert him. It was only fair. His poor old mother had always said, Think before you speak. Piensa antes de hablar. If he warned Quintaval, when they came for him in the morning Quintaval would not be there, ergo no execution. The only quandary, well, it was an immense obstacle, that is, would Cortés suspect him, Alvarado, as the one who told Quintaval and assisted in his escape? The consequences of that might be dire.

But then again, Alvarado rationalized, walls have ears. They truly did. Walls had ears and noses and mouths and tongues, for everybody knew everything. In this camp spies were as numerous as fleas. Surely this would not be the first secret that had mysteriously wound its way around. His fears mollified, Alvarado crept closer to Quintaval's room, but then, just as he was to enter, he heard several people talking.

"In less than an hour," Quintaval was saying. Alvarado could see through a chink in the walls—he could guess whose handiwork that wall was, sloppy Puertocarrero. He saw a tight cluster of men—Quintaval, Manuel and Juan, the two mute Indian servants from Cuba, Adu, and two other men from the infantry—speaking in hushed whispers.

"Once we get to the boat, you can navigate."

"Me? ¿Yo?"

Adu had no experience as a pilot and was not trained in the use of the compass, sextant, and other tools of navigation. He could not read the stars, had no maps of currents and winds, barely knew his starboard from his crow's nest, yet he wondered if it would be possible, if he were at the helm, to guide the ship beyond Cuba, positioning it as if for Spain, but diverge, rounding the overhanging head of West Africa, and make for home. Slipping by Cuba could be regarded as an error, a question of wind and current, out of his hands, and then, once nearing Spain, he could go south, with nobody the wiser. Nobody the wiser? Such a far-fetched idea. It was highly unlikely that he could deceive the others, and discerning his intentions, they would immediately throw him overboard.

It was a thought, an impossible notion, and sadly more. Adu, whose real name was Oduduwa, of the Yoruba people of the empire of Oyo, was first netted by Yoruba men from a neighboring village, then sold to the Ijo people, who specialized in the slave trade. It was Mande people who took him downriver to a place called Benin, where he was put into a prison run by black Muslims from a region farther up the Niger River. From the prison he was sold by an Arab Muslim from Timbuktu to an olive-skinned Christian Portuguese man from Lisboa, to a Spaniard from Seville, to an even whiter Englishman from Liverpool, and thence Quintaval in Havana, Cuba. He was traded for cowrie shells, copper rods, dyed cloth, three English pounds, Portuguese money, and Spanish ducats. To think of Mother Africa as haven, home, refuge, safety was to ignore what had happened to him.

"And Juan, you are the one to pull up anchor. The others will unfurl the sails at dawn when we are well away. There is a good breeze from the south. They won't even know we are gone unless one of them casts a backward glance at the boats."

"Master," Adu said.

"The plan is good, of that I am as certain as I am of my mother and the mother of Jesus and all the saints, and Jesus himself. Tan cierto como yo soy de mi madre, la madre de Jesús, todos los santos y Jesús. When we get to Cuba, I am sure that Velázquez, as soon as we report Cortés's grandiose and independent schemes, will dispatch a fleet to stop the vainglorious enterprise and bring them all home in shackles and chains, that is, those they do not slay."

Alvarado, poised beside the door, felt his breath catch and a cough climb up his throat. Dear God, what should he do? Did he want to be a killer or be killed? Of course he did not want to be killed, but how could he reconcile himself to being a killer. Father Olmedo had never spoken of Jesus's words on the matter, and nobody with any sense turned the other cheek if it meant decapitation unless, of course, they were a saint. But he was a caballero, was he not? God, he implored, give me a sign. Just a sign. Anything.

Then, lo and behold, a moth floated down from the night. It was a large moth, creamy white with paper-thin wings. It stopped in mid-flight and turned to Alvarado.

Dear God, Alvarado gasped, a sign, a real sign. He turned around without a word and tiptoed back to his room. An angel had settled it. He did not have to do a thing.

"Watch this," Adu said, looking up as the moth floated into Quintaval's room. He opened his mouth and did not even have to pluck it out of the air. It rested on his tongue, folding its wings for a moment, and then lifted away, a little damp on the feet, but none the worse for it.

Alvarado fell into a deep and guiltless sleep on his corn-husk mat as Quintaval and his group surreptitiously made their way to the ships bobbing in the Bay of Vera Cruz. Keeping to the shadows, wary of the moonlight, they reached the beach. They pushed two rowboats off the sand into deeper water. Dipping the cloth-wrapped oars into the smooth, silky water, they soundlessly rowed out to the ship farthest away from shore, the *Santa Teresa*, a nao, square-rigged with three masts. One by one the mutinous band climbed the ladder, got on board, and hoisted their provisions onto the deck.

"We have done it," Quintaval said. "Adu, to the wheel, be quick."

Suddenly a knife was at Quintaval's throat, the others were grabbed and their arms twisted behind their backs.

"Cuídate, mi amigo," Cortés said quietly. "Take care."

Isla, with great satisfaction, and Bernal Díaz, in a rare show of strength, and Puertocarrero, unusually lucid, trained their muskets as if they would not have to light the wick that exploded the gunpowder to power the bullet to kill their captives.

"We were checking the ships, Cortés," Quintaval explained.

"Very thoughtful of you." And then Cortés made a motion with his hand. Twelve Cempoalan warriors who had been waiting on the other side of the boat climbed up on deck, boarded, and pushed Quintaval and his men to the deck facedown.

"What say you now, Quintaval?" Cortés put his foot on Quintaval's back.

"You insist that we be in armor, Comandante Cortés, our equipment at the ready and constantly maintained. We were going to examine the boats for their seaworthiness."

Cortés pressed his foot harder on Quintaval's back.

"We are for Mary," Quintaval rasped, "y todos los santos en el cielo."

Cortés gave Quintaval a swift kick on one side, then the other, then kicked him over so that he lay splayed, his arms back in surrender.

"For Mary and all the saints in heaven? Not for me? Isla, do you think we should gut them here like fish or take them ashore, emasculate them, and make them mules?"

"Here and now, swift and clean, El Capitán, is what I suggest." Isla was always full of good ideas.

"Bernal Díaz, I hope you note the actions of the treasonous traitors well in your book." Cortés had the tip of his sword pointed at Quintaval's heart.

"The others are not traitors. I forced the slave and the others on pain of death," Quintaval protested. "Juan and Manuel are mute and cannot protest."

Although Adu's face was pressed to the deck and he could only see boards and knotholes, he had a sense of the open sea, could hear lapping against the side of the boat. The sound, so removed from what was happening on deck, was musical. He longed to sink down into the black water, wash off all concern, and end his life cleanly. Why waste his last minutes in words directed to deaf ears? Why give them the satisfaction of his sorrow? The other captured men, including the mute and deaf Indians, had started to wail and cry that it was true, that Quintaval not only was going to kill them if they did not obey him in his nefarious plot, but also threatened their wives and fathers, and those on down through the generations would be punished too if they did not go along with the plot. Adu had nothing to say.

Cortés hushed them. "If there is anything I hate more than a traitor, it is a coward."

Adu's father had died in great pain from what started as a cut from his prized possession, an iron blade set in a wooden handle which he had traded for crocodile skin and hippopotamus meat at a market upriver. The cut became a festering green sore, and the leg, which swelled to the size of a young tree, had to be cut off. His mother was dead already of birthing, only his grandmother and brothers and sisters were left, all of them taken into the compound of an uncle and his wives and children. Was his grandmother still alive? In Cempoala when Adu saw the old women at their work, he half expected to see his grandmother look up from the grinding stone. Sometimes on misty mornings, he caught a glimpse of a child's thin arm, a leg running into a row of maize, reminding him of his brothers and young sisters.

"Do you know what I am thinking?" Cortés said, holding his head up as if addressing the night sky's bright stars. "This is what I am thinking. Let us just sink these ships and have done with the whole idea of sailing back, sailing away from victory, once and for all. Nobody can *swim* to Cuba, can they?"

"We cannot sink the ships, Capitán." Aguilar, reluctantly dragged along on this adventure, was aghast at the idea of cutting off retreat. Troubles were compounding by the moment. He wished Núñez could stop the clock and turn back the hands to before he was "rescued." First Quintaval's punishment was decided with a roll of the die, then he and his compadres were to be hanged for wanting to go home, and now sink the ships? That would hurt them all. He saw the captains, the troops, the Cempoalan bearers following Cortés's lead, traveling deeper inland, trudging faithfully toward the steaming heart of the country. He pictured it as folly, as much so as climbing up to the lips of a volcano, the red lava below pulsing and popping into bubbles, then, as if in a trance, leaping into its fiery pit, where they would be boiled alive, their last yell unheard.

Isla, on the other hand, was in fine spirits. He had been the one to sneak off to Quintaval's window on the back side of the barracks and catch the villain and his associates in their treasonous conspiracy. He had not seen Alvarado on the other side. At the conclusion of his undercover work, what should he spy but a big white moth flutter through the doorway on the other side of the room. Not only that, but the savage, Adu, ate the moth as if it were the soft petals of a sweetly scented flower. The African was a cannibal.

"Perhaps we should have Botello interpret the moth incident," Aguilar had suggested when Isla made the report.

"I know what I saw," Isla insisted, "and I saw what I know to be true. My eyes did not deceive me. That moth was the devil, and the conspiracy in that room, the devil's own party."

"You say the moth was white."

"The devil, my dear Aguilar, has many disguises."

"Well said, Isla," Cortés said at the time, and without a moment's hesitation he summoned his most trustworthy. This loyal band followed the nefarious Quintaval along the path to the bay, then crept ahead, and from the far side of the beach got on board one of the rowboats, some ten Cempoalans following close behind in the event of a fight to the finish, and silently pushed into the water, reasoning that the last ship would be the one taken. They waited in ambush on the ship.

"What do we need ships for? We do not intend to go back," Cortés said now that the villains were caught. "Who dares argue against me?"

"To go back to Cuba . . . someday," Bernal Díaz began, then amended, "A means of leaving the country." He too did not fancy permanent residence in this barbaric place. How would he get his book published? "We need ships to carry the gold, El Capitán, to the king, to Spain." Bernal Díaz had never voiced an opinion contrary to Cortés's, and, having ventured these words, hoped he would not incur disfavor.

"Velázquez is sending ships, is he not, Quintaval?" Cortés asked, his sword point still pressed to the conspirator's heart.

"I have no idea." Quintaval was seeing in his mind's eye the roof of his fencing school caving in.

"Speak up, man. I think you have some idea."

"Cortés," Aguilar said, "should the worst come to pass, what I am saying is that a commander always plans for a way out. Without boats, we are marooned."

"Without boats, nobody turns tail. We must make our destiny, Aguilar."

"How will we be rich," Bernal Díaz asked, "if nobody knows we are rich?"

"Díaz, is your head so filled with ink you cannot think?" Obviously exasperated, Cortés gave Quintaval another kick.

"Gold does not float," Bernal Díaz continued in spite of himself. His boldness startled him. He looked about. Dear me, Bernal Díaz thought, I am all alone in my perceptions, except for those prone on the deck under the heel of the commander.

"A mere detail." Cortés looked down at Quintaval. "The penalty for treason, for rebellion, mi amigo, is death according to the law of the land now owned by King Charles, and we are all his vassals, do not forget. Sinking the ships is definitely within our appointed fealty to God and our mission here. God is good."

Quintaval reflected that even now, so close to his death, he was not of paramount importance. He was going to die and they were speaking of sinking the ships, mission, fealty. He had not paid a priest any indulgence fees, would that mean if he did not go straight to hell, he would linger in purgatory forever?"

"One ship *will* go to Spain to take the prizes already won," Cortés conceded, "and one other ship we will keep to have at the ready, the other nine down. We will let the tide beach the rest, the other nine. And for these mutinous dogs, fortunately we have a new jail built and ready."

"But we cannot all fit on one ship," Bernal Díaz objected.

"Bernal Díaz, are you telling me you are a coward like Alvarado?" They had left the hapless Alvarado behind sleeping the sleep of the just. "That you will go against God?"

"No, no, my lord and master. Who can go against God and those who serve him well?"

"Say no more then."

With great haste all the guns and arms and provisions were taken off the *Santa Teresa*, put in the rowboats, rowed ashore, then unloaded and hidden in the jungle, along with the canvas sails, ropes, rigging, ballasts, cannons, and all the other equipment that would be useful for the march to the interior, while Quintaval, Adu, Juan and Manuel, and the other men watched from the beach, their hands tied behind them. After the boats floated to the shallows of shore, Cortés planned to dismantle the posts and ribs, the bolts and ribbands, the cabins' chambers, and all the planking for use on buildings in Vera Cruz. As the sun came up, holes were drilled in the decks and holds of each ship. Four boats sank immediately. The other five listed precariously, and without anchor floated toward shore to beach in the shallows with the incoming tide.

Chapter 19

That morning, returned to the settlement of Vera Cruz, Cortés gathered the troops and announced in no uncertain terms that there had been some treachery in the night, that the boats had been destroyed, treason plotted, and that the traitors were to be hanged.

"Tears of Mary," somebody screamed as he happened to glance offshore. "Our boats."

None of the nine ships were entirely submerged. The bare masts wavered in the early-morning light like skeletons bidding adieu. The hulls wobbled as they struggled in the ripples of waves, their prows caught in sand. It was, Aguilar thought, a graveyard, a ruin, and he, who had dreamed of an end to foraging and tramping about, to sleep once more in a soft bed, wept at his own handiwork. If only he could close his eyes, go home, return, and be done with bombast and posturing, betrayal and deceit. How he longed for peace and quiet.

"Tears of Mary, tears of Mary," wailed the troops. "Our beloved boats."

"What are they saying?" Cuy asked Malintzin. They were with the women, packing for the long trip to Tenochtitlán. The troops' iron pots were tied up in cotton cloth to be put in wheeled carts pulled by the Cempoalans. Jaguar Claw's implements were hung between two poles placed over the shoulders of two Cempoalans. Bags of cornmeal were readied to be placed in slings to be borne on the back, fixed with straps over the foreheads of some Cempoalans. Alvarado was seeing to the horses which would bear the armored captains.

"Cortés says some traitors wanted to run away, and those same bad people sank the boats so they would not be followed." Malintzin knew, however, that the division between bad and good people was blurred in the camp as elsewhere, and it was very unlikely that Quintaval, even with Adu, Manuel and Juan, could sink the boats. She also knew that Quintaval was to be hanged. In the Spanish ranks, as in the Aztec, speaking against the general was punishable by death. But Quetzalcoatl would not have done such a thing. Yet to look clearly at what was true, it was true that Quetzalcoatl had been run out of his kingdom. On the other hand, since the boats were probably sunk at Cortés's command, did that mean he wanted to stay forever, settle down in Vera Cruz or Cempoala, grow his own maize, have his own household, get married?

"We do not want those faint of heart or not fully committed to our holy enterprise to live among us. We must root out dissident thought and deed and nip unlawful rebellion in the bud."

Sounds like trouble in the Garden of Eden, Francisco said to himself, for he dared not express his thoughts aloud.

Cortés, after staying up all night drilling holes in the ships, was so tired he could die.

"That is why today Quintaval and his slave, Adu, Manuel, and Juan are going to be executed for crimes against Spain, the city of Vera Cruz, the pope, the army of Christian soldiers, and for disobeying the commands of their captain. Their coconspirators and collaborators will have their feet chopped off. Not only did these villains plot against the laws of man and God, but in inglorious retaliation and disregard for the welfare of all, they have sunk our ships, the rightful property of Cuba." In complete truth, two of the boats had been paid for by Cortés, who mortgaged his substantial Cuban encomienda. Velázquez also owned two personally.

"They *are* going to stay here," Jaguar Cuy muttered to Cuy and Malintzin, standing by him. "With no ships there is no way for them to get away. They will stay, but not aboveground."

"There are two boats saved from the traitors' wanton destruction. With one, we will send gold to Spain, as gifts of the loyal subjects of King Carlos, and thereby gain his loyalty to our enterprise. The men who act as our emissaries in this matter will return with a fleet, a commissioned fleet if you will, so that those of us who wish to take our riches back to Spain under the aegis of the royal retinue in full regalia . . . Puertocarrero will be the captain." Cortés was improvising. ". . . and with papers establishing us as legal and official governors, as dons in possession of holdings . . . slaves and gold . . . vast vistas . . ." While Cortés saw himself ensconced as governor of Yucatán and all of Mexica lands, prince and protector of Spanish interests in the New World, when he had given the instructions to sink the ships, all he had thought of was preventing escape on the part of nostalgic deserters and consolidating the troops into one like-minded fighting unit. They would have to stand or die. No other way out. At any rate, a good execution or two would placate such yearnings and quell incipient mutinies.

"Puertocarrero gets to be the one to go to Spain with a letter and gold?" Aguilar protested to Francisco. "To represent Cortés, I mean us, before the king? He can barely speak the language."

"Mind your manners, Aguilar," Francisco cautioned. "Do you want a rope around your neck too?"

The troops arranged themselves so that everybody could get a good view of the hangings. It was to be the last entertainment before they left Vera Cruz.

"Núñez," Cortés asked, "what time is it?"

"It is seven o'clock in the morning." Núñez gave Cuy a look as she stood with the slaves and Cempoalan bearers, as if to say, Yes, it is horrible, do not be frightened. I will protect you.

"It is time then." Cortés signaled the drummers, and to the roll of drumsticks and the trills of trumpets, the culprits were brought out of the new prison and paraded for all to see—Quintaval, Adu, Juan and Manuel, and the others. It was in fact a beautiful morning, not rainy, not too hot. The two ropes for Quintaval and Adu were already dangling in invitation, and the stocks were set up for the feet-cutting of the others. Quintaval was first, Adu second. Father Olmedo was there to administer last rites.

"It is just a show," Malintzin said to Cuy. "At the last moment, it is not going to happen. The gallows are there merely to frighten, not for real executions."

"Is that so?" Jaguar Claw said.

"Traitors, traitors," the troops shouted in unison when they saw the bedraggled figures. Quintaval was weeping, Adu looked straight ahead without expression, and the others were screaming. Francisco ran off into the bushes and vomited.

"Cortés," Alvarado said, stepping forth from the back of the crowd, just returned from the horses. "Do you not think this is a bit severe?"

"Have we not had this discussion before?"

Quintaval shot Alvarado a look of disappointment. Alvarado was the source of the original betrayal, he knew, and he wanted Alvarado to live with that knowledge for the rest of his life. Francisco, returned from vomiting in the bushes, was ashamed of himself. He believed he should be strong enough to at least stand witness to the death of a fellow man.

"I answer only to God and king, and thus brook no opposition," Cortés concluded, silencing all objection.

Francisco knew the king was very far away and utterly oblivious of them here on the edge of the ocean. The king, soon to be the Holy Roman Emperor, had never heard of Vera Cruz; indeed, it had not existed until several months before, and Moctezuma and Tenochtitlán were not even words known in Spain, and perhaps not in Cuba or any of the other Indies. Had the Habsburg emperor ever seen a hummingbird, an armadillo, heard a howling monkey, seen a marigold, gazed upon a red as brilliant as that of a salvia flower? And God? Where was he? Could he not attend to what was happening right under his nose?

"Señor Cortés," Francisco said, "Don Cortés, I beg—"

"True, Francisco. You and your whole order are beggars, is that not what distinguished St. Francis, he and his famous alms bowl?"

"I am not sure that our dearly beloved St. Francis owned his own bowl, but he wished no harm to any creature, Don Cortés. Men grumble when they are together." Brother Francisco took a deep breath and continued, "Men complain of their lot, and are critical of those who lead. There are tiffs, who gets what and how much, who is best at this and that. It is merely human, and perhaps chastising Quintaval and his

friends, perhaps a period in the stocks, that ostracism would be sufficient for them to mend their ways and endear you to your troops. How
could they sink all the ships? Why?"

"So that we do not follow them in their escape, of course."

There was a hum of affirmation among those assembled, but also
mumblings and rumblings. It was not that they did not welcome the
spectacle of an execution. But truly, each of them, under their breath
or in the privacy of their tents, had voiced dissatisfaction, and could be
found culpable of doubt. Who goes to conquer a country with four
hundred men? Such a prospect could not help inspiring a qualm or
two. Nor did many of them believe that Quintaval was the one to sink
the ships. Such a ploy seemed beyond the capabilities of a handful of
conspirators who sallied forth in the dead of night. Steal a ship,
maybe, but destroy a fleet?

"I insist on a duel," Quintaval shouted above the grumblings.

"What?"

"Yes, a duel," Quintaval shouted again.

This surprising ploy was passed on. For a moment the troops were
dumbfounded.

"A duel?" Cortés exclaimed. "For a miscreant, a collaborator, a condemned man? Whoever heard of such a thing? Duels are fought over
honor, or, as in the case of El Cid, the fate of cities."

"If I am to be killed, let it be in an honorable way."

"Out of the question."

"Duel!" a shout went up.

"Duel, duel!" the crowd chanted.

Cortés looked at Bernal Díaz, who looked at Isla, who looked at
Alvarado, who looked away. "Jesucristo, a damned duel?"

"Duel!" came the shout again.

Cortés moved close to Isla.

"It is a rabble," Cortés whispered to him. "I do not know how to
control them."

"Do not show fear," Isla advised. "Never show fear."

"Que el mejor guerrero gane. May the best man win, Cortés,"
Quintaval called out. "I win and my men go free, the African too."

Cortés summoned his captains around him. "He is the best swordsman in Cuba, nay, in the Indies."

"The men he speaks of going free are good soldiers, swordsmen, Cortés. Can we afford to lose them?" This was Alvarado.

"Should I lose, be wounded or killed, you lose your captain. You cannot replace me."

"You will not lose," Bernal Díaz said. "For should we see that you are in straits, we will put an end to the duel—and to him."

"Tyrant!" Quintaval shouted out. He stood erect, his eyes clear. Perhaps all his sword practice was in preparation for this moment.

"That man needs muzzling," Cortés said. "By the rope."

"If you do not duel him," Isla said, "you will lose face, Comandante."

"We are in the army at war, Isla. Face is my least concern. Legs, arms, yes . . ." Cortés felt the press and smell of many bodies, the weight and heave of some three hundred strong, not counting Indian bearers, warriors, servants, and slaves. He saw Malintzin standing a little aside, her two friends beside her, the scrawny little Cuy, a rag of a woman, and the scurrilous Jaguar Claw, who must soon be put out of *his* misery. Cortés looked at Núñez, who was expressionless. Alvarado did not meet his eye. Bernal Díaz, head down, was scribbling in his book. Would history find Cortés a coward, a nobody? Cortés hated that idea. Isla gave him a dead-on stare.

"Duel," one of the troops said loudly again.

"Who said that?" Death to that man, Cortés thought, death and double death, and then let the devil take him straight to hell.

"Duel, duel," the shout went up in response, hundreds now implicated.

Cortés gave the signal to the trumpet players and the drummers, but they could not drown out the shouts.

"Duel, duel," came the chant on all sides. Even the Indians who did not know what it meant were chanting it. "Duel, duel."

"All right," Cortés acceded, and to his compadres whispered, "Duel it is, but you, Isla, and you, Alvarado, should I show the least sign of distress, put a finish to this fiasco."

Cortés turned to the line of condemned, turned to his troops, held his sword upright, kissed its hilt, which was decorated with intertwined snakes, and snapped his heels.

"Cut his ropes, throw him a sword. En guardia."

Supposedly a new man. Cortés. A man poised on the cusp of the future. Cortés. A man who espoused the importance of the individual, one who had read Machiavelli in translation, knew many Latin phrases, read all the latest romances for entertainment, a man who knew about Leonardo da Vinci. Cortés. Cortés embraced clocks and war machines, he secretly thought there was a place for Aristotle in heaven. This new man, Don Hernán Cortés, fought like a medieval street brawler who must use broadsword and dagger, two-handed slashes and swipes. Hernán Cortés was not one to abide by the elegance and moral imperative of rules and regulations if they did not suit him to a T. His game was archaic, sloppy, had no style. Not only did Cortés not subscribe to the rules of contained fencing, but he pursued his match well into the crowd, attacking Quintaval's back, aiming for his head and genitals two-fisted style, tripping his opponent up, kicking him soundly when he was down, and once Quintaval was upright again, he lunged for legs with his sword and with his dagger slashed wildly at the stomach.

It was a small matter, this duel, Cortés concluded, when he had Quintaval sprawled on the ground, spread-eagle in surrender.

"Preserve my honor," Quintaval begged. "Kill me now like a gentleman."

Cortés laughed and pointed his sword a little more deeply into his opponent's chest.

"To hell with honor. You hang."

"Spare the others. They will be faithful."

Thus, at eight o'clock in the morning as declared by one clock keeper Raphael Núñez, and noted by official recorder and would-be historian Bernal Díaz del Castillo, 15 de agosto de 1519, right before it started raining again, Quintaval went straight from the duel to the gallows. Father Olmedo told him he would absolve him of all sins on the spot and thus he would go straight into God's arms. As the ships still taking on water sunk with great sucking and gulping, parting wallows of water around them, Quintaval looked about, caught Adu's eye, and winked.

"Note this well, Maax," Jaguar Claw said. "Your lord and master Quetzalcoatl-Cortés is hanging his own man."

"This is what they do. That is their way, as sacrifice is ours. Cortés is just a man, Jaguar Claw."

"I see, not a god? Can we call him a beast again? Maybe Cockroach *is* a good name."

Alvarado, at the last minute, had not looked but buried his head in the flank of his horse, Alonzo. Brother Francisco got sick again. Botello took his guitar, went to the beach, and played a sad tune, something nobody recognized. Isla busied himself. Núñez went off into a corner. People could see him chanting something, bobbing his head. Aguilar read from his *Book of Hours* after checking the time with Núñez. First he intoned, "Ora pro nobis—pray for us, which usually was said after the recitation of the Psalms. Cortés, however, was exhilarated, simply filled with strength and determination. And entirely purged of his exhaustion, he must take Doña Marina immediately to mat, but on doing so, he found that his member, for all the inclinations it had, was not up to the task, and instead Cortés had to resort to aqua vitae. Unfortunately, then, the next day he had to start the glorious march inland, the path to glory and conquest, in the rain, with a nagging headache.

t eight o'clock the day after the execution of one Roberto Antonio Federico Quintaval, on the morning of August 16, 1519, as recorded by one Bernal Díaz, the Spanish left for Tenochtitlán, the great city of the Mexica.

16 DE AGOSTO DE 1519

We have 350 Spanish, 16 horses, 3 cannons, 2 harquebuses, 30 muskets, lots of gunpowder, thankfully kept dry, 100 crossbows, and 600 Cempoalans who carry equipment between two poles, drag carts loaded with canvas tent material behind them, and on their backs secured with straps across their foreheads, bear the weight of other supplies.

These numbers did not count Adu, who was not considered a man, and the increasing supply of women. Juan and Manuel, spared their feet, to have been cut off for conspiracy to commit treason, had used them to run away the night before, leaving their Spanish clothes behind them.

It was a two-day march from Vera Cruz to Cempoala, three days to Jalapa from Cempoala. Then the mountains began to rise sharply and the air cooled; rain became hail. On the fourth day they saw Xicochimalco but did not stop. Cortés had decided not to take the direct route, for after he had discussed the matter with Aguilar, Isla, and Núñez, it was deemed feasible to go through cities and villages that were enemies to the emperor and empire. These enemies would become, Cortés conjectured, friends of the Spanish. As they progressed to the heart of the country, toward the shimmering island metropolis of Tenochtitlán, he envisioned his ranks swollen with allies.

At first the weather seemed against them—rain that rotted the skin off your back some days, unbearable dry heat in other terrain that turned unmercifully cold at night. When the sky was cloudless during the day, the sun beat down on them with the vengeance of the Aztec god of war, Huitzilopochtli, and at night if it was clouded, the stars, which could have offered some company, did not show their faces. Sometimes the countryside was without a hint of vegetation. There were days so gloomy they felt haunted by bad memories and the visage of the hanged Quintaval. Even resourceful Botello seemed somber, subdued. Hunger kept Francisco's mind off his vocation.

It was not that Francisco did not want to love the land, for had not Jesus struggled with the devil in the desert, and had not the Hebrews labored through similar desolation for forty years? The people of Tenochtitlán, he knew, in their heart of hearts were waiting for word of a merciful God and everlasting life. What little he could do along those lines would be worth a hundred bleeding feet and a keg of growling stomachs. He vowed to persevere.

Bernal Díaz, discovering sand in his ink and too tired at night to write, got grumpy. Núñez worried about Cuy, who, always thin, had whittled down to a whistle. Aguilar, usually stoic, seemed lost without the company of trees, chattering monkeys, buzzing insects, and the continuous lapping of the sea. Father Olmedo was worried about Francisco. Only a monster could have assigned Francisco the tropics this trip, and from what Olmedo knew of monastery hierarchies, he suspected that Francisco was being punished for his sweet disposition, and a holiness that would rival an angel's.

Puertocarrero, who had accepted the captainship of the arduous journey across the ocean to take the golden artifacts and a long and very important letter to King Carlos in Spain, was spared the mountains and deserts. With an experienced pilot and crew, two barrels of wine, and another cask promised on successful completion of the task, Puertocarrero had parted ways with them when they left Vera Cruz.

Aguilar volunteered for the crew but was denied, declared indispensable to the trip to Tenochtitlán. It was so unfair. Nobody deserved to go to Spain more than he did, but he would have accepted his lot if the journey had not been so hard.

The army crossed a high range on a three-mile-long pass, Cortés named it en el nombre de Dios, which, trackless and rough, was full of grapevines and bees. Ascending to the central plateau, the air getting drier and the land more arid, Francisco, initially walking in the back with the women, fell behind the horses and cannons, and soon he was walking all by himself. He wished for a horse. Mary had a burro, he reflected, and St. Paul was on a horse when he was struck by the glory of his faith on the road to Damascus, and St. Francis, when he was sick, he had a burro too, but then he remembered St. Francis gave up his burro when he saw those less fortunate than he walking. Be grateful, mortal, to be on God's earth, Francisco chided himself, and trudged on.

"Botello," Adu said, pointing way back to the lone figure of Francisco.

Botello and Adu let the rest by, and then, supporting the large man between them, caught up with the group. Be grateful, mortal, for friends. And during a sandstorm, not a sprig of shelter to be seen, it was Malintzin who shielded him from the many stinging grains of sand-glass whipping against him. She let him crawl under her skirts. Be grateful, mortal, for this girl with a heart of gold. When they got to the mountainous region, the loose, grainy soil cut into the soles of Francisco's feet. He could see desiccated cactus clinging to crevices between rocks, and small, dry-brown lizards scampering over broken shale; scrawny rodents of an indeterminate kind stared at them, and every so often, curled up like unanswered questions, Francisco spied snakes. Higher, cooler, the earth was covered with pine needles, and the tree branches whooshing back and forth sounded like brushes sweeping the ground.

"Quetzalcoatl, the god of wind, is here," Malintzin comforted Francisco. "Take heart and breathe deeply. Wind before rain, first Quetzalcoatl, then Tlaloc." Be grateful, mortal, for rain.

They were received in the town of Xocotlan on a cold, windy day. The town, despite its thirteen temples, could not offer a feast, but the cacique let them sleep in the rooms of his palace and gave them blankets made of thick layers of scratchy maguey fiber. They were fed maize cakes, what the Spanish called tamales, filled with stewed prickly pear. When the Spanish left Xocotlan the next day, the cacique gave them little flat seeds from the red flower salvia, to be made into a drink or chewed. This was what was used by the message runners from Tenochtitlán. Called chia, it gave them strength. The cacique, who had thirty wives, also gave them slave girls, who immediately had to be baptized, and joined the increasing numbers of women who marched behind the Spanish, the Cempoalan warriors and bearers, and the male slaves.

Malintzin walked with the women. There were more of them now, Xocotlan maidens gifted to Cortés and his men, obligingly sampled one by one. There were nights when Malintzin was too tired to care if Cortés was with another woman, and times she did care, and felt her heart had been offered to some obscure god only to be stamped flat and tossed out. Her little victory in Cempoala over the cacique's niece seemed to have happened in some distant past, but she did not have the strength to protest or carry forth an argument. She was, these days, always parched, did not sleep restfully, and was not hungry. It was Brother Francisco who noticed this, and, drawing her to him, insisted she must eat to be strong and carry on. When she asked him why, she expected him to say something about his god, that she had to live because the god had died for her, but he said nothing of the sort. She had to live because he, Francisco, loved her.

The rougher the terrain, the longer the march, the happier Cortés became, and when the air was thin, it seemed he hoarded it all for himself alone. He chided everybody for their slowness and lack of good spirits, liked to go over the rules for conquest in the event that anybody forgot. Other than the continued wearing of armor, mass was required each morning, no blasphemy was allowed, no ill treatment of allies, no leaving camp, no gambling other than games organized by himself, and no sleeping on guard. Adu, although he had not been sold or given to a new master, understood that he too was to be governed by these rules. Since Quintaval's death, Adu had not even the spirit to yearn for freedom. It was the best he could do to stay in line, put one foot before the other. Truth be told, he knew he would not have survived a day alone in a landscape without water, and sometimes it was so hot and flat his eyes played tricks and saw what was not there. He saw Quintaval way behind or sometimes over them in the sky. When they ascended higher, Adu experienced mountain sickness. He gasped for air, and the captains had to bunch up together for warmth. A lone man would die of cold, Adu realized. Some of the Cempoalan bearers did die.

Yet as more time passed, the daily movement across the land, the sense of covering ground, going somewhere, penetrating deep into the heart of the country, ignited flickers of hope in Adu's chest. Not having to hear Quintaval's prattling permitted memory. There had been a time when Adu did not think of anything backward or forward, but here, in a country of brown men with their own ways, he remembered his long-ago capture as distinctly as the sky he could gaze upon each night seeded with white stars. The net crisscrossing his face, trapping him like a fish, had set grief upon him heavier than the death of his parents. In the hull of the boat, riding the big sea, knees to jowl, he thought he was suffering the tortures of the wicked in the afterworld or on the journey to the land of the dead. The Priestess of Death herself visited him often, and particularly in sleep she would brush her bony white fingers on his face. Wake up, Adu, and die.

Now, on the long trek inland, he realized that even on the coast when he was plotting his escape, he recognized the great affinity he had for all things Indian. The brown people, the cacique of Cempoala and his nobles, the craftsmen and townspeople were not slaves, not mere mute servants, dull animals slipping like shadows into Spanish kitchens, down Spanish mines, across Spanish plantations. The rhythm of the Cempoala day reminded him of home, how fishermen carried their catch in baskets of palm leaf, and how the women made jugs and pots from the wet clay of the riverbanks. The Indian shelters, earthen huts with thatched roofs, and even those houses with elaborate courtyards and large family groupings, were akin to what he had grown up with as a child. Adu liked Cempoala food, the sweet melons and peppers, corn mush eaten with fingers from a common bowl like kuku, their adornments of gold and bright turquoise stone, shells and silver, their brown skin. He liked the wet heat of the coast, the uncompromising sun, the strip of hot white sand that glittered like a thread of saliva around the shore. The jungle, with its overhanging greenery, was not a mystery to him as it was to the Spanish, who halted at every step, scared of what that little rustle in the bushes could be—a snake, a wild animal, some poisonous insect intent on stinging them to death. The spirits of the trees in the dark-floored forest welcomed him. And although he had never been upriver to the Sahara, where they had camels, he had heard of it, and thought it must be like the deserts they were crossing on the way to Mexico. As hard as it was to breathe in the mountains, as cold as the nights were, the air made him feel alive. He was alive. Adu, the New World whispered, make peace with me.

About two weeks out of Xocotlan, high up, on the flat central plateau of the country, with an elevation of 2,600 miles, near the volcano of Matlalcuéyatl, they neared Tlaxcala, a large city-state known for its animosity toward Moctezuma, the Spanish encountered about twenty Tlaxcalan scouts. In the vast plain, they had come to a set of huge boulders clustered together in a formation that resembled crude faces on a toppled head, as if a race of giants running away had left their skulls behind. Cortés halted his horse, and made the sign to his troops to halt. The Tlaxcalans had never been quite subdued by the Aztecs, Aguilar told him, and thus would be natural allies. Yet the braves within the narrow confines between the boulders were painted in war paint, blue like the wild tribes of England, and their tunics were red and white. Each man, well armed with bow and arrow, held a club in his left hand studded with sharp obsidian shards.

Malintzin was pushed forward to make polite overtures.

"Ten cuidado, beware," Isla cautioned Cortés, for he did not believe that Malintzin's words in Nahuatl were always a faithful rendition of the Spanish. That she herself was Indian was sufficient reason not to trust her. An Indian, and a woman. Moreover, Cortés's words in Spanish always struck Isla as unbelievable, as if their troops, now swelled to nearly a thousand, counting the Cempoalans, and with weapons and supplies, hauling cannons, were merely sauntering by, happened to be on the continent, just passing through, visiting, or, at most, on a pilgrimage, as if Tenochtitlán was Canterbury or Santiago de Compostela.

"The Tlaxcalas do not believe we come in peace," Malintzin told Cortés after she had finished the introductions.

"Tell them we are friends."

"They do not believe that. They say we are not their friends."

"Tell them we are guests of Moctezuma." For if they hated Moctezuma, as Aguilar had told him, they must fear him. If one was not a friend, it was best to be feared.

"We are under the protection of the mighty Moctezuma," she repeated.

With that, one of the Tlaxcalan warriors took his obsidian axe and hacked off one of the horses' heads.

"Dios mio, my beautiful baby," Alvarado screamed, and charging, cut off the head of the offending Tlaxcalan.

For a second, all stood still. Then Cortés, who had jumped down from his horse, took out his sword and shoved Malintzin behind him.

"Protect the women. Prepare for attack," he shouted to his captains. Killing a horse was ample provocation for war. Moreover, the Indians, who heretofore considered the horses immortal monsters, would now regard the Spanish as ordinary, vulnerable men, their war machines fallible.

"Prepare for attack." The word went back through the long procession like a line of dominoes falling back onto each other.

"Prepare for attack."

"Prepare for attack."

As the words echoed, bouncing off the rocky sides of the pass, the Tlaxcalans formed a phalanx, their obsidian swords raised in one hand, their studded clubs in another. One of them stepped forth and swiftly cut off another horse's head. Alvarado was aghast. How could anybody be so cruel? He stepped forth and killed the man on the spot.

"Attack."

"Attack."

The space was too narrow, the range too short for Spanish long blades, muskets, and cannons, and they had no room to cock and trigger their crossbows.

"Use your short swords, use your shields and daggers, war axes. Each man for himself, hand to hand."

"Each man for himself," echoed back among the troops.

Malintzin, pressed toward the back, was in a bunch of women who did not know if they should stand still, run, or surrender. They clung to each other, ready to die on the spot.

"Hit low, no mercy," Cortés instructed.

"Hit low, no mercy."

It was over shortly. Heads rolled, limbs were hacked off. The dust cleared, and at the feet of the Spanish lay a few Indian bodies; most of them, however, retreated between crags in the boulders, hurtling stones and insults in their wake, two carrying the two horse heads under their arms like trophies.

"They will put those horse heads on the rack of skulls outside of town to prove we do not ride immortal monsters," Aguilar said.

Alvarado wept. "I can take anything but the death of a horse."

"Contain yourself," Cortés admonished. While he did not have the feelings for the horses Alvarado did, the loss of a horse was strategically more costly than that of a man. Only fourteen horses were left. Furthermore, after their friendly encounters and hospitable reception all along the way, this attack was uncalled for. The Spanish, after all, Cortés reasoned, had done nothing to provoke it. Maybe it was merely a show of bravado, young bucks feeling their oats.

"This is the beginning," Isla said, rubbing his hands together in anticipation. He despised, as beneath his capacity as a soldier, lolling about in a hammock in a town square, the decadent hobnobbing with local officials, the work of ambassador and diplomat. He craved action, and had been with Cortés when a group of them from Hispaniola had captured Cuba, Velázquez, the present governor, as general. That the indigenous people ran when they saw them on their horses was disappointing and a well-kept secret.

Adu had never been in a battle and only handled a sword when sparring with his fencing teacher, Quintaval. The prospect of real fighting frightened him, for he had seen and experienced so much violence when he was captured and enslaved that he did not think he could strike a man with his hand, let alone with a sword. When Quintaval was hanged, he watched in horror as his master's legs continued to jiggle as if he were, though dead, running or mounting steps. And despite all the beauty of the country and people, the skull rack in Cempoala had been ample evidence that even here, as everywhere, men were cruel.

Chapter 21

All were accounted for, and that night Jaguar Claw, as chief butcher, cut up the headless horses. Some pieces were salted and wrapped up, other sections were to be roasted and eaten for the evening meal. Alvarado said he was not going to eat a single bite.

Cortés said, "Do not be such a baby," and went on to describe that when Genghis Khan had invaded Asia, his soldiers lived on mare's milk and sucked horse blood, and finally had to eat their horses, and when that source of food failed, every tenth man was killed and eaten.

"Cheery thought," Aguilar said with a shudder, for the dried fish and dried cherries and dried plums and bags of ground maize and beans were dwindling fast. One meal a day was the rule now. The ration of water had been cut from two quarts a day to one per man. If a man was still hungry, he had to eat grass. Horsemeat would be a rare treat.

The camp was set up beyond the clump of boulders where you could see an approach from all directions from far away. Poles were planted, canvas stretched, sleeping mats unfurled, the cooking area designated, and guards posted on the edges of the circle were to sound the alarm if even a puff of dust rose up on the horizon. It was a well-fortified camp; Cortés, no slacker in military matters, had it arranged according to Núñez's instruction. Cortés's tent was in the center, tents for his captains around his, tents for the rest of the horsemen, then the infantry, servants and slaves, cooks and women, and on the fringe, their Indian allies. Ditches were dug all around the camp, sharpened poles placed in them and camouflaged with loose dirt.

That night Alvarado had a stomachache and had to retire to his tent as soon as it was proper. Isla was cranky and could not be approached, not that anybody wanted to be near him anyway. Francisco's feet were bleeding.

"I should be taking care of you, child," Francisco said, his feet on Malintzin's lap. She had made a soothing and gluey salve of aloe for him.

"I am not a child, brother." He was brother and she was sister. But she did not think she could be both sister and child to him. Early on he told her she was all things dear to him, and that every friend was like a whole family. Had this other conversation occurred in the rain under the shelter of a big broad leaf? Or in a tent whipped by wind? Or in the stone room of a palace? Francisco always spoke gently to her. She and Cuy pecked at each other, did not mean ill, but were not altogether friendly all the time. And Cortés, well, Cortés, as he kept saying, was a man and did not waste time on cozy friendliness. While she said *his* words in several languages, he never asked her what she thought about anything or inquired beyond what was useful to him in terms of the customs and practices of the Aztec and Maya.

"Why did Quintaval have to die, Brother Francisco?"

"I cannot answer that, Malintzin."

"Is Cortés . . . ?" She tried to think of the right word. Her father had attended, as an official, sacrifices, accepting his responsibility as a dutiful citizen. To be a dutiful citizen was the best thing one could be. Yet the mother she admired as a child was the one who had run away in the woods to save her child from sacrifice. She would not be considered a dutiful citizen. She found the word. Good. "Is Cortés good?" she asked Francisco. Her mother's husband had not been good.

"No, I do not think so."

"But his are the ways of men and masters, most men, most masters."

"Yes, Malintzin. Most men are like Cortés."

"So there is nothing wrong with what he does?"

Francisco sighed. "Can most men be wrong, is that what you want to know? Yes, most men are wrong."

She was about to ask him more about the amount of wrongdoing one was permitted before it had to stop, and then who would be the one to say stop, when Botello appeared at the entrance to Francisco's tent.

"Ah, Botello."

"May I come in?" He ducked and crawled in on all fours. "I have brought you some crushed mint leaves in rosewater for those sore feet. You know, Francisco, you will have to reconcile yourself to shoes, St. Francis or no. And Malinche, I see you are well."

Botello, too, did not have a horse, but although lame in one foot, he hobbled along, keeping good pace with the troops.

"I must help with the evening meal. The horsemeat," Malintzin said, excusing herself.

It was not yet dark, but the sun was nowhere to be seen. Storm clouds were rolling over the plains. She hurried to the cooking circle to light the fires before it started to rain. But the preparation for the meal never got under way. Instead, a rippling peal of brass trumpets and then the roll of drumsticks broke into the gray sky.

"Men coming."

"Men coming."

"Twenty, maybe forty."

"What is it?" Cortés asked Aguilar, who was standing beside him.

A line of unarmed men filed out from between two distant boulders. At first they were just black silhouettes, but as they got closer it was a solemn procession of some sort. They appeared to be Tlaxcalan.

"Perhaps they are suing for peace or offering apologies," Cortés said.

As the Indians grew more distinct, it could be seen that they were carrying food. Arriving at the camp, they spread cloths on the ground and piled on top of them roasted turkeys, baskets of tortillas, bowls of beans, many avocados, dried peppers laced on strings, and jugs of fresh spring water. Then the procession turned around and silently marched back into the distance.

"I do not understand," Cortés said to Malintzin.

"There is no honor," she explained, "in fighting the famished. It is a rule of war."

"That was no war. A little raiding party, no casualties on our part. They realized the superiority of our forces and ran off."

"I do not think so, Cortés." She rarely called him Hernán. Despite their intimacy, which grew in the silence and darkness of their nights together, their days, except for her required services, were as if he had drawn a line in the ground with a twig telling her to stay behind it.

"Let the slave women taste the food before we eat it," he cautioned the troops.

The slave women sampled the food and did not topple over, choke, or die. No ill effects, the Tlaxcalan food declared safe, all sat down in front of their tents and feasted.

"You see," Jaguar Claw told Cuy and Malintzin as they cleaned up afterward. "Civilized behavior."

Malintzin was not speaking to him and tried not to listen to his venomous words. On the long march inland, he did not refrain from reminding Maax often of Quintaval's ignominious death.

"The Cockroach showed his true colors, did he not?"

Or: "Hanging? What an interesting way to die."

And: "You cannot be too careful, Maax, he kills his own and abides by no tradition. He truly believes he is a god with a god's power. You are handmaiden to a killer."

"You like killers," Malintzin replied in spite of herself. "Is not Huitzilopochtli, the god of war, your favorite god?"

"If you refuse to translate, Maax, refuse to pleasure the general, refuse to accompany him, what do you think will happen to you?"

"Nothing is going to happen to me."

"Just remember to worry." Jaguar Claw was anxious himself these days. He no longer saw the Mexica spies who had dogged their every move on the coast. Tlaxcala, he knew, hated the dominance of Tenochtitlán, and Cortés, by portraying himself as a friend to Moctezuma, had ensured attack. On the other hand, the Cempoala warriors, in full evidence on Cortés's side, were also known enemies of the empire. He wondered, since there seemed to be a full-scale battle of confused loyalties in the offing, if this was the right time for him to make a move against Cortés.

That night the campfires burned furiously, the west wind blew in, and the tall grass slanted in waves like women's crinkled hair or fuzzy cypress trees by the sea. The men had to sit at a distance removed from the section of the fire blowing out and in the other section did not receive the warmth they sought. Malintzin did not sit around any of their stupid campfires where the Spanish cavorted like eager young boys at a festival. She did not care to join the knots of common soldiers at their get-togethers or the captains' ring. She preferred to sit outside of all circles in the cold and dark, her skirt over her knees, hugging her legs. If Cortés wanted her to come to his tent, he would look over at her and nod. If he did not, she would sleep in her own tent or crawl in with Francisco, who suffered so much with the cold. Cortés did not look over that night. Rarely did he sleep alone. A tear started in the inner corner of one of her eyes.

"A little jealous are we, Malinche?" This was Isla preening like a peacock after his turkey dinner, grease on his upper lip. Isla had assigned himself the task of tromping around the camp checking the well-being of the captains and others in the immediate vicinity of Cortés's tent.

"I do not understand that word 'jealous.'"

"You do, Malinche, you understand it very well. Jealous as in you hate Cortés for being with another woman, hate the woman, and hate yourself."

Malintzin had been wary of Isla from the beginning. There was his long fingernail for one, and the position of his eyes for two, which, so widely spaced, were naturally suited to spying. His small head on a thick stalk of neck was like one of those big snakes that dance to the tune of a flute, and like Jaguar Claw's, Isla's mouth was fixed in a sneer. He laughed too often, and his mirth was always at the expense of another, masking in humor what was cruel.

"I am not jealous and I do not hate anybody."

"You love him, Malinche."

"I love Francisco."

"Oh, everybody loves Francisco, he is no threat . . ." Isla was going to say more along these lines but stopped. "Do you think the Negro is going to escape and run away to the Tlaxcalans?"

"No." She wondered if, now that Quintaval was dead, Adu would be the next in line for punishment. Juan and Manuel had already run away.

"Some might think I have a suspicious nature."

Malintzin did not reply.

"Cortés is married, you know."

"Pardon?"

"A beautiful Spanish woman, she lives in Hispaniola and heralds from the mother country, Spain. It is our custom to have only one wife." Isla turned to leave.

"He is married?"

"Well married. Happily married. Married, Malinche. Married by law." Everybody knew Cortés and his wife were miserable together, that he had been forced to marry her by her kinsman Governor Velázquez. "Cortés is the envy of all men of his country."

Malintzin's heart somersaulted. She had seen acrobats twist their bodies inside out and balance logs on their feet. She felt contorted. But married? Married? ¿Casado? She got up, stumbled, stood straight, clenched her jaw, and stuck out her chin. "I know he is married," she said, and walked back to the cooking circle. Except for the men on watch, people had retreated to their tents by now. The campfires that night had not been a success. It had been too gloomy even for smoking and drinking. Now it was late. Torches and candles were extinguished. She sat down again on the cold ground. The fire glowed in its ashy bed like an infected eye. The wind kicked up its skirts and howled like a mother who had lost her baby. Quetzalcoatl, she murmured, will you help me? I have nothing. Jaguar Claw had his vengeance, Cuy her Núñez, Francisco his god, each of them, the Spanish, the Cempoalans, the Xocotlans, the Tlaxcalans, all the captains, they had each other, they had their own names, their real names, their homes. Cortés had a wife.

She sat there, letting the great loneliness of the plains press in at her. It did not matter that Cortés was married. He would never have married her anyway. And if he did, he would take other wives, concubines, courtesans, mistresses, an auianime. Number one wives endured it—it was custom—because they had no choice, and sometimes they did not care because they did not care for their husbands in that way anyway. Some women simply waited it out, she knew, until their husbands were old and worn, too weary for others. Now he is mine, they would say, as if all that had transpired vanished like smoke in the air.

She heard footsteps, bare-feet footsteps. The demons have come to get me, she thought. I deserve it. I am not thinking as a woman should. I am not accepting the upper world, so the demons and the jaguar god of the night are going to take me down to the underworld. When people died, not those in war or women in childbirth, but people who died of age and sickness, they had to have a piece of jade to pay their way across the river under the ground, and a yellow dog to help guide their way. Here she was without a dog or jade.

"Why are you outside?" It was Adu.

"I like it." Adu could be so irritating. That he too was a slave did not endear him to her. On the contrary.

"I come from a warm place. It rains during the season of rain, but it does not get cold like this." He sat down next to her.

She did not care about his country, whether it was cold or hot, where he had come from. They were on the road to Tenochtitlán. Each day was another step in that direction, and when they got there, then what? Would she be given a house, her own land? She would not be Cortés's wife. In fact, nobody knew what would happen when they got to Tenochtitlán. Even Cortés, she ventured to guess, did not know what would happen when they got to Tenochtitlán. Francisco believed their entrance into the city would herald a glorious reign of love and reconciliation. Isla knew it would be a battle to the death. Alvarado hoped to import horses to the New World. Bernal Díaz anticipated being able to sit down in some palace room, complete his account of the conquest, have it sent by runner to Vera Cruz, and then sent by boat to Spain, where it would be published to universal acclaim. Malintzin thought it possible that the march to Tenochtitlán was a march to the mouth of the underworld, for if captured they would have to ascend the steps and feel the knife pierce their chests. If she were not used as a sacrifice, what else lay in store for her? No Aztec or Maya would have her. She was an auianime. A woman alone, at the mercy of all men.

"My parents are dead," Adu said.

She knew what was coming. It was: where I am from, parents dead, poor me, I am an orphan. She wanted to tell him he was talking to the wind.

"My whole village is gone. I am an orphan. You are an orphan too. We are alike."

"No we are not." Nobody saw her as an orphan, and although she was, she was not. "I am not an orphan." She was getting colder. If it rained they could fill their jugs, maybe even have enough water to wash their bodies. Clean, she could think better.

"If you are not an orphan, what are you then?" He should have let the matter drop.

"I am . . ." She could not say daughter of, wife of, mother of, grandmother of, niece, aunt. She did not want to say I am a slave, a prostitute, mistress to the captain sometimes. "I know how to speak three languages," she replied.

"You are blessed by your gods, very fortunate, very, very clever."

"No I am not." Stupid boy.

Adu was perhaps sixteen. She was nineteen. He seemed very young to her with his thin chest, gangly limbs, loping gait, breaking voice, and awkward manner of a not-yet man. His accent was different from the others', for he spoke as if he were poking delicately at the language, not letting it issue naturally from his mouth. She wondered if he dreamed Spanish dreams, but did not want to ask, for that would lead back to the story of where he was from, that he was an orphan, and she was one too.

"I am from very far away." Quintaval had a map in his study with continents the color of pears, the seas a faded blue. Spain was hanging down from Europe. Africa was gloriously alone. Asia, which took up most of the space, was across the sea from Europe. Quintaval said the map was old, for there were new maps made after Columbus showing the New World, a new sea. He pointed out Cuba. It was a tiny patch of land floating off from an unknown coast.

"It does not matter where we have been," Malintzin said, "for we are only here right now." Yet it was true that when the Spanish arrived in the floating temples, with their huge animals and funny language and inscrutable ways, she realized that the coast, the mountains, the capital were not the whole of the world, that very far away the people were different. Her people, the People, were only a part of the people. That knowledge made her feel at once bigger and smaller, as if she could puff up like the fish that can make itself into a spiked ball or shrink down to a tiny ant. And here was Adu, the only one of his kind, who was from somewhere else altogether.

"Why do you not wear shoes?" She thought he looked strange in the clothing of a courtier with short doublet, puffed skirt pants, big sleeves slit so the fabric underneath showed through, tight stockings, an iron breast piece going around his back and belly, and a bulky codpiece fitted between his legs—all this unnecessary cover and yet he had nothing to protect his feet. Francisco had no shoes either.

"I do not like shoes, so Quintaval did not make me wear them, but now . . . well, it would be nice to have some shoes and Quintaval cannot get them for me. He is dead."

"Yes, yes, I know." She did not want to talk about *that*.

"I hear things," he said. "I hear things other people do not hear. Sometimes I do not want to hear anything. I hear coyotes crying for love and I hear rats coming into the camp to find dropped food."

She could have told him a thing or two about hearing things. In the plains she could hear the wild whip of each sheaf of grass, their melancholy at not having trees near them. In the desert she could hear the one cactus grow toward the sun and cup the little water it had saved to drink later.

"I can hear my dead master moaning."

"He was not nice to you."

"In some ways he was awful, yes, that is true, but he was also very kind. I miss him. I have nobody else."

She could understand that. It was like that with Cortés. But Cortés was alive. When she was with Cortés, all she could hear was Cortés. With Adu, in her mind, she heard Quetzalcoatl, the real one, dance to a slow, heavy beat. He danced for rain when it was too hot, and when it was rainy he danced for the sun. She could put her ears to the earth and hear his heart.

"Now that he is dead, I can hear him moaning. To not hear my master moaning, I take little pieces of cloth and put them in my ears. I put little pieces of cloth in my ears."

She looked at him. "You do not have to say things twice, Adu. I understand you. But you still hear if you put cloth in your ears," she said. She not only heard grass and cactus, she heard the lisping of voices, a chorus of gossip, all the things people whispered in their tents. Now she heard the refrain like a dirge. Cortés is married. He is married.

"When you do something not to hear, it is not as loud, the sounds blend together and no longer pierce like tiny arrows pricking in your ear." Adu got up and dusted off his velvet doublet with his hand. "Good night, Malinche."

"That is not my name. My real name is Malintzin."

"Your real name is Malintzin? My real name is Oduduwa. Malintzin is a beautiful name."

"It is not that beautiful."

"It is. To me it is that beautiful."

Chapter 22

Cortés loved women, but he hated his wife. Save for social status, wealth, and legitimate heirs, his wife was a stone around his neck, shackles at his wrist, and ropes bound around each ankle. Ironically, he had a fondness for married women, that is, as long as they were not married to him. Experienced women were made for adventure. He also liked the deflowered, those who had fallen from grace as he had fallen as a lusty young fellow from balconies, tall stairs, trees, injuring, unfortunately, his back.

Before he met Botello, the soothsayer of the expedition, it was predicted that the death of him would be a jealous husband or that he would be hanged for killing his wife. He *could* kill his wife back in Cuba, Catalina, Señora Cortés, living high on a hill on his encomienda in a feather bed brought all the way from Spain, as if there were no fowl to stuff a mattress on the island. He had been unfairly duped into marrying her. Politics. Her cousin was the governor, his patron Velázquez.

On the other hand, Malinche, his own Doña Marina, had been a prostitute. That was what they said. Aguilar overheard Jaguar Claw reprimanding her in the Mayan tongue, calling her the whore that she was. No matter. In fact, Cortés took this as a challenge not only to the satisfaction of his pleasure, but hers as well. Women of the night were notoriously cold. Used to miming and mocking sensation, they were slow to kindle and ignorant of true sensation. They did not like their lips kissed, their eyes looked into, their names muttered with fondness. He was determined to bend this one to him.

Until Malinche, he had prided himself on one-night victories. He savored the chase, furtive glances by the fountain, the lingering touch on being introduced, flirtation in a baby voice, the exchange of amulets. Indeed, he had in dire times engaged the talents of soothsayers and sorceresses to further his interests. For example, in his favorite romance, *Celestina* by Rojas, a love-starred young man sought out a witch, Celestina, to make a love spell. When asked his religion, the hero of that book declared he had no religion but his beloved. Not that Cortés was anything but the most devout of Catholics and there was nothing he hated more than an infidel, yet he had room in his mind for such a pretty thought. He had room for lots of thoughts. One of his heroes was El Cid, a man dedicated to war, who fought for both the Catholics and the Moors, and of the pagans, he admired Alexander the Great for his ambition, and Julius Caesar, who was both politician and soldier. Then there was Roland, and in the British Isles, King Arthur. But King Arthur had been cuckolded by one faithful retainer, the golden Lancelot. Alvarado was his difficult one, the thorn in his crown, the bone stuck in his craw, the itch on his behind, the spur in his heel, and Malinche was, truth be told and may God damn her, she was . . . Cortés had to admit he liked her very much indeed. As appealing as other women might be, Malintzin was, after his first taste of them, much more appealing than any of them. She fought him, he could tell, resisted her feelings for him, but on the other hand, she would not let him ignore her or let him idle in the sloth of familiarity, would not permit him to let down his guard enough to lose his touch for courtship. With her he did not fall into sloppy habits of inattention. She kept him on pins and needles, on his toes. With her, he trod the light fantastic. All others could hardly inspire a mazurka. And whenever his other dalliances, those temporary entertainments entitled a man of appetites, began to harden her heart, he called her back and made her his again.

The next morning they broke camp, started up, forward ho, but their progress through other rocky configurations was impeded by an occasional arrow, a rain of darts, pebbles pelting their heads in bunches thrown from slings.

"Pesky Tlaxcalans." Cortés belatedly realized on their third day out that their initial skirmish at the pass with the braves was only the beginning of hostilities. If there was to be outright battle, he wanted to be done with it, but since the enemy was so elusive and their tactics so random, a hit there, a miss here, and then disappearance, he was not certain how to confront them. Wars were fought straight on, in lines face-to-face, that was the soldierly tradition. Moreover, despite the annoyances of the days, every evening, courtesy of the Tlaxcalans, a lavish meal would arrive.

"What time is it, Núñez?"

"Six o'clock," Núñez would announce, not looking at his clock, but sighting the procession of bearers appearing on the flat landscape as if emerging from a hole under the earth. These same people, daytime tormenters, delivered sage honey, quail, pumpkins, roasted frogs' legs, berries, a broad snake cut in chunks, still warm from being cooked to a crisp over the fire on sticks.

"They are fattening us up for the kill," Aguilar said.

"They cannot eat all of us," Alvarado remarked, although it was entirely possible.

A shudder went through the captains. Their dinner took place under a stretched canopy of canvas, the smooth plank and round wine barrels had been brought to support a table. Cortés had his Dante chair, which folded up and was highly portable. The captains sat on barrels and piles of things. The rest stood up in concentric rings fanning out from the core of captains, the Cempoalans and Xocotlans on their haunches. The Xocotlan slave girls and the Cempoalan cacique's large niece cooked for them when cooking was necessary. Torches lit the circumference of the outer circle. They were a little oasis of light and human order in the vast, empty landscape.

"We must bring them out," Cortés said to his principals. "They will pick us off one by one. So far we have been fortunate in not having any casualties, but they are teasing us and will aim to kill shortly. Their cowardly scheme brought to fruition will be a disaster for us. This food that comes to us seems a deliberate mockery intended to undermine our spirits. Is that why they do it?"

It was Isla who solved the puzzle. "Are you familiar with the ancient classics?" he began, holding out his long, limp fingernail, which twisted in and made everybody ill at ease to look at it.

"Yes, yes," all of the captains muttered, nobody quick to admit illiteracy.

"So you have heard of the Trojan horse."

"A horse?" Alvarado looked interested.

"A gift, a huge figure of a horse made by the Greeks and taken into the impregnable city of Troy. Inside the horse"—Isla lowered his voice—"the Trojans were hiding, and once inside the city walls, they jumped out of the horse and stormed the city. I suggest that we look our nightly gifts in the mouth."

"They are not poisoning us, Isla, otherwise the slaves would have died." Bernal Díaz's fingers were covered in gravy of a particularly slimy consistency. Was it from the snake? he wondered, it certainly was tasty.

"The ones who bring us food each night, they are spies, that is what I think," Isla held his long-nailed pinkie aloft. "They come to see how many we are and what weapons we have. They want to see what the horses can do, how many Cempoalan warriors have joined us. Do you not notice how when they come within the lines of the camp they look all about. Without a doubt they are counting heads, making an estimation of our firing power, gauging our condition, and accordingly are making ready for informed attack."

"Isla, I do not know what I would do without you."

"I hate to think of it, Comandante."

The next night Cortés accepted the Tlaxcalan food graciously, then set his men upon the food-bearers. Capturing all twenty-five of them, he had Isla and two others do the honors. Then the twenty pairs of cut-off hands were sent back in the baskets with the five remaining servers.

Francisco fainted and had to be revived with hot chili peppers dangled over his nose. Botello had to eat some morning glory seeds. Alvarado gagged into the neck of his horse. Father Olmedo said a quick prayer absolving the Spanish, but had to turn away from the sight. It *was* a bloody business. The men were given extra rations of wine. The Cempoalans and Xocotlans who had come along for the trip permitted themselves the rare indulgence of pulque. Núñez and Cuy retired to their tent early, as usual. Aguilar made do with tobacco. Cortés had to have Doña Marina, and only Doña Marina, that night. He was in high spirits but she was not, and received him with distaste. After he was done with her, she turned her face to the slanted canvas of the tent and dreamed of hands jumping out of their basket, skittering like crabs to her tent, up on her body, crawling over her belly like rats on a corpse. They went for her eyes, her mouth, her nostrils, her cihuaayootl, all the moist parts.

"Well," Jaguar Claw said when he saw her in the morning. He was seated on the ground, smoking from a small clay pipe a weed of the sort which calms nerves. "Your cockroach has unhanded the Tlaxcalans."

"He is not my cockroach."

"Your scorpion with his pincer claws?"

"Leave me alone, Jaguar Claw. They killed our horses." She had not meant to say anything like that.

"They killed our horses? Our horses? You own one of the monsters from the underworld?" Jaguar examined his own hands, securely fastened to his wrists.

"I did not mean that." She felt on the verge of tears but would not let herself cry in front of Jaguar Claw. Francisco told her to be kind to Jaguar Claw, for the man was not able to bend his ways with changing times. She asked Francisco if one should always bend with new masters, new places, although she knew that the posture of slavery was always the bent back. And what if Jaguar Claw was right, that one should remain faithful no matter what to one's people, one's town, one's early family. She wondered how far *Francisco* could bend.

The following morning, rather early, the camp just coming to life, the strategy session of the day in Cortés's tent still ahead, a sentry sounded the alarm.

Cortés looked up from his business behind a large rock. While he knew an attack was imminent, had invited it, he had been told by

Aguilar that before an out-and-out battle the aggressive tribe or city-state ritually presented weapons to their opponents and issued a declaration of war. The Aztecs and Mayans did not fight except at appointed times, and preparations were formal, not spur-of-the-moment. Moreover they did not fight to kill; rather they fought to capture, bringing live captives to the steps for sacrifice. Botello, who was stirring his tea, happened to glance in the distance. Alvarado, who was grooming his favorite horse and whispering endearments into Alonzo's ticklish ear, saw a cloud of dust. Isla, ever alert, twitched his nose like a nervous rodent. He smelled them coming. A mass of Tlaxcalans were running toward the camp full force at great speed with spears raised and arrows cocked. As they got nearer, some two hundred of them screamed a bloodcurdling battle cry.

"To the horses," Cortés commanded.

"To the horses."

"Poise harquebuses, cannons at the ready, crossbowmen behind, I lead, the principals make the form of an arrow, two, three, four, and so forth abreast. Uno, dos, tres, cuatro, cinco.

"Uno, dos, tres, cuatro, cinco, y así sucesivamente."

Cortés and his men were soon on their horses, and at the advantage of height and speed pursued the warriors, who had retreated as fast as they had appeared. The Spanish followed but could not find them. The Tlaxcalans had disappeared into a formation of boulders.

"This will not happen again," Cortés declared when they returned to camp. "That I can promise you. See to your weapons. Aguilar, as usual, you judged wrongly. I was prepared today to receive their declaration of war. Instead, we are attacked. Fie on you."

The day was occupied in oiling the metal of the muskets and the cock mechanisms of the crossbows. Swords were shined, horses exercised, and the captains spent the morning in Cortés's tent over a map and grid quickly devised by Núñez on the basis of a Cempoalan's specifications. This Cempoalan had, he explained through Malintzin, been to the capital and traveled through the area of the Tlaxcalans. Núñez thereupon, using a stick as a pointer and a piece of black coal on the piece of canvas stretched taut, mapped out a strategy and showed

Cortés how to proceed, and how each captain would be responsible for his share of men. In the first maneuver, the troops would not adhere to the unwavering line formation favored by the continental Spanish; rather they used the more cosmopolitan European style illustrated in war manuals and replicated by little boys with their toy figures—blocks of forty men across and long marched to the enemy. Núñez had studied this pattern and believed it efficacious.

While Núñez had not formally studied war, he was familiar with Machiavelli's writings on the subject and had had an opportunity once to glance at a copy of Leonardo's notebooks in the house of a rich and learned man. His carpentry he learned at his father's knee, his pilot skills honed on merchant boats in the Mediterranean. He looked far younger than his forty-five years and carried his knowledge lightly. His private concern now was to keep Cuy alive, nor did he himself want to die, and if only on the Spanish side by virtue of chance, he would do what he could to survive. Would any man do less?

Once the enemy was met, Núñez continued his instructions, his voice calm, the block formation would break and form a wide line which thinned and expanded according to the terrain. Men with short swords and shields attacked first and men with poleaxes and javelins second, the musketeer covering that row, and the cannons last, all must duck on the signal. The discharging of the weaponry was not to be simultaneous, but synchronized in such a way that the forward thrust was continuous, impossible to deflect.

Since Núñez had drawn up the battle plan, even though he was a Jew, he was permitted a sword, and a very good one at that. Alvarado said the steel was German, which he argued was better than Toledo steel. The next day, prepared for a major battle before dawn, the Spanish, in top form, met the Tlaxcalans head-on. But once again in the thick of it, the Tlaxcalans ran off and hid in the crevices of a small canyon.

"Damn, damn, and damn. On my conscience, I cannot abide their style of battle. Hit and run like mosquitoes. Like cowards. So irritating." Yet the Spanish, as before, did not suffer casualties, and that night, emboldened or perhaps frustrated, Cortés and his captains set out alone in dark, came upon a town, and raided and burned it, killing all who resisted and bringing back the women and children to be slaves. Cortés declared the town of Tzompantzinco pacified and free. Each surrendered prisoner was branded on the forehead and declared a slave for life.

The following day the Spanish force advanced to the edges of Tlaxcala without a trace of resistance. Then, with their talent for appearing and disappearing out of nowhere, filing three by three along the mountainous path which led to the city, a delegation of Tlaxcalans presented a message from the cacique of Tlaxcala. Through the offices of Malintzin, they announced that Tlaxcala was ready to surrender to the lord of Malintzin. The cacique wanted peace; the foreigners were welcome in his town, all the fighting had been a mistake, an error in judgment. Apologies were in order.

"It is about time this nuisance stopped." Cortés was wondering if some young ladies would be forthcoming, but just then Adu, looking up, saw a Tlaxcalan appear on the ridge. Was he simply a lookout? Then another man appeared. Several more took up positions, and another and another.

"Cortés, look." Adu pointed to what appeared to be one thousand Tlaxcalan warriors ranged above them. As soon as the conch-shell signal was given, arrows, stones, and spears rained down on the Spanish and hordes of shooting warriors bearing mallets spilled down from the ravines, attacking in full fury.

"God and Mary!" Cortés cried out. "It is a trap, an ambush."

"Go, Marina, go." He pushed Malintzin, who had been at his side, under the cover of a small ledge. "Alvarado," he shouted, "protect Marina, get her with the other women. Hurry." But before she could move a step, a Tlaxcala, sword raised, began running toward her. She was to be cut down. Stunned, paralyzed, unable to get a sound out of her throat, she knew this was her end, the moment of death. No, she wanted to plead, I am not finished, not finished with my life yet, not finished with anything. Yet it was to be. She was bracing herself for the blow, crouched, her hands over her face, when there was a sudden swishing sound. She dared not peek between her fingers. Then she did. The Tlaxcala who had started to attack her was lying at her feet, a knife in his back. Cortés shouted, "Get her out of here. Pronto, pronto." Alvarado took Malintzin's arm and pushed her through the crush of people to the back.

Then, still holding his dagger, Cortés threw his extra, the rapier he kept on his right hip, to Adu, who, as a slave, was not armed.

"Do your best," Cortés shouted to him.

At the sound of the conch-shell trumpet, more Tlaxcalans poured down from the hills, yelping like coyotes cornering prey. The younger warriors were painted red; their teeth were blackened, their hair loose and long. The generals were distinguished by tall headdresses of bright feathers, chests protected with plates of wood and thickly padded cotton. All, of course, were on foot, carrying spiked clubs, bronze shields, and short obsidian swords. A battalion of crack archers still on the high ground shot down at the Spanish in timed relay. Back, back through the crush, Malintzin was pushed farther and farther into the ranks, man by man, until she was in a press of women huddled in a tight circle, the Cempoala cacique's niece and Cuy among them. They were protected by a ring of stalwart Cempoalans.

"Cortés saved my life." The words spilled out of her.

"Have you seen my Raphael?"

"Cortés saved my life, Cuy."

The Spanish trumpets were sounded, the drumsticks rolled.

"Each man for himself," Cortés commanded.

"Each man for himself."

Why is it always each man for himself? Alvarado asked himself. He hated this, could not stand it. He supposed he could kill as well as anybody else, but he did not relish being in the thick of it. This was Cortés's element, not his. Only the prospect of getting killed kept him slashing and slitting, stabbing and sticking. Here a head, there an arm, in the stomach, take that and that and that.

"Por Dios y España!" Cortés shouted atop his horse, sword raised.

"Por Dios y España!" his troops replied.

"There is nothing like death in war," the Tlaxcalan general intoned in response from the front of his brave band. "Nothing like the flowery death so precious to him, Huitzilopochtli, who gives life; far off I see it, my heart yearns for it."

"Santiago," the Spanish troops called back for the patron saint of Spain, St. James.

"Santiago."

"Advance," Isla commanded.

"Advance," went the cry down the line.

Chapter 23

Adu found himself somewhere, not certain if he was in the front ranks or the rear guard. He was only aware of the men beside him, who were moving as one long snake into the widening fighting space. The Spanish, a moment ago pinned in a narrow chasm, halted, now crowded out of the narrow passageway between hills into the wide open. With the rest of them, Adu found himself moving forward. No time to execute the fine maneuvers Quintaval had taught him, no fancy steps and rules of order, but remembering to keep his body sideways, at a slant, never exposing his full front, he progressed with fast little steps, leading with the right foot, brushing to it with the left. Step, brush, step, brush, step, step, step. He kept his thrust level, a little lower than he would for a fencing opponent, for the Indians were shorter, and he kept his extension full-out, never with the elbow bent unless withdrawing his sword from a body. Sometimes he held the double edge of his thick fighting sword at the flat, good for quick gouges, or a slice down, top to bottom, high to low, or disemboweling, ended with a little twist. Adu swat, cut, lunged, thrust, dug in, pulled out, stepped forth again, twirled round, whipped the air, and took all comers with confident, steady strokes, long pierces, hacks, and even occasionally parrying forward, back, forward in, out, swoop, feint, double feint, retreat, attack, close rank, break rank.

At one point the Tlaxcalans divided their forces into four quarters. First the group called Place of the Hill fought; the next hour, of the Pines; the third, the White Plain; then Water took up position. Red bixa on their faces, the Tlaxcalans looked like devils to the Spanish. On the third day, the Tlaxcalan squadrons massed together and came in wings, accompanied by the blaring of conch-shell trumpets, the beat of snakeskin drums, and the low hoot of long wooden pipes. The Spanish responded.

"Rear guard forward," Núñez shouted.

"Rear guard forward," another captain repeated.

On cue, more men moved ahead.

"Reinforce."

"Reinforce."

Adu could sense the crowd around him and a swarm of men behind him. He was governed by the movement of the horde. Falling back with his line, then moving forward, falling with his fellow soldiers, and swaying in tandem felt like being part of an ocean wave or in tall field grass moved back and forth by a whimsical wind. The boom and smoking smell of cannons being discharged, the snapping sound of bullets, the winging buzz of arrows, the volley of the trumpet on and on made it seem as if war was all he had ever known. Only for one small moment of the continuous battle was he able to stand still without guard or threat. Somebody from somewhere pressed a leather wineskin into his hand. He tipped his head back and drank water so sweet it brought tears to his eyes. He handed the wineskin back. It was Cortés.

"Front line to the sides."

"Front line to the sides."

And then Adu was jostled, and could now see that the row of Spanish soldiers with their Cempoalan allies was no longer thickening, but again, as in their very first battle on the first of the three days, a clot of men fanned out to the sides, and the farthest reaches of the back guard came around single file, the line of them enclosing the Tlaxcalans in a long circle, their retreat cut off. The Spanish tightened the circle closer, closer, killing bunches in the middle.

"Quit the field."

"Quit the field."

The Spanish drew back. The ruckus quieted. There were a few more skirmishes here and there, a few prisoners taken, but in the main, in the middle, there at the end of the day, was a grisly pile of Tlaxcalan warriors beheaded, dismembered, bashed, stabbed, and sliced, eyes gazing unblinkingly into the distance. Spanish quarter-masters stepped gingerly through the mayhem, counting bodies and surveying the damage.

"Thirty-five of ours dead," somebody called out.

"Thirty-five dead."

Cortés did not think this should be announced quite so loudly, for the men would find out soon enough. There was no point in discouraging them. All in all, given the numbers of enemy troops, thirty-five casualties was a small number.

"God rest their souls. The day is won," he announced.

"The day is won."

"The day is won."

Adu did not feel like any day was won. He touched his arms, his legs. They were still attached to his body. He passed his hands over his chest. No wounds. While others on his side were exhilarated, he felt nothing. Some men were jumping for joy, hugging and congratulating each other. What he wanted to do was sink down into the ground and join the earth with the dead. Some of the Spanish soldiers wanted to go on into town and ransack Tlaxcala for treasure. They wanted captive women to do what they willed. They wanted to dive into some female flesh like bona fide conquerors.

"None of that," Cortés shouted out, kneeling on the ground. Immediately the lot of them fell on their knees, and while the Cempoalans stood upright, confused at the babbling, the Spanish gave thanks for victory.

"God," Cortés began.

And the troops replied, "God."

Then the men cleaned themselves off as best they could and on Cortés's instruction made camp, and the women set about preparing a celebratory meal.

"Cortés saved my life," Malintzin told Jaguar Claw, who, after being absent from the melee, suddenly appeared, ready to help in any way he could.

"I was about to be cut in two, and Cortés stabbed the Tlaxcala—"

"Of course he saved your life, Doña Marina." Jaguar brushed off his chest with the flat of his hands as if he were sweaty and dusty from rigorous combat. "Do you think he could do without his translator and interpreter?"

"It was more than that, Jaguar."

"Ah, he wants to marry you." Everybody but Malintzin had known that Cortés was married.

"I know he cannot marry me, but he did save my life, he did."

"Good, Maax. You live to die another day. I thought you hated him."

"I do."

"Of course you do."

"Where is Cuy?"

"Why do you ask me? I am not Cuy's husband," Jaguar Claw snarled.

"Cuy," Malintzin called out, looking through the huddle of women assembled to prepare the food. Tents were now being erected. Malintzin searched through the helpers. Cuy was not there. The captains were conferring in a corner of the battlefield; Núñez was not among them. Francisco, who had been corralled with the women, had not seen Cuy either. Adu was lying on the ground on his back, looking straight up at the setting sun. He had not seen her coming up on him. Botello was nursing the wounded—a few Spanish, mostly their Indian allies, the Cempoalas, the Xocotlans.

"Botello?" Malintzin called out. She did not want to go onto the field of battle, see the dead, the wounded, the blood, parts of bodies, the gore.

"Yes, yes, come over here, help me. Let us go through the fallen and see to the troops."

"Have you seen Cuy?"

"You do what I say, Malinche. Follow me. You clean out the wound, I will sew." Botello had torn up a shirt and walked with a bunch of rags on his shoulder to be used for wrapping wounds. He had his famous bag of herbs and whatnot.

Núñez appeared from behind a line of canvas and poles. "I cannot find Cuy," he said. "Have you seen her?"

"No, do you think . . ."

"Maybe she was wounded," Botello said.

"She was with the women, I saw her," Malintzin said. "She was next to the Cempoala cacique's niece. She was fine."

Above them birds careened, dipping down, rising up, circling slowly. Hawks, crows, and vultures.

"Help, help me," a faint voice in the spread of bodies called out.

"Cuy," Núñez screamed, and the three of them ran to the spot where Cuy was lying. She had an arrow straight through her leg, pinning her to the ground.

"Dear God," Núñez moaned.

"Nothing to it," Botello said. "All we have to do is pull it out."

"I cannot pull it out," Núñez said.

"What is it?" Adu had joined the search and then saw Cuy, who looked so scared he thought she might die of fear.

"I cannot move," Cuy said very, very softly, careful not to jiggle her legs and rip her flesh.

"My father had his foot cut," Adu said. "It did not go well."

Cuy looked up at Núñez. "Am I going to die, Raphael?"

"No, no," Adu said. "I can pull it out."

But when Adu examined the situation more closely, he could see that most of the arrow had gone through her leg and was stuck deeply into the earth. To pull it out would only cause more injury. What he had to do was pull *her* up through the remaining strip of wood at the end of the wooden shaft. He could cut it down near her leg, but still, to pull her up with her whole leg pierced would be excruciating. And the wound itself could ooze and swell.

"Núñez," he said, looking straight at him, his voice trembling, "we are going to have to take her leg and very carefully, without too much vigor and speed, letting the arrow stay fixed to the ground, not snapping it, we have to . . ." Words failed him.

"It will pain her terribly, Adu. We cannot do that," Núñez said.

"It will kill her if we do not. She cannot live with an arrow festering in her leg. We have to pull it out."

"Cuy is not going to die, is she?" Malintzin had started to cry. Cuy, however, was silent, her eyes big with fear.

"You are just a boy," Núñez said to Adu.

"I would be older if I could be older," Adu replied. "But I am not older."

Botello interrupted, "Tie a rag very tightly above the wound to stop the blood from coming out too much. Also look in my bag, Malintzin, for some rosewater. There is an egg in there somewhere. Yes, yes, and a stoppered jar of brandy. I have a real silver needle and real thread. We will need that, too. You will do fine, Cuy, my girl, up and around in a day or two." Botello smiled a gruff smile. "Nothing to it."

Malintzin took off her huipilli, spread it on the ground, and took the egg wrapped in moss and rosewater in a small glass bottle out of Botello's bag. She was surprised he could carry things so fragile on such a rough trip. She mixed the egg and rosewater together in a little clay bowl he had for crushing leaves. She soaked some rags in the brandy at Botello's instructions, found the needle and thread, and set them all on her blouse.

Botello said to Cuy, "I could give you some root for the pain, but we do not have the time for it to work. Here." He handed Cuy a block of soft wood to clench between her teeth. "Just bite down hard when the pain comes." He applied the tourniquet and drew it tightly.

Malintzin said, "Think of Quetzalcoatl, Cuy. Think of how brave he was."

Núñez said, "You will not die, Cuy. I will not let you die."

"You promise, Raphael?"

"I do."

Adu took one of Botello's knives and cut off the end of the arrow sticking up out of the back of her leg. Then Núñez and Malintzin held Cuy's leg steady.

"Are you ready?" Adu asked.

"Ready," Cuy answered.

Adu and Botello slowly and with great care, with Cuy's leg straight out at a fixed angle, pulled Cuy up, loosening her leg from the remaining part of the arrow embedded in the earth. This they managed without breaking the arrow or tearing up the wound.

"Done," Adu said, resting Cuy's leg back on the ground.

Cuy had not screamed nor were there any tears, but her face was drained of color and she had broken two teeth on either side of her mouth from biting down hard on the block of wood.

"Bless you, Adu," Núñez said.

Botello cleaned the wounds front and back, stitched up where the arrow had gone in and out, put the egg and rosewater mixture on those spots, and bound up the wound very nicely indeed. They bunched some rags behind her head and let her rest on the ground.

"Well," Adu said.

"Adu, I need a covering, please."

Adu looked down at Malintzin's bare breasts full and ripe, her nipples purple as grapes. Her blouse on the ground was streaked with mud and blood. The hem had been torn for a bandage. "Yes, yes, so sorry." Adu took off his own shirt. It was the one that matched Quintaval's, broadly striped taffeta, green and black. He fitted it over her head and pulled it down at the waist. "There we are," he said. Adu was holding the arrow in one hand. He touched her face with the other hand, bent in close to her ear, and whispered. "Malintzin," he said, "I have to tell you. The arrow is from a crossbow. It is one of ours."

"What?"

"Doña Marina," somebody shouted, "Doña Marina, the Tlaxcalan cacique is here. You are needed."

And suddenly Isla was by her side, eager to escort her through the field of death, up the little rise where the dinner was being prepared and the tents set up. It was late afternoon and the clouds gathered overhead. The Tlaxcala cacique in his fine feathers and trailing robe, and all the accouterments of wealth and power, with his fine nobles at his side, looked fitted out for a fiesta, not the least like the head of a defeated army. He held his head at a haughty angle as if he were obliging the lowly Spanish by presenting himself.

"Honored Malintzin, I see that you are a strong and powerful nation," he said to Cortés, "and we yield to your superior force. And I see that you have a few Cempoalas with you."

Malintzin translated everything but the honorific in Maya to Aguilar.

"Honored Malintzin, the Cempoalas hate Moctezuma, and yet you are Moctezuma's protected guest. Why is that?"

"He is calling you Malintzin," Aguilar said to Cortés.

"Tell him my name is Quetzalcoatl-Cortés, not Malintzin."

"It is a custom, their custom. You and she speak with one tongue."

"My tongue. Tell him I, Quetzalcoatl-Cortés, am his friend, the one and only Cortés. Friend to my friends. Death to my enemies. We are aware that Moctezuma has oppressed the peoples of this country, and we come from far, from the waters of the east, to free you all from your tribute, your slavery, and your sacrifices. We bring you word of the biggest god of all and we declare you vassals of the biggest emperor in the world. If you pledge your men, your support, we will overcome that perfidious force of evil Moctezuma and destroy Moctezuma."

The cacique listened carefully to what Malintzin had to say.

"We are poor people kept in debt by Moctezuma," the cacique began, and went on for some time, ending his speech with the words: "I have no choice but to accept your terms."

"They surrender," Aguilar said.

"Do they regard me as a god?"

"No, they see your men can be killed."

"No horses, though, were killed except the two at the beginning, thank God."

"They want to know your terms."

"My terms?" Cortés guffawed.

"Tell him food, wine, and women," Bernal Díaz slipped in.

Malintzin gave Bernal Díaz a withering look.

"Tell the cacique we want men, his strongest warriors, his most willing bearers. We have enough women, thank you." Cortés gave Malintzin a little smile. Yes, she smiled back. You saved my life. But then another thought crowded in next. He saved my life. Does that mean I owe him my life?

Chapter 24

The captains assembled that night in Cortés's tent for a postbattle analysis. The commander-general sat in his chair, the captains on the ground.

"What time is it?" Cortés asked.

"It is twenty minutes to nine," Núñez answered. He did not bring up that Cuy was wounded. Adu had shared the knowledge with him that she was shot by a Spanish arrow. Could it be that she merely got in the way, that the arrow was intended for a Tlaxcalan?

Bernal Díaz dipped his quill into his jar of newly mixed ink and wrote in his book:

17 DE SEPTIEMBRE DE 1519

"We won," Isla said.

"They fight for living captives," Aguilar countered. "Captives to be sacrificed later, so, Isla, we had the advantage from the beginning. We shoot to kill."

"I think they forgot the captive part in the heat of battle," Isla said. "I think that it was a matter of kill or be killed."

"They fight for their own country."

"Francisco, you are always saying something contrary. Let me correct you," Cortés said. "It is King Carlos's country, Spain's country, maybe by now, if King Carlos is declared Holy Roman Emperor, part of the Holy Roman Empire. In essence, we are fighting for *our* country. They are the insurgents."

"How could I forget," Francisco answered.

"Do not forget."

"You have not counted the Cempoalans who fought with us and the Xocotlans," Father Olmedo mentioned. "Many of them are dead or dying."

"Adu, the Negro, he was excellent in the field," Núñez added. Adu believed that the arrow in Cuy's leg was aimed at its intended target.

"You are right," Cortés agreed. "None fought better. He needs to be recognized. Let us reward him. I will fetch him myself."

Botello, Malintzin, Francisco, and Adu were threading their way between prone bodies, administering what comfort and help they could. The Cempoalans and Xocotlans had paid dearly for their alliance with Cortés. And now the fat of the dead Tlaxcalans was being melted down to pour on open wounds. Malintzin was preparing poultices of poppy, lemongrass, and concoctions of maguey leaves. Strips of clean cloth and splints of narrowed wood were being tied to salvageable limbs. Jaguar Claw, adept at butchery, was called to do amputations. He had been given an especially sharp ax for the purpose.

"Adu," Cortés said, stepping up from between the bodies of the slain and wounded.

Adu had not seen the general.

"Do not be frightened. I wish to see you in my tent."

Adu looked searchingly at Malintzin, then at Botello. They shrugged. Now it would happen as he feared it would. Adu felt his legs quiver as if they could no longer hold his weight. Was it to be a hanging? Would he get off with a whipping? Adu looked about frantically to see if there was a place he could run. There he was standing in a field of dead and dying Indians, several, no doubt, killed by his own hand. There was nowhere to go, nothing to be done, and he was truly of neither party. Out of place, out of mind. But he followed Cortés back to the big tent without a sword aimed at his heart or a musket trained to his head. He was shirtless and of course shoeless, as he always had been, and his sword was not his own. Obediently, like a good slave, he trudged to his fate. Did not the Priestess of Death set a time for every man? Should not he greet his death like a friend?

Cortés's tent was not the low crawl-in kind. It was tall and peaked enough for many men to stand in, a canopy in the front, flags, all the

trappings of a command post, a headquarters. Adu had seen something like it on the way to being sold on the Gulf, cloth houses with
rugs on the floor, sweets and syrupy liquids served on silver trays,
musicians engaged in song while all around chained people were being
bought and sold.

"You are a brave man, Adu," Cortés said, sitting down in his chair.
His lieutenants seated on the floor around him made Cortés look
more like a potentate than ever.

"I repeat: a brave man. You fought well."

Adu inclined his head a little.

"Do you understand me?"

"Yes."

Cortés liked his men to call him Cortés, but he did not like that
Adu did not say Capitán, Comandante, or General or even Señor or
Don. And the slave had something of the surly manner of his former
master, which Cortés did not admire, but he was not obsequious and
sniveling like the deceased Quintaval. His skin was very dark, and
with his body whittled thin, he looked like a charred stick. His lips
were very full, his nose widened as it approached his mouth. His
ears were small and pinned close to his head, his neck long, his knees
in their stockings knobby, and the muscles of his upper body, exposed
because he was wearing no doublet, were firmly developed, as were
his arms.

"I wish to reward you for service beyond the call of duty. I am
going to give you Quintaval's horse."

Adu did not know who had been riding it, and he knew that whoever was in the saddle would not fancy walking.

"I do not need a horse."

"You are to be one of my captains."

"Yo soy un esclavo. I am a slave."

"When this is over, I promise you more than your freedom."

Adu knew that Cortés could order him to do anything he wanted
him to do. A promise to a slave? What was greater than freedom? he
wondered. Adu watched Bernal Díaz make note of it in his book, the
spider squiggles and wiggles, his lines resembling the droppings of

bush rats, the dribs and drabs of dead insects. He knew that those signs meant a lot to the Spanish, as did the golden ornaments given to them by the Indians. But they were nothing to him.

"It is official. Bernal Díaz has documented it. It is officially noted. Your freedom when this is over."

"When is it going to be over?" Alvarado asked, and instantly regretted it.

"It will be over when it is over, Alvarado. It will be over when we liberate the Aztecs from their subjugation to the devil and his ways and their evil Moctezuma and his barbaric ways. What time is it, Núñez?"

Núñez looked at his clock again. "It is ten minutes after nine, Señor Cortés." He was worried about Cuy. She needed water and food to be brought inside the tent. He looked over at Adu.

Adu was thinking, A horse of my own. Horses were born to run, were they not? He could more easily run away astride a horse than on his tired, torn feet. He had not thought of running away again until just this night. It was as if his thoughts were made flesh, horseflesh.

"Here is your sword, Don Cortés, and I thank you for its use."

Adu presented the sword to Cortés.

"No, Adu, it is yours."

"Mine?"

"To keep."

"Thank you." Adu was very surprised. A horse and a sword.

"And I am wondering what is more than my freedom, sir?"

"Land, Adu, land."

Land? Adu was puzzled that Cortés could give away land, that anybody could own it, then give it. The earth was the earth's. "What land, may I ask, Señor?

"Emperor Charles's land, Spain's land, our land here once freed from Aztec domination. Each man will have an encomienda and slaves to work it. We did not come here to get our hands dirty with farming. Land, slaves, and gold. We have many friends now. The Tlax-calans fought us because they thought we were Moctezuma's friends. Now that our intentions are made clear, our forces include Cempoalans, Xocotlans, and will also now be composed of the Tlaxcalans. Together we are building strong alliances. We are on the move."

"I will accept the horse," Adu said quickly. He would accept, how could he not? To say no was only to have a word before his death, a final act of defiance that would cost him more than he could spare—his life—and all for the fleeting idea of victory. Adu remembered Quintaval's wink, and his great mistakes—talking too much, not understanding the nature of power.

"So glad you will accept the horse. You will be a caballero like the rest of us." Cortés looked around at his men—Alvarado, Núñez, Aguilar, Bernal Díaz, Isla. Farther Olmedo was one of them too. But there was that Francisco, a thorn in his side. "Anything else, Adu?"

Adu looked down at his feet. "I would like a shirt, sir, and some shoes, sir." His bare feet had been fine on the beach even when hot and on soft forest paths even when damp, but now that their way was getting so rocky . . . "Francisco, he too needs some shoes, sir."

"I do not need shoes," Francisco protested. "St. Francis did not have shoes."

"Be quiet, Francisco," Isla said, "before somebody cuts off your feet."

Adu looked at Núñez. He was wondering about Cuy. When his father hurt his leg, he became feverish and called out during the night for his mother. A grown man with a wife and children calling out for his mother. It was frightening what pain and fear could bring you to. A few moments before, he had wanted to run, and he could see himself running into the darkness, running on and on, never stopping until an arrow pointed through his back and out his heart. Núñez cleared his throat. Adu looked up. Núñez nodded. Yes, best not to say anything to Cortés and his captains about Cuy.

Chapter 25

In Cholula, they worshiped Quetzalcoatl and had a great temple in his honor. It was believed that the exiled and wandering Quetzalcoatl stopped there, making it his resting place before his final trip to the Eastern Sea. Accordingly, Cortés thought it would be a safe and welcoming place to stop. Situated within two days' march of Tenochtitlán, Nahuatl-speaking, tribute-paying Cholula was near the pass that went between Popocatépetl, Smoking Mountain, and Iztaccihuatl, Mountain of the White Woman, two volcanoes who were once, it was said, ill-fated lovers. The houses in Cholula were not rows of hovels set on the crust of the dusty, dry desert or dilapidated shacks holding fast to the side of a ravine. The temples and city buildings and all the homes were built in a series of terraced gardens with fish ponds in their courtyards, and everywhere there were flowers, even though the town was dry and cold. Cuy, whose leg was healing well, rode on Núñez's horse. Adu had put Francisco on his new horse and guided it. Both were in hemp-soled sandals, called huaraches, dug up from the Spanish store of supplies. The Cholulans graciously welcomed the large band of men, who were immediately presented with twelve young women as gifts.

"Take my dearly beloved niece, cousin, daughter," Maax whispered mockingly to Cuy. "Good for all occasions. She can cook, grind, sew, weave, carry heavy loads in the burning sun, if need be carry *you* on her back. Feed her a little bit and every night she will spread her legs without complaint."

"More women." Cortés beamed. But in truth, the growing number of women had to be fed, could not fight like soldiers, and, although providing pleasure at night and more hands at the cooking pots, were slowing the pace of the expedition. Isla slyly suggested that they be trained as Amazons, but Cortés, of course, would have nothing to do with that notion.

Malintzin watched Cortés watch the girls, gauging which one he would pick for his personal favorite. Would it be the one with the slightly protuberant eyes, the one with the smile of a child, the one with breasts pointy as arrow tips, hips low-slung? She knew what he liked. Good teeth, strong nose, big feet, long neck, thick pubic hair, but he was always open to variation, language no barrier. She told herself she did not care, how could she, he was a beast who hanged his own men, cut off hands, flinched at no brutality. He would never marry her, unless his wife died. On the other hand, he was just a man, was he not, a general acting the way generals had to act. Had he not saved her life? For that alone, she owed him loyalty, affection, dedication, and passion.

The housing for the captains in Cholula included spacious rooms built around courtyards overhung with vines of blue and white morning glories. Black butterflies and green and scarlet-breasted hummingbirds hovered over orange dahlias. Small covered walkways of stone flanked the rows of rooms. The mountain breeze was cleansing, bracing.

The afternoon of the first day, the Spanish and their Cempoalan, Xocotlan, and now Tlaxcalan allies collapsed with exhaustion, each man on his mat without need of company, except for Núñez, who kept Cuy by his side, never sleeping without his hand on her somewhere, in her hair or on her waist, his legs twisted around hers, his head nuzzled on her back. The other men teased him about it, he a slave to a slave.

Their first day in Cholula, the women, a legion of them now, were set to work unpacking belongings, sorting out the cooking utensils, which had gotten sandy, and airing mats and coverings. Jaguar Claw, also, was given little opportunity to rest, for he had to skin the newest batch of animals—large birds, animals low to the ground with reddish fur and long tails, the animals the Spanish called zorros.

"Did you know that the poison of frogs is not used on darts in battle because it can poison the meat?" he said to Maax. "They say Tenochtitlán is a city of gold. It gleams in the sun and Huitzilopochtli is well pleased." Jaguar Claw kept talking.

"Francisco says it is a city of God," Malintzin replied.

"Francisco does not know it is a city of *our* gods." Jaguar Claw, who had heard descriptions of it as a young boy, its avenues flanked by canals so that people could paddle up to their doors in their canoes. The temples of Huitzilopochtli, the god of war and the sun and the patron god of the Mexica, and Tlaloc, the god of rain, were the tops of a pyramid of one hundred and fourteen steps rivaling the Temple of the Sun at Teotihuacán. They kept the fire of the torches burning there day and night, and there was a secret room in the temple full of many treasures. Moctezuma's palace was the most elaborate palace on the face of the earth. He had hundreds of wives and concubines, and his own zoo with animals from all over the empire—jaguars, anteaters, pacas, pronghorn deer, agoutis, grisons, tiaras, zorros, wolves and coyotes, kinkajous, sloths and monkeys of many different varieties, peccaries, prairie dogs, gophers, and five hundred different kinds of snakes, sixty poisonous kinds, and crocodiles and great lizards, and the most delicious animal on earth, the small salamander axolote with gills in the shape of ferns. This was not to mention other fish and turtles and waterfowl, and an aviary with netting stretched over leagues of trees kept watered by the royal gardeners.

Moreover, Jaguar Claw had heard that the women in Tenochtitlán wore huipilli with elaborate embroidery and their skirts were of cotton finer than feathers. Their sandals were inlaid with turquoise and amber, held to their feet with ribbons dyed in red and blue and green. The women were the most beautiful in the empire. Jaguar Claw heard that in Tenochtitlán babies never cried, save those who were taken to be thrown down a well during the rain festival in honor of Tlaloc. And all the boys and girls went to school.

The first morning after their evening arrival in Cholula, Malintzin and Cuy went with the women to the river to wash their clothes and collect water in jugs for cooking, drinking, and cleaning. The jugs in

Cholula were black like those in Oaxaca, and the weave of their cloth included yellow and black colors along with the reds of the north. The old woman they went with said that, yes, their pots were from Oaxaca. The Cholulans got their salt from the salt flats of the Mayans, and for their own cherries which they pitted and dried, they traded pelts from the south and corn from the west. Feathers came from the southern coast. That was where the quetzal bird lived, his long green feathers reserved exclusively for the emperor. Goods that were woven or fashioned with care and all worked jewelry came from the capital, where the finest craftsmen in the empire worked in the warehouses of the emperor.

An old woman watched Malintzin when she took off her huipilli and cueitl. She watched her wade into the water with her clothes in hand. She had two of Cortés's white shirts to wash, one of silk, one of wool, his white silk hose, and his striped doublet with the zigzags down the middle and slashed puff sleeves. Cuy, still limping from her arrow wound, was shy and merely submerged herself with her clothes on, and, with nobody seeing her, took them off under the water.

"Who is your husband?" the old woman asked Malintzin.

"I have no husband."

"How is it that so fine a lady as yourself does not have a slave to wash your clothes?"

"I am a slave."

The water in that part of the stream was clear, and the sandy bottom scrunched and squished between Malintzin's toes. Black minnows swam between her legs, and many boulders bordering the water were perfect for laying out wet clothes to dry. Malintzin let herself pretend that Cholula was their final destination. She could see herself living in this little town. Why could it not be that easy? Sometimes, on the march, she felt as if her life was a road she had been traveling forever and she would never stop, never get there, never find herself anywhere in particular. After Tenochtitlán, if she lived through it all, then what would happen? She did not know. Botello, who could tell destinies by the lines in a hand and the way the leaves of their té de manzilla settled in the bottom of the cup, said that she would die young but the generations would know of her, and when she asked about Cortés, he waved his hand as if trying to dispel such an ugly thought.

"In life, we often do not receive what we want, and feel sorrow on that account," Botello told her. "Dear Malinche, we receive what we receive, and must learn to live with it."

Malintzin said she did not need the assistance of a seer to know that.

Botello sighed. "If you must know, Cortés is destined to kill his wife most brutally. He will be hauled up before our king and our courts for breaking the law. Generations will stamp on his name. He will not be given power because he is too powerful. He will die a disappointed man. And his very bones will be desecrated."

Malintzin did not think Botello was correct in that part of it, for how could Cortés break the law? He was the law. He would never die disappointed. "How will he kill his wife?"

"Choke her."

Somehow she could believe that, and her heart rose a moment before she checked herself.

The old woman at the stream now would not stop talking to her. "I hear you are not truly a slave, but a princess, that your name is Malintzin. Why do they call you Malinche?"

"I have many names," Malintzin said.

"I have never had an official name," Cuy said from her perch on the stone.

"You are both nice girls," the old woman said. "I would hate to see you die."

In the battle with Tlaxcala, Malintzin had feared for her life, and there had been other times on the march when she was frightened, but here, in this beautiful city, the gods of the underworld seemed dormant, quiet. Moreover, she no longer felt the nervous presence of the Mexica spies as she had at the beginning of the trip. As they neared Tenochtitlán the Tlaxcalas said they would have to pass between the mountains that belched fire and they would be so high they could almost touch the gods. Then they would have to travel under thick white rain so cold it piled up on the ground as if white feathered birds had fallen from the sky, and slept the sleep of the dead together stacked in layers. The Spanish called it la nieve, the snow. There were forests to transverse and mountains where you could not find your breath, the Tlaxcalas said. Malintzin wanted to stay still, close her eyes, and it would all be over.

"We are not going to die, old mother," Malintzin told the old woman, who was raving on about how pretty Malintzin was and how it was a pity she was going to die with all the rest.

WHILE MALINTZIN WAS washing his clothes, Cortés, with his chair and his desk set up in his room, was writing a letter.

"How should I begin, Bernal Díaz?"

"'Dear Most Supreme Emperor of the World.'"

"It is not respectful enough. How about: 'Most High, Mighty, and Excellent Princes, Most Catholic and Powerful Kings and Sovereigns'?"

"That sounds right." Bernal Díaz was wondering how the emperor was actually going to receive the letter. They had neither pigeons nor falcons, as the Moors used, and no bird he knew of could make the distance over the ocean to Spain. The Tlaxcalans and Cempoalans had runners who went to the coast, and the Mexica people had traders and runners, merchants and tax collectors go throughout the land, but once the runner got to the coast, what then? Puertocarrero had sailed away. There was the settlement at Vera Cruz where they had left the men, but nobody dared get on the only remaining ship in the bay. These days, Bernal Díaz knew, the sea was full of thieves, pirates, and Englishmen.

"They say, Bernal Díaz, that King Carlos is so holy he rehearses his own funeral, that his family and court put on black and must watch him step into his coffin, his arms crossed over his chest, his eyes closed, and sing his praises."

"Qué lástima. That is too bad. He is madder than his mother, Juana la Loca, then." Bernal Díaz wondered how Cortés, who seemed to know all the strange proclivities of the king, could revere him so much and conquer a continent on his behalf. But then the king was the king.

"Should I put: 'Dear Emperor Carlos, Moctezuma's empire will soon be yours. We have many curious items that will pleasure you'?"

"Keep using the word 'vassals'; he will like that."

"An excellent word, Bernal. Did you see the woman with the rabbit teeth in the Cholula batch?"

"I noticed her." Bernal Díaz liked to have a woman on his mat at night, but nowhere near him in the day. "A nipper." Furthermore, Bernal Díaz had heard of a disease the Italians got when they traveled and cohabited with savage foreign women, a terrible disease that started in that private area of the body, slowly crawled up to the head, and ate away the brain. He fervently prayed they did not have that disease here. It was strange, too, that of all the Indians he saw, not one of them had pox marks. Not one of them had ever gotten the pox. There had been a fair amount of it in his village in Spain, but he never got sick himself.

"SO YOU HAVE never thought of getting married?" The old woman at the stream persisted in putting her questions to Malintzin.

"As I said," Malintzin said, "I am a slave."

Cuy had washed her clothes, spread them on the stones, wrapped herself in Núñez's cloak, and gone on ahead, limping still, but getting stronger every day. She had gotten into the Spanish habit of resting at midday.

"BERNAL DÍAZ, ABOUT the gold, do you think we should mention an amount to the emperor?"

"Best first to talk about souls saved, then later, at the end, the gold, and not too exactly."

"Right, right you are. I understand."

FRANCISCO HAD FOUND a spot under a tree. He had washed himself in the stream before the women arrived, and instead of his heavy woolen gown, he had only a sheet of cool cotton over his body. The cold did not bother him. His new shoes sat beside him. Was this not paradise? How little it took to make a man happy, comfortable. He felt God so near to him it almost made him weep. Lately he knew he had been failing in keeping God in his thoughts because of the hardships on the trail. He kissed his wooden cross, prayed, and reminded himself that whatever happened he must keep the feeling of this morning paradise close to his heart so that he could take it out of his mind, as women gazed at miniatures in their lockets and drew comfort during bad times.

ADU WAS TROMPING about with Botello. "They say the cactus buds and white seeds of morning glory, called ololiuhqui or badoh, are good, and black seeds are used to produce visions. The sacred mushrooms, teonanacatl, and the jimsonweed are used for toothache and the poppy used for cough medicine. The cactus buds, the peyotl have stages—overexcitement, contentment, euphoria, tranquillity. Are you listening, Adu?"

Adu said, "I am listening."

"What is on your mind, Adu? You are *not* listening to me. What is wrong with you?"

"I believe, yes, I do believe, Don Botello, that I am of the age of coming into a man."

Botello stopped and looked at the handsome boy. "Ah, that means dreams. Who?"

"Malintzin."

"God pity you, boy."

"YOU ARE A FINE-LOOKING woman," the old woman said to Malintzin as they ascended the slope to the cooking area. She petted

Malintzin's wet hair approvingly. "You *should* be married. I have an unmarried son."

"There are many fine women in Cholula, little mother."

"Whores, every last one of them." The old woman spit. "My son has standards. He fell in love with a deer when he was a boy. Every night in his dreams he would wait for her. She had white spots on her back, tiny upright ears, and a small tail that twitched when she was excited. In his dreams they mated, made a home, and had children with the bodies of humans and the heads of deer, with hooves for feet. He was bewitched."

"WHAT I WANT to do is impress the emperor with the urgency of our mission, the great need the Indians have for Christ's love."

"Without God, my captain," Bernal Díaz said, "anything is possible."

"You mean, *with* God anything is possible."

"Exactly my thoughts."

"That is why we must be certain to have the approval of the king. He will agree to whatever we propose as long as gold is in there, on paper."

"IF YOU MARRY my son," the old woman said to Malintzin, "you will be spared."

"Spared?"

Malintzin knew the old woman was unsettled, not clear in her wits. Perhaps she drank too much pulque in the morning. It was permitted to old people.

"ONLY THEIR PRIESTS get to partake of mushrooms, buttons, seeds, Adu," Botello mumbled, his head down among the bushes as he foraged. "But I am a priest in my own right."

"Of what are you a priest, Botello?" Adu noticed the women coming back from the stream. Malintzin was walking beside an old woman, bending her head respectfully. He knew what the cruel men said about her. They forgot that she was a slave. She had to do what she was told.

"I am the priest of the earth, Adu, the grass, the trees, the plants, and hero of my own story, a long story it will be too." Botello could not tell his own fortune. Whenever he tried, a cloud came by, or the leaves in the bottom of the cup bunched together in unreadable clots. His life line on his hand was short, but his hand had been cut during a fight so that did not count.

"VASSALS," CORTÉS SAID. "What a beautiful word, so full of honor. You know, Bernal Díaz, the term 'El Cid' means Lord, but he considered himself just a vassal of the kings he served."

"Did not El Cid also serve sultans, that is, Moors?"

"In those days, Spain was not a united Christian country, Bernal Díaz. Besides, there are some good Moors."

"There are? Who?"

"Adu."

"I do not think he is a Moor, El Capitán. He does not worship Allah. He is like Botello, godless."

"The Muslims enslave their own converts, I have been told. Christians would never do that to Christians."

"I WOULD LIKE to get married someday," Malintzin admitted to the old woman, "if it was at all possible." The ceremony among the Aztecs involved tying the cloaks of the betrothed together. There were pictures in books of tied-together couples. It was sweet to see.

"I would hate to see you killed with the rest."

"What is it you are telling me?" They had come near the group of rooms where the Spanish slept the night before. The woman's ramblings were beginning to take form. "Let us sit down, old woman," Malintzin said, slowly easing the woman toward a large stone.

"If you marry my son, you will be spared."

"From what?"

"Truly he is strong."

"Is he like a jaguar, fierce and fearless?"

"He is strong like a tree who will not bend in a high wind."

"Handsome?"

"Not like Quetzalcoatl with his pale skin and ugly hair on his face. But like Huitzilopochtli when he is dressed for battle. He has the legs of a cougar, the arms of a monkey, and the body of a prince."

"His face, little mother?"

"His face. He fell in a fire, poor fellow, when he was a baby. They say it is a sign of holiness. The jaguar himself is spotted from getting too close to the sun. My son likes his tortillas served very hot and his beans well flavored with chili. He once ate the meat of tapir. His appetite is that of a warrior, and his hair is honorably cut for the captives he caught: three. We eat well in our house."

"How fortunate you are, old woman."

"I like to have my legs rubbed with duck fat and my hair combed with a brush of thorn in the morning. My daughter-in-law should do this for me. Also, our little plot of maize and our squash plants and tomato vines need care, for without a woman we have not made our quota of taxes in the last few years. We have three turkeys and several dogs. I would like our family to be able to sell cooked food at the market."

"A worthy goal."

"We are observant and do our sacrifices religiously."

"That is important."

"Tonight the women and children are going into the forest, Princess Malintzin, to hide until it is over."

"Hide? Why? When what is over?"

"So the women and children will not be mistakenly killed in the ambush in the morning. Come to our home after dinner." She pointed. "That is the house." The old woman indicated a rude hut, certainly not that of a warrior. One wall was nearly washed away. The thatch on the roof was worn off in several spots. Her turkeys were lean. One of the dogs was lame. "Come with us. You will meet your betrothed, and tonight we will hide, and tomorrow, after the battle, we will prepare for the wedding."

"The morning is the battle?"

"It is to take place in the zócalo, with the swiftness of wind, Quetzalcoatl's blessing."

"Quetzalcoatl loved peace. Is not Cholula his town? And our leader, Cortés, is really Quetzalcoatl-Cortés. Moctezuma knows he is the god returned."

"He is not Quetzalcoatl. Quetzalcoatl is not so tall and he knows our language and ways. He does not ride on top of monsters. Quetzalcoatl said: 'Defend yourself against enemies when the wind blows against you.' It is a sign. Lately we have had many strong winds. Quetzalcoatl said that 'he who does not fight is not a man.'"

"Where does it say that?"

"My son will capture many. Our family will be honored. Those lazy Cempoalans and the traitorous Tlaxcala and the dog people, the Xocotlans, and all the white hairy ones and the monsters they ride and their dogs will be set upon and slain."

"HAVE YOU NOTICED, Adu," Botello was saying, "that the birds in the trees by the stream were very anxious as we walked by? When the monkeys start chattering all at once, and the little animals creep down into their holes, it is because a terrible storm is coming. The birds are talking about it."

"YOU SEEM QUIET today," Cuy said to Maax when they knelt down to eat together at the evening meal.

"My flower time." All day Malintzin had been trying to get Cortés's attention.

"That old woman at the stream was certainly muddled," Cuy continued.

"Yes." Malintzin looked across at the men seated on benches at the table. Núñez, Adu, Francisco, Father Olmedo, Botello. Even Alvarado she would not like to see killed. Cortés? No more Cortés? Where would she go? What would she do? What could she do?

Chapter 26

Finally the meal was over, and the women took the plates away, cleaned them, and put them back in their boxes, the maize kernels were set to soak in lime, the dry beans poured into their own soaking jugs, the drying clothes fetched from the stones by the brook, twigs to light the fire in the morning gathered and covered, the fires dampened. The men, exhausted, had gone to their mats. No campfire tonight, for it was much too windy. Malintzin feared she would encounter one of the new women Cortés had chosen when she went to his room. Fortunately he was alone and sleeping.

"Cortés," Malintzin whispered, "wake up."

"Doña Marina, what is it?" He had been dreaming about people in Spain looking up to him.

"The Cholulas plan to kill us in the morning."

Cortés sat up. When he wanted to sleep, all he had to do was put his head down, and instantly he dropped down a few fathoms into the realm of deep sleep. He slept naked on his back, his arms outflung to his sides, his legs open. This night he had his cape over him. As he rose, he knew immediately that he was in a room in Cholula, New Spain.

"What is it?"

"Cortés."

"Ah, Doña Marina, my delight, how nice to see you." He put his hand on her back. She felt the familiar feeling. It was as if she were slipping into the heated water of the bathhouse, first her toes and then her legs.

"I have to tell you something."

Francisco had told her that he understood why she felt love for Cortés, for since she had been taken by Cortés she was no longer an auianime to many men. Of course she would be grateful for his protection. "Cortés is the strongest man. He commands attention. He is the father of our group. But on the other hand, Malintzin . . ."

Cortés sat up. "What is it?"

"When we come for our morning meal the Cholula men will sweep down on us, surround us, and kill us all. The women and children are leaving tonight."

"What are you saying?" He shook his head. His mouth felt gummy.

"They are going to kill us." She said that word, she realized. Us.

"Aguilar says Indians announce their battles, and present shields and spears. They do not attack without the formalities. What do you mean they are going to kill us? They welcomed us. This is Quetzalcoatl's city."

"Cortés, listen to me. Aguilar has been wrong before." She stepped clear of him so he would not touch her, distract her. "The Tlaxcalas did not announce war. They just attacked. An old woman at the washing stream told me, a woman with a loose tongue and wandering mind; all the women of the city are leaving tonight, Cortés."

"Neglecting their matrimonial duties?"

"I am telling you the truth. You are playing me for a child."

"No, no I am not." He moved toward her, put his hands on her shoulders, and looked her straight in the eye. "What should we do? Tell me, little one, what would Quetzalcoatl do?"

It was the first time he had ever asked her a question like that. Malintzin knew that Quetzalcoatl was not known for his love of battle. His city, Tula, capital of the Totonac empire, had been defeated, and he vanquished. While brave against the gods and endowed with great cleverness, he had never waged war successfully. His accolades did not include victories in combat. The old woman was wrong in saying that Quetzalcoatl would approve of them trapping the Spanish.

"Quetzalcoatl would have left in the night, quietly and quickly, he would leave the city to the Cholulas." Quetzalcoatl did not challenge people's cities and had no grandiose dream of conquest. He told men not to sacrifice men. "Quetzalcoatl would leave before he got ambushed. He would wait until the women and children of the town left after the evening meal, and after politely thanking the cacique, seemingly retiring to his mat, he would direct his men to leave one by one in the other direction. By the morning the Cholula warriors would not find anybody to fight. There would be nobody to kill. Nobody would have to die. Nobody."

"Not fight? Quetzalcoatl would not stand his ground and fight?"

"Certainly that is the best way to save everybody. That is what you should do."

"Are you telling me how to run my own war, to run away from my own war? Be a coward?"

Was Quetzalcoatl a coward? Why is that the worst thing?

"And have them call us women?"

"What does it matter what they call you? Why is being a woman the worst thing? I am a woman." But she knew that it *was* the worst thing, for if you were a woman, you had to have a man protect you, protect you against other men.

"Doña Marina." Cortés was putting on all his clothes now and had lit the candle. "You look so lovely, my dear, I could eat you. For now, I must pass the word, but I will come back later. Wait for me."

Malintzin took hold of his arm. "You will not kill the old woman, will you, or anybody?"

"A woman? Of course not."

Chapter 27

Under the cover of night, a contingent of their Indian allies, the Cempoalans, Xocotlans, and Tlaxcalans were sent out to surround Cholula so that it would be a two-pronged attack, inside and out. Their own women and Francisco were herded out into the woods east of the spot where the Cholulan women were hiding. Greatly outnumbered as they were, Cortés was nonetheless confident of success, for was not surprise the better part of valor? And their swords were sharper, their harquebuses more powerful than any spear, their matchlock muskets the most modern, and their crossbows faster than ordinary bows and arrows, they had horses, and simple fire—all thatched roofs lit—was the greatest weapon of all. In close quarters the horses could be deployed to gallop through, upsetting the Cholulan archers. Instead of the long rapiers, short swords and bucklers were to be used in the confined space of the zócalo. A volley of bullets, a volley of arrows, a volley of bullets, a volley of arrows, close in with spears, then swords hand to hand.

Malintzin was instructed to go with the Cholulan women and act as if she were in accord with what the old woman wanted her to do. She did go with the woman, but once in among the tall pine trees, the other women and young children there too, Malintzin had to tell the old woman, warn the other women of what was to happen. They could all go back into the town together and stop all the men.

"Mother," she said, pulling the old woman to her, "the Spanish have guessed what is to happen. Somehow they know that the Cholulas are going to kill them in the morning. Right now they, and their men, are surrounding the whole town. Let us go back into the town and stay in the zócalo so that neither side can fight."

"What? What are you saying? It is not possible."

"Alert your men, make haste to have them join the women and children, and you can all disappear into the forest together, and when nobody is in the town in the morning, there will be nobody for the Spanish to attack. They will leave."

"My son is a mighty warrior," the woman replied. "What you are telling me is not true, for how could anybody guess what our intentions are? Nobody in Cholula is a traitor. Nobody would tell."

"Old woman, tell the other women. What I say is true."

"Do you not see how many we are, a whole city against a band of barbarians?"

"And their allies—Cempoala, Xocotalan, Tlaxcala?"

"It does not matter. Quetzalcoatl is with us."

When Malintzin tried to warn the younger Cholula women, nobody could believe that Cholula would not be successful in a battle against the strangers. It was unthinkable. Moreover, Malintzin, as one of them (for was she not the commander's woman?), was setting a trap for them. Malintzin. Princess, they spat. From the provinces. She was a loose woman of loose ways, beautiful in looks maybe, but ugly inside. Thus a group of young, strong women, at least ten of them, encircled Malintzin and would not let her move from her spot on the ground. And so they spent the night—Malintzin and the women and children of Cholula—outside under the trees. The birds had already taken flight and it seemed that the few animals left had dug deep in under the ground. On plateaus and mountains Malintzin usually heard the red warbler and the oriole, and in the mountains she had grown accustomed to the smell of pine trees. But this night was too cold, too windy. The top tree branches hurtled themselves back and forth, would not rest, and the smaller trees bent and snapped. Everywhere it sounded as if a great giant, wrested out of his slumber, was moaning and groaning, and high up a whistling sound circled like a bird lost in its own song. Malintzin hunched down, drew a deerskin over her back, and tried to be her own cave, but her feet and hands hurt as if they had been left in a rushing stream. Her nose tingled, and her teeth ached with the cold. Then she heard the pad, pad, padding of an animal approaching her. Pad, pad, pad, pad. She dared not open her eyes. Pad, pad, pad. It got closer. She held herself so still it would think she was a fallen tree or a rock. Pad, pad, pad, it had somehow walked between the circle of women around her. Pad, pad, pad, it put its nose to her nose. She dared to open her eyes. It was a jaguar. She could not move, could not scream, could do nothing. The yellow eyes with its thin bar of black were like a snake's. It put its nose to her nose again, wiggled its whiskers, sniffed, and then, tail up, walked away.

Her mind tumbled like rocks sliding down a hill. It was a god. It was a jaguar. It was the jaguar god of the underworld. It was a Cholula dressed as a jaguar noble. It was Jaguar Claw come to kill her. No, it was a real animal, an enchanted animal. It was a priest transformed into an animal on a vision quest. No, no. It was a real jaguar who would protect her with his animal spirit.

She went to sleep, and in the morning she saw a large tapir rooting about for food and then was startled by two cacomixtles looking at her. The animals were wooing her, telling her she would not be hurt. That must be it. The women and children all about her were still sleeping, but when she got up they began to rise too. Yet they did not start a fire, set the water to boil, get the morning meal together. They sat waiting, and in a few minutes they heard the dying screams of men. Malintzin put her hands to her ears and curled up her body.

They looked at her and laughed, confident of the outcome, and an hour or so later, when it had quieted, they gathered up their children and prepared to return to their city. Malintzin hung back, rooted to her spot, and after a few minutes she heard their shrieks. This is my doing, she said to herself, and she forced herself to go and look.

Cholulan bodies and parts of bodies were being dragged to form a funeral pile. In battle finery, feathers and war paint, limbs hacked off, heads split, gaping holes in their chests, they were so extremely dead that Malintzin could not imagine them any other way. It seemed that for the whole world, for time without end, they had always lain there dead, dismembered, eviscerated, bloody. Why had she not seen them before, that pile in the town when the Spanish entered on their horses?

The old woman, her mother-in-law to be, so chatty at the river, went searching through the pile for her son.

"Where is he?" she cried. She grabbed Malintzin's hand. "Where is your bridegroom?"

Some of the Spanish had swiped off the Cholulans' penises and testicles and hung them, dripping blood, from their belts. Somebody was gathering ears to string.

"Where is my proud son?" the old woman moaned, her face ravaged by grief. "Who is here that knows him? Where is my son? My warrior, the reason for my life?"

Malintzin, like Francisco, had to vomit in the bushes, but the old woman would not be put off.

"My son is a valiant man, a strong man, have you seen him?"

Then they saw somebody coming out from among the trees.

"Jaguar!" Malintzin exclaimed.

"Living to fight another day," he said.

"My son, my son, where is he?" the old woman asked him. "Have you seen my son?"

A line of surviving men were brought out from the palace, their wrists tied behind them. Two guards pushed them forward with pikes. The woman's son held his scarred face high and looked straight at the sun.

"My son, my son." The old woman threw herself at his feet but he ignored her.

Stakes were set up by the Spanish, and kindling was gathered and placed at the bases. There was not enough thick wood for stakes for all fifty prisoners, so ten prisoners were tied together in a circle and put around one of the five stakes. None of the prisoners tried to run, which is what Malintzin would have done. It seemed a short distance from the stake to the forest, and while the man could quickly be brought down by an arrow, at least it offered a better chance, promised a less painful death than being pushed up against a stake and burned.

"My son, my son," the woman kept crying out.

"She should be muzzled," Cortés said.

"If I may translate," Malintzin said, stepping forth, "she says that her son is a prince, a prince who is a relative of Moctezuma. She told me that. And if he were killed, Moctezuma would take special pains to punish his executioner."

Cortés laughed. "Doña Marina, you outdo yourself with your translations. Her son is no prince, and if he were, he would be a prince no more. Do not make the mistake, my dear, of not knowing who your friends are. Were you not the one to warn me?"

"I am going to kill you," Malintzin muttered in Nahuatl.

"What is that, my dear?"

"Quetzalcoatl would not do this."

"If anybody is Quetzalcoatl, I am. And since I am not, Quetzalcoatl is a story for children. We live in a cruel world, and we must be men. Light the fires."

"Light the fires," went the cry down the line.

It took the whole afternoon to burn them all. The Spanish and the Cempoalans and the Xocotlans and the Tlaxcalans and all the slaves and servants and concubines watched. The Cholulan women and children had to watch. Núñez held his face still and put Cuy's head to his chest so that she did not have to see. He said, "To remember is to both suffer again and transcend suffering." Adu, like Alvarado, buried his head in the long neck of his horse, Alonzo, who pawed the ground nervously. Father Olmedo's lips were moving in prayer. Bernal Díaz, sitting on a rock, concentrated on his book. Isla stood with his hands held behind his back, his two feet spread out. He tried to appear stoic, but his lips trembled and his eyes blinked. Francisco was nowhere to be seen.

That evening, during the meeting in Cortés's new room in the palace, since the cacique had been one of the Cholulans killed, there was a lot of coughing because the smoke still hung heavily over the city. The air clogged the nose with the smell of burnt flesh and scorched thatch. All that was left of the town were women and children and the very old. These people, while the fires were still burning, were branded on their foreheads, for they were to be made slaves.

"Did you hear that one with the repulsively scarred face call out

'Mexica'? Isla remarked. "As if the army of the capital would come out and save him."

"They were all usurpers, rebels of the Great Emperor Charles V, king of the realm; they had rebelled, they must learn." Cortés was in a fine form.

"Hard to learn if you are dead," Núñez said.

"You are not a Christian," Isla replied. "You do not understand."

"He is a Christian," Botello put in. "He is a bona fide converso. I am not a Christian, but I ask Francisco, the most Christian among us, if he understands, and he does not understand."

"Francisco is an imbecile," Cortés said.

"I thank you from the bottom of my heart, Señor." Francisco stepped forth and steadied himself. "I aspire to idiocy, and by all means endeavor to overcome the haughtiness those of superior intellect assume. Such sin is a double sin, since the sinner knows better. Let not the working of the mind separate me from any man or creature. I abhor the idea."

"You are abhorrent, Francisco. You are so fat you cannot move, and so much the coward you supersede Alvarado. You are greedy and abominable. What good have you ever done anybody? You feel sorry for savages who kill their own in blood sacrifice? You, brother, would kiss your own killer? For shame, Francisco."

"So, Señor Cortés, as the lowest of the low, then, as are all whom I admire, beginning with Christ our Savior, I still do not understand the necessity of killing more and more people."

"My son, my son," came the voice. The old woman was still wandering the streets calling out for her child.

"She will haunt us," Isla said, "unless we silence her."

"Somebody get that old hag off the streets," Cortés commanded Bernal Díaz, who was happy to be excused. "Drown her in the brook."

"Sir, Capitán, Comandante, I am a writer."

"Bernal Díaz, your hands are as dirty as everybody's. Do as you are told. Tomorrow we leave this godforsaken place, comprende? Mañana nos vamos de este sitio del demonio. You are here now, not in the pages of some book."

Their departure from Cholula, however, was delayed by a few days. First there was thunder so loud it broke apart the heavens and lightning forked down from the sky as if in reprisal. The drops were so heavy they hurt the earth. All the flowers which had been blooming lost their petals overnight, their stalks pummeled to the ground. The mud walls of houses dissolved and ran into the streets, pooled with blood, strewn leaves, and assorted trash. Each family tried to claim their dead from the pile and the stakes, but it was too stormy.

"Tlaloc is angry," Jaguar Claw said to Cuy and Malintzin.

On the third day, the rain stopped and the sun came out with such force that to stand outside was to get struck down.

"The many dead warriors have gone up to the sky and joined the sun," Jaguar Claw said. "That is why it is so bright. This place will soon be a desert."

But in the afternoon, despite the risk, Francisco went for a walk. He was wearing his new shoes, so he was able to walk far. He was filled with an unusual strength, and he kept walking. That night he lay down under the stars, felt their companionship, and was not cold at all. The next morning he walked to a little plateau far outside of town. He was walking back to the coast, leaving the mountains. Well out of town, now on the flats, he came upon a wide, endless desert. By then he was quite thirsty. He lay down for the night. In the morning he took off his gown, his new sandals, and even the large wooden cross hanging by a cord around his neck. He felt like St. Francis when he left his home naked, not a stitch on his back. It was very hot. Francisco hobbled slowly, his arms outstretched, the hot sand blistering his feet. After a while he could no longer stand upright. He could see, however, quite well. Then he crawled, letting the sun lash his back with whips the color of blood. Foam spewed from his mouth, and what was left in his stomach came out as sour watery bile. He sang a little song, a last song he made up celebrating God's beautiful world. It was called "Ode to Cactus."

PART IV

ODA AL CACTO

Cacto con hojas de hule, bordeadas por los dos lados de filas de dientes afilados, yo te quiero.

Cactus with rows of sharp teeth edging rubber leaves, oh, two-sided saws, I love you.

Cacto con ramitas de largas y delgadas hojas, suave pelucita que protege la piel, como filas grandes de montañas de hormigas cruzando el terreno arenoso, tú eres mi inspiración. Pequeños cacto saliendo de la arena gateando, avanzando poco a poco, dáme tu valor.

Cactus with sprigs of long, thin leaves, soft hairs protect your skin like big lines of hills of ants across the sandy terrain, you are my inspiration. Small cactus easing out of sand, crawling, inching, give me your courage.

Cacto, como una almohadita cubierta de botones verdes con espinas suaves y amarillas entrelazadas, espinas que parecen una malla de encajes, amplias, como una hoja larga de agave que sirve de cojin cerca del corazón.

Cactus, like a little pillow covered with green buttons with soft interlacing yellow spines, spines like the mesh of interlocking lace, broad, long-leafed agave pincushion, dear to my heart.

Asientos ásperos con verrugas verdes y espinas suaves y amarillas entrelazadas espinas que parecen una malla de encajes, amplias como una hoja larga de agave que sirve de cojín cerca del corazón.

Stubby seats green warts with soft yellow thorns cactus, thorns like the mesh of interlocking lace, broad, long-leafed agave pincushion, dear to my heart.

Cacto de rojo profundo, sanguinolento, cacto que se extiende como chales del musgo, alfombra de cacto, cacto de cacto, ángeles, denme serenidad, cúrenme al corazón.

Cactus of deep red, blood red, cactus spread like shawls of moss, carpet of cactus, cactus of cactus, angels, give me peace of mind, heal my heart.

Cacto déjame mirarte, déjame morir mirándo a ti.

Cactus, let me look at you, let me die looking at you.

Dios te ha hecho con todo tu esplendor y toda tu gloria.

God has made you in your splendor and all your glory.

Amen.

Chapter 28

The first time Malintzin saw snow, tasted it, felt it on her head and shoulders, she felt tucked in the white breast of a giant seagull or caught in the white beard of some foreign god. The snow was above her, falling all around her, piling up on the ground. She could not breathe, it was getting into her nose; it was so cold it tingled. She looked up. The flakes were falling, tumbling, twisting, being shaken out of a bowl as big as the sky, winnowing down. The sky was a bowl of picked cotton fluff, fur, white feathers.

"Easy, easy, easy there," Alvarado said to his horse, calming him.

The snow fell on Malintzin's hair and stuck. She put her tongue out. It melted. She pressed her sandaled foot and made a print; her ankles stung with cold. She laughed and her tears froze on her face. Some of the Spanish were rolling in the snow; some were lying on their backs in it, fanning their arms. The horses started prancing playfully. But there was not much room to maneuver, for there they were, the Spanish, and all their allies on a steep slope, packed together on a high pass, between the two volcanoes, Ixtaccíhuatl and Popocatépetl, who in defiance of the snow were belching hot smoke, their lips red with fire. The valley of the Mexica lay somewhere below them. Their journey was almost at its end.

Malintzin, despite the cold, felt heated. Her head seemed to expand in an effort to understand and contain the idea of snow. It was something way outside the range of all her former experiences. Dear Francisco, she thought, please forgive me, I love the snow. It makes me happy. She wished he could have lived for a few weeks more to see this. Seeing snow would have made you live longer, Francisco. You need to live long to see everything. Without you, Francisco, who will

I tell the snow to? She believed he had dragged himself to some hidden spot to die like an animal craving privacy and peace in its last moments. Francisco had been her only witness, the only one who had known her, it seemed, since she was a child. Her sufferings, spare bits of happiness, setbacks, and small triumphs would now go unnoticed. Bernal Díaz, the official historian, would never record *her* life. Her friend Cuy, by turning to Núñez, turned her back on Malintzin and their girlish friendship. Cortés was not her friend. She had nobody. Francisco said once that when people died they could see the world from heaven, but Malintzin did not believe that, as she did not believe that warriors went to the sun to live with Huitzilopochtli. Life was the upper world and death was the underworld. Even the thought that Quetzalcoatl was somehow afoot and could live in a vaporous realm of the sky with visits to earth at a preordained time was more a fond hope than an entrenched belief.

"The snow," Adu said, throwing a ball of it her way. "Catch."

She caught the frozen ball and threw it back but it came apart. Adu made another one. She made a snow lady with a white head, a white belly, two white breasts, and black coal eyes. For hair she used twigs, and the nose was a stone, the mouth a line of seeds. She and Adu called her Señorita Payaso, Miss Clown. Because she was a naked snow lady, Botello called her Señora Desnuda. Malintzin wanted to make her a dress, but they did not have the time.

"Forward ho."

"Forward ho."

Gingerly finding their footing, the horses of the expedition began their zigzag descent through the mountains. A level spot here, another one right below, a ledge, a steady rock, the women held hands, wending their way down in a line, a little lower stopping and resting.

"Attention, halt."

"Halt."

They were still high up in the mountains. But the haze which had hung over the valley below parted. They could see the ring of mountains surrounding the flat floor of the valley, and in the valley was a lake, and in the lake was an island, and on the island, a city. Bernal

Díaz was so overcome by what he saw, he had to jot down some notes immediately.

9 DE NOVIEMBRE DE 1519

Tenochtitlán, Mexica.

I have never, nor has anybody in this party, seen such a grand conception made into a work of astonishing veracity. A magnificent metropolis on an enchanted island in the middle of a beautiful lake is spread below us and glitters in the sun like a bed of jewels.

Those who have dreamed of an Atlantis could not conjure such a splendid sight.

The city is joined to the mainland by three stone causeways.

Gaps in causeways are adorned with ornately carved wooden drawbridges.

Stone aqueducts of ingenious design line the causeways.

The sun illuminates everything and a glow emanates from the city like the eye of the world.

The tall pyramids of stone are painted in dazzling colors.

Bernal Díaz was really in a quandary. He did not comprehend how something as marvelous as this city could exist without Europeans, that is to say, how could it happen without European men at least seeing it, how could it be there all along without their knowledge? Or maybe it had simply not existed until this moment. Did not "discovery" make things real, the eye itself a conjurer's instrument? That a city of this sophistication could sprout up on the other side of the world without the perception of civilized white men was beyond a rational person's understanding. All these people here had gone about their business, and a fine business it was, without knowing him, Bernal Díaz, without the benefit of Christ. They did not know about horses or guns or Turks or King Carlos. Yet they seemed to have fared quite well. It was amazing.

As the Spanish and allied Indians descended into the valley and started across one of the three causeways, women and children swarmed out from their homes; administrators, officials, students, farmers, soldiers, street cleaners, beggars, and prostitutes crowded the streets; and on the lake itself and the many canals that radiated into the city proper, fishermen and laborers paddled forth to see the new-comers. The citizens of Tenochtitlán stared with great curiosity at the hoofed horses bridled and saddled, and, for this occasion, wearing straps hung with little bells, the gigantic dogs straining on leashes held by men with thick arms, the soldiers in bright metal armor carrying spears and pikes, packets of arrows on their back, shortened bows on their shoulders, all with long swords hanging sheathed on their left hips, some double-sworded, the unwieldy harquebuses, the cannons and falconets, and the Tlaxcalan, Xocotalan, and Cempoalan bearers and guards, and the small army of women who tramped behind.

Halfway across the causeway, the outsiders were met by an impe-rial Aztec procession led by drummers in white cotton maxtlatl. The beat was a slow, steady march. The drummers were followed by lines of august men in long tilmatli tied over the right shoulder blowing conch shells. Tromp, tromp, tromp. Toot, toot, toot. Then came two straight lines of men carrying tree branches to sweep the street. Finally, in the midst of a group of armed men, a canopied and cur-tained chair held up by two thick poles embellished with mother-of-pearl and turquoise appeared. As the chair was lowered onto the causeway leading from Iztapalapa to Mexica, the drumming became faster and more intense. Cortés jumped down from his horse. A mat of feathers was placed by the side of the chair. The Aztec people on the sidelines who were wearing shoes quickly removed them and cast their glances downward. The drumming stopped. The emperor stepped out. Cortés rushed up, ready to envelop him in a big abrazo. At that, a uniform gasp went through the crowd. Cortés was pushed back by the guards. The foreigner had presumed to touch the great Moctezuma. Moreover, the barbarian had not taken off his shoes as a sign of respect, and above all, he had dared to look Moctezuma straight in the face.

Malintzin quickly instructed, "Cortés, stand back, look down, take off your shoes. Do not touch him, never touch the emperor, do not look him in the eye."

That Moctezuma was noble, Bernal Díaz noted, was apparent in every feature.

Taller than Cortés, older, perhaps forty years old, finely muscled, strikingly handsome, he is a man without blemish. He wears sandals of jaguar skin, backs covering his heels and tasseled ties of gold thread around his ankles, the soles inlaid with jade. With a large cloak of finely worked feathers, he looked like an exotic bird about to take wing. Thin lips, purple in color, eyes set deep within high cheekbones, flat, long forehead, the Indian emperor wears more jewels around his neck and in his ears than a European potentate.

Bernal Díaz, although he had never met a European royal personage, thought Moctezuma's labret looked like a real emerald. On the emperor's head was a wreath of the rare quetzal feathers, the green as green as the emerald. He held a stalk of feathers made to look like flowers.

Aguilar could not help comparing the Aztec emperor to an Egyptian pharaoh of the Old Testament, for Moctezuma was similarly skirted in a white tunic, his smooth, toned legs were sun-browned, and around his biceps he wore tight bracelets of gold in the shape of encircling snakes. Indeed, with their pyramid architecture, tropical pomp, and the absolute reverence commanded by their monarch, the Egyptian-Aztec comparison did not seem far-fetched. The emperor was proud, haughty, cruel-looking. However, Adu, from his long tenure as a slave, was sensitive to nuance and mood. To him this priest-king had a tragic look. Moxtezuma's eyes held sadness; his posture, though stiff and straight, revealed fear. Had Francisco been there, he would have had sympathy for the man. Botello read death in Moctezuma's face, a proud man perceiving the number of his days. Malintzin kept her head low, as was appropriate, and did not look up from her bare feet. Her huipilli was plain, nondescript, of rough maguey fiber. Her hair was tightly wound around her head, pressed flat with two disks of thin silver, and she kept her arms and hands modestly hidden. To greet the emperor, she used her most formal Nahuatl, replete with exaggerated honorifics, calling him ruler of the world, a god incarnate, and ending finally with the sentence:

"I am the humble translator, if you will permit me the privilege."

"A woman?" Moctezuma's voice was deep and so soft she had to strain to hear him.

"Great Moctezuma, hummingbird king on the left, lord of Tenochtitlán, I am a mere woman, yes, and presume to speak, but I am not a commoner, rather I am the child of a nobleman, now sadly departed, in your service in the region east and south of here, in Tabasco. I beg your indulgence in permitting my presence in your company. If you will tolerate me, I will translate your venerated words of the noble Nahuatl language into the language of the visitors."

Moctezuma folded his arms across his chest. "Tell Quetzalcoatl that I have kept his kingdom ready for him."

"What did he say?" Cortés recognized the word "Quetzalcoatl."

"The great Moctezuma is addressing you as Quetzalcoatl, Cortés."

"Does that mean he truly believes I am Quetzalcoatl?"

"I do not know." She too had been shocked by the address. Anybody could see Cortés was not a god. The creases in his neck were caked in grime. A lone hair stuck out of his nose. Between his teeth were remnants of rabbit meat and vestiges of inadequately masticated tortillas. He smelled bad. And as a god, would he not know the language of his subjects?

Cortés, of course, was overjoyed by the pompous reception given to him by the emperor. For all his enthusiasm for the Habsburg emperor and king of Spain, Carlos, and despite his own tenuous claim to nobility, he had never been in the company of anybody of real social stature unless you could call the governor of Cuba important, which he did not. And this person, a king, the lord of the realm, ruler of thousands of people, nay, emperor of twenty-eight city-states of a geographical range yet to be charted ranging north, south, east, and west, a man richer than Midas, recognized that he, Hernán Cortés, was more than an upstart from the provinces, more than a failed law student or small island notary. Unschooled and outranked, he had not only been acknowledged as the man he was by a master general of great skill and intelligence, but placed in a pantheon of hero-gods. He liked this Emperor Moctezuma.

When the Spanish grew more familiar with the city, Bernal Díaz was to count seventy-eight major buildings, immense open courtyards, passageways, meeting chambers, granaries, storehouses, craft workhouses, monasteries, and shrines. On the loftiest pyramid were two temples—one to Huitzilopochtli, the patron god of the Aztec and the god of war and crops, and the other to Tlaloc, the rain god.

As was fitting, Quetzalcoatl-Cortés and his captains were immediately escorted to Moctezuma's palace, where, sitting cross-legged on the floor, they were regaled with welcome speeches delivered with great dignity by various dignitaries. Then they were entertained by dancers and musicians and acrobats of great skill who could juggle logs on their legs while lying down, and humpbacked jesters who reminded Cortés of the courtly dwarfs European kings were reputed to keep about them. Warriors dressed in the skins and heads of jaguars and carrying staffs and shields led a procession of old retired soldiers, and young eagle warriors sallied forth in anklets of claws, their headdresses made to look like giant eagle faces. Smelling of carnage and encrusted with tidbits of the long-dead and recently slain, their hair shaved on the sides and left long and uncombed in the middle and clotted stiff with blood and ooze, the Aztec priests formed a proud parade. Some in this grisly group wore human-skin robes from flayed victims, and their fingernails were so long they curled like Isla's pinkie nail. Alvarado was particularly frightened.

After the speeches, processions, and entertainment, a lavish dinner was laid out in the emperor's eating room on low tables before which the captains had to sit cross-legged. The menu included tamales of such fine texture they melted in the mouth like churned butter, mixiotes, meat steamed in bags made of maguey leaves, guacamole crushed and flecked with red and green peppers, roasted turkey, pheasant, partridge, quail, varieties of duck, and venison cut in thick chunks and basted with a most delicious chocolate sauce, a white fish marinated in lime juice, red snapper served with tomato sauce in the style of the east coast, guava, tamarind, sasaparilla, squash of various kinds, a stew made of corn and chilies, and fresh plums. Filled with this delicious food, they washed it all down with jugs of frothy cocoa brought in by beautiful young virgins. Moctezuma ate in the same room but did not eat with them; rather he ate, as was his custom, behind a golden screen.

Following the lavish meal, Cortés and his captains were offered the use of the public baths, which they politely declined, since too much bathing brought on the ague, and were instead taken to excellent sleeping quarters in a palace nearby, one which had belonged to the emperor Axayácatl, Moctezuma's dead father. The regular troops, servants, the vast entourage of women, and bearers and warriors from Cempoala, Xocatlan, and Tlaxcala were housed in modest thatched-roofed huts throughout the city, and the captains who wished the company of one of their paramours had to search high and low in the four separate wards carefully situated in an X in relation to the center of the town.

"Cuy? Where are you, Cuy?"

"Here I am," Cuy called out from an open doorway.

Núñez had brought Cuy some food from the table. As a slave, she was only served beans and tortillas, and thus relished the pieces of tender, well-flavored meat, but she was too exhausted to walk back to where Núñez was bedded, and even too tired to talk, she fell into a deep sleep right after she ate, Núñez alongside her. His sleep, however, was troubled by apprehensions; dreams which were untidy and unfinished drifted toward him like patches of the mist you see on the high mountains. He, with the other captains, not apprised of Cortés's plans, had arrived at Tenochtitlán after an inland journey of many stops and starts, somewhat at a loss. They had been in the land of the Mexica since March and here it was November. In their progress, their troops had gained thousands of Indian warriors. Of their sixteen original horses, they had fourteen. Their weapons were in mint condition and their gunpowder casks filled, for two men had lowered themselves over the lip of one of the volcanoes to scoop sulfur to replenish the supply. Still they were outnumbered by at least ten to one. Was there to be a full-scale war? Was there to be diplomacy and negotiation, a gentle, bloodless takeover? The emperor had treated Cortés like royalty, it seemed. Was the emperor merely extending the politeness required by custom, or was all the formal palaver masking less hospitable intentions?

Malintzin, too, was clueless. As official translator, she had been permitted at the celebratory banquet. Moctezuma's voice had been barely audible behind the screen in front of him, but it would have been rude of her to ask him to speak up, so she crawled close and put her ear to the bark paper embellished with gold leaf. The first thing Moctezuma asked was for her to describe Quetzalcoatl-Cortés in detail and enumerate all his godly qualities. She was tempted to warn Moctezuma, and she wondered that he did not remember that the historical Quetzalcoatl was of a retiring and humble appearance, whereas Cortés was boisterous and arrogant. Yet she held back, reminded of the skull rack below the temple steps, which was festooned with human heads, like decorations for a holiday, in various stages of decay, some clean skulls, others with flesh and hair still on them. Several were women. If Moctezuma truly believed that Cortés was Quetzalcoatl incarnate, she could be executed for blasphemy. If he was not, she could be punished with the others as a traitor guilty of blasphemy and a conspiracy to incite an insurrection. There seemed to be no way to have a truthful discussion.

Nahuatl, however, was a metaphoric language, one word capable of standing for several others or even signifying its opposite. Equivocation was possible, for each word in courteous court Nahuatl held the possibility of irony and even falsehood. Similarly, actions in the high culture of the nobility invited various interpretations. Could it be, she mused, that the great display of costumed dancers, trumpeting conch shells, trilling pipes, and pounding drums, and particularly the demonstration of warriors and priests greeting their entrance into the city and provided as entertainment was more a show of might than a sincere welcome? The reception might have been taken as mockery by the initiated. The emperor, surrounded as he was by wise men, advisers, scribes, and priests, could not truly regard Cortés as the god Quetzalcoatl. If he did, his wits were gone or he was in the grip of a poppy trance.

Malintzin had heard a long time ago in wild rumor that Moctezuma II, despite his adroit conduct of war, meticulous enactment of tribute, and stern requirements of submission, was subject to lapses of sense, plagued by afterthoughts, and had weaknesses of unusual sorts; for example, it was whispered that he was impotent and his "children" were not his own, and that at times he was unsure of his perceptions, prone to seeing omens in the most random of events. It was even hinted that Moctezuma made misjudgments. Sometimes, unbelievably, there was news of discontent not only among the tribute states but among the commoners of Tenochtitlán. Such a situation was not impossible, for it was claimed that the ancient city of Teotihuacán, site of the great Pyramid of the Sun and Pyramid of the Moon and the Avenue of the Dead, now grassy mounds, was burned down by its own people.

Given all these considerations, Malintzin's descriptions of the Spanish for the emperor's benefit were circumspect, circuitous, and painstakingly conscientious in portraying Cortés and his captains as neither gods nor men. They were as you saw them, she intimated, letting the emperor, since he was so astute, so very clever, come to his own conclusions. Certainly the insights of a mere woman could not compete with those of an august emperor.

She managed to comport herself with dignified confidence despite her sense of awkwardness and bewilderment. Were the amenities that were being observed, all the pomp and circumstance and excessive politeness, mere prelude? But to what? The fact of the matter was that the march inland was over. The conquistadors had crossed the causeway into the city and reached the mainland. After the long-drawn-out journey and the great anticipation of reaching the heartland, Tenochtitlán, they were here. They were at the golden city. What was to happen next? While Malintzin thought that civilities could continue for a while, she knew that sooner or later somebody's hand would be forced. Was Cortés going to take over Tenochtitlán and the whole empire of Moctezuma, or were the Spanish going to swing happily in hammocks for the rest of their days? Was there to be a bloodbath or a steam bath? Cortés, of course, was charming, very amiable, but at heart deadly. Moctezuma's nature was a puzzle.

Malintzin was of Cortés's party, surely, but her attachment to him had frayed to a weak thread. She could no longer say that Cortés was a man, therefore vicious, his faults the result of birth and custom. If that were true, there would be no Francisco, no Núñez, no Botello, or even an Adu. Aguilar was not cruel by nature. Puertocarrero had been a mere drunkard. And her father, who, while he had faithfully served the empire, at least had not invented sacrifice. The fact that Moctezuma and members of the Aztec ruling elite, the clique of nobles, were equally cruel did not lessen the culpability of the Spanish, nor did it serve as an apology for her own leanings and failings. That she was alone, a woman without a strong man, a person without alliances, a mere slave at the whim of a master—these facts could no longer suffice as an excuse for silent complicity. In order to think clearly, she had to separate the tender man who pampered her at night from the one who had hanged a harmless man at dawn, cut off twenty hands in the evening, and slaughtered a whole city in a morning. Cortés's hands on her skin brought visions of the severed hands, the ones in her dream crawling like crabs, molesting and torturing her.

She lay down that night on her mat in a little hut by the Grand Teocalli, the Templo Mayor, prepared to sleep. A shadow appeared at her doorway.

"What are you doing here?"

"Is that the way to talk to your better?" Isla asked.

Malintzin did not grace him with a look.

"Cortés wants you."

"I am sleeping."

The soldier stood over her prone body with his sword drawn.

"You dare?"

"Escaped slave, heathen traitor, girl puta." He leaned down, grabbed her arm, pulled her up, and spat right in her face. "You do as I say, malefactor."

Malintzin put on her cloak, flipping it out so that it swirled around her, whipping Isla on his eelish face. She stomped through the sleeping city in angry strides, rounded the palace of Moctezuma I, the Great Temple, and proceeded like a peeved child to the palace of Axayácatl, Moctezuma's father's palace. Across were the aviary, the Temple of Tezcatlipoca, and Moctezuma's palace. Torches were fixed in notches along the walls. They went inside Axayácatl's palace, ascended a stairway, and walked along an open corridor bordering a central court. And there, in a corner room, there he was, the god prone on his back, his mat placed on a ledge on one wall of the room, his armor resting on the floor, his legs bare. He had a little jar of pulque at his side, some tobacco leaf chopped up in a little dish ready to be placed in a pipe, his candles, a desk of sorts, and his famous chair. He opened his arms to her.

"Doña Marina, my love. Isla, you can go now."

"I am in flower," she lied as he drew her to his chest.

"No matter."

"My stomach hurts."

"Let me kiss it."

"Should I send for somebody else?"

"Now, now, Doña Marina, do not be a silly puppy. When you were a little slave girl in the kitchen, did you ever dream you would be received here like this, see, speak to, be near enough to touch the great Moctezuma? Did you see all that gold around his neck? What I want to know is where are the mines? That is key. Ésta es la llave. Perhaps in a little conversation with him, my dear. He seems to have accepted you. He likes you. Come here. You are crying, little one, why is that?"

"Francisco."

"I did not tell Francisco to walk away from our camp, go out and expose himself to death, boil himself to death, singe himself to death, whatever it was. Perhaps an animal ate his fleshy flesh, or some revengeful Cholulan got him in the back."

"You killed them all."

"The Cholulans started it, my dear. Indeed, you were the one who alerted us. Do not equivocate. You cannot have it both ways, either you are for us or against us, for me or against me." Cortés sat up with a sigh and rested his back against the wall. He hated demonstrations of grief, lack of fortitude, and while the emotions of women were laudable in song, he did not fancy an unpleasant encounter on this historic night. They were here in Tenochtitlán. She should be ecstatic. What he had previously prized in Doña Marina was her ability to venture forward, to adjust to new circumstances, to act without regard to misplaced loyalties, affections, sentimental memories. Was it not Lot who, though warned not to, looked back, and was it his wife who turned into a pillar of salt? Or was it his wife who looked back? Either way, a lesson there.

"This crying will not do, Malintzin. It is less than becoming and could cast serious doubt on our enterprise. Far from drawing sympathy to yourself, you will find that people resent your self-pity. Moreover, we must appear unanimous in all our actions. Beware of melancholy, black bile, the phases of the moon. Melancolía, bilis negra, las fases de la luna. We can have Botello bleed you, you would feel better."

"I do not want to be bled." She had observed the Spanish version of medicine. The slightest cough, and a vein was cut. A toothache merited extraction without benefit of pain-reducing poultices. A wound precipitated amputation when the placement of unguents and palliative plants would have proved an adequate cure.

"You do not want to be bled? Fie. You bleed yourselves in homage to your gods. Which one in particular demands blood? All of them are vicious as far as I am concerned. Tezcatpocapoac? Is he the most bloodthirsty? Am I pronouncing his name in correct fashion?"

"Tezcatlipoca."

"Is he also the one who requires that you throw somebody in the fire, drag them out half alive, and then cut the heart out? I have forgotten the exact sequence of torture here."

"That is Xihutechuhtili, the fire god."

"Sorry. And the one you throw crying babies to?"

"Tlaloc, so it will rain."

"Yes, yes, please forgive me. He sits up on top of the pyramid, next to Grandfather Huitzilopochtli, the war god, the great patron chief god of the Aztec. Was he not the one who killed four hundred of his brothers and dismembered his sister while she was nursing her child? And refresh me, who is our flayed lord?"

"Xipe Totec."

"Yes, good old Xipe Totec, who is celebrated with gladiator combat, except not fairly, for the captive is tied by one ankle to a stone disk and must fight three warriors simultaneously."

She did not want to tell him that she too found the gods of her people dreadful. She would not tell him of the woman in her town who met death in the forest with her baby rather than have him sacrificed, or that beautiful young virgins ran the risk of being sacrificed to the green corn goddess, or that her father, who did not die in war or sacrificed as a captive, had to abide after his death in the underworld for four years before he would be permitted to join the sun god and turn into a bird or butterfly, or that women who died in childbirth, although warriors in their own right, were buried at crossroads and doomed to haunt their villages. She did not tell him that there were people who believed the emperor and his nobles initiated the Flowery Wars not for reasons of piety, but as a means of controlling the empire through terror.

"Let me tell you your problem, Doña Marina. You love me so much you do not know what to do." He was packing his pipe. "You love me more than food, more than water, you love me more than life. You love me so much it is making you hate me. Your passion is too strong for your own good, or mine either, Doña Marina. Moderation in all things—Marcus Aurelius."

"Doña Marina is not my name. Ése no es mi nombre, ninguno de ellos es mi nombre."

"I know your name, come here, let me whisper it to you."

"No, I will not come to you."

"A little spitfire, are we? You want to die, is that it, this very night? Easy to do." He took hold of his dagger, which he always kept beside him. She moved away from him. He pulled her to his face and whispered hotly and wetly in her ear. "Puta. Puta." Then he twisted her arm behind her back and pinned the other one to the mat.

"No!" she screamed.

"No? Scream again, my dear, and you can join Francisco in hell."

ADU WAS SITTING on his mat whittling a little pipe out of a piece of wood.

"Hello," Alvarado said, peering in at his door.

"Hello," Adu replied.

"So we made it to the capital."

"Yes."

"Good dinner."

"Yes."

"Tomorrow, I hear, we go on a tour of the city."

"Hm."

"Too bad about old Francisco. Crazy to wander out without a hat."

"And Quintaval, too bad he had to be executed," Adu added.

"Well, Quintaval, yes." Alvarado looked down at the stone floor. "Yes, a bad business. Some would say he got what he asked for."

"And you, Señor Alvarado, what would you say? ¿Y usted, Señor Alvarado, qué dice usted? What do you ask for?" Adu looked closely at Alvarado, whose bottom lip quivered. The rims of his pinched nose reddened.

"I think I will go back to my sleeping mat," Alvarado said. "It has been a long day."

"Yes, it has."

FATHER OLMEDO WAS sitting with Aguilar while he said his eighth prayer of the day, his Compline prayer, which marked the coronation of the Virgin.

"I wish Francisco were still alive," Father Olmedo said when Aguilar had finished.

"He is with God, yes? Tell me, Father. Suicide is a very bad sin, is it not? Is not despair the worst sin?"

"I look upon it a little differently, Aguilar. I think Brother Francisco may be a martyr."

"Will the pope look upon it that way?"

"I think not, but for certain, Aguilar, our brother is with God, and thus beyond the reach of pope, prelate, emperor, king, commander, what-have-you."

"Did you see the rack of skulls, Father Olmedo?"

"I did indeed, Aguilar. Sobering."

ISLA WAS FILING his nails with a stone.

BERNAL DÍAZ WAS catching up on his notes.

BOTELLO, WHO MISSED Francisco terribly, thought he saw Francisco's face in the sky, outlined by a circlet of stars.

MOCTEZUMA HAD RETIRED early. While he often spoke to his advisers shortly before retiring, he did not do so this evening, for he wished to ponder the day's events alone. He did not know whether the man he had met was Quetzalcoatl in the sense of the old god, or the priest-poet, or the ruler of Tula returning, or if Cortés was a phantasmagorical creature designed by the malevolent trickster god to confuse him. Moctezuma was not certain of anything anymore. His life up to this point had been a series of omens, good and bad, each event signaled by the alignment of the stars, the flight of birds, the pattern of objects. Everything that happened was predicted, and his duties and responsibilities were in accord with tradition. The pattern of the year, each month containing a particular celebration and set of customs, was predetermined and a replication of the pattern of his ancestors.

This man, this commander, Cortés, this god, Quetzalcoatl, even with the omens preceding him, was utterly outside the boundaries of everything Moctezuma had been taught. He was so foreign that Moctezuma did not know how to respond to him, whoever he was. Moctezuma had not been trained to vary from the path appointed him. Wage war with other tribes, observe the gods piously, govern harshly and wisely. A god, he knew, could enter any person and do whatever he chose. Had not he, Moctezuma, been educated to honor the gods, gods who were exempt from human limitations. Was he not taught religiously how not to offend the gods, whatever the shape or form they assumed?

Another thing about this man Cortés, if man he was: Moctezuma had never encountered one, low- or high-born, who had such a sense of entitlement, such self-assurance, such careless boldness. Only a god, somebody not born as man on this earth, could be so contemptuous of custom and habit. Cortés not only had the haughty demeanor of a god and the unusual clothing of another realm, taking as his due all that lay before him, acting with celestial privilege, completely indifferent to the human hierarchy, but he did not seem to be aware of the cost of presuming to be a god if one was not a god. Heretofore people had feared for their lives in front of the mighty Moctezuma and dared not approach him in a whimsical fashion. This man, god, whatever he was, walked right up to him and had the nameless effrontery to look at him straight in the eye. It was not merely a matter of civility, which was certainly not minor, but the complete fearlessness of his actions. This person, or whatever he was, did not acknowledge degree, duty, or tradition, indeed his manner was closely akin to the outrageous and unsuitable behavior of gods not governed by human expectation. Who else could adopt such a manner with impunity? How did this person, this whatever he was, gather so many faithful followers to him, people who had known the reputation of the Aztec for generations and trembled before them. The Cempoalas, the Xocotlans, the Tlaxcalas, and the woman who spoke for this whatever he was, how was she so gifted if she were not an emissary of the gods?

Chapter 29

Jaguar Claw, as butcher to the conquistadors, had access to knives of steel with serrated edges, small axes, other chopping implements, scoops for gutting; he could put his hands on thin pointed instruments for piercing and popping, skinning tools, large grinders. He knew where the bone connecting neck to shoulder was located in a deer, monkey, any small running animal. There was not a lizard he could not gut in a few moments. Fish were child's play. And as a servant who was part of the entourage, particularly in the confusion of their first night in Tenochtitlán, he was allowed entry into the palace where the Spanish captains were sleeping. The question was which was the quickest, most quiet method to accomplish his task, for if Malintzin, whom he had heard was sleeping with Cortés this night, if she woke and caught him in the act, who knows what her actions might be? Then he would have to kill her too; without question he would have to do that. Not that he did not welcome the thought of getting rid of the traitor once and for all, but he decided it would be better to leave her alive, alive and accused. Execution of a woman was not that rare. He had seen female skulls on the rack. Were they common criminals or captives? Indeed a long time ago a princess of the Mexica, who was adulterous and had her lovers' likenesses made into sculpture was stoned to death for her crimes.

Keeping his knife concealed in a bag slung over his shoulder, he entered the palace as if he had been called upon to give a late-night massage, place hot rocks on a back, or administer to one of the white men in the capacity of a healer or comforter. He was a mere servant, a slave, one who did not look up. Nobody would stop him.

Like all sumptuous official buildings, the guest palace, the palace of the former emperor Axayácatl, was a maze of rooms wound around a courtyard. The floors and walls were made of precisely cut squares of stone so adeptly placed that not a wisp of wind or drop of rain could penetrate into the rooms. Cortés liked corner rooms, did not relish being in a line, and while others hung cotton cloths over their doors, he kept his door open out of respect for the Aztec custom.

There they were. Jaguar Claw gazed almost fondly at the couple, Malintzin's hip caught in the moonlight. Cortés was on his back, one leg thrown over Malintzin's waist, and one of her wrists was circled by rope bound to his wrist. What curious habits these white men had. Cortés's body sprawled out invited evisceration. The throat, however, that was the best way. Jaguar Claw had known animals with their intestines dripping out of their bodies running about bleating and howling. A human might do the same. Smothering with a mat would be quiet, but Cortés was strong and would thrash, waking no doubt Malintzin and others. Jaguar took out the knife he used to cut through the thick hide of a deer. The handle was short and easily gripped in the palm of the hand. He tiptoed into the room, holding his breath and keeping close to the shadows of the wall. Then he dropped down, and with the knife in his mouth crawled toward the mat. Malintzin turned, sighed, moved, felt the rope grip, and turned back. The rope tightened around her wrist. In her sleep she maneuvered back to her original position and began to snore lightly. The commandant let loose some wind. He was dribbling too. Stealthily as a rat, Jaguar Claw made ready to strike and slash.

Malintzin woke up and for a moment was not sure where she was. In her dream she was struggling and could not get free. Sleep was still in her mouth and her eyes were not seeing properly, but she thought she saw the large shadow of a big cat creeping toward her. Was this the jaguar who had kissed her in the woods of Cholula? She held her breath, closed her eyes tightly so that it would go away, then opened them again, but there it was, closer, not a cat. A man made ready to stab her.

"No," she screamed, "No!"

She swung her free hand up and knocked something out of the attacker's hand. It clattered to the floor.

Cortés woke up with a start. "What? What is it?"

"Jaguar," Malintzin gasped in Maya when she recognized him, "what are you doing here?"

Cortés grabbed Jaguar Claw's knife, cut the rope holding Malintzin to his side, kicked Jaguar Claw in the face, jumped up, reached for his arms, got hold of them, pulled them back, and then butted Jaguar Claw in the head with his own head. Wrestling Jaguar Claw to the floor, Cortés pressed him flat, got on his stomach, and, astride, held Jaguar Claw down, his hands pinned over his head.

"Why are you here? What is going on? Doña Marina, are you all right?"

"I am fine." Malintzin was shaking.

Getting up from the floor, Cortés pushed Jaguar Claw near the sleeping pad with his feet. Malintzin's teeth were chattering, but she felt hot all over. She was wearing her huipilli and cueitl, for Cortés had not removed them in his haste.

"Light the candles, stir up the coals." There was a small fireplace on the side of the wall and there were coals still glowing in its hearth. Malintzin's hands trembled as she grabbed a stick resting against the wall, poked the coals, and with the burning end lit several of the candles placed in nooks in the wall.

"So what do we have here?" Cortés looked down at the butcher with the twisted lips. The Mayan's eyes were glazed, not focusing, as if he were looking inward and no longer perceived the world around him.

Malintzin started to cry.

"For God's sake, this is not the time to weep. The villain was trying to kill me, Doña Marina, can you imagine? ¿Puede usted imaginar? Call the guards, for Christ's sake."

"Jaguar Claw," Malintzin said, "you did not try to kill anybody, did you?"

"Doña Marina," Cortés shouted, "do as I say."

"It is a mistake. He did not mean—"

"Help," Cortés shouted out. "Somebody come. Help. Say it in Aztec, Malintzin. Hurry up."

Already Malintzin could hear the soft pad of sandals hitting the stone floor, and soon the room was filled with Moctezuma's guards. Five grabbed Jaguar Claw and hoisted him upright.

"He, this slave," Malintzin said in Nahuatl, her voice faltering, "he wandered into the wrong room. He meant no harm."

"What are you saying, Doña Marina?" Cortés could not understand her words but knew she was telling a lie.

"The poor man is lost," she continued in Nahuatl, and then in Spanish said, "When I was a child, Cortés, I walked in my sleep. I walked right out of my house. You have to be gentle with people who walk in their sleep. My father would guide me back to my mat and rub my feet. When I woke up, I did not know where I had been."

"The man was going to kill me, Doña Marina." Cortés, standing up, revealed his limp genitals dangling beneath his dirty shirt; his hair was a matted mess. "I have been watching this scoundrel for some time and known he was up to no good. He is vicious, malicious, and bites the hand that feeds him. He does not know wrong from right. He is a butcher, a killer."

"He did not mean to, Cortés. Pulque, certain cactus buttons. People do not know what they are doing sometimes. Please let him go."

One of the guards moved closer to her. "Does the Malintzin want us to take him to prison? Should we wake up the emperor?"

"No, no, do not wake him," she replied in Nahuatl. "It is a big mistake. The fellow wandered into the wrong room."

"Does the Malintzin want to free him?" a guard asked. All the guards stared at her. Her hair, which had been modestly fashioned in flat disks for her audience with Moctezuma, had come loose, and her clothes were askew.

"You did not mean to hurt us, did you, Jaguar Claw?" Malintzin asked in Maya.

Jaguar Claw's eyes blazed at her in hatred.

"You were on your way to the cooking area and got lost, is that not so, Jaguar Claw?"

Had his arms not been held fast, it looked like Jaguar Claw would choke Malintzin.

"Aguilar," Cortés shouted, "Isla, Bernal Díaz, Alvarado, Núñez, Father Olmedo, Francisco."

"Francisco is dead," Malintzin said drily.

"Captains, rally to my defense. Will not anybody come, for Christ's sake?"

Isla arrived first, ready to serve, his sword drawn.

"This scoundrel, el canalla, tried to kill me, Isla, and Malintzin is pleading for his release."

"Maybe she conspired with him," Isla said.

"Cortés, have mercy," Malintzin begged.

"God is merciful, I am not."

"Rightfully so," Isla added.

"Jaguar has nothing. The man is harmless. Let him go."

"To try to kill me again?"

The guards shuffled their feet nervously. Aguilar arrived.

"Ah, Aguilar, our shipwrecked one. What is the fitting punishment for an ingrate murderer?"

Aguilar had been interrupted during his first good sleep in a long time. In his dream he was on a boat, a steadfast boat in calm waters, but in the distance, he saw clouds approaching. When last he was on a real ship out at sea, a squall stirred up from nowhere. The waves rose as tall as a church and hit the deck like unsheathed knives, the goats on board had bleated like women, and the men called to their Savior for mercy. The sea had its own will, nothing could stop it. One inky black wave curled itself around the boat and swallowed it whole. Aguilar was pitched from the deck far from the others. The darkness of the water and sky was so complete it was as if he were being thrown back in a time before God said, Let there be light. He was going to die a lone man in the middle of nowhere without the consolation of even a piece of ground to stand on. He could barely keep his head out of the water, could not help swallowing and choking. He struggled, tried to swim, and only managed to thrash about. It would be awful to drown. He imagined the bubbles coming from his escaped breath, his body twining down like a thrown bottle, the fish gathering to eat him. Then, amid all these fears, he became calm. He was going to die, that was certain, so he stopped struggling and yielded himself to death. Let it come, I am ready. Not that everything was tidied up in his life. Everything was unfinished, in disarray, but it did not matter anymore. All those small things did not matter anymore. He was beyond concern. At that moment he saw a large piece of wood floating right by him. He lunged at it, grabbed it, and wrapped himself around it. He saw in all that blackness a light line of sand.

"But you are alive, Comandante," Aguilar said to Cortés. Jaguar Claw was not a particularly pleasant fellow, but he was less of a threat than even Quintaval.

"Barely alive," Cortés nearly blubbered. "Doña Marina saved me."

"I just put my hand up and the knife fell down. I did not save anybody."

"But you did."

After the shipwreck, as soon as Aguilar could raise his head from the damp sand, he had searched for other survivors. Bloated dead men washed ashore like logs bound for the mill. Bits and pieces of the boat bobbed like toys in the waves. So he made himself a little house of palm fronds, sucked on crab legs in a kind of fevered glee, and when, three days later, he saw a woman gathering seaweed on the beach, he ran to her, and from that point he did not quite know what he was doing, for he had never been with a woman and was so glad to see a person and that it was a woman. It all got away from him. Since that time and since the term of his slavery, which he accepted as just punishment, he could understand any and all desperate acts. They come from deep within you and overtake the moment when it could have been different.

"He did not mean to kill you, Cortés."

"A man with a knife comes into your room, come now, Aguilar."

"He did not," Malintzin insisted.

"Do not plead his case." Isla was contemptuous of the whole

tawdry situation. His commander, the whore, the butcher. "Had this cur killed Cortés, you would be the one blamed, Malinche. Or perhaps you had some other plan in mind, you and Jaguar Claw."

"No, Isla, no, it was not an arrangement." Malintzin knew that Isla hated her with a passion that bordered on madness.

"Or maybe he meant to kill you too, Malinche."

"No, no, he did not, Isla."

Aguilar knew that Isla did not like Malintzin, or anybody for that matter. "Malintzin is pure of heart and clear of mind," he said. "And the Indian, he is ignorant, his humors out of balance."

"I am pleading for your life," Malintzin said in Maya under her breath to Jaguar Claw. "Look repentant."

"May you descend to the underworld."

"Jaguar Claw, listen to me, say something, anything. I am telling them you were on your way to the cooking area, that you stumbled into this room. All the talking you do, it has gone to your head."

"To my hands," Jaguar Claw replied.

"He says it is late. Where is the cooking place? He wishes to start the fires for the morning food."

The guards looked at her impatiently.

"I will take him." She had quickly wrapped Cortés's cape about her.

"Stop, Doña Marina."

"I ask one thing, Maax," Jaguar Claw interjected. "I want to be sacrificed like a warrior, not executed like a common criminal."

"Now what, begging for his life?" Cortés asked. "You are aware that by killing me he did not mean you well either, Doña Marina."

"You do not understand anything, Maax," Jaguar said.

"I understand enough to know nobody wants to die."

"You do not understand the extent of the threat, Malin*tzin*," Jaguar Claw said. "We will be obliterated, Maya and Aztec, and all of us who live in the forest, on the plateau, in the plains, the people who live in the north and south, our whole land, all our people, if we do not resist the power of the whites now. We will not merely be defeated, have a simple change of emperors, pay new taxes, go on as before. Our bones will be crushed, our temples ruined, our books burned, our art erased. Our world will become invisible. We will be less than ghosts.

"You have dreams of being a princess again. You attach yourself to a man you think is strong. You are ruled by your narrow little life, clutch at safety the way a marmoset steals his fruit. You too will be nothing, worse than dead."

"*You* will die, Jaguar, and not have a life, any kind of life."

"I will be with the sun. Warriors will chant my praises."

Malintzin shook her head. "You are wrong."

"What are you two talking about?" Cortés said. "My patience is exhausted."

Aguilar and Isla were still standing in the room. The guards still had Jaguar Claw in their grip.

"He wishes me to say good-bye to Cuy." Malintzin was wondering if, as Cortés had freed the tax collectors in Cempoala and been able to accomplish his many deceptions and ploys, she too could not enact a rescue for Jaguar Claw, she and Cuy?

"Take him," she said in Nahuatl.

"What a miserable night," Cortés said, throwing himself down on his mat.

"May I do anything to help?" Isla asked.

"You can leave. You too, Aguilar, leave me alone."

"I will go back to my own place too," Malintzin said.

"Remember we are getting a tour of the city tomorrow. And Doña Marina?"

"What?"

"Do not think of any plot to save that abominable Jaguar Claw."

"I am not."

"Isla?"

"Yes, sir?"

"Go with Doña Marina to her hut. Doña Marina, you have saved my life. I owe you my life. Thank you."

"No, you do not owe me your life."

"I am too tired for quibbling."

Malintzin glowered. She hated them all.

"Isla, do not let her out of sight."

"I will be fine, Cortés. It is not necessary to have an escort."

"And bring her back here tomorrow morning."

Jaguar Claw was taken down the steps to a windowless room to be imprisoned with thieves and drunkards. He kept repeating in Maya, "I am a warrior. A warrior." In his mind he was strong, for he had not flinched from his duty. He knew in time his heroism and sacrifice would be celebrated. The main thing was to die like a man.

The next day, without anybody knowing who started and spread the news, everybody knew what had happened. During the morning meal Malintzin told Cuy how she had a plan to save Jaguar Claw. She was going to beg Moctezuma's mercy.

"How will that look?" Cuy asked, spooning her cornmeal mush into her mouth as fast as she could and choking a little. "Jaguar Claw tried to kill Cortés, your master."

"When I plead with Moctezuma, I will beg as Indian to Indian."

"Indian to Indian? Moctezuma's wars are against Indians. Who else does he have to fight?"

"Cuy, I am a princess, I will remind him."

"Jaguar Claw will not appreciate your efforts and you will only endanger yourself by trying."

"I cannot simply let him go."

"What choice do you have? By the way, he was the one who told on you to the mistress when we were children."

"We are grown up now."

Malintzin wanted to tell Cuy something else that had happened to her the night of Jaguar Claw, something else that was terrible, but it was so awful she could not say it. That she could still care about Jaguar Claw, sit at a meal, have a conversation, that her mind still worked, her mouth could move, her feet walk, that people did not know what had happened to her simply by looking at her, was odd. She looked at her hands. They shook. Her lips could not fit around a piece of food. And if her mind was something of a home with sleeping mats, boxes, the griddle stone, it had all been upset, knocked down.

After the meal, Moctezuma on his litter, accompanied by handmaidens, pretty boys, handsome courtiers, and renowned warriors, plumed, bejeweled, and wrapped in resplendent robes, led the procession to the zoo, which was a ways west of the Templo Mayor and near the Tacuba causeway. The entourage walked slowly, Malintzin and Cortés on either side of the aloft Moctezuma, their eyes on the ground. Captains and their lady friends took up the rear. Moctezuma, ever the solicitous host, had Malintzin tell Quetzalcoatl-Cortés that he had been informed of Jaguar Claw's dastardly deed. Although the perpetrator was not one of his own men, he apologized that such an incident had happened in his father's palace, under his protection. Of course, being an immortal, Quetzalcoatl-Cortés would not have died, not this time, yet the very idea was galling. He, Moctezuma, was extremely embarrassed that such a rude thing had happened in Tenochtitlán. And why was it that Quetzalcoatl-Cortés walked when he could ride in a garlanded litter too. It would not do to put his godly feet directly on the ground.

"Renowned and magnificent Moctezuma," Malintzin began, for she knew that the sooner she approached Moctezuma, the better Jaguar Claw's chances would be. "I have heard of your power since I was a little girl. My father was an official, one of your loyal servants, and I too, in my humble way, am your most loyal servant. Your generosity and wisdom are known throughout the empire, and thus I am bold enough to ask you to let the person who was arrested last night go back to the Maya kingdom in the south, where he can tell all he meets of your generosity. He is a poor slave who last night was on his way to the kitchen, got mixed up, there are so many corridors, and walked into the wrong room. Today he finds himself in prison. It is so confusing, such a silly mistake."

"What did you say to him?" Cortés asked, coming around to her side of the litter.

"I complimented him on his beautiful kingdom."

"No, you are pleading for that rapscallion's pitiful life, and you will make our host unhappy and set him against us. Do you not see how fragile this whole thing is? One misstep, and he could have us all killed."

"Ask your master," Moctezuma said when Cortés had gone back

around to his place, "ask my honored guest how he would like to see the villian executed."

Malintzin repeated this to Cortés.

"Tell our host, Doña Marina, tell His Most High Majesty Moctezuma, that if Jaguar Claw could be executed by having his heart cut out, we would be pleased."

Malintzin said nothing.

"Go ahead, tell him. And if you do not tell him truthfully what I ask, I will strangle you myself."

Moctezuma replied that it was a great honor to die as a sacrifice, that a death on the steps was a mark of bravery, and that the heroes who submitted to the priest's knife went straight to the sun's house. It was an unusual request, and one which in usual circumstances he would not honor, but since they were guests, and Quetzalcoatl a god at that, and Moctezuma's kingdom was Quetzalcoatl's kingdom, he, Moctezuma, would abide by his wishes. Furthermore, Moctezuma said, Quetzalcoatl-Cortés, and his very special friends, could watch. Indeed he would take them up right now and show him where it would happen. It could be arranged for the evening's entertainment.

Moctezuma did not walk the one hundred and fourteen steps to the top of the pyramid, but rode in his litter carried by four men. Cortés insisted on walking, and Malintzin walked and all the captains huffed and puffed their way up. Catching their breath at the top, they could see the three causeways leading into the city, the road from Iztapalapa, the road to Tacuba, and the road from Tepeaquilla. They could see the fresh water which came from the Hill of Grasshoppers, Chapultepec, in the aqueducts. There were many canoes on Lake Texcoco, and the shores were lined with thatched-roofed houses. It was a market day and a big square was filling up with many people. Cortés declared that Tenochtitlán was more magnificent than Constantinople and Rome. London, Madrid, and Paris could not compare. And in the twin pyramids, the one they were standing on, the one dedicated to Huitzilopochtli, surely the tallest building in the world, right there Cortés wanted to build chapels in admiration of Mother Mary and set up crosses and little statues. Father Olmedo cautioned that it might be a good idea to wait a few days before broaching the topic with Moctezuma.

Then they were taken into a room inside with two altars. One had the figure of Huitzilopochtli, the god of war, made of paste and seeds and stuck with precious stones and pearls and circled with snakes made of gold. Around his thick neck was a jeweled necklace dangling with carvings of faces and hearts. Next to him was the god of the underworld, Tezcatlipoca. Before him, in a brazier, a fresh new heart moldered. The walls of that room were black with spattered blood, and there was one bright red new stain. Despite the copal incense burning all the time, the place smelled of recent slaughter. At the bottom of the great cu, as the tallest pyramid was called, there was a large kitchen area with blocks for chopping the limbs off the sacrificed men, which were served in a celebratory feast to the warriors who had captured them.

Moctezuma had a confession to make, he told Malintzin to tell her master. It was a little joke. The truth of the matter was that they could not watch the sacrifice of Jaguar Claw. It had occurred already. That very morning, as the sun rose, Jaguar Claw had been granted his unusual request. He had his heart cut out. Moctezuma pointed to the brazier.

"His."

Malintzin wanted to vomit.

"Your friend Jaguar Claw is already with the sun. Freshly bathed, dressed in great finery, head held high, he was marched with great dignity to his death. The fresh blood you see on the walls, that is his blood. His body, kicked down the one hundred and fourteen stairs, is being butchered as we stand. You will soon see his head on our rack."

Not only that, but Cortés was offered one of Jaguar Claw's thighs for the evening meal. Cortés declined politely. The Spanish were tired, he explained, the day hot, perhaps, Quetzalcoatl-Cortés suggested delicately, they could postpone their trip to the zoo and aviary until the following day.

Chapter 30

Within the city, near the district of temples and palaces, the aviary was a huge cage, except the nets enclosing and draped over the treetops were so high up and of so fine a weave that you were not aware that it was a cage. The imperial gardeners had planted palms from the coast, and in other spots the pine, oak, and alder of the high mountains. Little streams, picturesque waterfalls, piled rocks, and orchid flowers were landscaped into an idyllic tableau. Passionflowers whose nectar was used to induce calm in the agitated were artfully arranged to delight the eye. One pathway through the aviary was lined and overhung with clusters of angel's-trumpet trees. Another pathway, bordered with sage, led out to a vast savanna of grass and a small lake. The birds of prey were kept separate from the other birds, but otherwise each kind lived in its particular habitat. A lone eagle and its prickly pear bush, the symbol of the empire, had a pond and an island with a miniature model of Tenochtitlán of its own.

No other collection of birds gathered under the sun could rival the emperor's aviary, and scribes in the emperor's court had catalogued them all. There were parrots, macaws, toucans with thick, heavy bills, small green parakeets, hummingbirds, their tiny wings beating faster than the eye could count, neat brown finches and red warblers, and birds that did not fly much but ran in mincing or hopping strides, and swifts that kept their mouths open catching flies in mid-flight. There were birds which were indistinguishable from the foliage until they darted out. A black bird of modest size had a red bulge puffed out beneath its beak. There were mockingbirds, birds with yellow breasts and some with white patches on their heads. There were birds with white eyes, keeled tails, and crescents of white. There were cinnamon-colored sparrows, speckled birds, yellow-bellied birds with streaks of dramatic purple, and other birds with gray feathers, blue bottoms, ruffle-textured, sleek, peaked, blackbirds, and tanagers, and quail of all sorts. The collection included owls, buntings and magpies, wrens, pink flamingos, puffbirds, birds of turquoise color, some with patches of magenta, birds with red-and-blue-dotted fans on top of their heads, herons, pelicans, cormorants, seagulls, men-o'-war, kites and falcons, hawks, vultures, woodpeckers, and the very prized rare quetzal with its long green tail feathers, flat head, and red breast.

Malintzin should have taken great pleasure in their songs—the rough cawing, gentle cooing, the noisy croaking, cheerful chirping, chattering, gurgles, ripples of notes, melodies resembling those played on wooden flutes, choruses of chirps, scolds and gossips, twitters and trills. But the barrage of color and cacophonous sound assaulted her ragged senses. She closed her eyes and put her hands over her ears. The aviary made her sick.

Adu, separating himself from the captains, stepped up next to her. She jumped.

"I did not mean to scare you, Malintzin." He handed her two little pieces of cloth to put in her ears. She mouthed "gracias" and turned away. This was the official tour, their guide a courtier who specialized in birds.

"Are you tired, Miss Malintzin?" Adu asked.

"A little." She was exhausted, and only there because it was required of her. She would go back and tell Cortés all about it. He was spending the afternoon exploring the guest palace for secret rooms, hidden hoards of treasure.

"Come with me, Malintzin," Adu said. "Let me see you back to your hut."

Outside the netting, back on the streets and canals of the city, she did feel better.

"I can find my own way back, Adu." They had passed the district of temples and palaces parallel to the Tacuba causeway and were going around the marketplace.

"I would like to walk beside you, Malintzin. Would you let me walk beside you?"

When she looked up at the sun, now almost directly overhead, she imagined Jaguar Claw basking in its rays. He had taunted her, made her miserable most of the time, could have killed her, wanted to kill her, but all that seemed a minor annoyance in light of his limbs being eaten by priests, his torso fed to snakes in the zoo, and his head, the twisted upper lip open above his teeth, displayed on the terraced racks of the dead. She could not help reflecting that at one time Jaguar Claw had been a baby boy in some mother's arms, his face as innocent as a flower.

Then what happened to him? Were there too many babies? Had he been kicked as he crawled about, left to eat with the dogs, snatching what he could? When he took his first steps, was there anybody clapping? Did he acquire language only by furtive observation?

Malintzin softened her regrets with the idea that in some mysterious way death released Jaguar Claw from his misery. But in her heart of hearts, she doubted that the sun god had welcomed him as Jaguar Claw had anticipated, or that the sacrificed Jesus stood waiting with open arms, as Francisco portrayed the afterlife, or that Jesus's old father let Jaguar Claw sit on his right hand. An ordinary dead Mexica had to journey four years to Mictlán, find his way through fields strewn with obsidian knives, over mountains that moved, and across a raging river. But if Malintzin were to choose an afterlife for Jaguar Claw, she would have him resting in the eternal embrace of a mother who loved unconditionally and did not betray him.

"Are you well, Malintzin?" Adu asked gently.

"Well enough."

"You do not look well."

Two days in Tenochtitlán were like two months, and the odyssey from the coast to the city taking those many months seemed to have passed as one night's dream. For once she had no recourse, no possibility of rescue. Thrown back to her days as an auianime, she submitted to Cortés in silence, indeed was roped to him. So that night when Jaguar Claw appeared, knife in hand, why had she not just closed her eyes and let it happen? Just let him kill Cortés. Because, she told herself, Jaguar Claw would either have killed her as well or left her alive to be accused of the murder. In self-defense then? Perhaps. Was the deeper truth that she could not let Jaguar Claw kill Cortés? She did not think so. It could have been anybody beneath the Jaguar Claw's knife, she believed, and she would have raised her hand. One acted, then thought.

"YOU SAVED MY LIFE, Doña Marina," she heard Cortés say again as she and Adu walked to her room.

"We will become invisible, Malin*tzin*," Jaguar Claw had warned.

"I owe you my life, Doña Marina."

"Our books will be burned, Malin*tzin*."

"I am your fate, Doña Marina."

"Grant one favor, Malin*tzin*, have them sacrifice me as a captive warrior."

"Isla, would you see Doña Marina back to her room? We do not want any harm to come to her."

"We certainly do not, Comandante."

MALINTZIN LOOKED UPON the first night in Tenochtitlán as if she had fallen down a flight of stairs. Not the temple stairs, but some leading to the bottom of a deep well. She sank. She remembered Isla's cape lined in red brocade, how it billowed out behind him like the wings of a bird of prey, and how his light steps skimmed the earth like a demon ghost. His coyote teeth on either side of his mouth gleamed like sharpened daggers.

"Will the proud miss be all right all alone in the dark of the night in a foreign city?" Isla had asked in his snaky, sneaky voice.

"I will be fine." A fat white rat skittered against the wall of her room, pricked up its pink nose, and sniffed the air. Was it the soul of Francisco? The moon, full that night, mottled with gray splotches, entered her doorway like an uninvited guest.

"Thank you, Isla, for accompanying me."

"Are you certain, Miss Marina?"

"I am certain." Her doorway did not have a door, but she turned her back to him. He literally jumped on her and pushed her to the ground. Then he dragged her up against the wall.

"Not so fast, you little whore." His sharp knee parted her legs like a knife. He held her wrists down, pressed his full weight against her, then jammed into her so hard that her teeth chattered and she bit her lip.

"Dios mío, ayúdame," she cried out as searing pains sliced her from her groin to her navel.

"Shut up or I will kill you," Isla hissed through his teeth. "I will kill you if anybody hears, and I will kill you if you tell anyone."

Those words were an echo, not in Spanish but in Nahuatl—kill, kill you, kill her—an echo of a memory so distant, so frightening, that only its hem showed, the lift of its hem, the legs walking out of the room. The next night Isla used his hand with the long nail as if he wanted to scrape her clean of her female parts.

"YOU ARE NOT walking in your usual manner, Malintzin," Adu said.

"Adu, do not trouble yourself. I am fine." The marketplace the two had to go around on the way back to her quarters from the aviary was the most lavish marketplace anybody had ever seen. It was declared, by Bernal Díaz, a wonder of the world. Of most interest to the Spanish were the stalls where gold and silver were traded. Alongside the gold and silver were precious gems. Bernal Díaz noted emeralds as well as turquoise, rubies as well as coral, opals, pearls, amber ranging from dark brown to the translucent pale yellow, purple amethysts, red garnets. And next to the gems and gold was where the unfortunates were sold. Gathered from all over the empire, they were able-bodied young men, the ones who, having no property or means, sold themselves, and young women whose families could not marry or support them. Children and old people without family were for sale also. Some

were victims of war, and some were snatched and stolen. Some of
them were fated to be sacrificed. All were wretched.

"Slaves," Adu said to Malintzin.

"Like us."

"Do not be disheartened, Malintzin, our condition will change
with the conquest."

"So you are eager to become a slave owner yourself, Adu?"

"You say such sad things. Is it because Jaguar Claw died?"

"We are conquered already, Adu, and will remain conquered."

"You talk like Jaguar Claw, Malintzin. I advise you to be wise in
what you say. Quintaval is dead, now Jaguar Claw, and Brother Francisco may have died of his words too."

"Francisco's words were not poison, he did not have to eat them,
Adu."

"He had to live up to his words, Malintzin. He had to *be* his
words, and he could not live and be his words, so he had to die." Adu
had the long legs and stride of a young man in full vigor, but he slackened his pace to accommodate Malintzin.

"If I had my horse with me, I could give you a ride."

Since Francisco had disappeared and no longer needed a mount,
Adu rode on the horse Cortés had given him. All the horses except for
Alvarado's had been taken out of the island city proper to Coyoacán,
the region of the coyotes, where there was lots of grass and open sky.
Alvarado slept out there under horse legs, the smell of horse all around
him, the sounds horse sounds, and he had happy, horsey dreams. In
the city, crowds of people bumped up against him, and Alvarado hated
that, and they put their hands on his shoulders, and the prostitutes
called out to him, Cuaacualtzin, cuaacualtzin. Pretty, pretty.

"I like small markets, not big ones," Malintzin said.

"I too like the smaller markets, Malintzin," Adu answered.

Not so the captains. Bernal Díaz duly noted:

The Biggest Marketplace in the World
with the Most Gold.

Cortés had already casually inquired of Moctezuma through Malintzin about the bounteous supply of gold. Just curious was all. In truth, he was amazed that gold was not used as money or medicine in Moctezuma's empire. In his country, he told the Aztec, gold warmed the heart. Some people, he explained, were sick over the lack of it. Moctezuma had never heard of gold sickness and wondered that any kind of sickness should befall gods and their entourages. Flowers were what Moctezuma liked best.

Tenochtitlán was a city of flowers. Ordinary hut dwellers grew red and pink geraniums in clay pots outside their doorways. Some houses had roof gardens full of flowers in containers and hanging from poles. Outside the city center, at a meeting of the canals, a region called Xochimilco, there were the floating flower gardens. Originally the Aztecs planted vegetables there on woven-mat islands, gradually filled in an island, and made their city.

"You are limping, are you not, Malintzin?"

"My feet," she said, "hurt." She looked at him. A smile would have been too much, but she made her eyes meet his. "Do you have flowers where you come from?" Malintzin privately listed Adu as one of the men she could tolerate, and of those things in the world which gave her hope, like snow, flowers, tamales, the songs of the flute. Could she live on those things alone?

"We have flowers, yes, but they grow on their own; we do not cultivate them for their beauty. Of course, they are beautiful in any state."

They passed the temple with the skull rack. Malintzin did not look. They circumvented the palaces and went down a narrow street with a small canal in the middle. Even here, there were flowers in pots, and flowers bordered tiny plots of land used for a few tomato plants, a squash vine. Some people had their own turkeys and little dogs. But in the early afternoon it was quiet, and cool in the shadow of the houses.

"Here we are," she said. "Home." It was an ordinary dwelling of thick mud walls, a mat, a hearth, really everything she needed.

"What do you hope will happen after everything, Malintzin?" Adu asked. "¿Qué esperaría que pasará después de todo?"

She was surprised to hear that word, "hope," esperanza, not what will happen? ¿Qué irá a pasar?"

"I hope no killing, Adu. No slavery. Enough food. I hope that for everybody."

"Yes, I too. Do you wish me to stay with you, Malintzin, for the afternoon?"

THERE WERE THREE sources for the gold, Moctezuma had replied finally to Cortés's curiosity the evening before, after another fine meal. The three large gold mines of the empire were in the barbarous south where there were tribes of people who ran naked, ate their meat raw, consumed babies, had no writing, and were completely unaware of civilized behavior. These areas were not well known, and if Quetzalcoatl-Cortés wanted to locate them, Moctezuma would have to send guides to show him. It would take some time, Moctezuma cautioned, and involve a long trek not only through the habitat of barbarians, but through the lands of the elusive jaguars. Furthermore, Moctezuma confided, somewhere in the dense jungle there was a tribe of women who lived independently of men, if Quetzalcoatl-Cortés could imagine such a monstrous rejection of the gods and nature.

Cortés had answered Moctezuma that he knew of such women for they were famous in all the world and also in the sky domain of the gods. In light of such knowledge, Cortés could well understand that Moctezuma would not want to divert men best utilized in the capital to serve as guides, but he could also appreciate his proud eagerness to show his empire in its full glory. The good lived alongside the bad, Cortés repeated, haste does not necessarily make waste, he went on to affirm, so why not start on the expedition to visit the mines as soon as possible? He could dispatch some troops immediately if, of course, that would be in accord with Moctezuma. There was nothing, Moctezuma replied, he would not do for his honored guests. Cortés promised that along the way his men would find that tribe of women and root out every last one of them. Moctezuma thanked his good god friend Quetzalcoatl for his generosity, but he would like the ladies brought back alive as captives, for what a spectacle it would be for his people to see their hearts cut out. "Not *your* heart, daughter," Moctezuma assured Malintzin, who had translated the whole conversation.

NOW, IN THE afternoon of the next day, Cortés, knowing that Malintzin would be back from the aviary, asked Botello to fetch her from her little house to report on the aviary.

"She is indisposed," Botello told him. He had seen Adu go into her hut.

"Indisposed? Who does she think she is?"

"It is a woman's malady," Botello elucidated. "She needs to rest for some days."

"First Cuy, and now Doña Marina. Thank God I am a man."

MALINTZIN SAID IT would be all right for Oduduwa-Adu to stay with her for a little while, maybe for the afternoon. But first he had to take off his shoes, his huaraches. She said she wanted him to lie beside her, but with his feet at her head and her head at his feet. They must not touch. Not even their clothes could touch. Side by side but not touching, his feet at her head, her head at his feet, not touching. Yet she found herself clutching Adu's ankles, crying into his long beautiful feet.

Chapter 31

Isla was the one who thought of kidnapping Moctezuma.

"Then what?" Botello wanted to know. They had been in Tenochtitlán only a few weeks, and Botello had just met a nice woman and settled in with her in the Xochimilco region near the floating gardens. As far as he was concerned, he had found not only his place in Mexico, but, dare he say it, the love of his life, Cipactli. She was born in the month of crocodile. The captains called her the crocodile woman.

"With their leader rendered ineffectual," Isla continued, "the Mexica will have difficulty uniting, and if we threaten to kill their emperor, they will surrender. Not only could we get a king's ransom for him— all the nobles pooling their necklaces, bracelets, lip plugs, and earrings to have him returned safely—but we would be in a position to collect the tribute from the conquered city-states, all the wealth that flows into the capital."

"Kidnap the emperor with the army of the empire surrounding us?" Aguilar was weary of conquest. He had done his part. It was time to go home. "What time is it, Núñez?"

"It is ten o'clock in the morning, Señor Aguilar." Núñez was looking pale, drawn. Botello had been called to see Cuy twice.

"No, no, you are wrong, Aguilar. It is not a bad idea," Cortés mused. "We can hold him in trust, so to speak, and collect the tribute for him. Then later we will ransom him if need be. He is a demigod or something. I am certain they want no harm to come to him."

"You are the only god around here, Cortés," Bernal Díaz said not at all sarcastically.

"Exactly what I said, the man taken is only the emperor. Nobody can quarrel with that." Isla inspected his hands. His long fingernail had been broken, but he was growing it back.

"I would feel very strange about such an escapade, Cortés. Far better to attack them from the outside and make a run for it if we have to." Alvarado hated meetings and longed to be attending to uncomplicated tasks. Grooming, mucking, feeding, exercising.

"Alvarado, how can we besiege a city with only three causeways leading to it and an army standing within it?" Isla, initially reticent on the trip, had gained confidence since the execution of Quintaval, and here in Tenochtitlán he considered himself second-in-command, no questions asked. He strutted around the city like a prize peacock.

"Water is the key," Núñez said. He did not know why he said it, except that it was self-evident. He did not want war. He wanted to stay in Tenochtitlán. They had the best midwives in the empire there, and the most sanitary conditions.

"They are surrounded by water, Nuñez," Isla countered as if Núñez were soft in the head and understood nothing.

"What I mean is if there is a siege, water will be in short supply. We cannot drink the water of the lake, it is too salty, too brackish. They only have one water source, and it is Chapultepec. If the water supply is cut off, the city has to surrender." If the Aztecs quickly surrendered—and he knew they would, such a polite, gracious people—there would be an end to tension and distrust. People could get on with their lives. The only difference would be that Cortés would be emperor and his captains the nobles. Núñez remembered ancient Masada, how that fortress on the bare plateau was besieged by the Romans, and how, rather than be taken as slaves, the Jews killed themselves, mothers killing their children, husbands their wives and each other, until only one was left to tell the story. It would never be like that in Tenochtitlán. It could even be that the Tenochtitláns would be relieved to see a change of hands, and it could be done with a gentleman's handshake. What he wanted to do was to try his hand at corn, beans, have a few turkeys. It was impossible for him to own land in Europe.

Isla leaned forward and whispered something in Cortés's ear.

"Yes, yes, I know." Cortés nodded his head. Yet in all fairness, the expedition had benefited from Núñez's maps and construction plans. Núñez had piloted Cortés's ship. He was a very good carpenter. It was clear that he identified with the conquest because the man had no place to live. To go back to Spain or even Cuba or Hispaniola would risk being arrested by officers of the Inquisition. There was no better reason to promote the general well-being, Cortés believed, than individual interest, the need to survive.

"Exactly how will we kidnap the emperor?" Cortés kept his voice muted. This captains' meeting took place in the aviary in a picturesque spot resembling, to Aguilar's mind, a Greek amphitheater with rows of pristine white stone seats, a line of ceiba trees of great age behind them.

"We would not call it kidnapping," Isla said. "We simply extend an invitation." Isla thoughtfully rubbed his hands together. "These people are ruled by good manners, protocol, decorum. Their behavior is restrained, circumspect. Why not take advantage of it?"

Father Olmedo looked at Isla carefully. Like Moctezuma, the Spaniard had relatively little body hair. His "beard" was sparse, his mustache like that of a boy barely into manhood. His head of hair he combed straight back and it always appeared wetly plastered to his head. Father Olmedo thought Isla applied some kind of polish or grease. Nobody had yet seen him at toilet. Could he be tattooed, part of a mysterious sect related to the devil?

"We will give Moctezuma an invitation in all courtesy," Isla continued. "Our home is his home, our palace his, please call upon us in our quarters for a quiet dinner among friends. Your attendants are welcome, but it is really your own gracious company we seek, an intimate get-together. Candlelight."

"We can tell him," Cortés picked up, well pleased at the idea, "that he can run things as before, and it will seem that way, direction emanating from Axayácatl's, his father's, palace, and we the power behind the throne."

SINCE NÚÑEZ WAS at a captains' meeting, Malintzin got to visit Cuy in her room, actually Núñez's room in the guest palace.

"I have to tell you something," Cuy said to her friend.

"I know what you have to tell me, and why am I the last to know?" Malintzin knelt beside Cuy's mat.

"Is it not wonderful, Maax?" Cuy hardly left her mat these days. She already looked enormous.

"No, it is not wonderful. How could you be so selfish at a time like this? You have no mother to help you. You have nothing."

"I have Núñez."

"What can he do?"

"We are going to be married. We are a family."

Malintzin shook her head and mocked Cuy's voice. "He is going to marry me. He is going to help me, love me, take care of me." She shivered and hugged herself. "How foolish you are, Cuy."

Cuy, who had been rubbing aloe and cocoa butter across her fat little belly when Malintzin came into her room, stopped. "Just because Cortés does not want to marry you."

"I do not want to marry *him*. How is your leg? Is it fully recovered?"

"Yes." Cuy lifted her leg from the mat. Malintzin could see the place where the arrow had gone in and come out. The little wound was puckered like a mouth. "Any suspicions?"

"Yes."

"I too."

"Listen, Maax, Núñez and I are going to have a little piece of land, nothing bigger than what we can farm ourselves, grow maize, raise turkeys, a few vegetables, you know, afterward."

"Everybody and their little piece of land. I am tired of hearing about it. And you say 'afterward'? After what? A war that destroys everything?" Jaguar Claw once said that Cortés was a spider weaving a web, and that one by one the flies would be eaten. Now that Jaguar Claw was dead, his words had the weight of prophecy.

"You do not understand, Maax, because you do not love Cortés anymore."

Malintzin looked about. Cuy's bed was composed of several mats laid out adjacent to each other; cloth dyed in various tones of blue acquired at the market were hung from the doorway like a curtain, and bark paintings of birds and butterflies were set against the white walls. Some thinner gauzelike cloth was draped overhead as protection against mosquitoes. Cuy, the little bird, had made herself a nest.

"Why did you ever love him?"

"Because he made me feel alive." It hardly seemed sufficient reason now, but at the time it had been all the reason she needed. Before Cortés, she felt she was living in a muzzy, unclear world; it was like being at the bottom of a lake filled with algae. Cortés meant she came to the surface and breathed air. "He said he was going to set me free, but he already started to set me free."

"That is not why, Maax. I know why. You loved him because you are an orphan and you were looking for somebody to take care of you. What is a woman without a man, Maax? Can we live on our own?"

"*Your* answer, orphan girl, Cuy, was to become the mother of your own child?" Cuy's brain as well as her belly seemed to be growing. From somebody who had cried to leave her slave mistress, she had become somebody who thought on her own.

"I was fortunate in the father."

"You were."

"Did you feel like you were dead when you found out Cortés was married?"

"You think that I only care for myself?"

"Yes. How did you stop loving Cortés?" Cuy drew herself up, eager to hear.

Malintzin let herself fall back on her hands. "I stopped," she said slowly, trying to find her way by talking about it, "I stopped because he killed too many people during the day, however he could make me feel at night." She looked closely at her friend's pinched little face, straight shiny hair, and slanted eyes. "One day I woke up and realized he was a bad man, and that made me feel terrible. Maybe Francisco showed me a better way to become free."

"Isla is a worse man."

"I agree," Malintzin said.

"And Cortés is not all bad, Maax. He is very kind to Núñez. He is good to Alvarado no matter what he does. He does not ask his men to risk what he himself does not risk. Quintaval was a meddlesome fool and would have split the troops."

"The Tlaxcalas' hands, Cuy?"

"We were at war with the Tlaxcalas."

"The Cholulas?"

"For all their veneration of Quetzalcoatl, they were going to kill us. And Jaguar Claw was a menace to everybody."

"Cortés goes beyond war."

"What is beyond war? Kill or be killed, Maax, is that not the point?"

"Nobody went over to his country to make war and conquer it for their own."

"Our boats are not that big."

"You have gotten hard, Cuy. By pleading Cortés's case you condemn us all."

"You may have opened your eyes, Maax, but I, I use spectacles."

"Like Núñez?"

"If only Francisco had spectacles."

"Francisco was a free man, Cuy."

"Francisco was not free." Cuy propped herself up on her elbows. "Francisco could not live in the world his god had made. Far better to believe in gods who exact tribute, cruel gods in a cruel world. Far better to have reason for suffering than not know why you are suffering and expect somebody else to do it for you."

"I do not like to hear anything against Francisco. You have to leave me somebody, Cuy, to admire."

"I know." Cuy put out her hand and took her friend's. "I feel so sorry too."

They were both ready to cry for Francisco they missed him so much. Cuy, her older friend, the one who had taught Malintzin the ways of a woman, was now twenty-five years old by the Christian calendar, but she looked older, as if her life were more than half over.

"What I do not understand," Maax said, "is how Moctezuma is letting the Spanish stay as royal guests, is host to the very people who are going to take over his kingdom."

"He believes what is written, Maax."

"If I could write, I would write Malintzin is a god, fall down and obey her. But I know this. Moctezuma wants to believe what is written because the defeat has already happened in his mind. I can see it in his eyes. The people believe what the emperor believes because they are afraid or too lazy to believe anything else."

"You are not afraid, Maax?"

"I am."

"If there is to be a real war, which Núñez does not think there will be, our farm will be far away in Coyoacán, and you can come too."

"The land of the coyotes?"

"Núñez has a musket."

"Coyoacán is too close. Everybody would know where you were. They would find you out, hunt you down."

"Who would? One more stooped pregnant Indian woman, Maax, crossing the bridge at market time going out to the fields? Nobody would notice that."

"And Núñez? A white man?"

"Alvarado goes to Coyoacán regularly. He wants to start a horse farm there."

"The coyotes will eat up those precious horses. And the war will spread, Cuy. Xochimilco, Cuernavaca, Tacuba, Tlaxcala, Xocotlan, all of them will be in the war."

"SO IF WE invite Moctezuma to our quarters," Alvarado was saying to the captains, "why would he want to come here for dinner?"

"Have we not just gone through that?" Bernal Díaz thumbed back through his pages and, using his dirty finger to find the exact source, quoted:

Hospitality, gestures of goodwill among friends and guests, are paramount to the Aztec sense of propriety. Everything is done by the book, according to law and precedent.

"Where is Doña Marina, by the way?" Cortés asked.

"What I wonder, Capitán General," Isla put in, "is why nobody else around here has bothered to learn Nahuatl. Everybody is replaceable."

"She has done much more than translate," Aguilar said. "She has interpreted a whole culture, made it possible for us to be on an equal footing with caciques, with the emperor."

"If she can learn Spanish, certainly any man can learn Nahuatl, I am certain of that." Isla believed that he could accomplish anything if he turned his hand to it. As for the language, well, he simply did not have the time, engrossed as he was with empire-grabbing.

"I have learned a few words," Bernal Díaz said.

"Enough to talk to Moctezuma?"

"Not quite enough, Isla, I can say hello and good-bye, but soon I will have mastered their whole vocabulary."

"It cannot be soon enough. Isla has made a good point. The fate of a nation should not hang on a woman."

"Particularly when you get new concubines every day."

Isla had made a joke. Everybody laughed.

BOTELLO FOUND MALINTZIN in Núñez's room, which had become, he observed, similar to a Moor's fanciful tent with hanging cloth and designs, mementos, and a rug of thick woven straw. Next she would require a pet monkey or a parrot for her shoulder.

"I hate to be the messenger, Malinche, for they always bring bad tidings. I would like to be able to say, You are free. We are rich. God has arrived. Paradise awaits you. In fact, Cortés needs you. Come along."

"Botello, I want to ask you something." They were walking through the corridors of the guest palace, passing courtyards and patios, fountains with bubbling water, hibiscus bushes, trumpet vines, and warbling birds.

"Do you think Cuy will be all right?" Malintzin asked.

"Having a baby is the most natural thing in the world." He thought she might ask something else. He was worried about *her*.

"Yes, but in a war?"

"Maybe the Aztecs will surrender. Moctezuma is confused, perhaps a coward and possibly a fraud, definitely weak."

"He has conquered many enemies."

"When he was younger, Malintzin, and there are generals who stay far from the thick of battle. Cortés is unusual in that respect. Moreover, Moctezuma walks in the footsteps of his ancestors and will not deviate from their path. He lacks trust in his intuition and has no ambition. Already at the pinnacle of his society, he is, I must say, a conundrum, a bundle of contradictions." Botello's black curls obscured his eyes, and he always walked with his hands behind his back, his bad leg thrust before him, his shoulders hunched over as if his concerns were heavy, not related to the simple things everybody else worried about. He dwelled, Malintzin thought, not in a celestial realm like the one Francisco had talked about, but in something rooted in the dark earth, mysterious and old.

"You needed me?" Malintzin said archly when she saw Cortés and the huddle of captains in the aviary, some seated on the steps, others pacing up and down. Isla looked at the ground and shuffled his feet. She muttered a curse in his direction.

"What, what did you say?" Cortés asked.

"Oh, just something in Nahuatl."

"Yes, Doña Marina, this is what we have in mind. We are going to invite Moctezuma to visit our quarters, to partake of a little food in our company. It is only proper that he be our guest. We want you to propose this to him in the most polite terms, and very casually too. Perhaps you can comb your hair, put on your best skirt, make yourself suitable. You look terrible, by the way."

"This huipilli is not good enough?"

"Doña Marina, my dear, let us be pleasant and amiable to each other. I could not help it that Moctezuma gave me his daughter or niece or whoever she is, and it would hardly do to ignore her. She is a princess. Go back, change, make yourself pretty, if you please."

Señor Ciempés, Mister Centipede, a leg in everybody's business, but blind to the truth. She put on a clean cueitl with red threads and her huipilli with embroidered flowers. She put on her shell necklaces and combed her hair out, fluffing it up with her fingers. She picked up a stick of coal, outlined her eyes, rubbed berry juice on her lips and cochineal on her cheeks, and, sighing with the bother of it all, checked in her obsidian mirror to see if she was presentable enough.

"You look like a whore," Cortés said when she came out to meet the group on the way to inviting the emperor.

"That is what I am," she said.

"Do not be that way, Malintzin."

"What way?"

"I saved your life."

"I saved yours."

"Because I am showing favor to Moctezuma's daughter does not mean I do not care for you. It is my duty to oblige our host. I know and respect how jealous you are."

"I am not." She had not even been aware of Cortés's current interest.

"You are jealous."

When he said that, she could barely remember the pain she had felt at every new woman he looked at, yet even as recently as the night Isla had so kindly informed her that Cortés was married, she felt stricken. She was a little girl then. She was no longer interested. He annoyed her.

Aguilar cleared his throat. "Calma, calma. Let us invite Moctezuma for dinner and be done with it."

Ushered into Moctezuma's presence, she took off her sandals and kept her head down. He was sitting alone, playing a melancholy melody on his flute. He looked up at them.

"Yes, little daughter." Moctezuma sat cross-legged in a room of his palace, on the floor, his hair loose and long, a simple band holding it away from his face.

"Quetzalcoatl named all things," he said. "The mountains, all the forests, and caused the maize and cocoa to grow. In the time before the first man, Quetzalcoatl assembled bones from the underworld, infused his own blood in them, and taught his creation the arts of music and dance, weaving, crafts, the calendar, prayer, how to cultivate. As a man-god, he established the first city of our people, our land, the holy city of Tula, the capital of Tollon. He looked into a magic mirror, saw that he was old and ugly, was enticed to drink pulque, and sinned with his sister. A famine came upon the land, foreign invaders came from the east and the north. He was defeated. He went on a pilgrimage of atonement through the country, and finally, on the edge of the Eastern Sea, believing himself still impure, he put on a turquoise mask and a robe of feathers and made off on a raft made of snakes. Out in the sea he burst into flames and became the brightest star in the night. The date of his fateful return was predicted for Ce Acatl, One Reed, this very year. My heart, young daughter, is burning, smarting as if it had been washed in chili water. The circle has come around. It is the end of days."

His solemn droning and high seriousness grated against her ears. She wanted to say, As your heart is washed in chili water, so is my heart packed in snow. And if Lord Quetzalcoatl was such a noble and heroic man, how can you mistake Cortés for him? Instead, she said:

"Lord Moctezuma, we wish to invite you to our quarters as our guest, you alone, to join us in partaking of a meal, you sitting with us, your humble guests your hosts. We would be honored."

"Ask him when he can come." Cortés and all the captains had trailed behind her.

"We ask you when might be convenient for you."

"When is it convenient for you?"

Malintzin took a deep breath and ventured forth. "Great Moctezuma, you are in grave danger. Cortés is not Quetzalcoatl. He is a foreign invader. If you come to his quarters, you will never leave."

She conveyed these words in one tone as if she were announcing the coming dinner, detailing the menu. She kept urgency out of her enunciation.

"What did she say?" Cortés asked Bernal Díaz, who had bragged that he was learning Nahuatl.

"She said he would be delighted to be received in our quarters."

"Daughter," Moctezuma said, letting his gaze meet hers, an unheard-of privilege, "you warn me of what I know. It is my fate. Quetzalcoatl has been predicted. It is his time. It is my duty to pass the throne to him."

"Is not Huitzilopochtli your god? What does he say to you?" Malintzin never thought she would be invoking the name of the god of war. Moreover, Moctezuma had sacrificed Jaguar Claw among many others. Yet the emperor pitied himself and spoke in ponderous, self-important words. His doom was his country's fate, and it did not seem that he gave a thought to that at all. He was filled with a piteous self-importance.

"Huitzilopochtli is silent, daughter. But it is written that in One Reed the new cycle of the world begins, and we have had all the signs. The past has foretold it."

"What if Cortés is Tzitzimitl, a demon in the disguise of a god, a deception as desperate as the one that deceived Quetzalcoatl?" Malintzin was furious. Did not the emperor know she was telling him these things for his own good? Did he not realize what danger she was risking on his behalf? Was not "what was written" written down by a long-ago scribe, and was a told poem before it was written, and before that a dream, a vision, something so insubstantial it would drift away if not cut in stone and fixed down on paper. Or if "what was written" was an account of something that had happened, could not the teller of the account put in what he wanted? She knew the "history" Bernal Díaz was writing was a glorification of Cortés. Who was speaking for the Aztec, with their emperor less than useless? "The past is a story, Emperor, the past is over."

"The past is now, Malintzin, all times one. The past is prophecy, a map, and if it is a story, it is a story that needs to be told—and heeded."

He had been looking straight ahead, his eyes glazed. Then he turned to her, and for the first time let a snarl come into his voice. "You, you a mere woman, dare to insult and blaspheme the god you serve? You think he is not Quetzalcoatl? Have you ever seen such boldness, such a sense of entitlement, such different ways? He has crossed borders. Only a god could presume so much. Have we not been taught that he, Quetzalcoatl, was a man with a fair face, a man with a beard who would arrive from the Eastern Sea in a headdress similar to the clamped shell? Can we ignore what is so plainly before our eyes? His thunder sticks, the tunnels that shoot balls, the great beasts, the sharpness of their swords that have defeated every city he has moved through, is that not evidence enough? Can you explain it? You serve your master without belief and would betray him without a qualm. May I ask who *you* are? How is it you think you know more than the great scholars of our kingdom?"

"I have traveled with the invaders. I see what they are."

"Through what eyes?"

"My own."

"Our eyes carry our ancestors and all we have been taught. We see with the experience of our people. We see what the gods wish us to see."

"So when is Moctezuma coming for dinner, Doña Marina?" Cortés asked.

"Tell your master, little daughter, I will join him in a meal in his quarters today, this very day."

There was a mad scramble after that, for although the meal was to be served in the guest palace and prepared by Moctezuma's own chefs, the Spanish had to act as hosts and decide who would do what when and where. Alvarado would be the lookout. Isla would jump on Moctezuma. Adu would pin his arms. Aguilar would make short shrift of any attendants. Núñez would tie him up. Cortés would put a knife to his throat. Bernal Díaz would record the event for posterity. But they did not have to take those pains, for Moctezuma walked into the guest palace unguarded, attended only by one courtier, who put up the screen and served the emperor separately. After dinner Moctezuma dismissed his servant and thanked his host for the fine meal, which, of course, he had provided. When Isla grabbed him rudely, he did not resist. He did not have to have his arm twisted. He did not have to be clutched and pummeled, stretched or starved, drowned or burned within an inch of his life. He did not have to be put in chains or tied up. Cortés did not have to put a knife to his throat.

It was so simple. The Mexica emperor, whose capital city in the heart of the country was a wonder of the world, the man who ruled over four hundred cities and was the high priest of thousands of pyramided temples, the man who dictated the state religion and possessed vast tracts of land ranging up and down the coasts, up through the meat of the continent, lands rich with the staff of life, maize, tomatoes, sweet potatoes, tobacco, squash of all varieties, medicinal plants which cured pain and induced holy visions, and flowers so exquisite they brought tears to the eyes, lands bursting with gold and gems, a man who directed a far-flung and trained bureaucracy and a trained workforce which did his bidding—farmed the crops, built the architecture, fashioned the most beautiful objects—this man who was the commander of an army of hundreds of thousands, a man who had overseen the tortuous execution of thousands, this rich man humbly bowed to his fate and almost kissed the feet of his canny captor, Hernán Cortés, the only child of one hidalgo from Medellín, Extremadura, Spain, Cortés, Cuban fortune hunter, Cortés, first Latin lover, ladies'-man-about-town who had a way with people, knew his main chance when he saw it, and was not afraid of anything under the sun.

Moctezuma's courtesy was carried out in an elegant and graceful style. He behaved as if he were residing at his father's palace as a privilege and had merely transferred his court and official functions to a more favored location across the street. Cortés, for his part, assured Moctezuma, as a brother, a fellow man-god, that he could still act as if he were emperor, could continue for all practical purposes to perform his official functions, preside at festivals, meet with tax collectors and merchants, do the everyday governing. All Quetzalcoatl-Cortés asked was a small concession or two, mainly that administrative duties should be carried out under his, Quetzalcoatl-Cortés's, auspices and direction. Moctezuma was permitted his coterie, his wives, his servants, and granted the domestic accommodations of one of his rank; he could play his drum, smoke his pipe, read his precious books. But he could not collect his tribute of gold, silver, and gems for his own gain or that of his ruling elite. There was no immediate need of ransom, and it was better that it was not an overt kidnapping. The country's wealth would go to Spain, Cortés explained carefully to Moctezuma, would go to the biggest emperor of all, and also to his loyal servant, Quetzalcoatl-Cortés, and the land itself, in good time, would be divided, transferred, and governed by representatives of Spain—none other than Quetzalcoatl-Cortés and his captains. Only one other little alteration was requested, and that was that the sacrifices would have to be stopped and the heathen idols be replaced by humane crosses. And as soon as the people realized that it was a new era, the real God was to be worshiped throughout the land. Indeed Father Olmedo would begin lessons in the zócalo. As soon as all was set, new priests would be sent for, horses imported, cattle, blacksmiths, masons, carpenters, artisans . . .

"I will do all the hard work, Emperor Moctezuma. You will do the easy things, rule in name and custom until the time comes."

"Until what time, Quetzalcoatl?"

"Tell him, Malintzin, until Nueva España is established according to Christian principles. Tell him until the transfer of power is thoroughly and successfully accomplished, and the gold mines located with the kind help of his guides, and we receive sufficient tribute to make our keeping him alive worthwhile."

"Until the time they decide to kill you," Malintzin said to the emperor, "and then they will kill you."

Truly all Moctezuma had to do was give a signal of some sort to one of his thousands of soldiers and the Spaniards would be vanquished, become a mere faded page in the folding annals of Aztec warfare. But in the days that followed, Cortés and Moctezuma gave the appearance of becoming fast friends, for they were never apart. Small pleasure boats, single-masted sloops with pennants and awnings, were built by the Spanish for sailing on the lake so that the two leaders could go off shooting arrows at tame ducks and other waterfowl. At night the two men gambled at pitch-and-toss, the game the Aztecs called totloque, and like schoolboys, they frequented the pelota ball courts, with their enjoyment heightened by the high stakes of death to the losers. The chummy pair listened to music together, Spanish and Aztec. Pulque flowed like water. Shortly a secret room was found in the guest temple full of treasure. This is more like it, Cortés thought, we are finally getting down to business here. When the search parties returned with information about the location of the empire's gold mines, Núñez was put to work making maps and figuring out efficient mining methods. The Aztecs had merely scooped up silt in gourds, flushed it with water, and picked out the gold nuggets. If one dug deep, Cortés estimated, there was no end to the riches to be found.

Not only that: shortly heaps and gobs of golden objects worth some six hundred thousand pesos arrived in the capital as tribute, and all except the most exquisite jewelry was melted down and stamped. True enough, less food was collected, less cloth, less salt, less tobacco, less cocoa beans, less red beans, but while storehouses were not filled, there was enough to meet the needs of the population for the time being. Also, certain activities were less meticulously attended to. For instance, human waste, which had been carted away in canoes and used for fertilizer and the tanning of hides, was left neglected in the reed-covered outhouses, which smelled so foul they had to be abandoned. Natives quickly picked up the habits of the foreigners. Street sweepers did not bother to sweep—why sweep if you did not have to?—and canals clogged up with refuse—for when one was occupied by a foreign power, why bother? The animals in the zoo were not fed regularly. The big-cats got weak, their teeth fell out and their noses bled. The gardens and the aviary Moctezuma had established with great care fell into gross neglect: the tropical flowers from the coast withered, the numerous and various orchids wilted, and the luna flowers, which only bloomed at night, kept their petals tightly closed all the time. All that depended on the elaborate irrigation system turned brown. Only the cactus survived. Aztec books were burned, for those volumes of folding-out pages made of treated bark, as far as the Spanish were concerned, concerned heathen gods and a history best forgotten. Moreover, Bernal Díaz, who was in charge of literary affairs, considered Aztec writing hardly writing. Less produce, less production, the marketplace was not what it had been. The afternoon siesta started earlier and extended later. And why get up at dawn when there was nothing to do? The city slept in uneasy anticipation of imminent disaster, yet during the day no public mention was made of the fact that their august emperor was being held hostage.

Only when the sun went down were canoes paddled with silent urgency through the floating garbage to nobles' homes, and in emptied warehouses and obscure places far from the center of town young warriors met in secret. They gathered like huddled shadows in Tacuba, Coyoacán, near the swampy marshes of Xochimilco, and at Chapultepec, Hill of Grasshoppers, where the spring waters fed the aqueducts of Tenochtitlán. In subversive whispers, by the light of beeswax candles, an invention of the Spanish, they agreed that Moctezuma's mind was disordered, that he had been fed venomous poison or dazed by the sun or inhabited by the spirits of demons let loose by the earth-disturbing Spanish invasion. Everybody knew about disabling madness when the will was paralyzed and the wits scattered. That was what had happened to Moctezuma, people explained. There were cases of old people who wandered the streets or young men who were confused about their manhood or spirit women who seduced men to their destruction. Emperors were gods, true enough, but also people. Thus each warrior, as he returned to the quarters of his battalion, the common barracks, vowed to do his part in building an army independent of Moctezuma, one which would overthrow the Spanish and, if need be, kill Moctezuma himself.

Moreover, the rains had been slight that year, and in March of the Christian year 1520, coyotes came down from the brown, barren hills hungry for small dogs or babies left unattended. The starved animals crisscrossed the streets and streaked behind along the canals. They hunted fearlessly at the bases of the palaces and neighborhood temples, overran the ball courts, circled the market square, haunted and hunted every neighborhood in the city. Their howls petrified mothers. Fathers ran out of their houses armed with clubs studded with sharp blades made from the stones of the volcanoes. Then, right before dawn, there arose an even more dreadful sound. It was the weeping and wailing of a lone woman. It was, without a doubt, a goddess mourning her lost children, or even, the Spanish believed, the ghost of the woman in Cholula who was looking for her son. My son, my son, where is he?

Chapter 32

Moctezuma, appearing oblivious of the decay of his city, the unraveling of his empire, would begin his day sitting under a lime tree on one of the rooftop gardens of the palace compound. Moctezuma enjoyed sunning himself and sipping drinks made from the nectar of hibiscus flowers flavored with honey. He snacked on crunchy crickets salted and peppered with red chilies. He liked to have Malintzin beside him, not only as an obliging and attractive hand-maiden, but as official listener. Aguilar, who came along, as required by Cortés, had Malintzin translate the words for him, which he then transcribed in a book. Aguilar did not have aspirations along the lines of Bernal Díaz del Castillo, who envisioned that every European man who could read and afford his book, thanks to the new invention, the printing press, would one day be aware of who he was, none other than the brilliant author, Bernal Díaz del Castillo.

Rather Aguilar saw his book, or whatever it was, as being used in the schools the Spanish would set up for the indigenous people. Of course, they would learn the history of Spain in Spanish, and be able to trace the progress of the Christian message across the globe—that first and foremost—but they would also need to know their own history after the destruction of their civilization. He had reconciled himself finally to life among the Mexica as an important person, had a featherbed with a wooden frame made for him, and garnered the best and biggest candles for his bedside table. As minister of education, he would have a printing press brought from Seville, teach the Indians how to compress cotton rag and wash it out into paper, make ink out of local plants, set movable type, bind books and even read them.

Malintzin, too, fell into the routine of Moctezuma's rooftop recitations. Despite his bloodthirsty history, Moctezuma was a gifted storyteller, and while she knew the past was a story, maybe just a story, it was a good one and she believed much of it. Moctezuma's account of the wandering Aztecs, their journeys from their homeland, Aztlán, to the heartland, Tenochtitlán, depicted by footprints in the maps and pictographs, made her feel that there was a larger meaning to her own existence. She was not only from a wandering people seeking a place of safety, but her own quest, a destination free of dread and horror, corresponded to it. However, Tenochtitlán had hardly been her salvation. While Isla's attentions had slackened somewhat, Cortés's had increased. The less she could abide him, the more ardent he became. The more she hated him, the more he loved her. Cuanto más ella lo odia, más el la amó.

"Love me back, God damn you. Díme que me quieres, maldita." Cortés would pump all the harder, trying with his body to push through the wall of her indifference. She could no longer simulate interest. "Love me, damn you. I will not have it. No lo permitiré." He encircled her upper arms with his so tightly they bruised. "You are mine, do you understand? You are my prisoner, my love slave, I will not let you go."

Instead of tying her to him, sometimes he dismissed her. Those times were worse, for just when she thought he no longer would bother her, Isla might be lying in wait for her back at her hut like one of the snakes in the emperor's palace kept in huge broad-bottomed jugs cushioned with feathers. These vipers were fed mother's milk by lactating women.

For the sake of peace and quickness, she acquiesced like a child's doll of corn husks, her skin papery, limbs floppy, and she practiced her old trick of mind-skipping. Like a flat light stone thrown in still water, her thoughts bounced to the place and time when it would be over, although she knew nobody would save her. Nobody knew. And why would they want to know their commander's habits when it might cost them their heads or hands, their place, their meals, and why should they care? Botello had his crocodile woman. Adu, she believed, was occupying himself with the young women who flocked to his side wanting to touch his hair and stroke his unusual skin. He was polite, obliging, and did not take the native women as his due as did the other soldiers. Indeed he was a prize. She averted her eyes when he looked her way, acting as if she had never wept at his feet.

From the roof, sitting with Moctezuma and Aguilar, Malintzin studied the long line of women coming into town balancing baskets of fruit on their heads, leading children by the hand, pulling fat juicy dogs on leashes, and balancing cages of iguanas on poles between their shoulders.

In its heyday, a mere five months before when the Spanish first arrived, the market offered everything available in the empire—beans, chili peppers, tomatoes, amaranth, chia seeds, salt, turkeys, quail, rabbits, hare, deer meat, ducks, maguey honey and honeybee hives, avocados, manioc, wild plums, pumpkin seeds, frogs, newts, bark paper, incense, rubber resin, gums, limes, obsidian blades, lumber, animal skins, copper instruments, tobacco, pottery, pots, plates, bowls, and tubs.

Although supplies were dwindling, the market square was still crowded, and peddlers and food sellers plied their trade in the shade of the great pyramid and the canoes maneuvering between the refuge with bowers of flowers and ears of maize.

Above it all, on the azotea, Moctezuma sat in a chair made of reeds and rushes woven into a half hammock slung on wooden frames. He crossed one leg over the other and recounted his ancient lineage with patient pleasure. Below, in the shade of the wall, a band of beggars camped near a dumping pile.

When the Spanish had first arrived in Tenochtitlán, Cortés was happy to see beggars and prostitutes on the street. A real city, he said, like Seville. Bernal Díaz was gratified to see the slaves in the marketplace bound by collars on a pole, and compared the practice to that of Spanish towns where black slaves from Guinea were sold. Alvarado had said the canals of Tenochtitlán were like those in Venice, and one of the common soldiers said the Mexica market was more impressive than the one he had seen in Constantinople. The comfort of the familiar made the strange more palatable to them all.

"The Olmec, who were called the people of ulli, used the sap of the trees which grow on the coast to make balls, and they were the ones who began the ballgame."

Malintzin still used her little disk of rubber, inserting it before-hand if she had notice, but often Cortés would catch her at odd moments and not give her time. Isla never gave her time.

"The Olmec carved huge faces of their ancestors, and they had a calendar like the Maya, eighteen days to the month, twenty months to the year, the five days of darkness at the end. At that time, we Aztec started to come down from a northern lake city in the north called Aztlán, the land of herons. It was One Flint."

Meanwhile, Cuy's belly was growing. She looked like a turtle, with her legs and arms, small head sticking out awkwardly as if to make inquiry of the world, then retreating. Malintzin remembered her own mother pregnant with her brother, and it seemed to her that her mother had not been particularly tired or demanding. She had gone about her duties in her usual manner. These days Malintzin often thought of her mother, whether she was still alive. Her mother's son must be grown.

"We were guided by our god Huitzilopochtli, Hummingbird. He was a stern god, and we were then an ignorant and uncivilized people. The Otomi called us savages, dog people. Nonetheless, it was a begin-ning, and great things had been predicted for us. We established our first settlement near Tula, the region of Quetzalcoatl, although he had left long ago on the Eastern Sea."

Malintzin was often confused by the various tribes, who was who, and when they were, and which of them were still their own and not merely conquered people of the Aztec. The Maya were an independ-ent people, but their period of greatness was over and many of their great cities were in ruin. When she was taken to Bak in Yucatán and saw the long streams of moss hanging from the trees and monkeys playing in the ruins, grass covering the hallowed halls, she could feel the ghosts. She wondered if Tenochtitlán, whether the Spanish came or not, was doomed to suffer the same fate. Cholula had once been a great religious center commemorating Quetzalcoatl. Chichén Itza was deserted. Teotihuacán had been a holy city and residence of artists. Grass now grew on the Avenue of the Dead, and the inner temples of the Pyramids of the Sun and Moon were used as latrines.

Aguilar, the note taker and listening board, accustomed to sitting on the ground, sat on the rooftop cross-legged. He was letting his hair grow and kept it off his face with a band of cloth, and still tanned, could be mistaken for an Aztec man sporting Spanish clothes. He was cognizant of his shifting identity, did not disdain it, and in secret was fascinated by the story of the Aztláns. He had known before that they traced their ancestry to the Toltecs, who traced their beginnings to the Olmecs. The real Quetzalcoatl, a king of Tula, the Toltec capital, was chased out of his town by his enemies. Places where Quetzalcoatl had rested, slept, or had a meal were recognized by the Aztec people as holy sites along a pilgrimage route. The destroyed Cholula was such a place, and to him it was a mystery that Moctezuma, knowing of the devastation, could think of Cortés as the patron saint of Tenochtitlán.

Furthermore, Quetzalcoatl's headdress, its two shell-like portions clamped to the sides of the head, was actually an old Spanish helmet washed ashore from a trip previous to Cortés's and was put on a memorial statue of Quetzalcoatl as if it had been his very own hat. And another thing—the god Quetzalcoatl was supposedly born of the virgin Chimalman, who swallowed an emerald. Aguilar dared not explore how much that legend reminded him of things he had been taught as a boy and acolyte.

"In our first settlements, we dammed up the river and let the waters cover the plain. These lagoons became marshland and soon filled with rushes and fish, herons and other waterfowl. Our food was whatever we could scavenge—mosquito eggs, which we baked in patties, newt, axolotl, shrimp, frogs, tadpoles, birds, algae, fish. We began to feel proud of ourselves for we were making a settlement. But our god Huitzilopochtli regarded us and our new ways as haughty and disobedient, presumptuous and blasphemous, and he killed our leaders by ripping out their hearts. He commanded the priests to tear up the dam, and thus we were sent on our way through desert country south of Tula and commanded to fight the Otomi people. There we ate mushrooms, wild onions, nuts, yucca, wild honey, berries, mesquite pods."

During those first five months of Spanish occupation in the capital, before the noonday meal Father Olmedo conducted Christian lessons. This was done peripatetic style, as Jesus had imparted wisdom and pithy sayings in tiled courtyards, patios, on the street corners, under trees. Father Olmedo, using large pictures pasted on a series of frames that could be folded out much like Aztec books, spelled out the details of Jesus's life and message. Malintzin, of course, was called upon to interpret.

Jesus, in these pictures, was rendered squat and bowlegged by Father Olmedo's lack of perspective, and his flock, the sheep, were puffy barrels on stick legs. The sheep were an enigma to Mexica. Dogs were tamed and trained, turkeys fenced in, but larger animals—the big cats, the deer—ran wild.

When Jesus made loaves and fishes, he was more familiar, perhaps just a magician, perhaps an evil sorcerer, one who could put a spell on you, creep into your house, and steal your weapons and tools.

Jesus's betrayal Father Olmedo depicted by crude drawings of people whispering behind his back at a large table. Backbiters. Backstabbers. Now *that* the Mexica understood, for who was not betrayed every day in a hundred different ways?

Jesus's crucifixion was an unknown kind of execution, but that he should be executed, or that execution was unjust, was not a foreign concept to the Mexica. Partaking of a god's flesh and blood, however, rather than the god partaking of you, *was* a novel idea. It would be nice not to have to prick and slash your arm and leg, ear and nose, not to pierce your penis, your tongue, not to worry your whole life if you would be the next one to climb the stairs. And that one lived forever without wandering the treacherous terrain of Mictlán was welcome news indeed.

Then one day, as ordinary as the last, at the beginning of another lazy-hazy afternoon, Cortés received a message from Vera Cruz brought by an Aztec runner from one of the men left behind at the fort. Governor Velázquez's men, the letter went, had arrived on shore with something of an armada, eighteen ships, and appeared to be on their way to Tenochtitlán to arrest Cortés and take him back to Cuba in chains, where he would stand trial for rebellion and insurrection.

"They have come for me at last, the scoundrels." For days Cortés had felt out of sorts but not known why. He immediately took the missive to Botello at his new home in Xochimilco.

"If you had warned me, Botello, you lout." Cortés grabbed Botello by the throat of the tilmatli, the Aztec robe he wore now, along with the maxtili, the loincloth, and shook him soundly.

"Danger, Capitán, I did see danger," Botello choked out.

"It is about time you saw something, Botello. It is your job to alert me of developments." Cortés let the poor fellow fall to the earthen floor of his wretched hut.

"Ah." Botello looked up at the dense interweaving of his thatched roof. True enough, he had gotten wind of Cuban boats landing near Vera Cruz through his lady love, the crocodile woman, who as an herb seller in the marketplace, a woman of indefinite age and generous soul, was in touch with everything in the empire. As a matter of fact, everybody on the streets of Tenochtitlán knew that new "winged temples" were on the coast, that more silver-clad warriors on monster deer had disembarked and were in the vicinity of Cempoala. What Botello wondered was why Malintzin had not known, or why, if she knew, she had not told Cortés. He had assumed that Cortés was apprised of every last little thing. Certainly those at the moot court were talking of it.

"So you did see danger, did you?" Cortés did not think that Botello "saw" anything ever, not really, but he had kept him on because his predictions had proved entirely correct. Had he not foretold that the expedition would be a success, that Cortés himself would be fearless in battle? The old gypsy, in his vague and sloppy way, *was* gifted with intuition, showed great sensitivity to currents around him, and could usually be depended on to keep his ear to the ground. Yet why had this perceptive man failed him now when it was most important? Cortés had half a mind to dismiss the ruffian and punish him hard. Since sacrifices had been banned, it was dreary in the capital; a good execution could liven things up.

It was the time of day when Botello usually took a good nap in his hammock. On the move for most of his life, he now wanted to settle down in Xochimilco and prided himself on living on "the lake." I live on the lake, he would tell people. He had struck up curious friendships with others of his ilk—sorcerers, petty thieves, students with meager discipline and great aspirations, musicians, and poets. A few times, through his new friends, he had procured various plants and seeds which induced the most lovely inebriation. Partaking of such sweet herbs in a sweat house of one Xocono, a pulque maker, he had imagined himself in the form of a dove flying higher than the pyramids.

"What do you think I should do, Botello?" Cortés did not want to show desperation, but he was anxious, damn it. How could he conquer Moctezuma's empire and keep the pesky Velázquez at bay at the same time? Two fronts, fore and aft, were a general's nightmare. He decided that if he were to punish Botello, it would be after he proved totally inept and useless. First one thing, then the other. Velázquez, then Moctezuma, then Botello.

"Meet them head-on, mi amigo." Cortés was astrologically a Taurus. Botello thought his captain did look like a bull, with his large head thrust forward, protuberant forehead plowing the way, his broad shoulders a bulwark, narrowing down to a girlish waist, and a gait so bowlegged it looked like his big genitals got in his way.

"Meet them head-on? How so?"

"With baskets of food, pretty ladies."

"Botello."

"Just joking. I mean meet them head-on with soldiers. The Indian allies." Botello knew that Cortés, although wily and clever at court deception, loved nothing better than to be at the forefront of a rampaging horde. Machiavelli might be his mentor, but Genghis Khan was his hero.

"Can you tell if Velázquez himself is leading his men?" Cortés would have liked to personally cut off his patron's head.

Botello rumpled his forehead, put his fingers up to the creases, and adopted the stance of a trance. "I see, I see."

"Botello, just tell me."

"I do not think Velázquez is on this soil. There is a smallpox epidemic in Cuba he has to attend to, and he has sent an able captain in his stead." Botello heard this from his woman, who heard it through a former tax collector who heard it through a merchant who had passed, on his way south, near Vera Cruz and spoke to a cacique who traded tobacco for green glass beads with a member of the party left behind in Vera Cruz. This cacique got wind of the news through a sailor on one of the ships of the expedition against Cortés. Disease in Cuba.

Cortés, who had been standing in Botello's hut the whole time, now looked around. Botello's floor was pressed earth, the walls were earth, and the whole place made him feel like a damn mole. "How can you stand to live here, Botello? It stinks to high heaven."

"I like it well enough." Botello loved his new home. "I am on the lake." It was far better than shivering in some shanty in Seville or diving for coins off some slippery green-slimed dock, or grubbing for crusts of cassava bread in Cuba, or having to walk every day up and down mountains, some snow between your toes or in fear of red-hot lava spewing over you from some volcanoes on the way to Tenochtitlán. His residence was actually the home of the herb seller who had taken a fancy to him. In a swampy fecund region where the human waste was used to fertilize the floating gardens, the hut seemed to have emerged spontaneously out of the muck.

"It is so . . . so . . . damp here." Cortés would not have been surprised to see that Botello's big, splayed feet had taken on the webbing of a duck's. His woman, he had heard, was dark and wrinkled as old parchment, but her body under her robes was as supple as a maid's. Isla had said she was a witch, but Cortés, who knew about such matters, said: Every man to his taste.

"Yes," Botello mused in a cryptic voice. "I can see you will be successful in your venture against Velázquez's men." Botello was looking down into a pot that had been steaming on the hearth in the middle of the room. It was a simple recipe. A bunch of bay leaves, a cake of compressed sunflower seeds, a pinch of salt. You let the leaves boil, rise to the surface of the boiling water, then settle back down. When the seed cake disintegrated and spun about the boiling water like demented fish, you cooled the concoction. Imbibed by the light of the moon, mixed with honey and lime, this brew was good for digestion, coughs, blood circulation, a woman's flower time. It soothed heart and mind and gave one very hard erections.

"Are you absolutely certain I will defeat the lot of them, Botello?"

"On my mother's life." Botello's mother was alive, he believed, somewhere. He had left the caravan when he was a boy of ten, joined a band of footpads, honed his fortune-telling skills, and learned to swim and con a trick. Useful employments.

"Who should I leave in charge when I go to meet the army?"

Here Botello hesitated, stared into the pot again, and scratched his head and his balls. He was chewing all the time on a wad of cocoa leaves like a cow at its cud, a habit picked up from his woman. Cortés did not understand how a man who had been exposed to all the accouterments and niceties of Spanish culture could let himself go like that.

"Isla, I see, is the best one." Any fool could have told Cortés that Isla would be the best commander in absentia. While there were good reasons for not having him around at all, he could keep his composure. Capable and cruel, that was Isla through and through.

"I do not trust Isla."

"You can trust him to do what is best for himself, Don Cortés, which would mean keeping a stern peace in the city until you get back."

"Yes, but—"

"There are some men you cannot trust to do the best things for themselves, and they are the most dangerous, Cortés."

"What do you mean?"

"I mean the kind of man who, in throwing away his own safety, would endanger the lives of others."

"There is nobody like that. Each man seeks his own good."

"We would like to think so, Señor, but some men seek their own ill, and there are also men who, like sheep, follow their leader off a cliff."

"I am not taking anybody to a cliff."

"Did I say that?"

"Well . . ."

"And there are men like the mother pelican who would wound herself to have her chicks feed on her."

"Botello, men are not animals. We are in the image of God."

"And the animals, they are in the image of . . ."

"God imagined them."

"I see . . ." Botello smiled to himself. "And there are, Señor, those who would leave the pack, and those who would lock horns to achieve dominance, and I have heard of birds that lay their eggs in other birds' nests and birds that do not know an intruder when they see one, and . . . I could go on."

"Pray leave off. You make me think the world is a damn zoo."

"In lieu of Isla, I would suggest Aguilar. He is very smart."

"At books, Botello, but in governing? I am going to leave Alvarado in charge."

"Just what I was thinking." Alvarado, to Botello's mind, was the very worst of the lot for commanding. He was volatile and childish, tripped over his own feet, was scared of his own shadow, had topped the commander's lady, and was given to tics and antics unbecoming a gentleman. The man wished he had been born a horse, for God's sake.

"Alvarado in charge, Isla with me, also Bernal Díaz, of course, to keep a record of our victories. I will leave Adu. Núñez can stay because I am a good man and realize he wants to play slave to his slave. Aguilar can stay to impart a feeling of solemnity and respect for God and country. I count on him to maintain a high tone. Would you keep an eye on Doña Marina while I am gone? I will take most of my troops and leave eighty behind."

"Only eighty?"

"Some of the Tlaxcalans."

"I see, and you say keep an eye on Malintzin. Exactly in what way are my eyes to be kept on her, my amigo, if I may ask."

"Do not banter in lascivious jest, Botello."

Everybody but Cortés knew that Isla was raping Malintzin every chance he got. Meanwhile Cortés would not give her up. Botello felt that by not saying anything to anybody or intervening, he was contributing to her misery. But what could he do? Be killed by either man for speaking up? The best thing Malintzin could do was run far away. He told her this often.

"Dispatches will be sent regularly to Alvarado. It will not take long to settle the matter once that canalla, that rascal Velázquez, is gotten rid of—I mean, brought to trial under the authority of the emperor Carlos. Botello, let me tell you, my life is not easy." Cortés moved closer to the soothsayer and wagged a finger in his face. "But I do it for the common good. Far better to be a vassal of Emperor Carlos across the seas than subject to a petty tyrant near at hand, is what I think, for the Indians I mean. And for us, far better to have an opportunity for riches, fame, and land of one's own than to serve the needs and obey the commands of a man who is a usurper, for did not Velázquez take over Hispaniola from Columbus's kin and kind? My duty is to make Velázquez's lackey soldiers come to their senses and see the error of their ways in following that false governor, and for them to determine where their best interest lies, as you say, and surely if they are for themselves, they will be for me and our cause here. And which cause, I do not have to tell you, is God, glory, and gold. Gold is in the best interest of all good men. Glory is for the brave in heart and hand. And who can be against God except an infidel or the devil's legions? A skirmish for a show of strength, a manly battle or two, but mostly, dear friend, conversation, negotiation, good fellowship, I mean fellowship around the campfire. War is a game of wits, would you not say?"

"Indeed I would, but consider this—" Botello practically stepped back into the coals of his hearth. "People tend to resent the petty tyrant near at hand more than the vague figure of a faraway king simply because of that very closeness. We cannot endure the imperfect familiar."

"As always, Botello, you talk nonsense, aim to ruffle feathers, fluster the wits, and heat the humors until they boil over. Alvarado will be quite sufficient in command."

PART V

Cortés left for the coast with over two hundred of his men and hundreds of Xocotlans, Tlaxcalans, and Cempoalans to rout out Narváez, Velázquez's henchman lieutenant. He was uncertain of the numbers under the command of Narváez. Eighteen ships could hold a fair sum, but no matter how many, he knew his battle-honed group, his brave conquistadors, would be more than a match for them. From the information he could gather, Narváez's so-called soldiers had marched into Vera Cruz, had a skirmish or two with his men posted there, and were now on their way to Cempoala. Cortés planned to push the lot of them into the sea and burn their dastardly boats so that if they ever wanted to see the shores of Cuba again, they would have to swim. Those that succeeded could cry the tale of woe to their nefarious leader, one Velázquez, greedy, sneaky dog of a snake's whore, in their last living breath.

Alvarado had watched the expedition leave Tenochtitlán with a heavy heart. He did not relish being left in charge; it would change the rhythm of his day, affect his sleep, disturb his stomach, in fact each day would be an ordeal. His temperament was not the commanding sort, which was just what he told Cortés. Cortés had replied that he did not want to pressure the noble Alvarado, far be it for him to make a man do what he did not want to do. But confidentially, just between the two of them, Alvarado was the only one of the captains suitable for the task.

"Thank you, Capitán, I appreciate your confidence in me." Palpitations had already started in Alvarado's heart and were fluttering up his throat. He was surprised he could say a word without choking to death. The real reason he was chosen was because either nobody else would do it or Cortés did not trust anybody else, but why he trusted him, Señor Alvarado, was a mystery he could not fathom. His record was not illustrious to say the least. From the very beginning he had shown himself unreliable—racing his ship to get to the Yucatán coast before the flagship, fumbling through the whole thing with the unfortunate Quintaval, not to mention the little incident with Malinche.

"An opportunity for advancement, Alvarado, is not something an ambitious soldier turns down."

"I do not think I am worthy of such a great honor." And he was not particularly ambitious. At this point he just wanted to get out of it all alive, on horseback.

"How long do you think your mission might take, Comandante?"

"Hardly any time at all, Alvarado. One month. This is May. Give me until mid-June."

Any number of awful things could happen in a month. For this conversation they had been walking around the Templo Mayor and passed the rack of skulls.

"All those people lost their heads," Alvarado said. "Pity them." He noticed Jaguar Claw's newish skull.

"Ugly what they do to each other." Cortés had spoken to Moctezuma at length about having the sacrifices stopped, but Moctezuma assured him that power was kept, order maintained, and all made happy through such rites. Without the sacrifices, without something visible to fear, there would be chaos, revolt, class warfare. Cortés proposed the Christian God as a way to maintain civility, discipline, and the organized hierarchy. Moctezuma could be baptized, be a famous Christian convert. The Aztec emperor had to laugh at that. It has to be the fear of death, Quetzalcoatl-Cortés, you know that, to keep the people obedient. So on the days the conquistadors could hear the drums beating a slow dirge and the high piercing notes of the bone flute, they knew they should not venture from their rooms. Should they do so, they would be met with crowds of spectators, see the great urns set to boil outside the royal butchery, observe the fires blazing on top of the pyramid, the brazier receptacles for the hearts set out, and the long tilmatli, the cloaks, of the priests flaring up behind them, black and stiff with old blood. Then, when all had quieted down again, there would be a fresh trail of new blood from top to bottom and a new head to rot on the rack.

"I am leaving Aguilar and Adu as your trusty bodyguards."

"Adu is a slave," Alvarado protested. And Aguilar, at best, was reluctant; at worst, lazy.

"Adu has won his freedom through his bravery, Alvarado. Aguilar is one of our best minds. And Botello will be here."

"That is a comfort." Botello was a complete fraud as far as Alvarado was concerned, and, worse, could not handle a sword.

"Núñez too."

"The Jew?"

"Not only does Núñez carry the clock, Alvarado, he is our pilot, a carpenter of extraordinary talent, deft in battle, and a wizard at strategy. I would prefer to have such an able man at my side, but have generously left him with you."

"Botello lives in a hut with one of them." Moreover, Núñez in love was Núñez incapacitated. And now, with his woman pregnant, the three would be a drain on resources.

"Botello is at an advantage living in a hut. All the better to keep his ears on the pulse of the nation."

"But you say nothing is going to happen."

"How can anything happen? We have Moctezuma in our complete control. Tell me, Alvarado, nearly six months in this capital, and how many battles have we had? That is right. None. Doña Marina will be at your side for translating. Father Olmedo will be here for spiritual guidance."

"That is a relief." Malinche for translations? Had Cortés utterly forgotten his indiscretions with his mistress? Moreover, Alvarado had heard that she no longer responded to Cortés's attentions. Did that mean she was on the prowl for his, none other than Alvarado's, favor? No more trouble, he vowed.

"There is going to be a big fiesta here, you know. Think of me in the damp, mosquito-infested jungle while you are at the party. It is, I believe, the festival of the green corn."

"Is that when they decapitate young maidens?"

Cortés cleared his throat and kicked some refuse out of the way. The streets were getting as dirty as a European city's.

"My duty is to keep our interests safe, Alvarado, our gold in our own hands—that is, for Emperor Carlos of Spain—whatever that might require. Your duty is to stay, be charming and clever, eat and drink, smile all you can. The Indians think you are related to the sun god, you with your fiery hair are an incarnation of Tonatiuh. They love you, Alvarado, they do. Good heavens, you will be able to sail on the lake in one of our small brigantines, go duck hunting. You and your men will be indulging your every whimsy while yours truly will be in fierce battle against traitorous Cubans led by that son of a whore Narváez. It might rain. There will be mud and flies."

"Yes, as you said, mosquitoes. Do you know Narváez, Capitán?"

"Never laid eyes on the son of a ragpicker."

"Why did not Velázquez himself come to command his troops?"

"Smallpox in Cuba. An excuse for the coward not to challenge me face-to-face. Instead he sends his lackey, Narváez."

They stopped under a coral tree. To their right was a canal. Cortés had a big leaf of tobacco sticking out of his mouth. It had become a habit. In the morning, after the breakfast meal, he would have one of the Indians roll his supply for the day, which he kept in a small wooden box he had had made for him by one of the master craftsmen. One tobacco leaf after the morning meal, one for a morning walk, one after the afternoon meal, one after his siesta, and the one he took with brandy before going to sleep.

"Do you know the thought that still galls me, Alvarado?"

Now it was coming. He was going to castigate him for Malinche, that ill-fated night, which, if one wanted to be precise, had never really occurred since he was not able to bring it to fruition.

"Velázquez cannot accept my superior position here despite the fact that the emperor Charles IV, from all I have heard, looks kindly upon my initiative, my leadership."

"I thought he was Emperor Charles V."

"Fourth or fifth, he approves of gold. Are you surprised?"

When Cortés left for the coast, despite the quick ease with which he spoke of dispatching his enemies, he took with him rather a lot of artillery pieces that Indian bearers had carried for them since Cempoala—the petronels, small cannons, and the muskets and many powder flasks and cartridge boxes in addition to rapiers, parrying daggers, poleaxes, and halberds, hammers and maces, shields of steel with gilding iron, brass, and leather, and many crossbows of steel, wood, and horn. Cortés's favorite crossbow was decorated with ebony, ivory, and mother-of-pearl, patterned in twisted vines and birds in flight, dragons thrusting out their tongues in two curled prongs. He also absolutely had to take his wheel-lock musket, which had scenes in ivory of a walled town, a castle, and several naked round-bellied women dancing a jig. And he wore more than an armored breastplate and helmet, but also an armored skirt and gloves, and his horse was suited with a headpiece with little spiked protrusions in the front. Cortés's pennant, inscribed with the message "Brothers, let us follow the Cross, and by our faith shall we conquer," was carried by Isla. Alvarado thought they looked like Crusaders oft to wrest the Holy Land from the perfidious infidels. This was no doubt to be the battle Cortés had looked forward to all his life.

And despite all of Alvarado's fears, in the first week or two of Cortés's absence all went well, so that Alvarado was inclined to think his commander had been correct in describing the duties of occupation as paltry. The Mexica were preparing for the largest fiesta of the year, the one dedicated to the god Tezcatlipoca. It was the month of Toxcatl, May in the Christian calendar. Tezcatlipoca, otherwise known as Smoking Mirror, was the trickster god, the lord of the night who had tempted Quetzalcoatl with pulque. A god so devious required major appeasement.

Haircuts for the occasion were given in the great square, styled short in the front and left long in the back, and warriors who had distinguished themselves in battle were permitted to cut off all their long locks. The priests wore their hair shaved on the sides and front, with a stiff shock of hair in the middle of their heads. Women bought ointments, axin, or yellow earth for their faces, and stain for their teeth, and had their hair fixed in two loops ending in little horns in front of their heads. Holiday huipilli were brought out from wicker chests. The women who were to dance with soldiers had their cueitls decorated with hearts and a braided pattern. Some wore borders and fringes on their cueitls, and on their huipilli had patterns of fishes.

Flowers flooded the city from the countryside—purple irises, creamy lilies with their fuzzy yellow stamens, wild roses, baby yellow roses, pink cosmos, and bundles of blue lupine. The best feather weavers and jewelry makers from the tribute cities converged on the capital to make wands and headdresses and decorate maxtlatl. All cooking staffs of the upper class were engaged in planning the finest meat dishes—quail and deer and dove, pigeons and partridges, pheasants and wild boar. Sweet potatoes were to be roasted, and white fish prepared with crushed calabash seeds. The salamander axolotl stew was going to be mixed with yellow peppers, maize was to be cooked with pimentos and honey. All iguanas were rounded up, soon to be killed, basted with sage, and roasted on spits. Sea fish, turtles, crabs, and oysters were brought in from the coasts. The air was redolent of copal incense. Former shortages were forgotten, along with any possibility of famine or drought.

During these exciting times, Moctezuma was fitted with a new tilmatli, a blue-green, the royal color only permitted him, a beautifully spun white cotton maxtili, and new cactli with straps crisscrossing up to his knees. Jewels never before seen by the Spanish despite all their searching were brought out. Yet Moctezuma did not seem caught up in the joyous commotion. He was calm, sunned himself on the terrace each day, smoked tobacco, prayed, and continued to tell Malintzin the victorious story of his people.

When Cortés was gone nearly a month, it was the day in the Aztec calendar on which a perfect youth, called Tonatiuh, was sacrificed. He had lived one year like the child of the sun with beautiful virgins seeing to his every need. Fed the most delicious food and taught to play the most melodious tunes on the flute, on the day of his death he was dressed like the god and rowed out to an island on the lake to a small temple, and as he ascended the steps, as was required, he broke and cast down the flutes he had been given for that year. At the top he was sacrificed.

Alvarado chose not to witness this event. Moctezuma, although a prisoner himself, officiated when the youth's heart was cut out, and the legs and arms were brought back to the guest palace and cooked there by the royal cooks, braised first on a spit, kept moist by the continuous application of crushed tomatoes, and then beautifully served with a sauce made with chocolate, vanilla bean, peppers, and piquant spices. Moctezuma offered some to Alvarado, but he was sickened at the thought and indeed appalled by the whole celebration, although Malintzin told him it was a great privilege to taste some of the emperor's portion. In Alvarado's stead, Botello partook, and declared the meat tender and sweet as turkey.

Alvarado had never met the sacrificed youth but had seen him walking through the street, attended by his young ladies, and he had not appeared unhappy. By all accounts, he ascended his last steps in good spirits. Botello, trying to comfort Alvarado, said that he believed the god-man before his death was given a good dose of teonanacatl, the buttons of a cactus plant. The pink flowers of that particular cactus came out in May and could be found on the rocky ledges of mountains and canyons. Botello had gone with the priests to cull their crop.

Throughout the festivities, to culminate in a closing ceremony at the Templo Mayor, Cuy remained happily ensconced in Núñez's room. The best midwives in the city had been contacted through Malintzin and were ready to come at a moment's notice, and all the tools for the birth were assembled—the unused white cotton cloth to be spread on the floor, large pots to be put on the hearth so that the room would be filled with steam, and the little toys which would be given to the newborn, a tiny bow and arrow if it was a boy, a spindle and broom if it was a girl. Botello, with his bag of herbs and barber supplies, was prepared to assist if need be.

After the baby was born, the little family intended to move to Coyoacán. A small house was being built of adobe bricks. The thatch for the roof was to be woven by master craftsmen. The structure was in the shape of a square, the floors stone, not earthen, and like those of the richer Mexica, the house was built around an open courtyard. Although the structure was far from finished, Botello had already planted the perimeters with brilliant red salvia, marigolds, and white daisies with fuzzy brown hearts. Núñez, who was clever at such things, was carving a cradle for the baby. But Malintzin observed these measures with foreboding.

"Cuy, I have said this before. If there is to be a war, you are too close to the city." When Isla and Cortés left, Malintzin could sleep at night without starting at every little sound, but lately she was seeing death in her dreams. Tenochtitlán was razed, the pyramids toppled, the palaces dismantled, all statuary smashed, and the people of the sun brought low with sickness and starvation, their bodies clogging the canals and piled up on the once-beautiful avenues. In her sleep she wandered through the debris, picked up broken masks of clay, the stone of a pyramid, a smoldering brazier with a heart inside, a baby's dress.

"If everybody is to die in the city and near the city, Maax, why are *you* staying?"

Cuy spent mornings lying on her back watching her stomach enlarge, as growing children stay awake during the night trying to catch their legs lengthening.

"You can come to Coyoacán with us."

"We are both grown women now, Cuy. You are starting your family."

"Then flee on your own. This is a good time. Cortés is away. Alvarado could not find his own toes if they were not at the end of his feet."

Malintzin thought of the odyssey of the Aztec, the books Moctezuma permitted her to glance at when they were on the azotea. Little footprints in picture writing showed the long trek from Aztlán, the land of herons, to Tenochtitlán, each stop marked by a man seated with his mantle drawn around him. Conversation was indicated by curlicue clouds emanating from the mouths of the figures. There was something remarkable in that journey to her, walking, stopping, talking, moving on. The founding of the city, Tenochtitlán, the right place according to prophecy, was marked by an eagle on a prickly pear bush, a snake in its mouth. In map pictures, that emblem was at the center of the four directions.

"You are not staying because of Cortés, are you? Because of the habit of Cortés?"

"Because of the habit of my life, Cuy."

The first years of the Aztec settlement on Lake Texcoco, however, had been less than glorious, Moctezuma admitted. The lake was filled with snakes and mud and was completely inhospitable, but the Aztecs, who liked to claim they were relatives of the aristocratic Toltecs, were bound to stay where their god, Huitzilopochtli, designated. So they killed the snakes and ate them roasted on sticks, made floating gardens in the mud, drained enough land to build a great city, went on to conquer others and become the ruling force in the country.

"There are many paths connecting all the villages of the empire, paths well trod by running messengers, traders, and tax collectors," Cuy continued, trying to convince Malintzin.

While the little footprints of the Aztecs' journey were inspiring to look at, delicious to think of, a journey on her part, all alone, would be unthinkable. She imagined shards of sunlight on the dark forest earth glowing like broken gourds slick with water, shade so profound it swallowed you in a shiver, traps of sinking sand, poisonous plants, woman-eating animals. This was the place the runaway mother and her baby had died.

"Who would protect me?"

"Who is protecting you here?"

Malintzin thought it was all too easy for Cuy to give advice. She lay there like a big pumpkin set to pop.

"Think of it as snow, Maax. And you claim Francisco helped you to see differently?"

"Cuy, you are the one who convinced me Francisco was wrong. His people and my people—"

"*Your* people? Who is saying this? Maax, Malinche, Malintzin, Doña Marina? You sound like Jaguar Claw, sacrificed by Mexica for attempting to kill the enemy of Mexica."

"He went to his death proudly."

"Because he did not know better."

"We all have to die of something."

"Maax, you never wanted to die of anything, and particularly not on top of one hundred and fourteen steps with a knife in the heart. Your people, do I have to remind you, sold you."

"Maybe my mother sold me for my own good."

"Your own good?"

"Maybe it would have gone worse if I had stayed at home, that is what I am thinking now."

"Worse than slavery?"

"Perhaps I would have been stoned."

"For what? Only adultery merits a stoning. What are you talking about?"

"I truly do not know what I am talking about."

Cuy gave Malintzin a hard look. "The Maax I used to know always knew what she was talking about."

ALVARADO WAS IN his barn with his favorite horse, Alonzo. He had the body brush in one hand and in the other he held the curry comb, and starting at Alonzo's neck on one side, he worked down the shoulder and foreleg over the body and hindquarters of the horse. Then he turned to the other side of the horse, repeating the whole process—brushing, then getting the hairs out of the brush with the curry comb, brushing, then currying. He was working on the mane and was on the tail of the horse when the messenger arrived with the letter from Cortés.

25 DE MAYO DE 1520

Alvarado, I must tell you how we are faring, and express a warm greeting to you and all the captains. I trust Moctezuma is still in your company. Give him my fond regards. There has been a decisive battle with Narváez near Cempoala. Regards from the fat cacique.

Narváez, with his eighteen shiploads of men, promised to give two
thousand pesos to the man who could kill either me or Isla. Can you
fancy such a thing? Narváez got his eye poked out by a pike. I am
writing this on my own. Bernal Díaz is kept quite occupied with
the records and he has a nasty rash between his legs. Oh, by the way,
Alvarado, we are short of armor. Could you send some? Thank you
so much.

How could they need armor, Alvarado wondered, when he saw
them leave with just about every piece of armor in the whole supply?

We need barreras of iron.

Alvarado thought that strange. The barrera was the part of armor
that covered the mouth and chin with only a narrow slit for seeing out
so the jouster had to tilt his head down, find his mark, tilt his head up,
and blindly charge. Jousting was hardly an event in tournaments anymore, and if they were fighting near a river or swamp, headpieces like
that would be the last thing they would need.

The barreras are not necessary. I am playing with you, Alvarado. In
truth, we have everything we need. Our password while fighting is
"Espíritu Santo." Their password is "Sangre de Cristo."

Alvarado wondered which password God would hear and heed.

Our battle near Cempoala was in the pouring rain. Drats and rats.
We charged them with pikes. It was something, I will tell you that.
The artillery did not have time to fire more than four shorts. Balls
passed overhead, fife and drum sounded in the night. I shouted
charge. Arrows and muskets were discharged from Narváez's line.
Many of them were unhorsed. A little horsemanship would have
helped the lot of them, neither did they know how to fight.

Alvarado hoped that none of the horses were wounded. Terrible thing, a wounded horse. Would have to be put down. Far better that a man received a wound in the heart.

We gained ground, captured their artillery and their crossbowmen. Everybody was shouting victory, victory in the name of the Holy Ghost. We captured Narváez in the heavy rain. The fireflies were so thick it looked like the jungle was bejeweled. We won the day, or rather the night. It was a triumph of good over evil, pure and clear.

It sounded utterly chaotic to Alvarado, a mishmash of blunder and boast, but he knew that Cortés would never lose his head—literally or figuratively. Situations that would puzzle a Plato or St. Aquinas, Cortés could think through like a Euclid. He was like the best of the Moorish thinkers, or even, perish the thought, a Jew. Clever on his feet, never dismayed by disorder, and with a clear, unwavering understanding of his own interests, the man did not doubt. Completely at home in the most outlandish circumstances, Cortés opened the world before him like a well-loved book, a high romance, each page an adventure, yet the plot familiar as the Bible to a heretic. The man could fall asleep on a rock one moment, hack off people's hands and heads the next without the slightest hesitation, and wade through blood without trepidation. Everything was placed on earth for his use, and Señor Cortés thanked God for helping him who helped himself very well indeed.

There had been forty horsemen guarding the pass to their camp.

Alvarado was thinking of Narvárez's poor poked-out eye, a grisly, oozing orb atop a jousting pike. And was he wrong, or had not Cortés already routed the camp? Routed, secured, pacified, defeated, destroyed, annihilated, I win, you lose, we all die.

"Shackled, guarded, one-eyed Narvárez, leader of the insurgents, was still on the lookout for soldiers to rescue him," Cortés noted. He also made mention of a Negro named Guidela who arrived sick from the epidemic in Cuba. Bothersome. "We beat the kettledrums and fife, tambourines," Cortés boasted.

> *And thus we immediately went to the shore to remove sails, rudders, what-have-yous from their ships. And truth be told, the men who were our enemies initially have become our friends because of our infiltration, that is, as it is for men the world round, the promise of gold supersedes whatever else their original mission might have been. It did not take much to persuade them to lay down their arms and join our heroic forces to march in style with us side by side, making us a larger Spanish army by threefold or more. Bernal Díaz is working the numbers out.*
>
> *Yours in arms and fidelity, your comandante, capitán general, mayor of Vera Cruz, Hernán Cortés*

Alvarado did not know what to make of the letter. A skirmish, the war won? Somebody got their eye poked out, but what about fatalities? Insurmountable odds and victory against a background of dreary rain illuminated by fireflies, musket fire, the crashing of armor, horses up on their hind legs kicking for their lives. The usual exaggerations and glorifications, vague heroics at the expense of accuracy, reeked of Bernal Díaz's handiwork. And no word about the date of return.

In the meantime he, Alvarado, El Commandante's humble servant, had to go back to Tenochtitlán for the grand culmination of festivities. That meant speeches by visiting dignitaries and caciques, feasting, and that night the dance. For the captains, fiesta finery meant armor and plumed helmets, Aguilar in his velvet beret and droopy hose, except that he wore his hair like an Indian, swords on tasseled straps, some mounted, and in their midst Moctezuma, appearing in his glory as if host, not prisoner. It was to be something of a pageant, a costumed ball, midnight the hour of revelation, but not full disclosure, for the Spanish would remain wolves in sheep's clothing, making their entry as guests, not invaders, as liberators, not enslavers.

Chapter 34

The first thing that set Alvarado on edge that night at the culmination of the celebration in homage of Tezcatlipoca was the music and dancing. After a day of speeches in languages he did not understand, the dances were held in the coatepantili, a rather narrow area with steeped walls much like those of ball courts, so the sounds, rather than dissipating into the night air, were trapped and bounced off the walls in a bombardment of echoes. The five-toned flutes cut through the buzzing hum in dissonant, shrill tones and pinged against his ears like pins. Notched bones scraped with sharpened shells played an offbeat rhythm that set his teeth on edge. And what kind of bone was used he dared not conjecture. Then what had been bombarding and pricking his senses massed in his head like a bed of red ants swarming between skin and skull. A two-toned gong rang like a death knell, and the infernal drumbeats reminded him of everything unpleasant in life—dull aches before bedtime, his bowels giving way in the midst of company, his tongue thickening with thirst, and the time on the beach when sand got in his codpiece.

"What time is it, Núñez?"

"It is nine o'clock in the evening, sir." Núñez knew he should not leave Cuy alone in the palace, but they had all been hastened out, required to attend the ceremonies in their spit-and-polish armor. Núñez was in his best clothes too, his only clothes, breeches to his knee over blouse, tunic, belt, one bag of tools and another with the clock in it.

Alvarado looked to his left and to his right. Tall torches fixed in the walls of the buildings along the edge of the parading dancers burned fiercely. Braziers full of incense glowed like venomous bugs emitting a dizzying scent. The dancers, who now came forth, were painted in red and white, the women's faces yellowed and their teeth stained, and the men's costumes ranged from barely visible loincloths to the full skins of jaguars and big monkeys. Some people smeared in black bore the outlines of white bones, their faces painted like skulls. Some dancers were adorned with anklets of claws and belts of bones, headdresses of antlers. As they danced their repetitive steps in heavy foot marches, other dancers hopped and dipped light on their feet. Some of the men jumped high off the ground. Others were somersaulting. The lot of them were, to Alvarado's mind, lunatics let loose at a full moon. The flames of the torches blurred, separated, returned to blur, wavered. Alvarado felt he was going to vomit. Dear God, he moaned, let this be over with fast.

As soon as he uttered his prayer, he managed to regain his poise and was able to stand up straighter. Then he saw approaching him, carried on a litter upright, as the Virgin Mary would be carried aloft during religious processions in small Spanish towns, a statue of Huitzilopochtli made of amaranth seeds pasted with blood and honey. Around its neck, flapping behind it, was a cloak, a tilmatli, decorated with embroidered cactli, stylized shells, and butterflies. In one hand it held a bouquet of white lilies, in the other a fan. The most frightening aspect of this monstrosity was its grotesque head. With a hard bone beak, eyes of onyx or polished obsidian, it was a giant hummingbird face. This horrific visage was followed by a troop of people covered in scaly snakeskins. The tempo of the dance quickened, the music crescendoed, the chants blended into one ringing reverberation. Then abruptly the quickened pulse slowed and the dancers, like tired old men, began to dance the undulating, sinuous, convulsive, dreadful Dance of the Snake. Sweat ran down Alvarado's back. He was burning with fever and a chill set his teeth chattering. His feet, clammy and slippery, could hardly hold his weight, and the backs of his hands broke out into little red bumps. The hair on the nape of his neck stood on end. I am turning into a snake, Alvarado gasped, his throat clamping shut. Fighting for air, he began choking as a group of dancers roared toward him wearing skirts of dangling snakes and iguanas. They moved in, then out, in, out.

"Get Alvarado out of here, something terrible is going to happen!" Malintzin shouted to Aguilar over the noise. Alvarado's face turned bright red and he began to gasp for air.

Then Alvarado screamed, unsheathed his sword, and, with his eyes squeezed shut, began swinging right, then left, right. In one clean slice he cut off the head of a snake man. Left, he severed the arm of a snake woman. A jaguar man lost both his legs in one fell swoop. An eagle man was dismembered. Chopping and hacking his way, Alvarado went for the drummers, decapitated several, the pipe players, severed fingers from their hands, hands from arms, hands, arms, legs, feet, of each and every dancer he could reach.

"Stop, stop." Aguilar was stunned, numbed, nearly paralyzed with shock. "Stop, in the name of God. Pare, en el nombre de Dios." As soon as he could move, he ran forward and threw himself at Alvarado, but Alvarado, in the grip of a frenzy, kicked Aguilar out of the way and, whipping the air overhead with his bloodied sword, moved forward, cutting a swath through the crowd as if scything wheat. Thrusting like a blind madman slashing his way with a cane, he stabbed all before him.

"Sound the retreat." Aguilar scrambled up and took command. "Retreat, retreat." But in the confusion it sounded like retrench or reconnoiter or relieve or retrieve or redeem the honor of Queen Isabella. Gross disrespect for the rules of engagement and outright rebellion broke out among the troops. Without command, they mustered forward, stumbled, and fell into the fray. Was not the festival merely a façade, an evil plot to ambush the Spanish? They had suspected as much. One by one, each man did his share, hewing down dancers, musicians, visiting caciques, cooks, wood carriers, fishermen, tortilla makers, basket weavers, runners, merchants, everybody brown, bronze, red Indian. The hapless Aztecs, dressed for a festival, unarmed, and trying to climb the walls, were chopped down. Women trying to flee with their babies had their bellies ripped open, tripped, and fell on their own intestines. Babies were held aloft on the tips of swords. Bloodcurdling cries rose up between the pyramids, screams echoed about like those of deranged beasts caught in a tunnel.

Father Olmedo, his skirts twisted about his legs, holding the cross on the string around his neck before him like a talisman of peace, waded through the carnage pleading, "Stop, stop, for the love of God."

Adu, who did not know what to do, attempting to herd a group of Indians to safety, saw that instead he had driven them toward slaughter, and became an unwitting witness to their deaths at the hands of his fellow soldiers. Aguilar, trying to maneuver, had to step over the bodies of the many dying and bleeding, and out of mercy had to deliver the final blows.

"Back, back to the castle. No more," Aguilar shouted again and again.

Malintzin scrambled under fallen bodies for shelter. Would the Spanish mistake her for one of the Aztecs? She *was* an Aztec. Where was Cuy? Where was Núñez? Their allies, the Tlaxcalas, having never seen a war conducted in such a haphazard and cowardly fashion, fled in fright. Indian blood dripped along the stones of the cobbled streets, crept along like worms after a rain, sunk into the pressed earth. Certainly it was a spectacle that would appease the most savage of gods. Canals ran red. Great blotches of red spattered the sides of the buildings of the Templo Mayor of Tenochtitlán. Dribbles of fresh blood dripped from low-hanging cornices like tired rain.

"It is I, Doña Marina, yo soy Doña Marina," Malintzin screeched in Spanish as one of the troops made to stab her.

The peal of the trumpet signaled withdrawal.

"Back to the palace," Aguilar commanded. "Recoil."

"Recoil," went the message through the ranks. "Retreat."

Somebody hoisted Malintzin up from the ground by the wrist. It was Father Olmedo.

"See to the women," he hissed at her.

She stumbled forth, and with her back to the walls of the stone buildings, first the palace of Tlillancalqui, and into the temple precinct, passing Moctezuma's palace, exposing herself as little as pos-

sible, she inched toward the guest palace, for by now the Mexica warriors, those not slain, had grabbed up their swords and shields and
were initiating an offense. Stones, darts, and arrows flew. The Spanish
were beaten back, then back some more. Malintzin, panicking, found
herself in a crush of people. Pushed down to the ground among the
dead and dying, she scrambled up and made it to the entrance of the
guest palace. Moctezuma, shielded by a ring of Spanish soldiers, was
shoved before her. She lurched forward, and in the jostle heaved herself through the doorway.

Adu was already in the largest courtyard instructing soldiers to pry
stones up from the floor with their pikes. Other men, in relay, were
carrying the stones and piling them up into a barricade over the back
doorways and the few windows. Núñez was directing a group of men
who were placing the sleeping mats as shields in front of all the open-
ings to the individual rooms and the entryways to the terraces. Cortés's
precious chair was placed in front of Núñez's room, where Cuy cow-
ered behind a barricade of pieces of armor, boots, and cloth. Flustered
slave women ran about in circles, Tlaxcala bearers huddled in a distraught clump on the far side of the courtyard. Wounded soldiers,
stretched out flat on the floor of the patio, cried out for water.

"Cuy, Cuy!" Malintzin shouted. "Where are you?"

Cuy, behind her barricade, held an ax in her hand.

"Cuy, are you all right?"

"Has the war started? Are we going to die? Is my baby going to
die? Tell me no, Maax. Where is Raphael?"

Adu came up behind Malintzin. "Botello needs you."

"Cuy, I will be back. Stay calm." Malintzin saw Botello kneeling
before a small pot over a fire in the courtyard brewing medicines.

"Stir this," he said. He was making balms of jalap and sasaparilla.

Father Olmedo, walking among the prone men, searched for those
in need of last rites.

"All accounted for," a voice cried out.

"All accounted for," came another voice.

Aguilar stood in the middle of the chaos. "Let us thank God," he
said, falling to his knees, and all of them who could intoned:

"God, who art in heaven, hallowed be thy name. Thy kingdom come, thy will be done, on earth as it is in heaven. Give us this day our daily bread, and forgive us our trespasses as we forgive those who trespass against us. Lead us not into temptation, but deliver us from evil. Amen."

When they finished their prayer, an eerie stillness surrounded the compound.

"What are we going to do?" It was a pathetic, weak voice coming from somewhere in the group.

"Yes," came the chorus, "what are we going to do?"

Aguilar stood up and commanded: "Alvarado, come forward."

Alvarado had sequestered himself behind a pile of cut wood.

"Alvarado, come forward."

Little sobs escaped Alvarado's lips.

"Did you hear me? Stand forth, you fulsome coward."

Uncontrollable sobs.

"Do you wish to be dragged out from your lair?"

A torrent of sobbing.

"Alvarado, I am talking to you."

Alvarado crawled forward on all fours, rolled over like a submissive dog, and lay in front of Aguilar.

Aguilar kicked him several times. Alvarado curled his body up like a bug, protecting his private parts.

"They were demons," he pleaded.

"Do you realize what you have done?"

"They were coming for me."

Aguilar shook his head. "Este hombre necesita a su madre. This one needs his mother."

"They were going to massacre us."

"With what? Feathers and flowers? *Now* they have their weapons, their swords and slingshots and blowpipes, and bows and arrows, and thanks be to you, Alvarado, we are trapped in here. *We* are the besieged. *Your* doing. *Our* deaths, on *your* hands. So help me God, I could kill you."

"Kill me, please kill me, Aguilar, I deserve it."

"Oh shut up."

"If you do not, Cortés will . . ." Alvarado stood up. His reddish hair was streaked with blood. His pretty face was bruised and scratched up. He looked as if he had come straight from hell. "Cortés will—"

"Kill you? I hope he does."

"No, he will—"

"Save us? Rush back to rescue us? Oh, everything will be wonderful again. We will be back to our hammocks and frothed cocoa, slave girls and golden trinkets. Quick, send a runner, fetch Cortés to come and save us."

"I only meant—"

"Alvarado, you damn fool, we will not even be able to get him word of this. He is on the coast fighting Velázquez's men, leaving us here under *your* able command, and we, we were invited to a party, for Christ's sake."

"A party with human sacrifice," Alvarado found the courage to add.

"You should be the last one, Alvarado, to complain about human sacrifice. Right now you just pray, pray hard that you have not brought us to ruin by your impetuous ways. Our Indian allies have fled in fear. We are alone, eighty of us here, with a few wounded Tlaxcalans. By some miracle none of us Spanish were killed. By some miracle, Alvarado."

One of the men of the troops said, "We had to kill the Aztecs, Aguilar. Kill or be killed. We killed them. We did it. It was a victory."

"A victory, you idiot? It was manzata, a vast killing of defenseless animals. It was a slaughter of innocents. Kill, kill, kill? Is that your slogan? Look at that bold soldier before you. I present Capitán Alvarado. A pathetic rag, a trapo."

Alvarado hung his head.

"And if you cry, if you cry again, you disaster, I will ram my sword through your cojones. It is too late for tears, too late for repentance." Aguilar shook his head wearily and sighed. He was rescued for this? He looked out at them. What a sight. Savages in their finery. But there was nothing to be done. They were here now. "We must make the best of it, men. Get Moctezuma, he is our only hope. Gentlemen . . . let us play the last card."

The shackled emperor was hauled out of the room where they had put him and led up to the rooftop where he sunned himself every morning, Malintzin and the soldiers following close behind. As soon as they stepped forward so they could be seen, a flock of arrows sang through the sky, landing at their feet.

"Back, back." Aguilar pushed the group back under the overhang. "Now tell them, Malinche, shout it out in your strongest voice, tell them we will kill their emperor if they do not give us safe passage through the city."

Malintzin stepped out and stood straight and tall. No arrow fell. A vast silence surrounded her.

"Go on," Aguilar said. "Tell them."

She took a deep breath and used the cone-shaped instrument to project her voice. "We will kill your emperor. Let us through, let us leave town."

Moctezuma was pushed forward. His hands were tied behind his back. A knife was held to his throat. Then, across from the guest palace, from the top of the palace of Moctezuma I, a group of warriors stepped out. One of the nobles began speaking. Everything else quieted.

"What is he saying?" Aguilar asked.

"Kill Moctezuma, they do not care. They have a new emperor."

"It is a bluff. Moctezuma is related to the gods."

"They say they have a new emperor. It is Moctezuma's brother from the royal line going straight to the sun."

"Tell them we will kill their emperor Moctezuma, Hummingbird on the Left, and all their gods will punish them for letting their son Moctezuma die."

She did this.

There was silence.

Another man of their party, a priest by the look of his cloak and matted hair, gave a long chant. Afterward all that could be heard were birds from the aviary.

"What did he say?"

"He says, Aguilar, that we are intruders, invaders, destroyers. We pretend to be friends, but we are plotting to overthrow them, despoil their women, rob them of their rich stores of food, melt their beautiful jewelry, deface their city. We have nothing to give them but grief. He says that Moctezuma is a coward, not fit to rule, that his brother, Cuitlahuac, is declared emperor, and that they will kill us outright or capture us and sacrifice us. He says that we will all be dead soon. That they will tear out our hearts, eat our flesh, drink our blood, and suck on our bones." Malintzin stopped. There had to be some way, she was thinking, of getting Cuy out of this.

Aguilar slumped. He had not asked for this, for any of this.

Moctezuma seemed dazed and unaware of the drama uncoiling around him.

"Your Highness, Your Highness"—Malintzin grabbed the emperor's shoulders and shook him—"Your Highness, you must say something, tell them something. We will be killed."

Moctezuma could hear her and knew what she was saying, but it did not make any difference. He had started to take the journey inward, the one men make when they are about to die. He had no interest in all that once was most dear to him—flowers, the song of a bird, his books, poetry, the feel of clean water on his body, the froth of cocoa. Moctezuma no longer cared the cares of the world.

"Get Moctezuma back inside," Aguilar commanded. "We still need him no matter what they say." The guards, Moctezuma, Malintzin, and Aguilar returned to the large courtyard where the Spanish were waiting. Some were seated cross-legged among the wounded. Others leaned against the walls, still others sat on the stairs, their arms on their knees, wringing their hands. All had taken off their armor. The pieces lay like shed shells, discarded husks.

"You disgraced yourself today, all of you, save Adu, who is not even one of us," Aguilar announced. Truly he was too weary for anger, but he felt he should express outrage. It was a form of bravery.

"What happened upstairs?" Núñez asked. "Will they give us safe passage?"

"Núñez, your job is to keep time." Aguilar said, ignoring his question. He turned to the rest of them. "You brought dishonor on our country, our king, our God. If we had time, I would have you all hanged for disobeying orders, for larceny, for assault, for stupidity, but we have no time. While the Indians are out there haranguing us, I want twelve of the musketeers to reply with some musket fire and six crossbowmen to shoot arrows. Do this within the shelter of the overhanging ledges. Do not expose yourself or risk yourself, just keep them distracted. Do not waste ammunition. You, Father Olmedo, quickly pen a letter to Cortés explaining our dire straits. Cortés is either in Cempoala or Vera Cruz or on the path back. You, Alvarado, will sneak through the barricades, out the back entryway. You are to be the one to deliver the message. Make your way to Xochimilco, go by way of Mixcoac, take your fastest horse, ride for your life, ride for *our* lives. We will give you a pouch of chia seeds for fatigue."

"But my horse, what if he should be—"

"Damn your damned horse."

"His horse is his bride," somebody in the crowd said.

They all laughed.

"No time for idiocy, men." Aguilar caught himself sounding like Cortés. "Listen here, listen now, listen close."

They huddled together, each man touching the other. Father Olmedo, who had gotten his quill and ink powder, mixed it with water in a little jar, unscrolled a sheet of paper from his supply, and began to pen the letter. Núñez, who had returned to his room to check on Cuy, came out again.

"What time is it, Núñez?" Aguilar asked.

Núñez drew his clock out of his shoulder bag and opened the silver casing protecting its face.

"It is ten-thirty at night, Aguilar."

Aguilar had missed his evening prayers. All was in utter chaos. He would take slavery any day. And now the damn wind had started up. Jesus Christ and Mary. Were the elements also to conspire against them?

Malintzin listened. The wind. Quetzalcoatl. Tlaloc would be close behind. And so saying, great gusts ripped around the palace, making the torches set in the cornices of the patio walls burn in ferocious whooshes and snaps. Then the torches were extinguished. A stillness fell like a cloak from the sky, smothering the points of the pyramids, muffling the topknots of the aviary, and erasing palaces and architectural wonders. The silence rolled down from the hills into the valley and spread along the surface of the lake. Then a drum began beating somewhere, a hungry animal from the zoo roared, and in the hills the coyotes were assembling for their nightly foray. Malintzin heard the Aztec warriors outside the palace shuffling between the buildings, the lone cry of a baby, the flow of water in the aqueducts, the soft lapping along the shores of the lake, and she even thought she could hear the maize in Xochimilco stretching their stalks to meet the sky. The scent of bodies being cremated seasoned the night with the smell of burning fat. She looked over at Adu. He nodded.

So it has come to pass, Aguilar was thinking, the unthinkable. He remembered Cortés's vision of the waterwheel with some buckets full, others empty. Fortuna. "To despair is to commit the gravest sin," he said softly in the dark courtyard. Above him was a square of sky seeded with stars. He looked back on his misspent life and realized he had always been preparing for siege in one way or another, the final resistance to fate. He lifted his chin and addressed the troops.

"We are not the attackers, as we had envisioned, men. With one blunder, Alvarado has put us on the defensive, and you, you sheep, followed his lead. *We* are the ones encased in the walls, *we* are the beleaguered, the ensnared. So be it. We must keep cool heads and not falter in discipline. When Cortés arrives, he will have not only defeated Velázquez's troops but won them over to our side. I am certain of that. He is a man of unusual talent. What I am suggesting—and note this well in your missive, Father Olmedo—is that Cortés bombard the city from the outside, and that when the Mexica are engaged in battle from outside their city, we here, trapped in this building, can escape, join Cortés, and make a finish to this wretched business. That is my hope."

"Three cheers for Alvarado!" somebody piped up.

"Todavía no, no hurras por favor. Not yet, no cheers yet please."

"Maybe Cortés is losing." This cheery note came from Botello.

"Losing," the cry took up.

"Never," Aguilar shouted back, and as he said it he believed it. "Nunca. Do you know your capitán general, your comandante? Do you?" Aguilar raised his two fists in the air. "Has he ever lost?" Aguilar realized he was playing the demagogue, pretending to a bravery he did not possess, but if he were to have faith in one person, it would be Cortés. Whatever the man's faults, there was no soldier more brave, no commander less intent on leading his men, and if there was any man who could wrench victory out of the jaws of defeat, it was Cortés.

"Has Cortés ever lost, ever given up?" Aguilar raised his fist in the air. Much hung upon his own words, his manner, his ability to convince his men, sway their lot, give them hope. Their very lives depended on it.

"No," came the answer. "No, Cortés has never lost."

"Well then, enough said. Reinforcements are on the way. Adu, you check our arsenal store, count the crossbows, muskets, cannons, gunpowder, the whole of it. Estimate how long we can hold out. And you, Malinche, go with the women to the cooking area. See how much food we have stored, food, fuel, and more importantly water. Put tubs and buckets in the patios and on the azoteas and in the open courtyards to catch any rain. From now on we are on rations. Can we do it?

"We can, we can," came the response.

"Can you do it?" Aguilar asked Núñez.

"I can, but my wife, Cuy . . ." He gathered himself. "I can do it. We can do it."

"I know you can do it. Can you, Adu?"

"Sir, I can do it."

"You, Botello?"

"I wish my Cipactli were with me. But I can."

"Malinche?"

Malintzin, as a slave, had subsisted on grubs and worms. The Mexica people when they first came to Tenochtitlán ate grubs and worms. There were still people in the city who lived like their ancestors. They did not wear labrets and elaborate featherwork, shoes, cotton, were not permitted to smell certain flowers, had never eaten meat.

"Sí," she said. "Yo puedo."

"A cup of water a day except for the wounded and the little mother-to-be. May God, Mother Mary, sweet Jesus, and all the saints in heaven help us."

"Amen," the troops answered.

Chapter 35

Núñez did not think he was going to die, for if he died, Cuy would die, and the baby would die, and that was not possible. Centuries, eons of his people and all of Cuy's people had since the beginning of time gone into the making of this baby, and he, Raphael Núñez, would not allow this baby to die. He assured Cuy and three times a day he praised God for bringing him to this moment of life. So he did not feel desperate and thought only patience was required of the situation. He spent most of his time lying down beside Cuy telling her stories about the earlier parts of the trip.

When they'd left Cuba at the end of March 1519, he said, their first stop on their one-hundred-and-twenty-mile trip was the island of Cozumel off the southern coast of Yucatán. There had been two previous expeditions to the Yucatán coast before this, and one to Panama. At that time, the Spanish occupied Cuba, Hispaniola, and Jamaica. None of these former explorations had yielded any evidence of Amazons. But the men were, as red-blooded soldiers and savvy sailors, open to anything. When, lo and behold, they climbed the stone steps of the small island temple, Cortés and his captains encountered startling clay figures of women wearing snake skirts and belts of hearts. Not only that: the walls of the stone temple were smeared with freshly spattered human blood. Not only that: the floor was littered with dismembered human bodies. The men's torsos were cut open. The hearts were cut out.

"Dios mío," exclaimed the most timid of them, Alvarado. "Amazons have done this."

"Proof of the awful truth," Father Olmedo pronounced, pinching his nose with one hand and making the sign of the cross with the other.

"Amazons ahoy," Puertocarrero called down from the temple to the troops assembled at the base of the small pyramid.

"Man-killers," went up the shout among the troops, four hundred strong.

Botello said he did not believe that women had necessarily been the butchers and flesh-feasters. But let them think women, why not? The whole thing was fascinating to him—fertility goddesses, human sacrifice.

"An Amazon charnel house where they sacrifice their captured men and cut out the hearts to offer to their Amazon goddess," Cortés declared, trying to be sturdy and stalwart in front of his captains despite the reek of the abattoir. Their first stop, their first "discovery," had to be this, Jesus Christ and Mary. Enough to dishearten a diehard bullfighter. Cortés was already angrier than a blood-starved flea because Alvarado, the pilot of one of the eleven ships, had raced ahead of the fleet, gotten lost, and finally caught up to the other ten ships.

Since Herodotus, Núñez told Cuy, there had been sightings of Amazons, the one-breasted warrior women who waged war on men and mercilessly kidnapped them in spring for breeding purposes, Cortés informed them all. Indeed stories of these savage women and their lurid, barbarian practices were known to every red-blooded sailor and brave-hearted discoverer. In hopes of finding a mention of them, Cortés as a young man had avidly perused accounts of Marco Polo and John Mandeville, and later the records of Columbus, and the written exploits of the Portuguese Vasco da Gama, and Amerigo Vespucci's adventures on the southern continent.

"I think they are cannibals too," Bernal Diáz said, daring to examine one of the corpses. "See, no hands."

"No arms either, Bernal Diáz," Isla added.

"Cannibals ahoy," Puertocarrero shouted to the troops.

"Man-eaters," chorused the troops.

Adu braced Quintaval's shoulders with his arms because for all his brave talk, his master was of a sensitive nature. Adu was grateful, too, that the gentle Brother Francisco, too heavy for stair-climbing, had remained at the bottom of the pyramid under the shade of a ceiba tree with the troops. Even he, who had memories of fellow slaves being thrown off ships chained to each other, found the sight of these bodies, the poor men violated so they had not the privacy of their own innards, extraordinarily cruel.

"It is a temple dedicated to she-devil worship," Puertocarrero said, taking out his wineskin and shooting a skein of the red liquid down his mouth to drown the disturbance in his stomach.

Núñez gazed out the one window cut in the wall of the temple, seeking solace in the waves curling ashore. Even Isla, who flinched at very little, had to go out to the ledge surrounding the temple for a breath of air. Still a little queasy but not wanting to appear less than manly, he went back into the temple room and observed Alvarado shivering inside his boots although outside the sun bore down on them like a malevolent, flat-faced disk. Alvarado was a coward, Isla knew. Yet, interestingly, the young man had the presence of robust good health, a man with a ready joke and a rousing song. Just then Bernal Díaz cried out and pointed to a corner of the room. He had spied a small clay sculpture of men plugged into each other rear to front, twenty of them all in a row.

"Dear Mary and all the saints in heaven!" Father Olmedo exclaimed. "Sin compounding by leaps and bounds."

"Sodomites ahoy," Puertocarrero shouted down the pyramid.

"Puertocarrero, cállate la boca, por favor. Basta," Cortés warned.

"Sodomites," chorused the army below with great glee.

Francisco, hearing all the commotion, shrugged. In truth he had known of a few such practitioners in the monastery, and from all outward appearances these brothers seemed the same as those among the group who carried on with women. He, Francisco, was not a participant either way, any way. Not a handsome man, fat in fact, an ear tattered, his nose broken in two places, and his left shoulder unreliable and in constant pain, he did not expect to be attractive to anybody, although that was not why he entered the monastery. His decision at age ten was a practical matter, for he knew if he were to grow up, it had to be beyond his father's reach. Francisco simply sought safety. Within the monastery, he found God's pure love.

"Let us make haste to leave this place," Cortés said. "It is haunted."

"Haunted," Puertocarrero shouted down.

"Haunted," the troops relayed.

The spawn of hell, witches newly released from hell. Bernal Díaz planned to word it in his account of the conquest in just those words.

"Not human, these Indios," Isla concluded.

Earlier, aboard the flagship, there had been a discussion among the captains about the humanity of the Indians. Quintaval, who had been educated in the classics in Spain, said that Aristotle believed that some men were not truly men, but less than men, and so that as a kind, these half men were suited by nature to be slaves. Hearing this, Adu, although only fifteen, thought, but most prudently did not say, that Indians, whatever they did, like all men, were by nature men, as each animal in the forest was monkey or bird, cat or snake. It was slavery that made men pieces and shadows of themselves, their beings tied to the whim and will of a master. Francisco, countering Quintaval's quoting of Aristotle, pointed out that St. Augustine would hardly hold with inborn inequality. He could also have mentioned St. Francis's observations about the sanctity of all God's creations, but St. Francis was regarded as something of a lunatic among the men of the expedition.

Now Cortés, turning to his captains in the temple, said, "Oh, they are human, those that do these things, cutting off arms, legs, hearts."

"I am not going to let my heart get cut out," Quintaval said. His teeth had stopped chattering, and he had finally found his voice. "Or my limbs hacked off and eaten. I want to die in bed, safe and sound, I do, all in one piece. Our trip was commissioned by Velázquez, governor of Cuba, to rescue anybody from the former two trips, get slaves, and investigate the rumors of gold. I say we have done our duty. We can return to Cuba and report back that we found no gold, no slaves, that it is a savage country with an enemy beyond bloodthirsty. Fini."

"Bloodthirsty, meat-hungry," Puertocarrero relayed to the troops.

"Bloodthirsty, meat-hungry."

"Cálmense, everybody. Puertocarrero, you stop playing the fool, and you, Quintaval, you, remember yourself, man." Cortés pointed his finger at Quintaval and gave him an evil look. He felt he could kill and dismember his captains, one and all, then and there. "We will not brook cowardice in our midst. Nobody is going to cut your heart out or hack off your limbs. We are, after all, soldiers inured to hardship. What we see is the work of infidels in need of Christ."

Infidels, Núñez pondered. He had noticed before they ascended the steps that the small huts in the village below the temple were empty of people but not long vacated. There were no dogs, no turkeys walking about, yet good dried peppers were strung in garlands across doorways, and there was fresh water in large jugs in the shade of trees. Fish were laid out on drying racks. He noted an abandoned loom, one side tied to a tree, a red pattern in progress, as if the weaver had just stepped out of her harness. Moreover, the bodies in the temple were freshly killed and not decayed. He was certain that their every move in the temple had been observed by the infidels. Infidels. A Muslim term for "other," and now the Christians were using it too. If the Indian infidels captured them, could he somehow convey to them that he was not a Christian and therefore should be spared, infidel to infidel?

"This is a mission of exploration, Cortés, not conversion, not conquest."

"Quintaval, as a Christian in all places, at all times, you have a duty to bring His Word."

Adu also knew they were being watched. He could see them hiding, the people of the village, in the branches of trees, in bushes, behind stones. If the Indians attacked and the Spanish were captured, would the Indians free him? Could he explain to them he was just a slave without a will of his own and of no particular belief other than in the gods that lived in all, each plant and drop of water, each man and woman, the snake and even in the teeth of Death?

That night the captains, having their evening meal in the *Santa María*—hard cassava bread, jerked pork, olives from Spain, guava from Cuba, fresh fish caught that day and roasted over a fire on the beach, and an extra ration of wine which Cortés thought they deserved—discussed the events of the day. It had been conceded early in the meal that the cannibal killers were not necessarily Amazons.

"Wild men," Bernal Díaz guessed, although he had already written women in his book.

"Wild men live in forests," Francisco said, "not jungles. They are the ones who walk away, leave home and farm, and wander off to be hermits." He had a natural sympathy for such men.

Botello, the soothsayer, ate not only the flesh of the papaya but the little black seeds and chewed on the hard rind. Alvarado, his wineskin out, tipped his head way back, and let the wine pour out in a long, smooth arc. The candlelight on the long table flickered as the boat rocked. And the moon, full and pasty, hanging over the black waters, and resembling Botello's pitted face, seemed an eavesdropper at their evening meal. Adu and Juan and Manuel, Quintaval's two mute Indian servants from Cuba, were the cooks and the servers and the washers of the crockery and wooden spoons. Each captain, of course, carried his own knife, wiping it clean on his stockings after use.

"The wild men of Europe live in the woods, grow woolly beards, and scare lone horsemen on the road," Botello continued, as if beginning a ghost story. Nobody in the crew would confess to having met a wild man.

"What do wild men eat?" Alvarado asked. He had heard that they relished juicy young children.

"Mushrooms," Botello answered. "They eat mushrooms."

"Are you a wild man?" Isla asked Botello this with his usual lack of diplomacy.

"I have known a few wild men," Botello answered circumspectly, digging at a piece of rind caught between his teeth with a cracked and dirty fingernail.

Núñez knew there were madmen who could not live in cities and that Amazons did live somewhere in the world, but he did not believe, as some did, that on this or any continent he would find men with feet growing out of the top of their heads, their eyes on their bottoms, or that he would encounter a legendary group of Christians led by somebody named Prester John. Some said the Indians of Yucatán were a lost tribe of Israel, for earlier explorers had sighted pyramid structures like those the Hebrew slaves built in Egypt. Indians not from India, as Christopher Columbus insisted. Other Indians. Did not hot sun make all people brown?

"We of white noble blood have been sent by God to civilize these beings," Cortés said, holding his wooden spoon upright as a specter, "so we must not fear them." He spoke those words with confidence not only as a Christian but as a hidalgo.

Quintaval knew, and had told Adu on the ship between Havana and Yucatán, that Queen Isabella had bestowed knighthoods in Spain without regard to inherent, long-standing qualities, and thus Cortés's family standing was acquired for services rendered in the war against the Moors. *His* family, the Quintavals, on the other hand, could trace their beginnings to landholdings in the Pyrenees, and the family pedigree could be traced back more than six generations, and if it had to be proved in an Inquisitional court of law, there was no Moorish or Jewish taint in his line. So not only was Cortés an upstart, one of these newly minted lower nobles, but the rest of them sitting there had as little if not less claim to fame. Alvarado's family, for example, came from Italy, trekking the whole way with their old mothers on their backs. That is what Quintaval had heard. Isla, now, he was a strange fellow. Nobody knew where he came from, and his Spanish, could that be an Italian accent? Was he perhaps an Italian mercenary in Cortés's pay?

In point of fact, Cortés admired the Italian writers—Dante, who described purgatory to his satisfaction, and the supreme Don M., Señor Machiavelli, who described the necessary conduct and strategy of a prince or one who would be prince. Princeliness, according to Don M., was not necessarily inborn, but rather a collection of attributes to be learned through instruction and acquired through practice.

The next day the Spanish traveled up the coast, rounding the nose of Yucatán and stopping at a river. As they were loading fresh water on their boat and hoisting the anchor to continue their travels northward, Puertocarrero, one of the watches, spotted some feathers sticking up in the bushes.

"Cortés," he shouted. "Feathers ahoy."

"Cortés," the cry went up. "Feathers."

"Now what is it? Birds in trees?" Cortés was not in a mood for foolishness, but he had told his men to be vigilant, to wear armor at all times and always be prepared for battle, as uncomfortable as it was. He was on horseback, and he and Alvarado and Quintaval galloped up to the place on the beach to see what Puertocarrero was so flustered about.

"Do you see?" Puertocarrero pointed.

And at that very moment a bunch of bright red feathers flew at them, as if some scarlet tanagers or male cardinals were staging a frenzied bird attack, but the sharp points and long shafts were not bird beaks.

"Arrows," screamed Alvarado, who barely escaped one aimed at his leg.

Another bunch of arrows landed in the sand immediately in front of Cortés's horse, and then, with a great yell, a group of Mayans started to run at them armed with clubs spiked with cactus thorns and obsidian spikes.

"Call to arms," Cortés shouted.

From the side, jumping out from behind the dunes of sand, streamed hundreds of Indians.

"Short swords, short swords," Cortés commanded. "Strike eyes, faces."

They had practiced with short swords. Long swords took too long to extricate from their sheaths, leaving the swordsman at risk, and were not good for close fighting.

"Slash, cut, slash, cut, thrust."

"Slash, cut, thrust," chanted the troops as they did just that.

The Indians, wearing armor too, but only of matted cotton, with insufficient defense against Toledo steel, were soon routed, Núñez told Cuy. But this early group returned, their ranks fortified by more of their men. And now the Spanish who had been hauling the casks of water on the beach dropped their loads. They charged, blades thrust in front of them. In formation behind them came the crossbowmen, who with their cocked bows, notched and governed by tightly wound springs, shot off fifty arrows at two-second intervals at Isla's command.

"Shoot, shoot, shoot."

The cavalry, which had horses grazing in the meadow when the first signal was sounded, bolted for them. On board the ships, cannons were loaded, and eight men with the four harquebusiers, and the many pikemen with their long pikes, lowered themselves into the row-boats. The men with the long axes followed. The guns and the har-quebuses, as unstable as they were on their tripods in the small rocking boats, were aimed and fired. The cannon fuses were lit and the can-nons discharged, and although falling far short of their mark, the large black balls terrified the Indians and many fell back. Moreover, they were completely intimidated by the great size and dangerous hooves of the horses.

"Release the dogs," Cortés called. On shore, in tall cages, ready to be loaded back into the boat, were ten dogs of a large and ferocious breed, mastiffs which had been starved and taught to chase down and tear people apart.

A short time later, when Bernal Díaz combed the beach to count the casualties for his book, he was able to write that only one of the Spanish had been killed and few wounded, and without too much exaggeration, eight hundred Mayans lay dead in the field. Their chief soon appeared, attended by an entourage of nobles. They were, like the warriors, in a sort of loincloth knotted and draped in the front, but they also wore capes over their bare backs woven in elaborate geomet-ric patterns, and sandals which appeared to be of deerskin and fiber. Their headdresses were elaborately braided feathers, and they had heavy jeweled plugs under their bottom lips so their mouths hung open like those of petulant children. Their foreheads were elongated and their noses arched. In surrender, they politely offered baskets of dried fish, beans, squash, and plums, and, wrapped in cloths, piles of their thin, waferlike bread made of maize. One basket was filled with seagull quills, and inside the narrow funnel of the quills was gold dust.

"Did you see that?" Bernal Díaz said to Francisco. "Gold."

Evening fell and the slain lay on the battlefield of sand, which, scorching hot earlier, was cooling off, darkening with shadows and dampening with each small break of a wave. Bundles of rubbery kelp

lay strewn about like the dark hair of deranged women, and the bubbling fingers of the incoming tide reached and lapped gently against
some of the bodies. The dogs had been caged up again, not permitted
to eat the corpses, and the weapons were in various piles—the crossbows, the pikes, the poleaxes, the guns, their fixtures, shields, and
swords back in hilts, knives back in boots. The melancholy of evening
quieted everything.

Each man had his story, which he would later tell aboard ship
within the close cluster of his mates, the candles lit, the boat listing,
with wine on the table, the familiar soft strumming of Botello's guitar,
the high piping notes of Alvarado's flute.

Francisco told of standing behind a rock during the battle praying
like mad clutching his rosary, and opening his eyes for a moment only
to see a man backing into him, one of the Indians. "Stop!" Francisco
said. The man turned suddenly, knife raised, and then the two of them
stared at each other. Francisco was frightened, terribly so, but at that
moment all his fear seemed to rise out of him, leaving him dry, almost
marooned, it seemed, on an island of serenity. I am going to meet my
death. I am going to see the face of God. That is what Francisco
thought. They both had dark brown eyes. Francisco smiled a little.
The man drew back, as if the smile were an attack, an affront. Then
he came closer so that he could take in all of Francisco's many imper-
fections, the crooked, flattened nose, the raised shoulder, and the
heavy, lumpy body. Francisco smiled more broadly. "Am I not ugly?"
And then the warrior left.

"Why did you not kill him?" Isla complained. "He was the enemy."

The Mayans came back a second time the next evening to gather
their dead from the forlorn beach. Accompanying the chief this time
was a group of twenty young women roped together so that they had
to walk in tiny steps in order not to choke each other. The chief nodded, and with eyes lowered, they passed slowly from the Indian side
over to the Spanish. The sun on the horizon was bleeding into the sea.

"We do not sacrifice," Cortés said to the defeated cacique.

"He does not understand you," Bernal Díaz said.

Alvarado stepped forth, indicated with his fingers a cut throat, a heart wrenched from a chest, a blow to the head, a sword in the chest.

The cacique understood, then shook his head no. Then he made the motions of sweeping and then of sex by having a young man step forth and reveal his genitals in the direction of the women.

"Ah . . . slave women," somebody whispered. "They are giving us slave women to pleasure us."

Cuy was among them. She was crying, then looked up shyly. Núñez liked her immediately.

And she liked the story immensely, half believing the baby inside her could hear and understand.

Chapter 36

By the time Cortés returned to Tenochtitlán from his battles on the coast with the troops sent by Velázquez, the besieged Spanish and their women had been holed up in Axayácatl's palace for over two weeks. They had almost run out of food, had little water left, and were greatly disheartened. Rocks, clots of dirt filled with pebbles, and sharp-edged broken pottery had been hitting the palace in a continuous barrage. If anybody ventured out onto the roof, he would be the immediate target of dozens of zinging arrows. Any day now, it was feared, there would be a final attack—their meager, half-starved conquistadors and a few Tlaxcalans against thousands of well-fed, trained warriors. What could they do? They sat around playing cards and dice, gambling away what little they had—their daggers, their boots, their belts, their helmets and armor, doublets and hose, then their homes in Cuba, their wives, and all their children. Father Olmedo gave his food ration to Cuy. Botello strummed his guitar occasionally, sad tunes in minor keys, never finishing a song but leaving off in the middle, a befuddled look on his face. He spent his water ration on a hibiscus in the courtyard, talking to it as if it were his child and last hope in the world. Separated from his herb seller in Xochimilco, Cipactli, the crocodile woman, he mourned like a widower. Adu kept his strength and spirits up by running the whole indoor perimeter of the palace each morning and night, up and down stairs, lifting heavy stones, and practicing his fencing with Aguilar as he had been taught by the long-dead Quintaval. Father Olmedo heard more confessions in those few days than he had during the whole trip. The collective sins of the conquest rose up higher than any pyramid seen in the world.

Moreover, every curse word that had ever been thought up, and new terms involving mothers, dogs, goats, swine, and bodily functions, were composed on the spot. Some of the men had taken to carving their names on the stone walls—Juan, Rodrigo, José, Federico. All the gold they had collected from their expedition not already parceled out to Cortés or sent to the emperor back in Spain was stacked in a room, and certainly it was a great deal, but nobody cared anymore how much it was. It could not sing to you, talk to you, comfort you. You could not eat it, drink it, use it to get warm by, keep cool with; you could not make love to it, and it could not love you back. As of the last two days, some men had started whimpering that they would rather die by their own hands than be taken as captives and have their hearts cut out. Núñez cautioned against that idea. Father Olmedo said it was a sin. Aguilar said he would have none of that kind of talk, concentrating on his *Book of Hours* and certain prayers he had held fast to when he was a slave of the Maya. He and Núñez played chess for hours on end using a little chess set Botello had carved. Cuy, expecting to give birth daily, knew she would not have enough milk to feed a baby. She gave herself up to prayer—to the Spanish gods, Núñez's big god, and to the old gods of her people—Tepeu, Pakat, Pauahtunes, and Nacxit Xuchid, one of the Maya names for Quetzalcoatl. Malintzin took refuge in sleep. She slept all the numbers on Núñez's clock and woke up tired again.

Cortés arrived in Tenochtitlán on St. John's Day in June 1520. He had run into the Tlaxcalans, Xocotlans, and Cempoalans on his way, the ones who had fled the capital when Alvarado had started the carnage. Awkwardly, without the use of a translator, they tried to explain what had happened. Cortés also picked up an additional two thousand Tlaxcalans, who were eager to break the yoke of Mexica, and of Narváez's men he had added thirteen hundred soldiers, eighty crossbowmen, eighty musketeers, ninety-six horses, one-eyed Narváez himself, and a sick black slave. Somehow, though, Cortés had not encountered Alvarado. As it turned out, Alvarado had never gotten much farther than Coyoacán, where he was detained by a lame horse, and then he got lost in the vicinity of Chimaluacán, sat down under a ceiba tree for a few days, cried, was taken in by some sympathetic villagers, consoled by some maize cakes, and had to get his second wind before he started out again. Thus Cortés, uncertain of the situation, having left in peace, returned to a completely silent Tenochtitlán. His Indian allies, thousands strong, waited near Tacuba.

A loud pounding on the barricade over the front entryway of the guest palace one early morning rudely awoke the besieged conquistadors. Aguilar, in his hungry delirium, still half asleep, thought it was Death come to get them all, and he rolled over and covered his ears.

"For Christ's sake, let us in," Cortés shouted.

Aguilar sat up with a start. "Cortés, is that you?"

"None other, you lazy lout. Open up."

And there he was, El Comandante in the flesh in all his armored splendor on a good strong steed, and behind him troops and more troops.

"God has heard my prayers!" Aguilar exclaimed. "Happy day."

"What in hell is going on here?" Cortés could not believe his eyes—a barricade, thin Aguilar practically a skeleton, the place in a damn mess.

"Cortés is back," went up the shout as mats, pieces of wood, and assorted junk were cleared away so that a free passage could be made. Cortés elbowed his way in. Isla came in second, then Bernal Diáz with his book, the one-eyed Narváez, and hundreds of others. The many horses, so many they could fill three stables, were led to an open area on the first level of the palace. There were so many men that it was standing room only.

"They let you in to trap you here with us," Aguilar said, a moment before relieved beyond words and now worried. "That is why you got through. Where is Alvarado? Did he not warn you? Dear God, you are a miracle. Please forgive me." Aguilar fell down on his knees.

"Get up, Aguilar, you know I hate groveling." Cortés had not expected anything like this. How could things go so wrong so quickly? He had only been gone a few weeks, a month at most, a month and a few days. "Father Olmedo, what has happened here? My conquistadors have become a ragtag parade of fools and indigents. What a fine bunch they are. Where is Alvarado? I left him in command. Where are everybody's clothes?"

Indeed many of the conquistadors were naked, having gambled away their clothes. Father Olmedo, though still in a habit, was as bearded as a bear and could not help scratching himself.

"Señor Cortés," Father Olmedo began, "something terrible has happened."

"Out with it."

Father Olmedo, as quickly as he could, told him about the festival, the dance, how it had sent Alvarado into a frenzy of killing and how others joined in, and then how they were chased into the palace and could not go out, and how wretched was the day.

"Where is Moctezuma?"

"In a room. But they have a new leader."

"Where is Doña Marina?"

"Sleeping."

"It is morning. Get her up. And you"—he pointed to one of the unclothed—"Where are your clothes?"

"They have been won."

"Won? Preposterous. Get them back, and everybody get dressed and cleaned up."

"We do not have enough water," Aguilar said.

"You, Father Olmedo, you look like you need a good delousing."

"We have no water to use to clean ourselves, and hardly any left to drink."

"No water? And whose idea was that?"

"God's, sir. There is no rain. We thought there would be rain on the first night, but there was not a drop. Just wind and more wind."

"You sound like a bunch of farmers. God is on our side, but he does not reward stupidity. A bunch of you go outside to the square with some buckets and—"

"They will kill us," Aguilar protested.

"So rather than risking a few arrows, you are all going to stay in here and die of thirst and filth?"

"Respectfully, sir, it is more than a few arrows."

"Of course it is more than a few arrows, Adu. Why are you not in armor?"

"José, he owns my armor, he won it."

"José, give Adu back his armor; I want to see everybody's own armor on everybody's own backs. Aguilar, so you are in charge here? What have you been doing?"

"Playing chess, Comandante."

"And Núñez?"

"Playing chess with Aguilar, sir," Adu said.

"Where is Núñez now?"

"With his wife, sir," Aguilar answered.

"Aguilar, I cannot believe what I am hearing from you. All this disarray, no discipline, and to think that you were graced by your Maker with some wit. Have you not survived shipwreck, the jungle, slavery, what-have-you, and yet you let yourself degenerate into . . . this"—Cortés waved his hand, indicting all of them, the naked and the filthy. Only Adu looked at all lively and alert.

"Sir, I never thought you cared much for cleanliness," Aguilar said.

"I have lived among the Indians long enough to prize it. And are you not thirsty? You do not venture out to get any water? You have no food? This is ridiculous. Nobody is going to starve. Cortés starving? Nobody is going to capture us. Cortés in a cage? Nobody is going to kill us. Cortés killed? Let them try. They would not dare. A few weeks without tortillas and quail, tobacco and wine, and you are vermin-infested, weak-kneed, ready for the knife? Are you men? Or are you women? And speaking of women, did I not ask somebody to get Doña Marina up off her mat? What are the other women doing? The only person who can sleep late around here is Cuy. Has the baby arrived? Not yet? Stubborn bastard."

"With all due respect, the baby will not be a bastard. Cuy and I are married, Señor Cortés." Núñez stepped forth gingerly. Like Adu, he almost looked like himself, for he was in his proper clothing, his breeches on, his tunic fastened, his white hose smooth, his spectacles sitting on his nose, his handkerchief in his pocket.

"Married, Núñez? When did this happen? And why was I not invited? You could not wait until I got back? Padre, is this your handiwork?"

"Sí, Señor Cortés." It had not been what Father Olmedo would call a totally Christian event. The ceremony had hints of pagan and, dare he say it, Jewish practices, but they were all going to die soon anyway, so what did it matter? God was God, he would not mind a few words of Hebrew, the reference to Moses and Israel, a canopy, the stomping on pottery. Aguilar had acted as notary, and it was officially noted down in lieu of a legal certificate. Cuy had stood up with help next to Botello's hibiscus, which appeared to be thriving through it all. Núñez had worn Aguilar's old velvet cap for his wedding. Surprisingly, Botello had been able to strum some Hebrew melodies which Núñez sang, although Botello himself could not help being the pagan he was, resembling, Father Olmedo thought, Pan, and the men, taking back their clothes for the occasion, had danced about in pairs as if they were men and women. The real women were not in the mood for dancing. Somebody shared some tortillas he had been hoarding, and a pot of beans they had been saving up for their last meal was consumed. Malintzin, standing beside Adu, had cried a little. Of course, everybody wished that Francisco had been there, but he was not, or if he was, he was lurking invisibly about behind a pillar, a big smile on his big face. And they wished the situation had been a little more favorable, but it was not. You take joy when and where it comes, Father Olmedo had declared. There was a little wine left. It was a wedding.

"Hm."

Then they heard a timid knocking at the back entrance.

"¿Qué es éso? Un ratón? What is that? A mouse?" Cortés asked.

"It is I," said a small voice, "Alvarado. Let me in before I get shot in the back."

"Do not let him in," Cortés commanded. "He has betrayed all of you."

They could not say otherwise. It was true. Alvarado was beyond consideration.

"Comandante, for all his sins, he is one of us."

"Él nos ha costado, he has cost us, Father Olmedo," Cortés said. "Sí, mucho."

Isla nodded in agreement. He had been standing behind Cortés all the time with a wicked smile on his face as if he knew that the minute Cortés turned his back, disaster would befall them all. Bernal Díaz had already settled himself on a step and opened his book to a new page. Alvarado was to be listed among the infamous.

"Oh well, let him in."

Father Olmedo nodded at Aguilar. Aguilar went to the back entrance and parted a mat. "What do you want?" he asked Alvarado.

"Please, Aguilar. I lost my way. Please forgive me."

Aguilar sighed, pulled some mats down, and let Alvarado pass through.

"God will reward you for your good deeds," Alvarado said, scurrying in and inconspicuously joining the outer ring of men attending to Cortés. He took on a pensive, distracted air as if he had been there all along.

"Bring Moctezuma in here, or is he too busy sleeping, playing chess, or falling down on his job as an important hostage to see me?"

"He is in his room, Capitán. He is in a melancholy state."

"Not the only one around here, it seems. Bring the female dog they call Moctezuma out, let us make him work for his keep. Get Doña Marina off her rump. We will bargain with the new emperor. Moctezuma's brother, Cuitlahuac? Let us see if we can weasel our way out of this prison. We will offer Moctezuma back. We still have the gold, right? And where is my chair, by the way?"

"We broke it up to use as a barricade for Cuy's room," Father Olmedo explained.

"You broke up a good Spanish chair? You know, Aguilar, your strategy—and I am amazed that Núñez did not correct you—is amiss. You hole yourself up because you are being besieged? Wrong, wrong, wrong. When besieged, you do not help your enemy by exaggerating your sorry condition, to do so is to make it worse for you. Deprived of air, you should seek air. Well, never mind. Any other chair to be had?

No. Well, let me take off this armor and sit down on a damn Aztec mat. Get some woman to twist it into the shape of a chair. We have a few supplies with us, it turns out. The fat cacique thought of all of us here and sends his fond regards, and we have some dried beans and peppers, tortillas, and tomatoes, dried fish, which, as you know, is very good here, and a cask of wine, about ten barrels of water, and look here"—Cortés reached in his pouch and drew out a little drawstring sack—"tobacco."

A great cheer went up.

"Long life to Cortés. Viva Cortés."

"Alvarado, I see you hiding behind a pole, acting innocent. You made it to Coyoacán and back, it seems, in one piece, your heart in your breast, am I correct? Were you not commander in charge? Did I not leave the fate of our expedition in your hands?"

"Sir."

"You know, Alvarado, that when we get back to Vera Cruz, I am going to have you arrested for dereliction of duty, at least that, and then, well, the charges are too numerous to enumerate here, but consider yourself relieved of your post."

"Sir."

"We need all the horses. We need them here, so you, since you are so talented with the species, will have to take some men with you, get our horses grazing in Coyoacán, and bring them here."

"But—"

"I am glad you wish to be of use, and I suggest that you leave right now. This is not a time to dawdle and pick our teeth. And Botello, we have a sick man. We have brought him on a stretcher. Please see to him."

Adu, who regularly helped in attending the sick, went along with Botello, but when he saw the man who had been carried in, he stepped back in horror. The black slave had pustules all over his skin and his lips were swollen shut. Some of his sores were oozing blood. His eyes were open but he seemed blind.

"Do not get close, Adu," Botello said, pushing his friend away. "I have seen this before."

Chapter 37

With Cortés back, people who had barely moved in the last few weeks began to scurry about energetically. Women got out their twig brooms and began to sweep like Quetzalcoatl intent on purifying the world. Water was set to boil in pots. Father Olmedo was given some peppermint herbs to apply to his fleabitten hide. Cortés, of course, was in the thick of it.

"Núñez, I want you to take some men, many men, and, using all your tools, and bricks if necessary as hammers, make a covered cart."

"A covered cart, Señor Cortés?"

"Yes, a cart covered with boards in which men or women, as it may be, can sit. Leave small holes for muskets and crossbows and spears. Think of it as the armadillo they have here, or a turtle with his shell, on wheels. Two horses to pull, women inside. Make as many of these as you can, and not wider than the causeway. Start now."

"The wheels?"

"Use barrels, the rims of barrels, anything. Put your mind to work, man. Your wife's life is at stake. Do you understand? Where is Doña Marina? I have been asking for her."

Malintzin stumbled forth, dazed, sleepy, and in a weakened condition. She had been giving her water and food ration to Cuy.

"Get the woman some water, for God's sake. She is our voice. Do you not know enough to take care of La Lengua?"

Malintzin was given a jug of water. Somebody had to tip it back for her.

"Not too fast. You will vomit it."

Malintzin looked at Cortés.

"So, my love, glad to see me?"

"There is no hope for us, Cortés." Her voice was dry and hollow.

"Yes, yes, I have heard all that nonsense." Cortés turned to Aguilar. "Tell the other women to start cooking immediately. We need to get people on their feet before we start negotiations. Double the wine ration."

Cortés put his arms around Malintzin and gently lowered her to the ground.

"Truly, you do not look well. But you must listen to me. I want you to talk to Moctezuma. As soon as we all eat, we are going to send Moctezuma out to talk to them."

"The nobles and priests have formed an army, Cortés, it is no use." Malintzin was so tired even swallowing took effort. His words came faintly and sounded foreign, as if they emanated from somebody else. "When we took Moctezuma out on the terrace, they threw rocks. They think he has betrayed them."

"Ah yes, betrayal, how it rankles."

Cortés looked so robust and spoke with such gusto that she was overwhelmed. His health was almost blinding. She wanted to shield herself from him as one seeks shade from the sun.

"Drink, eat, and do not rest. You need to move about, build up your strength, and not give in to weakness." Cortés spoke sternly. "It wounds my heart to see you this way, Doña Marina. Left to your own resources, you might have died while I was gone."

She heard him but did not believe him. Wounds my heart? These words came out of Cortés's mouth?

Some soft beans were brought to her. Cortés mashed them with a spoon, mixed them with his spit, and lifted the spoon to her mouth.

"Try this. Eat slowly." He masticated a piece of tortilla, spit the moist ball into his hands, and fed her with his fingers. "Little bites. That's a good girl."

"You are only being nice to save the men."

"Save you too, Doña Marina, or have you not noticed where you are?"

"Tell me what you want me to say."

"A little civility, if you please. Dear Cortés, sweetheart, what would you like me to say?" Then Cortés called out to his men. "Where is my speaking tube? She will need it."

With help on both sides, Malintzin followed Aguilar and Cortés to join Moctezuma, who was being held by two soldiers out on the highest terrace. Immediately there was a rain of arrows and stones, and insulting shouts.

"Revered Mexica," Cortés announced, "we want to talk."

Malintzin repeated his message in Nahuatl, trying to muster her loudest, most solemn voice.

It quieted. A noble, his hair cut in the fashion of a successful warrior and wearing a diadem, clearly only an emperor's prerogative, stepped out onto the terrace of the temple.

"Cuitlahuac," Malintzin whispered, "Moctezuma's younger brother."

"So what does the twisted and forked tongue want to say?" Cuitlahuac directed his stinging insult straight at Malintzin. "We will kill you, one and all, suck the marrow from your brittle bones, and spit you out."

"Before you do that," Malintzin said on her own, "we will kill your brother Moctezuma."

Cuitlahuac laughed. "My brother, the great Moctezuma, has betrayed the people. He is a woman who wants to die on her comfortable mat. She is old, her mind muddled. Your leader, the usurper, foreign invader, uninvited guest, occupier of our land, murderer of women and children, is not Quetzalcoatl. Far from it. He is worm excrement."

Moctezuma, standing beside her, propped up by two soldiers looking dead already, perked up at the name Quetzalcoatl.

"We request safe passage," Malintzin continued, undaunted, "and we will let Moctezuma live. We only wish to be gone, to go back where we came from."

Cuitlahuac laughed. He resembled Moctezuma, but was more finely muscled and of a tighter demeanor. "And where do you come from, Forked Tongue?"

"If you give us safe passage, we will leave you all the gold."

Cuitlahuac laughed.

"We will pay you tribute from our land across the sea."

"*Our* land? Your land, Malintzin? Have you ever been there? Do they grow maize there? If it is so wonderful in their land, why did they come to our land, why do they want our land?" He sounded so like Jaguar Claw that Malintzin had a momentary feeling that he was Jaguar Claw come back alive.

"Most certainly you do not wish to see your older brother dead." As she said this, she recalled that royalty routinely killed their male siblings over the rights of succession. Her argument was flimsy, of no account. She felt faint but mustered her strength. "We have much gold which we can give you."

"You offer our own gold to us? They have corrupted you, little mother."

"We will pay you tribute from our land far away over the Eastern Sea. We have beautiful fabrics and articles made of metal much sharper than obsidian. We will give you thunder sticks and our tall deer so that the emperor never has to touch the ground again. Our cooking pots and shovels are made of this hard material. We have tools and many medicinal herbs and all sorts of dyes of the most brilliant colors. We have other animals that can pull wheeled carts, tools which can cut trees down in a day and smooth the boards." Malintzin was exhausting herself. She held Aguilar's arm for balance.

"Continue your tiresome song, woman, and your tongue will fall out. We will consider your offer," Cuitlahuac said. "Send over an emissary for negotiations."

Malintzin related Cuitlahuac's words to Cortés. She was wobbling.

"One man, only one man," Cuitlahuac repeated. "And do not send the woman."

Malintzin turned to Cortés. "They do not want me. Who will we send to negotiate?"

"Botello."

"Botello? Not Botello, Cortés. I will go."

"We will send Botello. Say no more. Botello is perfect."

"We are sending," Malintzin shouted, her voice quivering, "our medicine man, a man who lives with your people, whose wife is of your people, a man who knows the secrets of the earth and the heavens. He already knows words of your language. He is in great sympathy with your ways."

"Your ways, you say, princess? You are no longer one of us?"

"No. Yes."

"Very well. Send this pale demon over. Send him when the sun is midway in the sky."

The new emperor and his coterie turned and disappeared into the altar on top of the pyramided temple.

"Do not send Botello," Malintzin begged. "He has no chance, Cortés."

"Not true. Botello is invincible, eternal. He can work spells on them. Botello is the best one. He lives among the floating gardens, he speaks something of their language and dresses in their flimsy clothes. Botello is simpático. Doña Marina, get the damned gypsy."

She went inside and down the stairs. The troops were assembled, all of them crowded into the courtyard, looking up at her, expecting some announcement.

"Botello," she called from the stairs.

"Yes, I have something to tell the commander," Botello replied, "immediately."

Malintzin, holding on to the side of the wall, felt the world darken, and then her hands slipped, her legs gave way, and she collapsed, rolling down the last steps into the courtyard.

"Doña Marina, Doña Marina." Cortés ran behind her. "Doña Marina." He knelt down beside her, took her face in his hands, and put his ear to her chest. "She is breathing, thanks be to God. Get her to a room."

Aguilar and Cortés carried Malintzin down the steps into a room and spread her on a mat. Botello had followed.

"Doña Marina, my pet, my love." Cortés slapped her gently on each cheek. "Do not die. Please, Doña Marina."

Malintzin's eyelids fluttered. She saw Cortés's face very close to hers.

"Gracias a Dios." Cortés wiped her brow with his hand. "Tú vives. You are alive."

Propping her head with his arm, Cortés had her sip some water.

"Doña Marina, you need to get well, my little pet. Botello, she needs a strengthening tonic. She needs to be bled and her humors adjusted."

"I need to tell you something, Cortés," Botello said.

"You need to mix some tea for her, Botello, crush some herbs, make something that will give her strength. Do we have any leeches?"

"Mi amigo, I need to speak to you privately."

"We cannot have her walking about unassisted."

"Sir."

"What is it, Botello? Can you not see that Doña Marina needs your care?"

"May I speak to you privately?"

"Very well."

The two stepped over to a corner of the room.

"The black slave brought from the coast died," Botello whispered.

"So, one less to worry about."

"He died of pox, Cortés, the smallpox."

Cortés closed his eyes and his head drooped. He pinched the bridge of his nose with two fingers, muttered an oath or two, and bit his lip. "Dear God," he murmured, "spare us." Then he brightened. "I have been around the pox before and so have most of the men. We do not get sick from it. It is no matter. Did anybody touch him?"

"Adu."

"Hm, not good. The Africans are vulnerable to foreign diseases, also the Indians. We must keep our allies away from it. Tell Adu to bathe himself well. See to it. Do this quietly. Let us not panic the men. Adu is a good warrior, one we can ill afford to lose."

"There is something else," Botello said.

"God in heaven and all the saints, man, what else could be wrong?"

"The baby is coming. The girl's baby is coming."

"That is woman's business. Do not bother me with such nonsense."

"We have no midwife here."

"We have dozens of slave women, concubines, what-have-yous, surely there is one woman among us who can deliver a baby. You yourself should be able to do it with one hand. It is a natural process, nothing to be frightened about." Cortés stopped, then remembered. "Botello, I have something to tell *you*."

Botello did not like the tone of Cortés's voice.

"You have served us well."

"My duty," Botello said modestly.

"And we are grateful. You are a man of many abilities and have a rare talent for making friends wherever you are."

"Thank you, sir, but I need to attend Cuy. It does not promise to be an easy birth. She is very weak and the baby very large. Spirits, too, are low around here, as you have observed. Mind and body must work together and this is the most important of women's work. Indeed, human work, if we are to be—"

"It will be a half-breed, Botello, if it lives. Not only that, but of Jewish blood, a mixed-up bastard mongrel."

Botello had not thought of it that way. "They are married, sir." He himself was of indeterminate race. And had not Cortés taken some interest in the matter of Cuy's health?

"The thing is, Botello, we have chosen you to be our negotiator with the new emperor."

"I?"

"You are the most qualified. Tell the emperor we will give them everything we have, and all we ask is safe passage. Come back straightaway. Report what they say."

"Me? But I do not speak the language."

"That is not entirely true. I understand you have a woman, live in the city, and consort with their poets manqué, students, and such."

"But this would be official. I only speak a little. Un poco"—he held up his fingers to an inch, then narrowed them to half an inch—"poquito. Why not have Malintzin? She is your official assistant. I do not mean you should put her in peril, not at all. They will not hurt a woman."

"They do not want a woman. They want a man."

"Then you are the one to go, Cortés. Clearly you are the obvious choice."

"I am needed here, Botello, is that not obvious? I turn my back one minute and see what happens? The men are nothing without me."

"I am needed here too. A woman is going to have a baby. We had a sick man die within our walls of a very contagious disease."

"That is different. Remember I am the commander, Botello. Remember Quintaval."

"I remember. But Señor, the Indians will die of smallpox if we do not take extreme precautions."

"Well and good."

"Our allies?"

Cortés paused a moment. "No, no, I do not mean them, they will not die, they cannot die. And do not say a word about this smallpox to anybody. There are too many problems here for one man to handle. Do not confuse me."

"Cortés."

"You must do as I say on penalty . . . You know, Botello, for the greater good, we all have to make small sacrifices."

"*Small* sacrifices?"

"Think of Santiago, the patron saint of Spain, who fought the Moors."

"Did he live?"

"I do not remember. But I do remember that he was a hero. So when you go over to the Aztecs, tell them that there are secret stores of corn here in the palace, and that there is enough hidden away to feed the city for weeks, for months, forever."

"They will not believe that."

"If it is said with enough authority, people will believe anything. People all alike are not interested in truth or anything else except a firm, steady hand, a confident smile, and a warm voice. Do not prevaricate, stick to your statement, show no doubt. They will believe you. They will end up wanting to buy that corn we do not have and they do not need. You have convinced people that you can tell fortunes,

Botello. You can make anybody believe anything, I am certain of that. Tell them they are Moctezuma's personal stores. Tell them that what we have will make them hearty lovers, great warriors, eternal beings. Tell them that the gods came down from the heavens, spoke to us last night, and told us to share our secret stores out of the goodness of our hearts, and all we wish is to go in peace."

Botello gave Cortés a hard look. He looked at the men in the courtyard, those sitting on the stairs and in the entranceways of the rooms. The women were cleaning and packing the pots. A group of men were tying mats onto the sides of small platforms. They had taken the metal rims of the wine barrels to make wheels for the buffered carts.

"So when are they expecting me?" Botello, in all his soothsaying, fortune-telling, heaven-gazing, and tea-leaf-reading, had not antici- pated this. He knew very well that Cortés was selfish, mendacious, a man who lived without the slightest wavering of will and never had a drop of regret. But he had always counted on Cortés's loyalty to his men. Quintaval's inglorious death should have indicated to him the lengths to which Cortés would go. But he had forgotten. Quintaval, the coast, all of that, only a year or so ago, seemed ancient, as if it had happened in an innocent golden age.

"When the sun is directly overhead, you go, Godspeed."

Botello walked down the stairs slowly and made his way over to Núñez's room.

Núñez was wiping Cuy's brow with a wet rag. A woman was set- ting out a clean white cloth on the floor.

"What time is it, my good fellow?"

Núñez took his clock out of his sack. "It is eleven-thirty, Botello."

"By the looks of it, Núñez, she will be another six hours at it. I may not be here when it happens. Leave it up to the women. They will know what to do."

"But Botello, you have to be here. We cannot do it otherwise."

"Babies do themselves. It will happen whether I am here or not."

"You will be here, where else will you be? We will not be leaving here, we will be here until we have safe passage. Cortés said—"

"Núñez." Botello put his hands on Núñez's shoulders and steadied him. "Cortés is sending me across to negotiate."

"Negotiate? They are not going to negotiate. They hate Moctezuma. This is ridiculous. Cortés is asking you to do something futile. He is sending you to your death, Botello." Núñez, who had been kneeling beside his wife, got up, took Botello's arm, and drew him into a corner of the room. "Do not go. Refuse to go. You are to be the sacrificial lamb. Do you not see? You cannot simply walk to your death in obedience to Cortés's whimsy."

"Is that not what we are all doing? Is that not the duty of a soldier? Generals and kings are notorious for their ability to sacrifice their young men."

"But you are not young."

Botello laughed. "True, maybe all the more reason, then, that I be the one. To stay, Núñez, would be to be labeled a coward, which I do not care about, but I would also be hewn down in front of my friends by my own commander." Botello smiled. "I must go, Nuñez. I must. It is my time. You are the timekeeper. It is time."

"A clock is an instrument, Botello, not God. It is a mere machine. God never says to lie down and die. There are no appointments. God says to survive until you cannot. That is your duty, your most important duty—that and to hurt no one."

"In truth, my friend, I have hurt many. We are in the army, how can we hurt no one, how can we not die? Do not trouble yourself, my good fellow. I have seen the future, and you and Cuy and the baby will survive it all. You three shall live." Botello was making this up, as he did everything else.

"I know we will," Núñez replied.

"Believe me, I was not given the gift for nothing. And I am going to leave you some things in my bag." Botello took the bag from over his shoulder. "My red pouch: inside sleeps sleep. A pinch is enough for a full night's rest. The green: in the green bag is something for pain. It is a weed best smoked, like tobacco. In the yellow bag, you see it is only a mold, but it clings, it does, when put on a wound, and should she tear around her opening, press it there. In the event that it is dreadful, have her chew on these seeds. However humble they may look, Núñez, and I will, if I may, take a few myself, I may need them, you can never tell . . ."

"But you say it will not be dreadful."

"No, it will not, but in the event . . ." Botello turned away, a sob lodged in his throat. "I must say good-bye to Father Olmedo, Malintzin, Adu."

Malintzin was sleeping when Botello stopped by. All the better, he thought, going on to Father Olmedo's room.

"Father, I am leaving now."

Father Olmedo fell down on his knees and started to pray.

Adu had to be held back.

It was hot when Botello stepped out into the sunshine. Bright and clear. A good day to die, no doubt, but Botello's legs, which he had hoped would see him across the street with some sort of dignity, nearly faltered. Two Aztec guards came up, took his arms, and assisted him. They did not take him straight up the steps, as he had thought, but led him to a small doorway in the side of the palace. Unlike the brightness outside, the hallway was cold, and smelled of moist earth. It was like entering a cathedral, the eyes unaccustomed to the dark, or a tomb. Botello knew that he was not entering death, not quite yet, for that would happen in the open, on top of the pyramid. He would be stretched out, and his last sight would be of the priests with their clotted hair, his last smell their fetid rotting-skin cloaks, his last sound the dirge of their snakeskin drums. He would have to be brave. Then he would not have to be anything anymore.

Chapter 38

Malintzin had never been permitted to go into a birthing hut. Because of her profession, she was considered tainted, bad luck. But the moment Cuy screamed out, "The baby is coming," Malintzin, who had been weak and ill herself, rose from her mat, drank a cup of hot water, ate a piece of dry tortilla, and went to join the six other women, all young slaves who had been gifted to the Spanish along the way. They were now to serve, in the absence of Botello and the professional healers in Tenochtitlán, as midwives.

Other women were crowding in. Everybody wanted to see. The woman in charge, in a gruff Nahuatl, barked instructions to the others. It was the fat Cempoala cacique's niece, the woman Malintzin had been so jealous of in Cempoala. No longer simpering and flirtatious, girlish and foolish, the niece seemed to know what she was doing.

"Men banished." Emerging from a cloud of steam like a goddess, the niece shooed out all the men, including Núñez. Malintzin, as Cuy's closest friend and translator from Cuy's Maya into the niece's Nahuatl, was permitted entrance, but was told to stand back as the boiling pot was carried to the edges of the room. The room was filled with a thick vapor like a sweat lodge or a misty valley of dreams where nothing was as it seemed. It was all foreign, fascinating, this women's world, to Malintzin. A birthing mat had been unrolled. A cotton cloth was stretched over the door, and candles made by the Spanish of scented beeswax lined the perimeter of the room. The niece in charge and several others washed Cuy carefully with cloths dipped in bowls of hot water and then lathered her with the human fat of dead enemies. They scraped her skin with skin scrapers and her teeth with twigs scented with peppermint. After washing her hair, they greased it with butter made of cocoa and duck fat. They rubbed fat on her female opening so that the baby would just slip through. Then Cuy was prepared to walk, Malintzin on one side and the cacique's niece on the other. As was the way, Cuy was not allowed to squat quite yet or lie down. When she was ready to deliver her baby in a crouched position onto the cotton cloth, the placenta and afterbirth were to be carefully saved to be buried by the hearth.

Cuy had to be a strong warrior woman, the cacique's niece explained to Malintzin. Cuy's duty was to produce a warrior, a captive, or, if deemed by the gods, the wife of a warrior, the wife of a captive.

"A baby," Malintzin countered. "Let us do that first."

"During the process Cuy will be possessed by the spirit of Cihua-coatl, the serpent woman, and she will feel the birth like the splitting in two of the earth goddess by the two sky gods, Quetzalcoatl and Tezcatlipoca. Cihuacoatl's body was torn in half into the sky and the earth," the niece continued, repeating the famous lines. "Originally flowers and herbs grew from Cihuacoatl's hair, and from her skin, grass, mountains from her shoulders, and wells and springs from her eyes. Her foods were human hearts and blood."

Malintzin did not translate all of this into Maya. In her estimation, reference to violence done a goddess would not bolster fortitude. The mother-to-be was limp and pale, like a little bird whose wings had been clipped. She was in a daze of pain. Each contraction wrung her out.

"Will I live?" Cuy asked Malintzin softly.

"Yes, you will live. Think of the time when you have a beautiful baby in your arms."

"The baby shall live too?"

"You both shall live."

"Do you promise, Maax?"

"I promise."

The cacique's niece told Malintzin that Cuy was participating in something grand and noble, that she, a mere girl, would be taken by this event into time like the stars above and the great sea of the east. Her body, let her be aware, would contract and relax of its own will.

The pains would not ask her permission, but would come like canoe paddles pressing her sides, and squeeze her like the rubber bands of hule ballplayers wore. They would tighten, loosen, tighten, loosen, to push out the baby. Cuy would be like maize ground into the stone and made chaff, an iguana cut and pounded into strips of meat, an armadillo hit over and over again with an obsidian-studded club, a flower squeezed dry of its nectar, a maguey scooped of its pulque, a turkey plucked of its feathers, a butterfly dismembered of its wings. She would join all women in her suffering.

"You will be fine, Cuy. Every person you see has come out of a mother." Malintzin gave the cacique's niece an angry look.

"Maax," Cuy whimpered as a spasm gripped her, "help me."

"I am right here, Cuy. You are not alone."

"I am alone."

"No, you are not alone. Your baby is not alone. There are many women here, they all know the joy of birth." In truth, none of the young women there had had a child. Yet, as young as they were, they had seen many births in their towns and villages, and they felt a bond with Cuy as if she were their sister.

"This is different, different from any other pain. This is worse, Maax, they have no idea."

"They do, they do." Malintzin gestured for one of the other women to take up her post at Cuy's side. Then she went to the water jug that had the coldest water, dipped a cloth in it, wrung it out, and pressed it on Cuy's forehead, rubbed it around her neck, and cooled her cheeks and chin. "Make your mind jump over the pain. Do my pain game," she said to Cuy. "Make your mind go to the place where it is all over. You and your baby, two and two together." Malintzin cooed a little song.

"I want to lie down," Cuy begged. "Just let me lie down." Her legs buckled.

"Do not let her lie down," the niece said.

"Not yet, Cuy."

"I beseech you in the name of my mother to let me lie down."

Malintzin did not say, as was true, that Cuy had no mother.

"She wants her mother," Malintzin told the niece.

"It is natural to want your mother or seek comfort in the name of the goddess Ciucoatl Quilztli at these times."

"Let her stop for a moment," Malintzin pleaded.

"No, the baby," replied the niece, "must be loosened from its cage."

"Just for a moment to gather her strength."

They lowered her onto the mat and valerian root and aloe mixed with duck fat was gently smoothed on her female opening and she was given some chia seeds to chew and her cracked lips were dotted with drops of water. Then she was hoisted up again.

Somebody wrenched open the cloth on the door and poked his head in.

"Raphael Núñez, my husband," Cuy cried out, "save me!"

"No men, men out, out. Go to your place." The niece flapped her hands, shooing Núñez away.

"Is she all right?" Núñez asked. "¿Está bien?"

"Is she all right?" Malintzin asked the niece for him.

"She is wonderful," the niece replied. "Never better. She is doing what the gods have fated her to do; she is fulfilling her destiny as a woman. Let us not consider this a sickness. It is a health, the most healthy thing one can do."

Malintzin said, "No se preocupe. Do not worry."

And so it went, walking around and around, Cuy crying and screaming, begging to rest, contractions clenching her body faster and faster, twisting her right and left. At intervals she was permitted to squat over the cloth. Finally, just as she was about to right herself to walk around again, a great splash of water came out from between her legs, and involuntarily she crouched, gave a great push, and the baby slithered out, a slimy, bloody baby. The cord was cut and knotted, and the niece intoned the chant for baby girls.

"As the heart stays in the body, so you must stay in the house; you must never go out of the house . . . you must be like the embers of the hearth." When she washed the infant, she prayed to Chalchiuhtlicue, the goddess of water. Cuy, relieved, never so tired in her life and happier than she had ever been, closed her eyes, her baby curled up beside her wrapped in a clean cloth.

"You did a good job," the niece complimented her. "A beautiful baby."

"It was not that hard, was it?" Malintzin whispered in her friend's ear, although to her it seemed very hard indeed. Toward the end of the delivery Cuy had panted like a dog and pleaded to be put out of her misery. But there she was, Cuy still Cuy, Cuy cleaned, Cuy with rags bunched between her legs to staunch her flow, Cuy's baby born. "We are now on the safe shore."

Núñez had been allowed in, and he knelt beside Cuy, kissed her hands, and thanked her for the child, this blessing, their child, and he wept a little, could not help himself. "My beautiful wife, my beautiful daughter, our little family."

"It still hurts, Raphael."

"It will go away, Cuy, my darling," he said. "Soon."

"Do you promise?"

"I promise."

"You will be better in a day," the niece said in Nahautl. "But the mother must not leave this room until the naming ceremony."

"You will be better in an hour or two," Malintzin translated, aware that very soon, in a night or two, they were all going to escape the palace and try to get over the causeway to Tacuba unseen by the Aztec. There would be no time for naming ceremonies.

"It is over, Cuy. All the months of waiting, the discomfort . . ."

"I do not feel it is over, Raphael. Something is wrong."

"Quiet, rest, Cuy, just rest."

But something *was* wrong. Cuy's body started to heave again.

"It is coming again," she said. "The pain is coming again."

"Cuy, the baby is here. Look." The child was pale and had lots of black hair. Two little legs pumped the air, and feet and toes and arms and hands and fingers, they were all perfectly formed. The little girl scrunched up her face, pulled back her legs, and cried.

"No," Cuy shrieked, "no! Take her away."

The niece quickly handed Malintzin the baby and put her hands on Cuy's belly. She looked at Malintzin in alarm.

"What is it?"

"The afterbirth came out already," the niece said. "The baby is fine."

Cuy convulsed into a ball of pain.

"Steady, steady." The niece put her hands around Cuy's belly and placed her head on Cuy's chest. She parted Cuy's legs. "Let me look. I will not hurt you, little bird. Let me look." Then she looked up at Malintzin.

"Something else is in there," she said.

"Something else?"

"Another baby."

Malinche turned to Núñez, who was holding his baby girl. "It is another baby."

"Get it out, get it out!" Cuy screamed. "Get it out. It is killing me."

"On her feet," the niece commanded.

"On your feet," Malinche said.

"I cannot," Cuy cried. "Do not make me."

"Do not torture her," Núñez pleaded.

Cuy's face, which had returned to its warm brown color after the birth, now drained and turned ashen. "Raphael," she cried. "Me voy a morir. I am going to die."

"No," Malinche assured her, but when she looked at the niece's face, the large woman turned away and would not meet her eye.

"Set her down. Hold her legs down."

Cuy kicked and struggled.

"Tell her she has to hold still," the niece said. She called two women over to hold Cuy's ankles. Then she spread Cuy's legs, put one finger in the birth canal, and with the other hand pressed Cuy's stomach. Cuy's screams could be heard throughout the palace.

"What is going to happen?" Núñez asked.

"It feels wrong, the position is wrong," the niece said to Malintzin. "Lift her up. Let us shake her, shake it loose."

"Shake her," Malintzin translated into Spanish. The niece and another strong woman grabbed Cuy's arms and shoulders, pulled her off the floor, and shook her until her teeth rattled.

"It hurts so much," Cuy sobbed. "Save me, Raphael."

"Get the man out of here," the niece said. "He will distract her from her work."

"Núñez, go, go," Malintzin said. "Take the baby with you."

"Let him stay. Let him stay."

"I will be right outside, Cuy my love."

"Put her on the mat," the midwife said. "Spread her legs again."

The two helpers took Cuy's legs, spread them far apart, and with Cuy shrieking in pain, the midwife tried to put her hand up through the birth canal, but she could not manage it.

"I am not feeling the head. I can feel folded legs. The child is large, too large. It is in the wrong position."

"What does that mean?"

"I will have to cut the stomach open. Get me a sharp knife."

"What, what?" Cuy cried.

"She says the baby is stuck," Malintzin said.

"No, no!" Cuy screamed.

"Tell her," the niece said, "that the baby will have to come out that way or it will die."

"But Cuy will die if you cut out the baby."

"She will die anyway."

"She will die for certain?"

"From the pain, from the blood, she will die. The only other thing is to cut pieces of the baby out from below. Then the baby and mother die together. We cannot kill the child to keep the mother alive."

"We can."

According to belief, Malintzin knew, the real father of the child was not Núñez, not a mortal, but Tezcatlipoca, the very strange lord of the here and now, and the husband and wife, the temporal mother and father, had, by the act of intercourse and release of their fluids, merely helped the baby along. The continual implanting of male seed was necessary for two or three months after the conception to make the baby grow, but after that period of time, the temporal father had to stop. If the labor was difficult, it meant that the father had continued to have intercourse after the allotted time.

"Ask the earthly father what he wants. He is the one who caused this," the niece said. "Through his immoderate actions he has brought this on himself."

"Maax, what is she saying?"

"You have a beautiful daughter to live for, Cuy, one who needs you, and you have a husband."

"Tell the white father to come in," the niece said.

"Maax, Maax," Cuy groaned, "I am going to die."

"You will not," Malintzin insisted. She got up and parted the curtain at the door. "Núñez, come in here."

Núñez handed his newborn daughter to one of the women waiting outside and stepped in.

"It is this," Malintzin said in Spanish. "Either they cut the baby out or they cut Cuy open and take out the baby. Either they save the baby or they save the mother."

"Save Cuy," Núñez said. "Save the mother. It is the law."

"Raphael," Cuy groaned, "I want to die. Help me die. Please help me to die. Take away this suffering."

Father Olmedo, who had been waiting with the cluster of men, stepped forth into the room.

"Can I do anything to help?" he asked.

"Get Cortés in here," Malintzin said.

"We are going to save you," Núñez said, "but the baby, the one inside, Cuy, may have to be sacrificed if—"

"No!" Cuy screamed.

"You are letting her suffer while you are talking," the niece said.

"Cortés is coming," Malintzin said.

"What does he have to do with it?" The niece was furious that a man would usurp her authority.

"Help me die, save the baby," Cuy whimpered. "Please, please, somebody help me."

"El Comandante is coming," Malintzin said, returning to her friend's side. "Cuy, you can have other babies."

"I do not want other babies. I do not want anything. Just help me to die, Maax, please, if you love me, help me. I cannot stand the pain." Cuy twisted to the right and to the left, her body a swirl of agony, her hands clutching the air. "Help me."

"My precious, my love, do not give up. I love you." Núñez touched her stomach. Cuy shrieked in pain.

"Many women have to sacrifice themselves in giving birth," the niece said. "When they die, they haunt the crossroads."

"Hush," Malintzin said. "Do not bring up that falsehood."

"Some say two are unlucky. One would have to die anyway."

"Be quiet, woman."

Cortés entered the room, Adu behind him, then Aguilar and Bernal Díaz. "Women, good afternoon, what is going on here?" Cortés was in armor, his sword strapped over his shoulder. He had no hope that Botello would be successful in negotiation. It was a tactic. They would be escaping under the cover of night.

"Get Botello back," Malintzin said. "He must still be alive. I have not heard the drums."

"Botello is unavailable. What is the problem?"

"Explain it to him," Malintzin said to Núñez, for she was at a loss for words.

Núñez mumbled a bit, wept, shrugged his shoulders, and fell into Cortés's armored chest.

"I see," Cortés said, holding Núñez at arm's length and looking into his eyes. "There was a great man named Julius Caesar. A great captain, a great ruler, he was born of his mother through cutting her open."

"Pero la madre no sobrevivió. But the mother did not survive," Núñez said.

"Hm. Yes, I do not know, that is maybe so." Cortés ruminated, stroking his chin. "I understand about Botello. Too bad Botello is not still with us. He could stitch her up well. But what is *is*, sí? And what is to be done *is to be done*, and done fast. Adu, get Botello's bag."

"He took his bag," Adu said, his eyes narrowed.

"No, no, not the medicine bag. The one by my desk. His barber tools. In any job, we need the right tools, a sharp blade, am I right? Take my sword, for instance. Pure Toledo steel. Sharper than their obsidian. It is steel that wins wars. Horses that win wars. Also in Botello's bag you will find a steel needle, and real thread, none of this cactus thorn and maguey fiber. Who is the best stitching woman in this compound? Malinche, ask among the women. And none of this on-the-floor birthing. Proper, up-to-date methods. Get some men to bring in my desk so I can see what I am doing. Good, and fetch the decanter of aqua vitae by my mat. We need to give Cuy enough brandy to drink so that the edges are worn off. How does that sound, Cuy my girl?" Cortés crouched down and smoothed Cuy's hair, which was plastered to her forehead by sweat. "The right tools, the proper spirit, little darling. Give us a smile like a good girl. And will somebody please unhinge me." Cortés held up his arms. One of the birthing helpers undid the buckles to his metal breastplate and took it off.

"Go, go!" he shouted to Adu and Malintzin. "Do not stand around with your mouths open."

"Does she need a block for her mouth?" Núñez remembered that when Cuy was shot by the arrow she had lost teeth biting down on a block.

"No, no block. We want to hear her scream. Screaming is good. Screaming is life. We want to keep her alive and know she is alive."

Cortés took off his doublet and silk shirt and stood bare-chested in his cloth codpiece, hose, and boots. "No point in bloodying a good blouse. This is more like it. Open the door. Get some good fresh air in here, God Almighty, it is suffocating, and snuff out that nauseating incense. This is not a church or a brothel. No wonder the girl is crying. Jesus, Mary, and all the saints. And listen, she needs something that will tame her nerves, Núñez, the herbs they use for the captives before they cut out their hearts, does Botello have that?"

"Botello left some mushrooms."

"No, no, no visions. It will confuse her. We must dull the pain, but she must be able to concentrate on her task, know her task, work with us. Oh well, a little brandy, brandy will do the trick."

"Raphael," Cuy moaned, "please help me die. Please, I do not have enough strength, no more strength. Dying is not the worst thing. I will die of it anyway. Please."

Núñez knelt beside Cuy and took her hand. "Cortés is going to save you."

"I will try," Cortés said. "I will do my best. I will do it. Courage is what you need. Be a bull, my girl, be a bull. "

"She is a strong woman," Núñez told Cortés.

"I am certain that she is. Where the hell is Adu?"

Cortés turned back to Cuy. "I will not let you die. Do you hear me?"

Cuy, who had almost faded, mustered a whisper. "I do not want to die."

"Of course not, perish the thought, banish it."

"Forgive me for wanting to die. I do not want to die."

"What is she saying?" the niece asked. "And why are all these men in here? The goddess will be angry, close up the little bird's womb. She will bring death and devastation down on all."

Adu appeared at the doorway with Botello's barber bag. Malintzin followed with the seamstress she had found.

"I do not want to die," Cuy said, another contraction gripping her.

"What is that?"

"She does not want to die," Malintzin said to the niece.

"It is her duty to die if that is her fate. I thought she said she wanted to die. Two babies. One must be sacrificed. The mother must die for such an affront. Somebody must die. It is the way. Somebody must pay."

Cortés's desk was brought in, it was a board and two barrels. A clean cloth was put across it. Cuy was hoisted up. And Cortés took a sharp razor out of Botello's bag.

"What is going to happen to me?" Seeing the blade made Cuy more terrified than ever.

"Cuy, Cortés is going to . . ." Malintzin could not say it.

"The gods will punish her for this," the niece said.

"Drink some," Cortés said, holding Cuy's head up and making her swallow some brandy, but she choked and could not swallow.

"Oh well, a waste of some good brandy." Cortés wiped his hands on his hose. "Are we ready?" He held up the razor, which even in the dark, sequestered room gleamed. Adu hung back in the shadows. Aguilar and Bernal Díaz got well away. Isla put his head between the doorway and the curtain.

"Get him out of here," the niece said.

"I will see you later, Isla," Cortés said sweetly. "Hasta luego, Isla."

"Do not cut her stomach open," Núñez said. "I insist that we save her."

"The pain is too much for me," Cuy shrieked. "Help me to die, Maax."

"What does she say?"

"She wants to live," Malintzin said.

"I thought she wanted to die, as is necessary," the niece said.

Cortés smoothed his beard, scratched himself, and fell on his knees.

"Dear God, help me to do what I am about to do. Spare this woman's life, deliver her baby in one piece. I ask this in the name of your Son. Amen."

Cortés stood up, smiled, and gave all attending an encouraging nod. "All right now. We are going to make room for the baby to come out. Cuy, mi amiga, I am not going to cut your stomach open. Adu, get over here. Hold one of her legs down. Doña Marina, you do the other. Spread them wide. Wide, and do not let her move them. Doña Marina, tell her I am going to cut her down there, not the stomach. I am going to widen the opening. It will hurt, hurt terribly, she will lose more blood, but she will not die, and the baby will not die. Nobody, if I can help it, is going to die. I will not let her die. Tell her that, Marina. Tell her she will need her hope, her will, her strength, and her faith in me. Tell her to trust me. She has to take on my strength." Cortés put his hand over hers and squeezed. "Do you feel that, Cuy? That is my strength going into you, you understand, comprende? Be strong. Be brave." Cortés cleared his throat. "Ready? Hold her down. I will cut her and make room for the baby. There will be a lot of blood, but it is only blood. If I can get my hands inside, I can pull it out, get the baby out if I can reach in. I will, with God's help, do my best. She is going to scream. But the screaming will be good. It will mean she is still alive. Do not be frightened of a little screaming, a little blood. And Núñez, you hold her hand. Do not faint. Your wife is counting on you. As soon as I am done and have the baby out, Doña Marina, stanch the blood and have the woman sew her up. She is not going to be torn to shreds. She will not split open or die of it. It will be fast and simple. It will be one clean big cut which I am going to make. Much neater. Now keep talking. Talk to her. Talk to me. Nice weather we are having these days, what do you think?"

"It is beautiful weather," Malintzin answered.

"I remember one summer when I was a child," Cortés said. "It rained every day of the school holidays. I was so angry I asked my mother to make the rain stop."

"I want to die," Cuy said. "Just cut my throat and put the mat over my mouth. Get it over with. Help me, help me die. I cannot endure the pain." She was whipping her head side to side, biting her lips raw. She pleaded to all the gods and even to the Christian gods, Jesus and Mary, and she cried to the God of Abraham to put her out of her misery.

"Stay with us, Cuy," Cortés said. "Hold fast. We will not let you go."

The pain was beyond endurance. It was worse than anything, anything ever, and then, there in the fetid little room, surrounded by her husband, her best friend, El Comandante, Adu, and the niece, in the midst of the unendurable pain, and dread as thick as mud, as easily as a thin curtain parting, Cuy caught a glimpse of the afterworld. It was not the underworld of demons and horror, not the one where mothers who died in childbirth went.

It was twilight, the sun was setting, there was a path between the trees. Very still. Very peaceful. Quiet. There in that place, that was death. There were black silhouettes of the trees with shiny black leaves after a rain. The sky was pink, and the path going over a hill was small but distinct. She knew what she was seeing and she knew suddenly that to die was not terrible, not hard. All she had to do was yield to it. She felt sad for Raphael, for Maax, for her baby girl, but she was not sad for herself. *Others have been this way, and I too can do it.* Then, with what she thought was her last breath, she let out a howl.

"I do not like it when it gets very hot. Warm, mild, in between is my choice for weather. Núñez, do you remember the dust storms in Spain? Terrible. We used to crawl under our mothers' skirts. Remember those dust storms? Atrocious."

"I do, Señor Cortés, I do indeed remember."

"Do they have dust storms where you come from, Adu?"

"Yes, Don Cortés."

Malintzin felt that her own heart was being cut out. "Cortés, Cortés."

"The air in Tenochtitlán is thin, have you not noticed? But refreshing. One more little turn of the hand. Got it. Here it comes." Swift, determined, not afraid, not squeamish, and despite all the blood, putting one hand within the lips of her vagina so the cut would not penetrate beyond her skin, he drew the razor down with his other hand. Then he reached inside, and with a neat hook and twist of his hand he reached into her, was able to turn the child, and brought the child through the birth canal.

"Tie it, tie the cord." The niece moved forward and did her job. The baby was born, it cried, Adu burst into tears, Núñez was stunned. "See to the mother, see to the mother. Stop the blood, stitch her up. Be quick, quick. Apúrele, rápido."

Núñez, who had felt Cuy's hand loosening, had gripped her harder, harder still, and now the hand that had almost been slipping out of his clasp tightened.

"Get some needle and thread. Sew her up, sew her up."

The niece stanched the blood and cleaned the wound off, and while Cortés held the flaps of skin together with his fingers, the seamstress stitched. She was deft, quick, a professional. It took all of five minutes if Núñez had had the wherewithal to look at his clock.

"I am alive," Cuy cried out before she fell asleep. "I live."

"Dear God," Cortés said, "thank you. Gracias a Dios." He fell on his knees. Núñez kneeled beside him. Adu went on the other side. Malintzin held her hands together in Christian fashion. Thank you, Mother Mary.

"Will you get up off the ground?" the niece said. "We need to clean up around here."

"She lives!" Malintzin shouted out as she pulled aside the draping over the door. "She lives. The child lives. A boy lives. A girl and a boy."

"She lives!" went the shout. "He lives. She lives. She lives. They live. El vive, ella viven. Viven."

Then the niece intoned:

"Dear son . . . you must understand that your home is not here where you have been born, for you are a warrior, you are a quecholli bird, and this house where you have been born is only a nest . . . your mission is to give the sun the blood of enemies to drink and to feed Tlaltchutli, the earth, with their bodies. Your country, your inheritance, and your father are in the house of the sun, in the sky."

"Hush," Malintzin spat. "None of that."

Bernal Díaz noted the event in his book.

30 DE JUNIO DE 1519

A daughter, Claudia Núñez de Tenochtitlán, and a boy, Noah Núñez de Tenochtitlán were born in Tenochtitlán to Señor Raphael Núñez de Seville and Señora Cuy Núñez de Tabasco.

Chapter 39

They left the next night as soon as the sun went down. The horse's hooves were covered with cloth, no tapers lit, the troop armored breastplates were covered with dark cloth, helmets draped in black, everything shiny and bright hidden, all sound muted. They were like figures from the underworld creeping out of the palace, phantom figures, Cortés in the vanguard, the gold, lots of it in bars and objects—rings and earrings, lip plugs, earplugs, and nose rings, bracelets, necklaces, pendants, masks, fans, all sorts of ornaments and small statues—in bags and on covered stretchers on poles carried by two men and shielded by horses on both sides. The cavalry, the infantry, then the rear guard cautiously, like ghosts and sleepwalkers, mourners and wraiths, tiptoed, single file, in four long lines from each entrance to the palace, then they joined up. The causeway to Tacuba allowed for only four men or two horses abreast at one time.

It was eerie how quiet this human train was, the migration of night creatures spilling out into the streets while the population slept, only the monumental buildings standing in silent witness. Fortunately the guest temple was very near the Tacuba causeway. They had to pass the palace of Moctezuma I and the zoo, and go across the bridge of Tecautzinco. Malintzin, Cuy, and the babies were in the one padded cart finished in time, its wheels muffled by strips of rubber found on a ball-playing outfit in a palace closet. Malintzin felt she could hardly breathe in the enclosed box. Cuy, with her babies pressed to her nipples, prayed they would not cry. There was not the hint of a whisper or scrape of boot or light cough, and the frontmost group—Cortés, Alvarado, Aguilar, Núñez, Father Olmedo, and Isla—were halfway across. It seemed they were going to make it, escape undiscovered, when out of the night, an Aztec woman cradling her colicky baby on the street, saw them and cried out:

"Mexica, awake!"

Immediately warriors, who must have been sleeping in the bottom of their canoes along the causeway, popped up and started to row frantically toward the silent parade of Spanish. Armed with their bows and arrows, spears and clubs, and screaming battle cries, more warriors poured out from their houses and fortresses at the base of the causeway. The warrior students in the calmecac, the seasoned soldiers from the barracks, and from all around the Spanish, the Aztecs began throwing sticks and stones, shooting off blowguns and arrows. Others, civilians of the city, like beavers gnawing through wood, dislodged the wooden bridges from the causeway, and with long wooden crowbars with hooked ends they took up the stones supporting the causeway. The exit to Tacuba was obliterated, as was the return to Tenochtitlán.

"Save the gold," Cortés commanded. Most of the gold was in the rear guard carried by the soldiers from the Narváez expedition. Overloaded, even if there had been someplace to go, they could not have made it. Cortés, seeing this, changed his command.

"Dump the gold. We will come back for it."

But most of the men would not part with their gold, would not give it up for anything, and, hugging their riches to their breasts, were picked off, falling off the causeway into the water. Of those not wounded, some could not swim, and even those who could sank to the bottom of the lake, weighed down with their loads. Cortés felt, for once in his life, at an impasse. Shooting the harquebuses, which had to be set up on tripods for balance, was not feasible, there was no time to ignite the gunpowder in the muskets, and getting close enough to spear the Aztec in the canoes was next to impossible since the canoes could be maneuvered like dragonflies skirting the surface of the water. The captains in the vanguard, the first group, Alvarado, Núñez, and Isla, had made it across before the causeway was torn up, and galloping their horses into the cover of a pile of big boulders, they waited for the rest of them to catch up.

"I am going back to get Cuy," Núñez said.

"And I Cortés," Alvarado said.

"I will stay stationed here and wait for the others," Isla said.

Cuy and Malintzin in their box cart were in the middle of the procession, their way in front and back cut off by the destruction. The Mexica were pulling apart the road so quickly that soon the two women with the twins, already at the mercy of the storm of arrows, were on a meager island of the causeway with nothing left to do but jump off or be shot down.

"Cortés," Alvarado shouted out, "stay fast, I am coming."

Cortés had been thrown off his horse but was standing firm on a piece of unbroken bridge. Many Aztec were surrounding him, but they had not shot an arrow at him, wanting to take him alive as a prize for sacrifice. The circle of Aztec warriors tightened like coyotes drawing in to close off their prey.

Malintzin got Cuy out of the box cart, she and the two babies, who were strapped with cloth to their mother's chest. The two women hid under the cart, hoping not to be discovered. But they had been sighted almost immediately. Pock, pock, dozens of arrows peppered the corn-husk stuffing of the piled mats, and the whole structure wobbled in the onslaught and tipped, falling over into the water.

"We have to swim," Malinche said.

"The babies," Cuy protested.

"It is our only chance." Malintzin could see the shore on the Tacuba side. It was not far away, and if she could catch hold of a piece of wood, anything that floated, she holding one baby, Cuy the other, hefting their bodies up and keeping their heads above water, one hand on the wood, they could kick their way to shore. Cuy was so weak from the birth and the loss of blood she could barely move, so there was no other way to do it.

Núñez, seeing them slide into the water, on the safe side jumped from his horse, ran into the lake, plunged in, and, pushing one of the wine barrels that had come loose from its bearings and was bobbing on the surface, drove it toward the women.

"Grab hold, Cuy. Give me one of the babies, you hold the other."

Several canoes headed toward them. Bodies, Mexican and Spanish, hit against them as they tried to make headway. The black lake was streaked with bright crimson. Cuy got hold of the barrel. Núñez took the baby. Malintzin pushed the other baby to Cuy, thrust herself away from the barrel, and, to deflect attention from the babies, shouted out in Nahuatl, "Kill me, kill me, I am the Mexica princess Malintzin."

One arrow struck her arm. She sank down.

"Maax!" Cuy screamed.

Alvarado was stranded on an island of stone some six feet from where Cortés was standing, he too on a piece of the broken bridge, a ring of Aztecs in canoes all about him.

"Go back, my friend," Cortés commanded. "Go back, save yourself."

Alvarado had lost his sword. The dagger he kept in his boot was gone too. The only thing he had was a pike. As one sometimes acts unknowingly and with grace in extreme circumstances, Alvarado undid his armor, picked up the pike, dug it firmly in the exposed soil between the stones, and vaulted over to Cortés. Just as he landed near him, two arrows pierced his arm.

"Hail Mary, full of grace," he gasped.

"Alvarado, Alvarado." Cortés reached down, tried to hold Alvarado's body up, and felt it a deadweight falling and pulling him down into the dark water.

"Jesus, help me." Swiftly Cortés unbuckled his breastplate, sucked in his breath, extricated himself, took a deep breath, dove below the surface, took hold of Alvarado's head, and began to swim underwater toward the Tacuba shore. The lake was full of dead horses. Father Olmedo, who was almost on the Tacuba side of the shore, had slipped off his robe and, looking like a long white worm creeping out from under a rock newborn and fragile, hip-hopped over the pieces of the causeway, made it over to where Aguilar was cornered, and, jumping into the water, pulled Aguilar by the leg in after him, swimming with one hand and dragging Aguilar with the other. He surfaced quietly after a bit and pushed Aguilar safely toward the shallows of the shore.

Isla, on the safe side of the causeway, sheltered by a thick bush, watched it all.

Malintzin's wounded arm was of no use, and each time she went down under the water she had less strength to push off the bottom and hit the surface. So this is the way it is to end, she thought, a great calm overtaking her. She had forgotten about the baby, she let everything go. She had struggled so long she was almost relieved to be dying. She knew she was not going to survive anyway. Botello had told her that she would die young. But it was such a pity, especially now, now of all times.

Cuy, who had reached the shore, cried out, "My baby girl, my baby, save my baby!" Was she carrying her daughter, who had somehow escaped her grip? Did Maax have her? Núñez pushed the baby boy into Cuy's arms and dove. The water was choppy and black and overlaid with canoes. The bodies of horses and men bombarded Núñez. He could not see a thing. But he kept swimming, would swim to the end and bottom of the earth if he had to, certain that he was being directed by some divine guide to his daughter, the newborn light of his life. Noah, his son, had not drowned in the flood and was in his mother's arms, but Claudia, where was his Claudia? Núñez's own arms were so tired he did not know how he could move, but he persisted, risking arrows, spears, and being hauled up into a canoe as a sacrificial captive. After what seemed like a long time, his mouth full of water, his eyes stinging, he had to wade back to the shallow water and rest a minute before going out again. He did this so many times it seemed as if he were a dream, a lifelong dream of swimming, not finding, losing, sitting on the sand, going out again.

Isla observed as best he could in the darkness, and within the shelter of the bushes, Núñez's futile efforts. Then he saw Cortés standing upright on the beach. He looked like Proteus emerged from the depths. Next he made out Aguilar and Father Olmedo, who were running about on the sand calling out, Núñez, Núñez. Adu was walking out into the waves breaking in ripples on the shore, dragged something out of the shallows, and threw it over his shoulder. With his load he looked like a leviathan standing up on end, in the dark only his eyes and teeth white. Isla saw men of the troops and some of the women slaves huddled together. Then he noticed that from the shore Adu could see him hiding in the bushes. In fact, the abominable Negro was looking straight at him.

Malintzin felt herself being pulled up and thrown over a broad shoulder.

"My baby, my baby!" Cuy cried out. Her plaintive wail pierced through all the battle cries, shouts, and commotion. "My baby, my baby!"

"Cuy," Malintzin gasped when Adu set her down on the sand, and she did not remember anything more until she became conscious again.

It was dawn. The survivors, those who were left of the troops, were crouched down in a huddle behind the rocks. Adu leaned over Malintzin.

"Bring a torch, let me see her wound."

"Where is Botello?" somebody asked. "He can operate."

But across the lake they heard the boom of the drums, and on the tallest building, the pyramid to the war god, Huitzilopochtli, and the rain god, Tlaloc, two fires were roaring high. It was a sacrifice morning. As soon as the sun came up, the one hundred and fourteen steps would be climbed.

"Oh no, oh no." Malintzin could not contain herself. It had to be Botello.

"Shh." Adu tried to comfort her as he looked out across the lake. The causeway was destroyed. Bodies of Spanish soldiers bobbed up in the water, those who were not attached to their gold had already washed up on the sand. They were like victims of a gigantic shipwreck. An empty canoe floated ashore. And then a man who had been lying in the bottom of the canoe rose up.

"Botello. It is Botello." Adu jumped up and ran to meet the canoe. Núñez was sitting with Cuy and his son trying to regain his strength to go back into the water and search for his drowned daughter. Cortés was sitting in the sand weeping. Father Olmedo and Aguilar were praying. Isla was still in the bushes.

"Do not say anything," Botello said, handing the baby girl to Adu. "She is alive and well. I scooped her up before she could go under. Give her to her mother. Say nothing about me."

"Botello. Wait."

"I am no longer one of you." Botello lay back down in the canoe, and dipping his oars as if they had fallen to the sides and the canoe was drifting, he headed back to Tenochtitlán.

Adu shouted from the shore, "Your child, Cuy, your child is safe."

Malintzin, her shoulder broken and her arm dangling uselessly, hobbled up to the rejoicing parents.

"How was she saved? Who saved her? What happened?"

"Quetzalcoatl saved her," Adu said. He did not sit down with the rejoicing parents. "I have something to attend to, and I will be right back."

"Where is Alvarado?" Aguilar asked a few minutes later.

The sun was coming up. The slow beat of the drum could still be heard. Cortés sat with his legs splayed before him in the shallow water, remains of the crossing floating around him. He could say nothing, do nothing. His eyes were glazed with tears, his will was gone.

"He cannot be dead," Aguilar said. "Alvarado cannot be dead." Aguilar started to run along the shore, turning over the bodies that had washed ashore.

"Look for the hair," Father Olmedo called out, joining him, knowing it to be fruitless. "The bright hair."

They recognized many of the men, their arms outstretched as if seeking salvation on the beach, meeting the morning God open-armed.

"Alvarado is not here," Father Olmedo said.

"Wait," Aguilar called. He knelt next to Cortés. Alvarado was lying beside him.

Alvarado was on his back, his legs splayed, his beautiful hair fanning out from his face like seaweed. They did not see his chest move.

"Poor Alvarado, so misguided."

"Nonetheless a Christian," Father Olmedo replied. "A bad Christian, but a Christian."

"A terrible Christian, but I forgive him all his sins," Aguilar said.

Alvarado blinked, sand in his eyes.

"¿Un cristiano terrible?" he said.

"Alvarado!" Aguilar exclaimed.

"The horses?"

"Some left."

"My Alonzo, Luce, Liliana?"

"Did not make it."

"Dear God," Alvarado moaned.

Cortés had not seen the resurrection of Alvarado. But he had stopped crying and roused himself. He stood up and put one foot in front of the other, then the next. He was walking up the beach looking for each of his men so they could have a decent burial. "Isla?" he cried. "Where is my right hand, Isla?"

"He is killed," Adu announced. "I was looking for him and found him with an arrow in his back."

Malintzin looked at Adu, then looked away.

"Strange," Aguilar said. "I thought of all people, he would be one to survive. An Aztec arrow must have found its way to shore."

"Look," Father Olmedo said, "look who we have here."

"Alvarado," Adu said, smiling. "Alvarado accounted for."

Cortés could not restrain himself. He was simply happy. Suddenly all did not seem lost after all. He gave Alvarado a big abrazo. "Do you think I would let you die, you rogue?"

"I do not remember how I got to shore," Alvarado said, "Or anything much. I was on the causeway, then I was in the water, then I was on the shore. Now I am here."

"Gracias a Dios," Father Olmedo said.

"The gold? And where is the gold?" is what Cortés now wanted to know.

"I lost my book." Bernal Díaz joined the little circle. "I lost my book," he moaned. "All my work."

Everybody stared at him. "Your book, Bernal Díaz?" Father Olmedo said. "You are crying for a book? Some have lost their lives."

More stragglers who somehow had survived were staggering up onto the shore.

"Where is the gold?" Cortés repeated.

"At the bottom of the lake," Aguilar answered. "Many of our men have died rich."

"Maldiciones. We will return to dredge it up and get every last piece." Cortés stamped his foot and raised his fist. "Núñez, are you here, are you alive?"

"Alive, sir." Cuy was holding the babies.

"Ah, he is here, our timekeeper. That is very important, muy importante. Time and boats, a clockman and a carpenter. Listen, my captains, I have an idea. We will not go unavenged, no indeed. We will not forgo what we have intended to do."

Cortés was dripping wet, his hair plastered to his head. He had no horse, no sword, no gold, no land, and nothing to eat. His glorious army had been defeated. "Núñez, you will design boats in Tlaxcala that can be dismantled, we will carry them overland, reassemble, and attack from the lake. We will be sailors. And men"—Cortés raised his fist to the sky—"bit by bit, we will assemble more allies. The Tlaxcalans, the Cempoalans, the Xocotlans." He looked around. "Where are the Indians who were with us, where are they?"

"Many have died, Cortés. Others have . . . I do not know."

"No matter. We will replenish their ranks. I stand here today, on the morning of June 30, 1520, and I say to you: Bernal Díaz, do not cry, we will get you another book, more paper, pens, ink, I remember everything. I will tell you, and furthermore you can continue to make note of our valorous crusade to bring the Word of Jesus and the benefits of civilization to these barbarous people. They will pay for this insurrection. We will level their city, decimate their country. We will redeem our gold, all our gold and more. This is our country under God and pope, king and law. We will take it back from the rebellious rebels. New Spain is our Spain."

Nobody was listening. As the sun rose higher, more bodies washed ashore, bumping against the rocks. Troops, horses, Aztecs, flotsam, the tide foamed red. Father Olmedo led the bedraggled group in prayer.

"This has been a sad night, a night of tears, a night of sorrows," Father Olmedo said. "Noche Triste."

Bernal Díaz would have written, had he his book, his pen, his wits:

30 DE JUNIO DE 1520, NOCHE TRISTE,
TEARFUL NIGHT, SORROWFUL NIGHT.

Cortés could hardly wait until the prayer was over, but Father Olmedo was rattling on as if they did not have to flee for their lives. One more word or two and they would gather what they had, pick up, and get on the road. He had his Malintzin, his Núñez and Alvarado, Adu, his Aguilar. It was too bad about Isla.

"Yes, men, it has been a night of sorrows, Noche Triste," he started up again as soon as the amen was uttered. "We have a long trip ahead of us." Bodies strewn in the wet sand, the drums on top of the temple of sacrifice beating their dirge, blood running thicker than water, but Cortés on the beach assumed the same posture he always did when delivering a speech, right foot forward, his stomach sucked in, his chest thrust out. "We have lost many of our bravest men." He threw out his arms in a dramatic gesture. "Dear God, please receive them. But this I promise you, you the survivors"—he raised his finger in the air as if addressing a rapt audience, members of his court, a schoolroom of good boys—"we will be back."

Cuy had dried off both babies, bundled them up, and was nursing them at both breasts. Father Olmedo now was lying on his back as Francisco liked to do. Aguilar was thinking that once they got to Vera Cruz there would be some way for him to get to Spain, if only to take a letter to the emperor penned by Bernal Díaz. To think he had considered making Tenochtitlán his home. Adu looked at Malintzin. Would her arm always hang down from her shoulder? Was there any way for it to be cured? Every time she lifted her hand she winced. He could feel the pain as if it were his own.

"We will build a huge catapult to hurl boulders into the city. We will cut off all food going into the city. We will cut off the water supply at Chapultepec. We will starve them. Mexica will die of thirst. We will lay siege. We will reduce their city to rubble, take over the empire—"

"Pardon," Father Olmedo said. "Should we not bury our dead?"

"Never fear. Never yield. Nunca, nunca. No time, no time." Unfortunately most of the soldiers from Narváez's troops were dead or worse. Cortés could hear the sacrifice drums beating. It was the hour of the heart. Botello, poor fellow, no doubt had been marched up the steps. And then Francisco had died in the desert. Others had died too. Maybe four hundred men, and the Indian allies. He did not count. Quintaval, the cobarde de mierda. Francisco. Botello. And now Isla, how mysterious it was that he died once he had made it to shore. But there was Doña Marina still alive, still standing. She looked like a drowned rat. One shoulder was raised, the other dipped lower. Lovely breasts, though. Those big eyes. Strong legs. She was, he hated to admit it, crucial, the heart of hearts, a queen.

"Let us start on our long walk back to the coast. The Aztecs think we will go home, home to Cuba, Spain, but the empire of Mexica, that is our home, and we will be back to claim what is rightfully ours."

"Cortés," Malintzin said, "before we start—"

"I know, your shoulder. The first night, at the end of this day, I will see to it. A sling, perhaps a little bleeding."

"No, it is something else."

"What is it? You know I am distressed, my patience nearly at an end. All my tobacco is wet. We have no food. We will be pursued. You wish to thank me for saving the baby and Cuy? I am happy to be of service. The boy will grow up to be a fine Spanish soldier, the girl a Spanish mother of soldiers."

"I cannot come back when you return to Tenochtitlán, Hernán."

He looked at her incredulously. "You are still my slave, Doña Marina."

"I cannot," she said.

"So defiant, Doña Marina, and you constantly forget your place. You cannot tell me what you are going to do. Do not think otherwise. You are not free yet. I cannot do without you, and that is that." He stamped his wet boot and water squeezed out.

"I am pregnant, Hernán."

For a moment, El Comandante was struck dumb.

"I am pregnant," she said again. "Estoy embarazada." Using her right hand, her good hand, she patted her stomach. "Embarazada. Pregnant."

"A child? ¿Un niño?"

"Yes."

Then he smiled. "A child, an heir, a son." He had a daughter or two in Cuba, and he noticed that some of the slave women were pregnant, but that was different. "My blood. A child of New Spain, the New World, the new nobility, the first child conceived, the first Christian boy, that is, rooted, bred, and born in the new country. I am well pleased. It is the right time, the right place." He moved forward to hold Malintzin, to hug her and kiss her. Interpreter, translator, mistress, mother, woman. Death all around, and now life. God was most definitely on his side. But as he reached for his little slave, she stepped back.

"No, no, do not be frightened. A squeeze will not hurt the baby. Do not think I will press myself upon you in any way. Gentle, gentle, I am a gentle man. You must take good care of yourself, Doña Marina. By all means you must not tire yourself. I just wish we had a horse left for you to ride on. As soon as we defeat the Aztecs and return to claim what is ours, my son will rule this land, and his son in turn. The House of Cortés." Then he turned to Núñez, for the sun was climbing higher in the sky and soon it would be swelteringly hot. "Do not lose heart, men, we will conquer. We *will* conquer. Núñez, what time is it?"

Núñez no longer had his clock. It was somewhere at the bottom of Lake Texcoco. Still, he answered as if he knew the hour, the minute to the second.

"Cortés, it is time to stop."

Chapter 40

I t was one of those cloudless days in New Spain, four years since Noche Triste, three since the final defeat of Mexico in June of 1522. It was 1525 and Malintzin was twenty-five years old, Cuy was in her thirties, and little Martín Cortés, Malintzin's and Cortés's son, was all of three years old. The sky was of so benign a blue that on that day one could not imagine it filled with lightning or hail or even night. The worst one could picture was soft rain in midmorning. Malintzin was in the kitchen of her home in Coyoacán instructing the servants. Guests were coming, flowers had to be arranged, incense placed in the corners of the room, tortillas rolled out. Cuy and Núñez and their children were expected, the Cempoala cacique's niece and her family, Father Olmedo of course, and Cortés would be coming to fetch Martín for a visit to his home in Cuernavaca.

Malintzin's house was a large three-story block building painted a burnt red, the roof flat with open cedar beams across to funnel off water, the ends decorated with carved ram's heads with rounded horns and vacant eyes. Plates in the shape of the sun decorated both sides of the two front heavy oak doors, and there was a bell on a drawstring for guests to announce their presence.

As Malintzin went from room to room checking to see if all was in order, little Martín stumbled after her. The child, named after Cortés's father and nearly three, was bowlegged and sturdy; he was a darling. Everyone who saw him loved him immediately, but he was not the child she was pregnant with on the night of sorrow, the Noche Triste of June 1520. On the long trek back to Tlaxcala, Malintzin suffered a miscarriage, and in her grief and desire for a child, came to Cortés's mat every month after her flow. Finally, nearly a year later, she conceived again. Although legitimized through the intervention of the pope and baptized by Father Olmedo en el nombre del Padre, in the name of the Father, del Hijo, of the Son, del Espíritu Santo, of the Holy Spirit, Amén, little Martín was considered a mestizo, a mixture, less than Spanish by some.

"Mistress Malintzin, Mistress Malintzin." One of her servants bustled into the kitchen. "There is a poor old woman at the door, and a young man, and they insist on seeing you."

Malintzin knew immediately who they were.

There had been signs.

A nest of baby birds had fallen out of a tree in her courtyard. Some of her best tomatoes had shriveled on the vine. Pumpkins had burst. And the week before, it had been so hot nobody dared venture far. But when Malitnzin actually saw them she was shocked. Her mother, aged beyond recognition, was dressed in a loose maguey fiber gown, and although the weather was warm, she also wore a heavy rebozo like an old person who can never be warm enough. She had no shoes and her toenails were yellow, cracked, and long as talons. The son, however, affected the Spanish style with mismatched doublet and hose, long cape, boots, and a ridiculously floppy velvet hat much like Aguilar's old cap. Her brother had grown into a silent, surly youth, and beneath his heavy eyebrows he had his father's disapproving gaze.

"Daughter," the old woman sobbed with a tremolo, as if she had not spent a single moment without thinking of her long-lost child, her recovery a lifelong quest.

"Madre, Naantli," Malintzin said, stepping forward to give her mother a big abrazo. Tears welled up in her eyes. She could not help it. "I have missed you."

Childbirth had not changed Malintzin; if anything, it had enhanced her beauty. Her face was striking, her body slim, her posture that of a princess. She had many suitors, but she considered that part of her life over. Passion had flared up when she was young and nearly consumed her. Now she knew better, and her energies were devoted to her son, her household, and her collection of artifacts. She knew that she had not truly experienced love until she had a child. Moreover, she owned her own home. Furnished in the Spanish style, it provided every comfort. Her chairs were covered with leather from Oduduwa's ranchero in Oaxaca. Mainly Oduduwa raised bulls for the corrida de toros, an entertainment and ritual originating among Moorish soldiers. A man, a bull, death. The Spanish loved it, and what was left of the Aztec nobility loved it, and the Tlaxcalas loved it too. Oduduwa also trained horses for caballeros. Alvarado, now governor of Guatemala, had a monopoly on horse importing on the continent and was Oduduwa's supplier.

"And this is my grandson?" Malintzin's mother cooed affectionately, but Martín put his thumb in his mouth and would not come out from behind his mother's skirt.

"What is his name, the precious boy?"

"Martín." The child had straight black hair cut in bangs all around and slanted black eyes, and he was dressed in little white cotton breeches to his knees tied in multicolored tassels, a loose overshirt gathered at the neck, and perfect little huaraches tooled by Núñez. Shoemaking was one of his many pastimes.

"Martín, come to your grandmother." The old woman leaned forward with her arms outstretched.

But Martín thought she was a witch, started to wail.

"María," Malintzin called to a servant, "take Martín out to play, would you? Gracias."

"Such a beautiful house." Malintzin's mother, undeterred by her grandchild's reception, made herself comfortable, sitting down on the stone floor. Malintzin's brother chose a chair. "And you are so famous."

"I am famous?" Her mother had said the word so that it sounded like defamation, yet Malintzin at that point was neither famous nor infamous. Bernal Díaz had not rewritten his book, *The Conquest,* lost at the bottom of Lake Texcoco, so accounts of her role in the conquest were scant. Furthermore, when it all came to light, she knew that little notice would be taken of her translating and interpreting. What could be said? She had been a slave, a woman. On the other hand, Díaz had at the ready the names and coloring of all the horses used, and Cortés's valorous fighting style, and Cortés's popularity with the troops, and there were a few others things he could recall if need be, but a prosperous landowner in Guatemala, he only occasionally put pen to paper in the serenity of early evening after a little aqua vitae and a nice cigar.

"So," Malintzin asked her mother, "are you well?" She noticed that her mother splayed her legs without concern for modesty, and when she spoke, spit gathered at the sides of her mouth. She had the smell of the hearth and her skin was lank, hanging on her bones in fringes.

"Do you have anything to drink?" the old woman asked her.

Malintzin clapped her hands. A servant brought some juice made of tamarind in three small earthen jugs on a wooden tray.

"We have not eaten today," her mother said.

The servant brought in plates of soft tortillas drizzled with honey.

"We have not had a full meal in days," her mother said, wiping her mouth on her ragged sleeve.

Malintzin told the cook to heat some beans and chop some tomatoes.

"Am I well, you ask, daughter? I am well enough." But the old woman answered in a sorrowful voice, and she went on to enumerate various incurable maladies. She could no longer see very well or hear very well; her legs ached day and night. She had a pain in her chest, in her stomach. Sometimes she could not move her bowels. Sometmes she woke up because her heart was beating so loudly. Often she wondered why she was alive. She would not be alive for long, that was for certain.

"They say you travel, Mallalini, that you went south to Honduras and farther away than that, to Guatemala, that the Spanish have taken all the land, that Cortés is to be emperor of the world."

It surprised Malintzin that her mother could even say such words. Honduras, Guatemala, Spanish, Cortés. As an Aztec woman, her mother had pledged her life to loom, broom, spindle, and hearth, to the growing and grinding of corn. However, it seemed that even in the south now, even in remote inland villages, people were speaking the new language. The Maya in Chiapas were holding out, but it would only be a matter of time before the whole continent belonged to Spain.

"And you have grown into such a fine young woman, Mallalini."

Her mother's hair was white as snow, and it had thinned so that her head showed through, shiny and vulnerable as a baby's skull.

"Do you forgive me for selling you, Mallalini?" Her mother furrowed her brow and breathed in so that her nostril looked pinched. She cocked her head to one side like a child asking to be forgiven for spilling her food.

"It puzzles me . . ." Malintzin hesitated. Malinche, Maax, Doña Marina, and now Mallalini hesitated. It was the question of her life, something she had wanted to know for fifteen years, and yet she hesitated. She took a deep breath. "I would like to know why you sold me, why you betrayed me." There, she said it.

"You have not forgiven me. I can see that." Now her mother was the petulant child.

"I want to understand." How could her mother have sent her away? Was she not as delightful as Martín, did her mother not want to shield her from all ill, would she not run away into the forest to keep her from harm, even live among the monkeys? "It was because of your husband, was it not? You did not want him to harm me anymore. Is that not why?" Malintzin's hair was done up nicely in tight buns pressed flat with fat from a pig, scented with crushed roses, and studded with turquoise stones. She wore a necklace of amber beads, a small scorpion trapped in one. Her feet were entirely covered with cow leather and her soles were raised from the floor with a soft padding of cotton. Her meticulous appearance belied the turmoil within her.

"I sold you . . ." Her mother looked around. The walls of Malintzin's home were covered with straw baskets woven from all over Mexico. They were, along with pottery and masks, part of Malintzin's collection of artifacts. She had managed to save some Aztec books, too, before they were burned, some ornaments before they were melted, some pottery before it was smashed.

"You sold me because . . ." Malintzin wanted to hear, I sold you to save you from my husband's nightly mistreatments. I did not know what to do, my dear daughter, so that when the slavers came along, I realized I could free you from his clutches and send you far away. I sold you out of love and concern.

"I sold you, Mallalini, because you brought disharmony into our home. You were always too much the princess. Do you remember how you were? You were arrogant. You knew everything. You thought you knew more than your own mother. Your own father spoiled you, and you would not submit to your stepfather. You would not obey his rule, the man of the household. He told me you were incorrigible, you had the ways of a woman, a grown woman, you were . . . I am sure you understand as a grown woman that a woman has her place, and a girl child—"

"Where is your husband now?" Malintzin asked quickly, for she thought she might cry, be weak.

"He is dead. It was the smallpox."

"That is unfortunate. I hope he did not suffer much."

"The smallpox is a terrible disease."

Brought by the African slave from the Cuban expedition launched to overturn Cortés, smallpox had spread like fire. By the time of the siege of Tenochtitlán in 1521, more than half of the Aztec within the city were dead or dying of the disease. Moctezuma's brother, who was elected emperor even while Moxtezuma was still alive, died of smallpox. The defense of the city and command of the Mexica troops had been taken over by Cuauhtémoc, another relative, who, when his people were defeated, asked to be killed, but was instead pardoned and then tortured. It was smallpox even more than drought, when the water supply was cut off, and famine, when food could no longer be brought into the city, that had won the war for the Spanish. Over 240,000 Mexica were found dead after the Spanish siege. Bodies were piled up and decomposing, the nearly dead apparently left to digging out blades of grass between the stones. Starvation was rampant. Some said that 40,000 Mexica died throwing themselves in the canals with their wives and children so as not to be taken as slaves. Of the Spanish allies, 30,000 Tlaxcalas died. About 60 Castilians were killed. It turned out, however, that while the city and people were defeated in the name of God and glory, little gold was to be had. Cortés ended up reverting to the old currency of cocoa beans to pay the regulars of his troops.

"This big house, Mallalini, it is all yours?"

"Yes."

"You own it, live in it, all by yourself?"

"Yes. Yes, I do." Malintzin was carrying on this conversation as if all were well. She tried to remember the mother she must have loved once. But all she could summon was the image of nighttime undone hair. Her mother's hair had looked like a big nest of crow feathers. And when she was a little girl, her mother had seemed like the great furred animals, a legend of the north, one of the ones who towered over men, could run faster than a dog and climb like a monkey, was greedy for honey but did not make a sound. Truly, Malintzin had been frightened of her. And it amazed her that this woman, a dribbling old woman, could still wound.

"It is a big house, Mallalini." The old woman looked around, coveting, claiming.

"Yes."

"Big for one person."

"I have a son."

"I mean for one grown person, it is a big house."

"I have lots of guests."

"I suppose you do." Her mother's mouth gathered at the side like a rotting fruit. "People these days are fortunate to have a roof over their heads, since the war."

Sometimes Malintzin liked to walk through her home numbering things. The floors were made of large flat gray stones sanded smooth and even. The adobe walls, whitewashed on the inside, were thick, so it was cool in the summer, and during the rainy season the rooms were heated by large fireplaces built into the walls. Her kitchen was a room with a wooden table in it and chairs with seats of rushes. Her mat was raised off the floor, cradled in a wooden frame with legs and ropes across. Each night the ropes had to be tightened with a crank. Martín had a small one in his bedroom. And each night she said, "Sleep tight, do not let the bedbugs bite," and then she would give him little pinches and tickle him. "Hijo, hijo." "Madre, Madre." Her pillows were stuffed with duck feathers and in her main room a candelabra made of two metal rings hung from the ceiling on iron chains and could be lowered with a pulley to light the candles set in the hoops. Cortés had insisted that Martín have a little crucifix over his bed, and in the hallway wrapping around the courtyard there were little niches in the walls sheltering small statues of the Virgin Mary and small obsidian carvings of the Aztec gods. In her bedroom Malintzin had a large stone carving of Quetzalcoatl in all his feathered finery holding a broom. Mirrors set in tin cases with little doors with places for candles were placed on the walls of the room with the big wooden tub for bathing. This is mine. My house, my things. I, mine, me. Yo, mío, mí. She owned those words, now, personal pronouns, possessives. She owned her life. She owned herself.

"Alaminos, your brother," her mother said, "has grown into a fine young man, has he not?"

"He has a Spanish name?" Malintzin had forgotten her brother's original name. And he has been so quiet sitting there in her home that she forgot he was even there.

"I changed his name. Tecayehuatzin sounds so . . . Aztec."

Then Malintzin remembered. Tecayehuatzin, her brother, although the suffix -*tzin* was for people of noble lineage, and *his* father was not a noble. She wondered if this boy could speak for himself. Then she remembered that her mother had once been a very quiet person. Her silence was complicit with the unspoken, the unmentionable.

"You never married, Mallalini?" Her mother said these words as if they were an accusation *and* judgment.

"No. I do not want to be married," although Malintzin remembered a time when she aspired to the state of matrimony with the desperation of a drowning person clutching at a twig going downstream.

"Nobody wanted to marry you?"

Malintzin gave her mother a wary look. She wanted to say, This is my house and you must respect me in my own house.

"I do not know and I do not care."

"You must be very lonely." Her mother put a drop of solicitous sadness in her voice, as if for fifteen years she had been concerned with her daughter's loneliness.

"I am not lonely at all. I have baby Martín and friends."

When Oduduwa traveled up from Oaxaca, the two of them would take mats up on the roof and sleep under the tent of the night, looking for stars, shapes and patterns. They always tried to locate Quetzalcoatl. For part of the year the dead god would live as the evening star, then he would disappear into the underworld and reappear as the morning star. Quetzalcoatl, people would say, is coming down to earth on his big temple-ship.

Aguilar came on Thursday evenings to drink wine and talk about the book of Nahuatl poetry he was compiling. They did not go to the rooftop as she did with Oduduwa, but stayed in her bedroom. She liked the sound of that—bedroom, cuarto de alquiler. Her coverlet, a cubrecama, was pure white cotton with small embroideries on it of various figures—the goddess Tlazolteotl, Tezcatlipoca in black and red guises as merchant, warrior, and ballplayer, a Tarasca noblewoman being escorted to her wedding, a Mixtec in a maxtlatl. The Cempoala cacique's niece had made it for her.

Moreover, Father Olmedo visited after mass on Sunday afternoons. They talked about Francisco, the good old days on the road. It delighted him in the middle of Sunday dinner to shove everything aside and partake of her as another dish. She could never have guessed he had so much imagination. "Father Olmedo!" she would squeal, both of them laughing their heads off.

"The child's father is, that is to say, Mallalini, he is . . ."

"Rich and powerful?" She knew what her mother was hinting.

"You are on good terms?"

"Yes, we are." She had made peace with her child's father. And from the beginning Cortés had concerned himself with Martín's welfare, importing for him, before the infant was even able to sit up, a small horse. Strapping the child to the saddle, Cortés would lead the docile little pony around his courtyard by a rope, and he spoke excit-edly of the time he would teach Martín to shoot a gun. Cortés's palace in Cuernavaca, an area a little ways outside Tenochtitlán of so temper-ate a climate the air was sweet, was made of stucco painted a lemony yellow. Jacaranda trees shaded benches along the sides of the walls of the courtyard, intertwining their branches on the terraces above.

Cortés's wife, Catalina, who came from Cuba after the fall of Tenochtitlán, was thin, modest, and quiet, hardly the imperious first wife of a viceroy or governor, as Cortés hoped to be. Unfortunately she died in her sleep one night after an argument with Cortés about the treatment of slaves. There was a rumor that her death was not quite as natural as Cortés maintained, but Emperor Carlos did not pursue the charges. While he was not concerned with small matters, the king, fearing Cortés's energy, his autonomous manner of thinking, the very things which distinguished Cortés as a general, appointed him to only minor positions of power. Spanish bureaucrats were brought in to rule New Spain and represent the throne across the sea. Cortés, Carlos esti-mated, had been good for conquering but would be bad for the close, inglorious, and above all and always *obedient* work of running an empire.

"So your brother is thinking of a position in the new government," Malintzin's mother said, as if this were not the purpose of her visit.

"Is he really? The new government?"

"You are the one who is in touch with the important people, Mallalini."

The important people. Once a year the important people all got together. Cortés called it All Souls' Day, a day when all the spirits came to visit. But as far as everybody else was concerned, All Souls' Day was the Day of the Dead, or rather the two days of the dead, November 1 and 2 in the Spanish calendar. On those days they wel-comed Francisco back to earth and Botello, who died in the siege in his mud hut entwined with Cipactli, his Aztec soul mate. Cuy and Malintzin honored Jaguar Claw. Cortés insisted that they honor the death of Isla too. So those of them who lived near Tacuba, where Señor Isla met his unfortunate end, made a shrine. According to custom they were supposed to put out food Isla liked, and little mementos. But the fact was nobody knew what food Isla had liked, so Malintzin, Cuy, and Núñez picked out rotten, smelly melons, a stack of tortillas fuzzed with mold, dead frogs with their poisons intact, enough beans to bloat and float a corpse, and a very rare Spanish fruit called an apple, a manzilla, with a grub in it in honor of Isla's Christian origins.

They made a little effigy of Isla, a doll with a small head, bone snake eyes sewn on the head like buttons. Mosquito larvae were put in his miniature codpiece, scorpions between his tiny toes, lice and rancid duck fat were smeared over his cloth head for his hair. Father Olmedo added a little slip of paper from John: chapter 10, beginning with "Verily, verily, I say unto you."

"As I said, are you listening to me, Mallalini?"

"Yes, I am listening." Malintzin could not bring herself to call this woman, sitting in her house as if it were her own, Mother.

"Your brother is thinking of a position in the new government. He is very talented."

"What can he do?" Malintzin thought of mothers and their sons. The mother in Cholula who had wanted her to marry her son, and how people in Tenochtitlán heard the same cry every night in the zócalo, their buildings in ruins, not a stone left unturned, a national palace and a great church built over the rubble of palaces and temples.

"Your brother is very intelligent; he learns fast. He can learn anything. He is studying Spanish."

"Is that so? ¿Habla español?"

Her brother did not say anything.

"¿Un poco"—she held her fingers up to an inch, then narrowed the distance—"poquito?"

Her brother tried to smile, but it was an expression he had not mastered. He had not the labios for it, and she could picture him having to eat in quick, small gulps and having to drink lapping like an animal.

"It would be very sisterly of you to assist us, but, what can I say, I raised you to be generous and kind, and I knew we could count on you to honor family connections. We have traveled far from the coast, as you know. We need to rest, stay until your brother obtains his rightful position. When we get on our feet, get on our feet—"

"Your son can carry you back," Malintzin said. "He is young and strong." Had not Botello and Adu carried Francisco, and Alvarado carried his mother over mountains?

"Carry me back? Surely you are joking. Carry me back on his back?" The woman's laugh was double-edged.

Malintzin got up from her chair, came over to her mother, and kissed her on the lips fully and passionately.

"You are going back."

"We have nothing to go back to, Mallalini, The wars—"

"I will provide a home for you, yes, you and your son, but you must not stay near me."

"But we just got here, Mallalini. Such a short visit, daughter. Are the beans ready, the ones being heated? Do you not have some hammocks which could be strung up? Certainly you do not want us to go. Blood it thicker than water. I would like some water. Did I hear that you are boiling some beans? This is such a large house, and you only have your son."

"And you have one too."

"You are a wealthy woman, a woman of means, you got to speak out before important people."

"Never my own words. I spoke for others." Malinztin got up from her chair, leaned down, and put her face near the old woman's face. "Now I speak for myself. I tell you, go. Go away before I do something we will all regret."

"Come now, you must admit slavery was good for you. You learned a lot. Where would you be if I had not sold you? Look who you met, all that you accomplished. Your hands are soft, you have shoes. My husband warned me about you, your ingratitude, your—"

"María, could you see our guests out, and call Juan. You may need some assistance."

"You will provide for us, that is what you said, a house, a house on the coast with several rooms, and a garden, yes, a garden, some animals. An old woman needs some help. A slave—"

"María."

"Madam?"

"Get rid of them."

QUETZALCOATL SLEPT UNDER a big ceiba tree, his back resting against the trunk. The branches leaned down so low that roots sprouted from the ground, making a circlet of spires, the tree creating its own forest. Quetzalcoatl was having a dream, a dream as real as Malintzin's childhood nightmares, but not peopled with the demons of the underworld. Rather the dream was about Cortés's big comeback, the final, mighty siege of Tenochtitlán, in the Christian calendar year of 1521. In his reverie the Indian bearers obligingly carried the parts of newly made brigantines which could be ingeniously reconstructed easily and assembled on the shore of Lake Texcoco. Moreover, the Spanish possessed catapults, bombards which could shoot cannonballs made of stone, fire in containers that could be thrown by slings, giant bellows capable of projecting flames in whooshes, small handy muskets without the need of supports, and ample gunpowder made of sulfur scraped from the lips of the Popocatépetl volcano. Not only was their weaponry more than sufficient for the task at hand, but also the troops were newly fortified by more warriors from jealous city-states convinced they could make an end of their imperialistic neighbor, Mexica.

After skirmishes and pitched battles in bordering cities, Cortés closed off the Mexica water supply at Chapultepec and blocked the entry of any food through the three causeways. Smallpox was already ravaging the population. Moctezuma's brother, Cuitlahuac, who had been emperor for a short while, perished of the disease. The remaining animals in the zoo were eaten. The plants in the gardens withered, curled up, and died. Famine raged and bodies overlay each other in the streets like cords of wood. A few survivors subsisted on mud, dust, tufts of dry grass between the stones, stones sucked to grains of sand. The new emperor, Cuauhétmoc, in a last-ditch effort, dressed and armed the women as warriors to fool the Spanish as to the Aztec numbers. The siege lasted ninety-three days; the official surrender took place on the morning of August 13, 1521.

SOME BELIEVED QUETZALCOATL could change form and, like a shape-shifter, an anualli, a cunandaro, be anything he wanted—a plumed serpent, the quetzal bird of the air, the coatl, primeval earth lizard, a snake-dragon reborn each season through the shedding of his skin. Could Quetzalcoatl be the jaguar of the Olmec, whose coat was spotted like the stars in the sky, and was he able to spread his wings like the great world-bird, rising from his own ashes to hover among the stars of heaven?

QUETZALCOATL'S SIESTA COULD have taken place at two o'clock in the afternoon if it were to be noted by Núñez on his newfangled clock, retrieved dripping with moss from the depths of the lake, and the day any day, for it could be both then and now, here and there, time and place compressed to the eternal moment.

Acknowledgments

The faithful attentions of Frederick
Slaski made this book possible.

I am grateful for the expert and kind
assistance of Jill Bialosky and Lucy Childs.
I am also indebted to Evan Carver,
Alfred Guillaume, Michael Kouroubetes,
Ceres Madoo, Leander Madoo,
Stephen Dunn of the Eastern
Frontier Society, Liliana Quintero,
Amy Robbins,
and Lynn Williams.

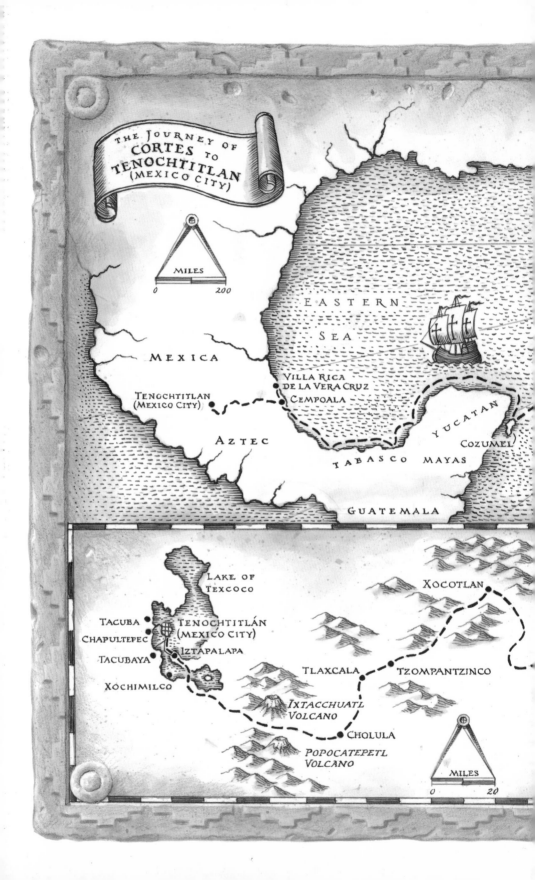

THE JOURNEY OF
CORTES TO
TENOCHTITLAN
(MEXICO CITY)

MILES
0   200

EASTERN

SEA

MEXICA

VILLA RICA
DE LA VERA CRUZ
TENOCHTITLAN
(MEXICO CITY)   CEMPOALA

AZTEC   YUCATAN
                                                COZUMEL
                    TABASCO   MAYAS

GUATEMALA

LAKE OF
TEXCOCO   XOCOTLAN

TACUBA
CHAPULTEPEC   TENOCHTITLÁN
                (MEXICO CITY)
TACUBAYA   IZTAPALAPA
                                TLAXCALA   TZOMPANTZINCO
XÓCHIMILCO
                        IXTACCHUATL
                        VOLCANO
                                        CHOLULA
                POPOCATEPETL
                VOLCANO   MILES
                                            0   20